"Vale to Bridge, report!"

Tuvok answered her. *"Stand by, Captain. Commander Sarai is in contact with main engineering. We registered a momentary particle surge six milliseconds before the warp matrix collapsed."*

"Reports coming in from all decks . . ." Troi was already checking her own panel. "Several minor injuries . . ."

"Tuvok," Riker broke in, "what was the nature of the particle surge?"

"Source unknown at this time, Admiral," reported the Vulcan, *"but it appears to be a broad-spectrum burst of tetryons."*

Then, with a blinding burst of exotic radiation, a ragged-edged rip sliced across the dark and opened wide. Great sickle-shaped arcs of lightning in grotesque, alien hues emerged from the fissure, lashing out in all directions. Wild pulses of uncontrolled gravitation swept out from the newborn anomaly and slammed into the starship, spinning it like a dinghy in a stormswell.

Briefly overwhelmed, *Titan*'s inertial dampeners failed, and Vale felt the deck fall away from her as the briefing room inverted.

STAR TREK
TITAN™

SIGHT UNSEEN

James Swallow

Based on *Star Trek®* and
Star Trek: The Next Generation®
created by Gene Roddenberry

POCKET BOOKS
New York London Toronto Sydney New Delhi

Pocket Books
An Imprint of Simon & Schuster, Inc.
1230 Avenue of the Americas
New York, NY 10020

This book is a work of fiction. Any references to historical events, real people, or real places are used fictitiously. Other names, characters, places, and events are products of the author's imagination, and any resemblance to actual events or places or persons, living or dead, is entirely coincidental.

This book is published by Pocket Books, an imprint of Simon & Schuster, Inc., under exclusive license from CBS Studios Inc.

First Pocket Books paperback edition October 2015

For information about special discounts for bulk purchases, please contact Simon & Schuster Special Sales at 1-866-506-1949 or business@simonandschuster.com.

The Simon & Schuster Speakers Bureau can bring authors to your live event. For more information or to book an event, contact the Simon & Schuster Speakers Bureau at 1-866-248-3049 or visit our website at www.simonspeakers.com.

Manufactured in the United States of America

10 9 8 7 6 5 4 3 2 1

ISBN 978-1-4767-8316-1
ISBN 978-1-4767-8320-8 (ebook)

HISTORIAN'S NOTE

This story takes place in early 2386, seven years after the *U.S.S. Enterprise*-E's confrontation with the Romulan praetor Shinzon (*Star Trek Nemesis*). Only a few months have passed since William T. Riker was promoted to rear admiral (*Star Trek: The Fall—The Poisoned Chalice*) and Kellessar zh'Tarash was elected president of the United Federation of Planets, following the assassination of Nanietta Bacco (*Star Trek: The Fall—Peaceable Kingdoms*).

One

It wasn't the first time on this assignment that he had felt like he was out of his depth. The plain fact of the matter was, the alien starship was like nothing he had ever seen before.

Recruited right out of the Tech Clutch on Selay, Ythiss had left his homeworld and clan nests to go to Starfleet Academy, and by the skins of his ancestors, he had graduated with honors. Ythiss liked to think of himself as an intelligent sentient, full of all that fix-anything attitude that Starfleet liked to encourage in its engineers. But this ship didn't conform to any kind of layout he had ever encountered, not in space or in textbooks. For starters, it seemed to be made largely of *wood*.

A rangy, muscular humanoid dropped out of the carved hatchway in the overhead of the corridor, falling to the planked decking in an effortless three-point landing. "Here," she said as she stood up, handing him a rope made from woven vegetable matter. "Help me with this."

"As you wish." The lieutenant blinked his large slitted eyes and cocked his serpentine head, taking up the slack she offered.

A member of the Dinac species, Guoapa was the commander of the vessel, although the duties she performed on her ship would have been the remit of a subordinate engineering officer like Ythiss on a Federation craft. When he had told her that, the canine-like female let out a barking snort of amusement. *What kind of fleet gives command to those who don't have their paws in the engines?* With that comment, the Selayan had immediately warmed to the alien captain, and from that point on Guoapa had insisted on having Ythiss as her assigned liaison. She hardly spoke to the lieutenant's commanding officer back on the *U.S.S. Whitetree*, much to Captain Minecci's chagrin, but after a while both the Starfleet and Dinac crews had found a comfortable balance for their association.

Ythiss waited for a nod from Guoapa, and they hauled together. The rope snapped taut and his earspots captured the sound of ceramic pulleys turning somewhere up inside the hatch. The lieutenant knew that their actions would—so he hoped—kick off a manual release of the intercooler vanes folded along the outside of the Dinac pinnace. Observed from a distance, Dinac ships had a beauty to them that Ythiss thought quite fetching. Sculpted to be warp-streamlined, they sported gossamer energy-collector wings that reminded him of the great rainmoths that swarmed in the cooler months on Selay.

He hauled and did as he was told, but Ythiss was still bothered by the fact that the *Whitetree* had spent nearly a month with the Dinac and he was no closer to understanding the peculiarities of their faster-than-light drives.

It was an odd blend of warp technology that had elements of Gorn brute-force motors, Vok'sha slip-gen engines and certain types of older Romulan systems, all in a mix that was quite unique. Ythiss found them utterly fascinating, to the point that he was spending far too much of his time on board the pinnace trying to fathom them.

When the engines had suffered a emergency shutdown, catapulting them from warp velocity in deep space, several light-years away from the Dinac home system, he was actually a little *pleased*. Not that the ship might be damaged—of course not—but pleased that he would have another excuse to slither around inside the drive core and get an up close and personal look at the alien tech. The *Whitetree* had quickly come about to take up station alongside and a repair party led by Chief Medeiros was already aboard, shoring up environmental control on the lower decks. Aside from a few bumps and bruises reported by Doctor Shull, the only thing injured so far was Dinac pride.

Heavy gears clanked into place and locked, and Guoapa gave Ythiss the bob-of-the-head gesture that was her equivalent of a thank you. The Federation's cultural survey notes on the Dinac had made it clear that the aliens were a proud species but a practical one. They had not come looking for Starfleet's help, but they had willingly accepted when it was offered. Ythiss let go of the rope and sucked in a breath. He felt more tired by the exertion than he wanted to admit; over the past few nights, the Selayan had found it difficult to rest, and he put it down to his mind being overly focused on the alien warp drive system.

The surveys said the Dinac most closely resembled a bipedal version of a Terran animal known as a fox, with short fur covering almost their entire bodies, tall triangular ears and large eyes above a pointed snout lined with small sharp teeth. Ythiss sometimes despaired of the inevitable comparisons between xeno races and faunaforms from Earth, a direct result of the fact that a disproportionate number of Federation exobiologists were Terran-born humans. He was from a race that was most often described as cobra-like, although he had seen one of those snakes at a nature reserve on Benecia Colony and been vaguely insulted by the comparison.

However you wanted to describe them, the Dinac were a vital people with a bold spirit that Ythiss found invigorating. They were new to the galactic stage, despite having developed a more or less reliable form of interstellar propulsion decades earlier. Until recently, they had been content to remain within the bounds of their home system, but now their government had expressed the wish to become an associate member of the United Federation of Planets. As part of the first steps down that road, the *Whitetree* had been assigned to the Dinac as part of a technological and cultural exchange.

For their part, Starfleet was not only helping to forge an alliance with a new species, but also getting a valuable opportunity for teaching into the bargain. The *Whitetree* was a small *Saber*-class starship seconded to Starfleet Academy and the majority of her crew were midshipmen on their first cadet cruise. The Dinac mission was the ideal opportunity to expose the next generation of Starfleet officers to the kind of challenges—and wonders—they would meet after graduation.

For a moment, Ythiss recalled his own cadet cruise, and his mind wandered back to what seemed like an epoch long past.

So much had happened since then. The Borg Invasion, his experiences serving aboard the *U.S.S. Titan*, the rise of the Typhon Pact and, most recently, the fallout from the assassination of Federation President Nanietta Bacco. Months later, with a new leader and a new sense of purpose in the UFP, Starfleet had renewed its commitment to exploration, and once his tour on the *Whitetree* was up, Ythiss hoped to return to the forefront of that endeavor. But he also understood the importance of showing the cadets that Starfleet's core strength was in its willingness to explore and make new allies, not just to exist as a defensive force.

However, none of that would happen if they couldn't get the pinnace under way again.

Guoapa was speaking into a microphone tube sewn into the collar of the multi-pocketed utility waistcoat she wore. Untranslated, the Dinac language sounded like a collection of high-pitched yaps and howls, but the tone was plain enough for Ythiss to surmise that she was giving someone orders. In response, the wooden deck beneath them gave a shudder and the craft lurched as the engines failed to start correctly. Guoapa's teeth bared in annoyance.

Ythiss opened his tricorder and took a scan, simultaneously patching into the *Whitetree*'s external sensors. He immediately saw the problem. "There is considerable subspace particle interference in this area. It is obstructing the initiation of a viable warp matrix."

"As if the engine is choked, yes." Guoapa sniffed. "In a dozen voyages, this has never happened before. Usually, resetting the wings will free the matrix to form, and—"

The engineer-commander never got to complete her

thought. All at once, braying alarms sounded down the length of the tubular wooden corridor, and Ythiss's nasal slits twitched as he detected the release of an alert scent into the pinnace's atmosphere. In the same instant, crimson warning flags unfurled across the tricorder's compact display screen as the energy readings peaked alarmingly. The sensor relay from his ship suddenly cut out.

The lieutenant's talon clacked on his combadge. "Ythiss to *Whitetree*, do you read me?"

A garbled mess of noise answered him, barely recognizable as a voice. Unable to pick out any words, he sprinted the short distance to a porthole and pressed his face to the glass.

As he was an inherently exothermic life-form, the temperature differential of the fluid in Ythiss's veins was negligible; but still he instinctively recalled a human aphorism about the figurative chilling of one's blood when he saw what was happening to the *Whitetree*.

The spade-shaped ship was falling. Out in the silent darkness, space itself had ripped open, a great wound in the void bleeding streamers of bright, violent energy. As a warp engineer, Ythiss was dreadfully familiar with the bestiary of spatial anomalies and unpleasant stellar phenomena that could affect faster-than-light vessels. The highly trained, calm and collected part of his mind registered that this was most likely a type-gamma subspace rift, of at least Magnitude Seven on the Ros-Sina-Michael Scale. The rest of his thoughts crystallized into a single, unspoken cry: *My friends, my crewmates are on that ship.*

The first of many gravity distortions radiating out from the rift struck the Dinac pinnace, and Ythiss felt the vessel shake and roll. He tried to pull himself away from the porthole, but he could not tear his gaze from the unfolding horror. The *Whitetree*'s engines were surging, the glow from the impulse grids flaring brightly as the ship tried and failed to escape the savage pull of the newborn singularity. Lashes made of light whipped the outer hull of the ship and left ugly tears in their wake as compartments underwent catastrophic depressurization. Slowly, agonizingly, the Starfleet vessel began to slide back toward the raging maw of the rift.

Behind him, he could hear Guoapa shouting commands, and where his claws touched the wall of the pinnace he could feel the vibrations as the Dinac ship failed over and over to activate its own drives and flee. Meter by meter, the *Whitetree* was swallowed whole by the ragged mouth of the spatial fissure, consumed along with a handful of escape pods that had ejected in hopes of breaking free of the pull. Fountains of exotic particles briefly flared into the visible spectrum, marking the instant of the *Whitetree*'s disappearance.

The distortion waves kept on coming, pounding the pinnace's hull like storm-force breakers against a seawall. Wood groaned like a living thing and overstressed supports burst into sprays of splinters. Ythiss felt the craft lurch again as it too now began the slow, inexorable drift toward the rift's event horizon.

Lights were going out all down the length of the main corridor, and frost was forming on the ports as life support shut down. Ythiss felt a paw on his shoulder, and he turned to see Guoapa, wide eyed and desperate. "I am so sorry," she blurted. "Did we cause this?"

He was still trying to form a reply when the anomaly gave a final pulse of energy, before it swallowed itself and vanished. A heartbeat later, a last aftershock ripple of stressed gravitons pulsed out across the darkness and struck the pinnace head-on.

The wooden deck came flashing up to meet Ythiss, and then there was pain, then nothing.

When he awoke, it was dark and wintry, and the lieutenant had no way to reckon how much time had elapsed. The tricorder was damaged, many of the sensing functions ruined by the subspace discharge or from the sheer physical damage of being hurled across the interior of the Dinac ship.

Ythiss was dimly aware that he had broken some bones in his leg, but the pinnace's internal gravity had dropped, and that made it easier to manage the injury. Guoapa found him as he came out of unconsciousness, and he realized she had moved him to a different compartment. Other Dinac crew members and a couple of familiar faces from the *Whitetree* huddled there, keeping close together to make the best use of body heat. Breath formed bubbles of white vapor as he exhaled. The air was polar-cold, raking at the inside of his chest like knives. The deep chill made him sluggish, and Ythiss cursed his saurian biology.

"All primary systems are blacked out," Guoapa was saying, with a grim set to her ears. "Drives do not answer. Communications appear nonfunctional. We shifted some battery support packs to power life provision, but that will not last long. A span-day at best."

Ythiss accepted the bleak news with a nod and peered at the tricorder. The readings were confused. "Is this . . . everyone?"

"It would seem so. Some tiers of the ship were released to the void. No reply from them." He could sense she was maintaining a firm rein on her emotions for the good of her crew, but the lieutenant had come to know the Dinac female well enough over the past few weeks to see that she was furious at their circumstances. "So, we preserve who is here until we can do so no longer."

He nodded again. "That effect we witnessed. It was . . . external. Caused by something outside . . . both ships." His thoughts were slow and glacial, and Ythiss's scaly face twisted in a scowl.

For an instant, Guoapa's spirit seemed to lift briefly. "I feared that we might have made this thing. These new iterations of our engine designs are still untested. We could have—"

Ythiss shook his head. "No. I think . . . we were in the wrong place. At the wrong time." He shuddered at his own understatement. *Such bland words to be the epitaph for nearly one hundred officers, noncoms and cadets.* A sickly feeling washed over him as he came to the realization that he and the handful of survivors around him would soon join the lost. Either the air would run out or the cold would take their lives. Here, far between stars at the unexplored fringes of the Alpha Quadrant, rescue would never come.

The Dinac captain seemed to intuit his thoughts. "Lieutenant Ythiss. You and your Starfleet came so far to befriend us. I regret this is the result of it."

He was finding his way toward a suitable reply when the tricorder let out a strangled bleat. Ythiss looked down at the screen. The scanner was registering a number of life-forms closing in on their location. "Guoapa . . . are you certain there were no other survivors?"

"On my world, I swear it."

The scan returned odd, off-kilter results. *Not carbon-based life. Some strain of organic the damaged device cannot read.* He tapped another key, activating an overlay. There were no resonance traces from transporters, nothing to indicate another vessel out in the vacuum nearby. *If we have been boarded, where did they come from?*

In the corridor outside the compartment, ice-rimed wood creaked and groaned as weight settled on it. Someone was moving closer.

Ythiss pulled himself up and took a step toward the sealed hatch. "Hello?"

On the other side of the hatch, something made a sharp, metallic noise like the snapping of bones.

"So . . ." Admiral William Riker glanced over his shoulder as they stepped out of the transporter room and into the main corridor. "How many messages did it take to wear him down this time? Ten? Twenty?" He raised an eyebrow. "Fifty?"

The thin, gangly Caitian walking at his side absently pawed at his face, smoothing the black and white fur there. "I'm not certain I have the count, sir."

Riker allowed a thin smile. "Mister Ssura, I don't believe that for a second. You're my aide *because* you know everything down to the *nth* percentile. I know you know exactly how many times I had to put in a call to Admiral Akaar's office for this meeting."

"Indeed, sir," allowed the lieutenant, his ears twitching in apology. "But it has been my observation that my overaccuracy in certain conversational situations is off-putting to some. I am attempting to be more . . . colloquial."

"And also you think it doesn't matter?"

Ssura's head fell in a shallow nodding motion. "There is that." He gestured with the padd that never seemed to leave his grip. "It is well known that Admiral Akaar is not the most communicative of superior officers."

"I hadn't noticed," Riker deadpanned. The reality of it was, the towering Capellan admiral had an entire Starfleet to run, with hundreds of vessels to oversee, the borders of an interstellar nation to patrol and a far frontier to explore. The concerns of one man—and one command—were probably quite a way down his priority list.

Still, Will Riker had hoped that ascending to the first rung of the admiralty would have made a difference—but he quickly learned that even within Starfleet's top brass, the pecking order was as rigidly enforced as it had been between the first class and fourth class on his first day at the Academy, if not more so. He smiled again as he thought of a favorite phrase of his old friend and former commander Jean-Luc Picard: *Plus ça change . . .*

The corridor they followed described a circular arc around the interior wall of Starbase One, the great spindle-shaped space station orbiting high over Earth. As they continued, the bland walls gave way to a vertiginous view through great floor-to-ceiling panels of transparent aluminum. The massive space-bay of the dock extended away beyond the windows, and floating out there in null gravity were a half-dozen starships of various configurations. Most of them had the pearlescent hulls of Starfleet craft, although Riker glimpsed part of a streamlined fuselage in terra cotta shades.

Ssura noticed his attention. "From the Vulcan trade delegation," explained the felinoid.

Riker nodded, mentally ticking off all the classes and registrations of the ships with the same care he had shown as a boy growing up in Alaska. Back then he had been poring over pages in the *Starship Spotter* guidebook; now he had a vessel of his own, although the *Titan* was elsewhere, at Utopia Planatia over Mars. Still, a little of that thrill he had felt in his youth came back to him as he watched the ships at anchor. Each one was a story waiting to be told, the beginning of a voyage as yet uncharted.

And that was why he was here: to get his own story back on track.

A turbolift took them down a few levels to the secondary docking ring and a maintenance gallery that protruded from the interior wall of the space-bay. As Riker entered, he saw the sweep of an oval primary hull out past panes of projected holographics. A large cruiser-scale ship was docked there, an older *New Orleans*-class vessel, and he could see workbees and shuttlepods floating over the hull, making final precruise preparations.

Riker looked away and found Admiral of the Fleet Leonard James Akaar standing like a gray-haired sentinel in the middle of the room. He was addressing two junior officers, quietly enough that Riker could not hear what was being said. One of them seemed familiar to him, a dark-haired Efrosian woman with commander's pips on her collar, but he couldn't place the face. At her side, a male lieutenant wearing the mustard-yellow undershirt of an operations officer chanced a look in his direction and gave a wary but respectful nod. The younger man was unknown to him, and Riker couldn't immediately identify his species either. Humanoid, but sporting vertical lines of scales on his forehead, earlobes and throat. Riker made a mental note to question Ssura later on the two officers; as an aide-de-camp, the lieutenant's precise and fastidious demeanor had its advantages. The Caitian was almost as good as a library computer.

As if he had suddenly caught Riker's scent, Akaar turned his back on the man and the woman and fixed him with a cool, level gaze. "Will," he began, without preamble. "Walk with me."

"Sir." Riker fell in step with the taller officer, unconsciously straightening the uniform tunic he wore with a tug on the hem.

Akaar led him out of the maintenance gallery and on to a catwalk tube that extended for a good distance over the saucer section of the docked starship below. If not for the tripolymer support struts holding clear panels in place about them, Riker could have imagined they were in the open air high above the hull, like ancient mariners atop a galleon's mast.

"The *Tokyo*," rumbled Akaar, indicating the ship. "She's undergone a substantial refit from stem to stern. Barely a square meter of the original spaceframe has been left untouched."

Riker nodded. The well of the Federation's resources was not infinite, and sometimes older ships found themselves serving far beyond their original projected terms of service, reinvigorated with new technologies and upgrades. The *Tokyo* would have been a contemporary of the *Enterprise*-D when her keel was first laid, and here she was decades later, about to serve again. "I know her captain. Christopher Jones. Good man."

Akaar returned the nod, coming to a halt. "He and

that Andorian XO of his will be taking her out for an extended cruise. Four years, deep exploration."

Something in Akaar's tone made Riker tense. The reason he had pressed for this meeting, the reason he was here now, the reason he had always felt he had been in Starfleet, was to take on just such a mission. For a while, he'd had it, holding the center seat on *Titan* while the ship pushed back the frontier and went, like the old fleet maxim said, *where no one had gone before.*

But that had fallen away from him in the wake of the events that unfolded after the assassination of President Bacco. Maybe it was some kind of karmic revenge for all the times he had refused promotion to captaincy over the years, but Riker's elevation to flag rank had come completely out of the blue, and on some level, even after months on the job, he was still trying to process that. Becoming an admiral had been the choice of others—of Akaar and officers like him—and Riker had done his best to make the role fit.

He understood that the promotion had been about expediency, about the need for the right man in the right place at the right time. And he had taken on that responsibility, helping to bring the architects of the plot behind Bacco's murder to justice and pulling the Federation back from a darker, more hawkish path. But it was still hard to make everything *connect*. In all his plans for his tomorrows, Will Riker had not thought much further than the bridge of the *Titan*, and the love of his wife, Deanna, and daughter, Natasha.

Even now there were moments when he looked at himself in the mirror and half-wondered when this would all come to a halt. *Okay, Riker. Joke's over. Give back the rank tabs.*

Akaar showed no sign of smiling, however. "I gave all due consideration to your request," said the admiral, as if he could read the other man's mind. "Proposal denied."

Riker's heart sank, but he buried the reaction deep. "Just like that?"

"Just like that," Akaar repeated. "You want to put the *Titan* back on her original mission plan, get your ship out to the Vela Sector again and pick up where you left off." He shook his head. "No. That is not going to happen."

"Sir . . ." Riker began.

"You're not a captain anymore. You don't get the luxury of heading off to parts unknown and digging in the dirt of strange new worlds. Accept it and move on."

The blunt delivery was no less than he expected from the Capellan, but still Riker felt a flicker of annoyance at the dismissal in the words. "I told you, sir, I'll do whatever the fleet asks of me. That's the job, that's the price of wearing the uniform." He drew himself up. "But I joined Starfleet to serve to the *best* of my ability. And frankly, I'm not sure I can reach that when the mission is all about handshakes and trade agreements. I'm not a diplomat. I never have been. I leave that kind of thing to the people who are actually good at it, like my wife."

Akaar made a small noise of agreement. It was the last thing Riker expected. "Interstellar relations are not your strong suit. That's undeniable. Your report on the situation on Garadius IV made that clear. Vice Admiral Peters was not happy."

Riker suppressed the desire to wince at the mention of the mission to the disputed planet. Dealing with the manipulative, antagonistic beings on that world had tested his patience almost to the breaking point.

"And then the recent situation with the Cytherians and that so-called 'summit . . .'" Akaar let his words trail off. "Something that everyone involved wants to put behind them."

Riker colored slightly. What some barrack-room wags had nicknamed the "Takedown Incident" had not exactly been a walk in the park for the newly minted admiral. Along with officers of similar rank from a handful of other galactic powers, Riker had been coerced by elements within an ancient alien civilization to wreak havoc across a dozen star systems, and the fact that he had been used as a proxy against his will was still raw, still a source of both anger and embarrassment. It was another reason Riker wanted to get back out there, to brush off the stigma and return to where he could do the most good.

"I know you think you were promoted too quickly," Akaar continued. "And there are others at Command who feel the same way. But what's done is done. I chose you because I know you will do what the fleet asks of you." He gestured toward the *Tokyo* again. "Jones and his crew will be picking up where you left off in the Gum Nebula. The *Proxima* is already on its way out there, and they'll be taking on *Ganymede*'s mission."

"You're recalling all the *Luna*-class ships?" Riker frowned.

"Not recalling. Re-tasking. Part of it is political . . . One reason is that the Romulans are sending probe ships out to Vela as well. We know the Typhon Pact view the *Luna* ships as heavy cruisers more than explorers, and the last thing we need is to create a new way to antagonize them. Smaller ships, more of them, won't read like a threat." The Capellan shook his head. "The fact is, mission profiles all across the quadrant are undergoing a revision. Stem to stern."

Riker held back a question. He had heard rumors of a change rippling across Starfleet over the past few weeks. Some were saying it was because of the undue influence exercised over the force from the president pro tem after the Bacco assassination. Ishan Anjar, the ambitious Bajoran politician who had stepped into Bacco's shoes after the assassination on Deep Spacc 9, had been a key player in the very conspiracy that brought about her brutal murder. He had justified it with old, familiar rhetoric, cloaking self-aggrandizement with patriotism, claiming that Bacco's peaceful policies would ultimately weaken and destroy the United Federation of Planets. Even though he was now in prison, Ishan's influence still persisted in some corners. *So Akaar's putting our house in order*, thought Riker.

Once again, the admiral of the fleet demonstrated his near-uncanny ability to anticipate questions before they were asked. "One day I woke up and found our best and brightest were all becoming hawks. That cannot stand, Will. It is imperative that we show the new generation of officers and noncoms coming up after us that belligerence is not the Federation way. We are a postwar society now. What we do in the next few years will define us for decades to come."

"I understand." Riker nodded again. "We need to lead by example."

"Just so. You have proven time and time again that you can not only do your duty, but that you also think outside the box. It's a trait you've passed on to all your people on the *Titan*. And that is why I need you, and that ship, close at hand." His tone softened slightly. "But perhaps we'll ease back on the diplomatic missions for now. I have something else in mind." Akaar's hand disappeared into a pocket of his long uniform tunic, and it returned with a small padd. He offered it to Riker.

"New orders, sir?"

"And then some. I've given you license to shake things up a little. It does come with some strings attached, of course."

Riker kept his poker face as he paged through the orders, skimming the content for the high points. One term leapt out at him, and he read it aloud without thinking. "Sector commander . . . ?"

"It may not be the mission you *want*, Will," said Akaar. "But it's the one you *have*. Make it work."

"Aye-aye, sir." Sensing that he was being dismissed, Riker turned to walk back down the gantry, but Akaar put out a hand to halt him.

"One more thing." The Capellan inclined his head toward the maintenance gallery, where Lieutenant Ssura was waiting patiently with his paws crossed in front of him and the two other officers Akaar had been speaking to were still standing at attention where they had been left. "*Two* more, actually."

It was then that the missing pieces of information Riker had reached for moments before now came to him. First, that the species the young lieutenant belonged to was a race called the Skagarans, beings who shared a world called North Star with a colony of displaced humans. And second, that the woman with commander's rank was Dalit Sarai, a former Starfleet Intelligence officer who had directly aligned herself with Ishan Anjar's aggressive policies . . . and become a pariah because of it.

Two

As Ensign Torvig Bu-Kar-Nguv entered the holodeck, the optical augmentations in his eyes automatically adjusted to down-filter the bright glow from the data streams that filled the chamber.

The Choblik blinked. It was a lot to take in, and even for his cybernetically enhanced brain the pace of the digital interface was too fast to process. Pillars of bright binary code extended down from overhead to deck, each a waterfall of data streaming from dozens of different sources. Gigaquads of information flashed past, and in the middle of it stood a static humanoid figure, a strange sketch of a being made up from simple mathematical shapes.

The only features on the figure's spherical head were an inverted triangle of black dots, and it had eight limbs rather than the more typical four. Six sets of fingers were interlaced before its torso, and Torvig was reminded of images he had seen of beings at prayer.

Communing. Yes, that was the term. The entity before him was in communion with the endless tides of information invisibly washing back and forth through subspace all around them.

"Greetings, Torvig." The voice resonated from all around him.

"Hello, White-Blue. How are you today?" He glanced around. "You seem, um, busy."

"I/We are engaged," came the reply. Some of the pillars of data faded away to decrease the clutter in the holodeck, and the glow in the room fell to a more ambient level. The holographic humanoid looked up at the engineering officer; the gesture, in point of fact the avatar itself, was purely for Torvig's benefit, as the being existed in the bioneural circuits built into the walls all around them. "Gratitude expressed for the new co-processor matrix you provided. I/We have been able to improve functionality by a factor of twenty-three percent."

"I am glad I could help." Torvig hesitated. "I was wondering if you had given any more thought to what we talked about."

"The Daystrom Institute," said the hologram. "Affirmative. I/We are preparing a simplified version of my program to submit to them for examination. A nonsentient proxy, to be exact. I/We hope it will be of use in their research."

"That is good, I suppose . . ."

The hologram continued. "In addition, analysis has been completed on the components of the malicious software weapon we recently encountered at the Kinshaya transmitter array. I/We have fully deconstructed the code base and configured several possible countervectors for it, should the weapon or something of similar scope be deployed again." White-Blue's voice briefly took on an indifferent tone. "A crude manipulation of subspace communications technology. That system is better served to unite disparate life-forms, not to inflict harm upon them. I/We have sent the relevant files to your data queue. Perhaps, with Admiral Riker's permission, you could pass them on to Starfleet Command."

"Of course." Torvig was still finding it hard to assimilate the changes his friend had recently gone through, even if White-Blue seemed to have little or no issue with them.

When they had first met, SecondGen White-Blue was an artificially intelligent machine mind inhabiting a robotic "droneframe," a member of a synthetic species that called itself the Sentry Coalition. The AI had asked to accompany *Titan* on its mission of exploration, and for a time it had become a valuable asset to the crew—and a friend to Torvig, whose own origins as a partly artificial life-form had given them both a common bond.

Then White-Blue had apparently given up its existence to save an alien world, but Torvig had never been able to accept that. Instead, he sought out a way to reconstruct the AI's software—a goal he might never have been able to achieve if not for a risky process that had bonded the dead machine intelligence with an advanced hologram program. As much by chance and luck as pure science, Torvig's friend had come back to life. But this new iteration of White-Blue was not the same being, not really. Existing now as pure data, the AI "lived" inside one of *Titan*'s holodecks in a form far beyond organic or mechanical instrumentality.

"Are you okay down here?" The question sounded odd as it left Torvig's mouth. "Are you, uh . . . *lonely*?"

The hands unfolded. "Friend Torvig, your concern for this construct's emotional well-being is appreciated. Your support during this period of reintegration/redefinition has been invaluable." White-Blue paused. "I/We are fully aware that the existence of the primary iteration was terminated, and that the existence of this iteration would not be extant if not for you. Gratitude is expressed. You have given this construct a second chance at life. A great gift, indeed."

Torvig felt as if a weight had been lifted from him. "I am . . . glad you feel that way. I was not sure that bringing you back would be the right thing to do."

"It was. And in return, this construct wishes to offer you something."

The ensign held up one of his bionic arms. "That is not necessary . . ." He trailed off. "Wait, what *kind* of thing?"

"Observe." White-Blue extended his hands and the rest of the data pillars folded away to nothing, replaced by scaled-down virtual models of what looked like a heavily modified version of a Starfleet class-one sensor probe. "This is an adapted spaceframe constructed from Federation components, a microtranswarp drive and several new custom bioneural modules based on Sentry design protocols." With a gesture, the largest projection came apart into sections, becoming an exploded technical diagram in three dimensions.

Intrigued, Torvig peered deep into the display. "You have increased the range and the sensor acuity. And the processing system and data storage capacity is far larger than any other probe I have seen . . . Too large, in fact."

"Negative. It is correct for the mission profile I/We have designed."

"Which is?"

White-Blue pointed at the probe. "If Admiral Riker will permit it, this construct will download its full program into a probe unit. A complete transfer of consciousness."

Torvig's eyes widened. "But what about your droneframe? It is still in storage, down in engineering . . ."

"I/We have evolved beyond the limits of that shell. Chief Engineer Ra-Havreii has often expressed the desire to dismantle this construct when he believes I/We are not listening. He has permission to do so with the droneframe. It is no longer required. The transwarp probe will enable this construct to achieve what I/We have always desired. To *explore*." There was a hint of awe in the synthetic voice. "Aboard *Titan*, this construct cannot meet its full potential. You and William Riker have helped I/We achieve so much, Torvig. Interrogative: Will you do so once again?"

The ensign felt a pang of sadness but covered it quickly. "If that is what you want . . . But I hoped there was more we could learn from one another."

"There is. We shall." White-Blue brought up a new series of images, and Torvig recognized the design of an advanced neural interface mechanism. "You can accompany I/We. This cyberlink will enable you to directly download your organic mind into a positronic neural net carried aboard another transwarp probe."

"What?" Torvig's throat went dry.

"Choblik neural architecture is highly compatible with this design," White-Blue went on, apparently unaware of the pallor creeping over Torvig's snout. "It would be a relatively painless process."

As he watched, the interface device went through a

simulated download cycle. Long reader needles designed to penetrate deep into brain tissue extended from the inner surface of the unit, and the Choblik unconsciously ran a hand over his furry scalp. "*Relatively painless*," Torvig repeated, in a dead voice.

"Affirmative. In addition, your life span would be extended indefinitely." White-Blue paused. "You once said that you joined Starfleet to see the galaxy. This is an efficient method by which to meet that goal."

"I am grateful for the, um, offer," he managed, fumbling for the right words. "But I am not sure I am ready to completely discard my organic body just yet."

"The offer remains open," White-Blue replied. "As *Titan* will no longer be engaging in its exploratory mission in the Vela Sector, it may represent the only opportunity you will have to—"

"Wait, what did you say? The mission is canceled?" Torvig reeled back, shocked by the AI's casual mention of the fact. "How do you know that?" The ensign had heard talk aboard the ship that Admiral Riker was meeting with Fleet Admiral Akaar that day to determine the future of the *Titan*, but as far as Torvig knew, no official announcement had been made. He studied the hologram carefully. "Please tell me you have not been entering secure Starfleet databases without permission . . ."

"Negative." White-Blue seemed affronted by the suggestion. "You have made your strange needs to restrict various kinds of data very clear to this construct. Those boundaries have been respected." Panels of information snapped into existence all around Torvig, everything from bills of lading to spatial observations, unclassified communications logs to equipment requests. "Using pattern modeling, I/We have observed multiple indicators congruent with standard Starfleet Command mission deployment strategy. By analysis of several thousand information traffic sources, this construct has been able to determine that *Titan*'s next deployment will be within the bounds of known Federation space, probability plus or minus five-point-five-one percent."

Torvig caught a piece of the data streaming past on one of the panels, a request to Memory Alpha from the science teams aboard *Tokyo* for all of *Titan*'s mission logs for their time in the Gum Nebula and beyond. "Oh." Now that the AI was pointing them out, Torvig saw all the circumstantial evidence indicating that White-Blue's prediction was likely the right one. He felt a sudden sense of disappointment. "But . . . we were going *back*. To see the cosmozoans again, the Squales, even your people . . . We are not finished out there."

"It would seem your commanders have other plans," said the hologram. The data panels faded away and the image of the fearsome-looking neural interface device reappeared. "Interrogative: Perhaps you wish to reconsider?"

"Level with me, Deanna." Commander Christine Vale looked over her shoulder at *Titan*'s counselor and chief diplomatic officer. "What's your husband thinking?"

She gave a half-smile. "You know it doesn't work like that, Chris." Troi tapped a finger against her own temple. "Empath, not telepath, remember? There are times when Will's like a closed book to me."

"I hear that," said Vale, taking a deep breath. "More so, these days. I guess that extra weight on the collar is heavier than it looks." She gestured at the three rank pins on her maroon-colored undershirt.

Both women looked away across the starship's primary landing bay as an alert chime sounded and flashing lights began to blink around the wide hatch that dominated the compartment. Standing at a console nearby, Petty Officer Tabyr ran her long-fingered hands over the panel, and with a hiss of pressure shift, the hatch started to drop open like the drawbridge of some age-old castle. Troi could make out the glittering membrane of a force field barrier holding the atmosphere of the ship safely in place. Beyond, there was the void of space and a fractional arc of rust-red: all that was visible of the surface of Mars from their high orbit. A Type-11 shuttlecraft glinted as it caught the sunlight from distant Sol, turning inbound toward the starship.

Vale glanced along the line of officers, and without a word from her they all drew up into a more formal stance. Deanna's husband had never been one to stand on ceremony, and his promotion to admiral hadn't altered that, but she knew Vale and the others had nothing but respect for Will Riker and they wanted him to know it. This was going to be an important moment, and it needed a little gravitas.

Christine had, as was her wont, done something new with her hair for the occasion. The cut of it was intriguingly asymmetric this time around, with a thread of bright copper standing out among the rest of her tresses. Standing to the first officer's right was the next man down the line of command on board *Titan*, the ship's tactical officer, Commander Tuvok. As always, the Vulcan's dark face was steady and unreadable; to Troi's empathic senses he was like a calm oasis amid the shifting sands of sensation that came from the others around her. Outwardly, Security Chief Ranul Keru was as stoic as his Vulcan counterpart, but beneath that impassive surface the unjoined Trill was all controlled energy and directed strength. He caught her eye and gave Troi a warm smile. Filling out the rest of the group of department heads were Aili Lavena and Sariel Rager, the Pacifican and human females having served at *Titan*'s conn and ops stations with distinction since the ship had first left spacedock.

To Troi's left, *Titan*'s chief medical officer, Shenti Yisec Eres Ree, shifted lightly on the talons of his feet, his tail making slow, lazy motions back and forth. The Pahkwa-thanh saurian sniffed at the air and made a low grunt deep in his throat. "I smell anticipation," he said quietly.

"That's one way to describe it." Last in line was Commander Melora Pazlar, *Titan*'s science officer. Anyone who didn't know the Elaysian's species would never have guessed that she came from a microgravity world that forced her to wear a g-suit beneath her uniform at all times. Deanna could tell that most of the expectation in the room was coming from her.

There should have been one more person waiting on the landing apron, but as usual Chief Engineer Xin Ra-Havreii had made his excuses and refused to leave the warp core for what he had called "a cursory meet-and-greet." The ship was at the tail end of a few minor refits, some of which had been started when they had been summoned back to Earth before Will's promotion, and never closed out. Ra-Havreii claimed he was ticking off the last important elements of those upgrades, but it was a convenient half-truth he could use to prevent himself from leaving the private little kingdom he had in main engineering.

Thinking about Xin made Troi glance at Pazlar again. The ongoing semi-romantic relationship between the Elaysian science officer and the Efrosian chief engineer had as many peaks and troughs as a sine wave, and if the shipboard rumor mill was to be believed, it was deep in the low phase right now. She filed that fact away for later consideration. Troi's diplomatic duties also extended to her own crewmates.

There was a low thump of displaced air as the shuttlecraft *Armstrong* crossed over the atmosphere barrier. Through the canopy window, Troi saw Ensign Olivia Bolaji in the pilot's chair, deftly bringing the small craft to a careful halt on the deck. As the hum of the impulse engines faded, a hatch slid open and Troi broke into a smile as she saw Will.

He found her immediately and returned it, but in that instant Troi knew that something was amiss.

"Admiral on deck!" snapped Vale, bringing the assembled officers to parade-ground attention. A synthesized bosun's whistle issued out of the air, piping the admiral aboard with the familiar three-note tone.

"Good to be back," said Riker, stepping down. "As you were, everyone."

Troi saw him glance over his shoulder. She could sense other people in the shuttlecraft, but he had clearly asked them to wait inside for a moment. The joy at seeing her husband again faded.

Vale seemed to sense it too, and the other woman gave her a quizzical look. Will saw the unspoken question and raised a hand to take control of the moment. His lips thinned. "Okay. Let's get the bad news out of the way first. Starfleet has taken our mission away from us. We're not going back to the Vela Sector. In fact, we're not going back to deep space, at least for the foreseeable future."

He let that sink in, and Troi felt the faltering of the collective emotions around her like the sudden ebbing of a tide. Over the past few days, the mood of *Titan*'s crew had been upbeat and optimistic. There wasn't anyone aboard the ship who wasn't anticipating a return to the vessel's first, best destiny: the chance to go out beyond the edges of mapped space and into uncharted territory. *They want to make some history,* Troi had told him at dinner a few days earlier. *They want to do some good.*

"Yes." Riker nodded at them. "Believe me, I know exactly how you feel. I'm not happy about it either. But orders are orders, and what Command asks of us is what we do." He stepped forward, meeting the gazes of his officers one at a time. "We've gone through a lot in the past year or so. Changes for good and for ill. But we have weathered it, and emerged stronger. And I firmly believe that is because this ship is one of the finest in the fleet. From the very start, *Titan* was created to be a microcosm of the United Federation of Planets. No other ship in Starfleet has as diverse a mixture of species and member citizens serving side by side as *Titan* does. We've made it work." He broke into a grin. "No, better than that: We've made it *thrive*. When *Titan* went out to the Gum Nebula and all points beyond, we took a piece of the Federation along with us. Not just the ideals of the charter and the intentions behind it, but a living and breathing example of what we are and what we can accomplish. And I'll grant you that it feels like we're leaving things undone out there, but we're not. Other ships are going to take up the baton we're handing them. They're going to learn from what we have done, and because of *Titan*'s achievements, Starfleet is going to be a better place. We have affirmed the principles of the Federation. We are what people can point to when they say *united we stand, together we are greater*."

Riker's passion, his certainty, was infectious. Troi felt the tide of emotion shift again as the honesty of his words reached every one of her crewmates. She met his gaze, and he showed his wife the smile that was only ever for her.

"I know you want to make some history," he said, drawing on Troi's past words. "I know you want to do some good. And we will. *Titan*'s new mission means she won't range so far from home as she has in years past, but that won't make what we do any less vital." Riker tapped the admiral's rank tab on his collar in a manner that was almost self-deprecating. "I have a new assignment. I'm no longer Admiral-Without-Portfolio. As of zero-nine-hundred hours today, Greenwich Mean Time, I am now an acting sector commander, Alpha Quadrant frontier zone."

Keru, Lavena and Rager were nodding, taking it in. The area of space Will referred to was toward the far perimeter of the UFP, where nonaligned worlds, smaller independent galactic powers and fringe star systems were plentiful. After the chaos of the Borg Invasion, those sectors had been left largely to their own devices by Starfleet, but with the Typhon Pact now a very real presence and the Federation still rebuilding itself, they could not afford to keep looking inward.

Riker continued: "I'm sure you probably know that Sector CO is usually a job for someone of commodore rank, posted to an orbital starbase or a planetside outpost, but Admiral Akaar has given me some *latitude*." He grinned again. "I'm retaining *Titan* as my flagship and mobile base of operations, and from here I'll be keeping watch over the whole thing. You all know me. I'm not one to fly a desk. I like to feel the wind at my back."

With his pause, Riker invited comments, and Pazlar was the first to speak. "It'll be patrol missions from now on, then?" She couldn't keep the disappointment out of her tone, no matter how hard she tried. "Sir, what about our expeditionary operations?"

Tuvok answered for the admiral: "There is much of the frontier sector that offers scientific curiosity."

"I imagine we'll be doing a little bit of everything," Riker replied, glancing between his two officers. "We're not going to stop being explorers, Melora. *Titan*'s too good at that to not use her. But we're also going to be peacekeepers, sentinels, rescuers . . . whatever we need to be." He looked around at the bulkheads of the ship. "What I talked about before, that standard we have established: It won't be off at a distance. We're going to help set the tone for a Federation that has taken some hard knocks in recent times. *Titan* isn't just a starship, she isn't just a tritanium shell keeping a few hundred organic beings alive in the darkness. She is the principles we have chosen to abide by. We're going to stick around for a while and remind people what makes us greater. We are going to lead, to teach, to defend, to uphold *by example.*" He seemed to run out of words; but it was enough.

"Good pitch, Admiral," offered Vale, breaking the silence that followed. "I guess I'm convinced."

"I'm not done yet," said Riker, and he turned back toward the shuttle and beckoned to the people waiting patiently on board. "I brought more than just words."

Three other officers had also disembarked behind the admiral; the first was Lieutenant Ssura, the long-limbed Caitian who had been assigned to Riker as his aide during the Bacco crisis. He bobbed his head in greeting as the admiral explained that Ssura would be permanently transferred to *Titan*, to continue to serve in his present role. The next was a Skagaran lieutenant who hauled a cloth kit bag over his shoulder, a dark hat with a wide brim dangling from his fingers and a large, strangely shaped thing made of leather in his other grip.

"Is that . . . a saddle?" said Keru, out of the side of his mouth.

"Indeed," offered Tuvok. "Curious that a junior officer would use so much of his personal baggage allowance for such an object."

"Matching hat too," Vale added, noting that Troi was studying the young man carefully.

"It's called a Stetson," said the counselor.

The lieutenant had a rangy build and unkempt dark hair that didn't hide the lines of scales common to his species. He realized he was being watched and came to attention. "Captain," he said, addressing Vale as the next most senior officer present after Admiral Riker. "Lieutenant Ethan Kyzak, reporting for duty. Permission to come aboard?" He had a drawl to his manner that Vale couldn't decide if she found charming or showy, and she frowned.

"Granted, Mister Kyzak."

"The lieutenant here is going to be joining us as an operations officer." Riker glanced toward Rager, the ship's senior ops manager. "Sariel, can you come forward?" He beckoned to Lavena at her side. "Aili, you too."

Ree's snout came close to Vale's ear as the two *Titan* officers crossed in front of them. "Do you know who that is?" The doctor was indicating the last person to exit the shuttle, an Efrosian woman with a flat, humorless expression that marred her otherwise ordinary face.

Vale counted three commander's pips on the Efrosian's collar. "No idea," she whispered back, "but she doesn't look very happy to be here."

"Perhaps she didn't hear the speech."

Vale was going to add something, but Riker had drawn himself up and was speaking again. "The changes in mission profile for the *Titan* are not the only ones that are being made today. Others will come in the days ahead. But here and now, I'm taking advantage of an admiral's prerogative to initiate some changes myself." He took a breath. "Lieutenant Sariel Rager. Lieutenant Aili Lavena. You have both served this ship and Starfleet with integrity, courage and skill. It is therefore my honor to promote you both to the rank of lieutenant commander, effective immediately, with all the responsibilities and privileges therein." Vale heard Lavena release a small gasp of surprise as Riker presented a single gold pip with an obsidian-black center to each of the women.

Rager accepted with a salute and obvious pride. "Thank you, Admiral!"

"Thank you, sir," said Lavena, her eyes shining.

"You two have earned this a dozen times over," Riker told them, meaning every word.

Vale glanced at Troi. "This is turning into an interesting day. Remember last time that happened?"

The Betazoid gave her a look. "I don't think Will's finished."

When she turned back, the admiral was staring straight at her. "Commander Christine Vale," he began. "Step forward."

She did it automatically, her body obeying the order before she had realized it was happening. Her thoughts raced to keep up. *What now?* she wondered. Part of her dared to build a hope, and she crushed it before it could form. *What is he doing?*

Riker's even manner became formal. "Attention to Orders." He beckoned to Ssura, and the Caitian handed him a padd to read from. "Let the log show that as of this stardate, I am standing down from the post of commanding officer of this vessel, and in turn I set my flag to be carried aboard her until such time as I choose otherwise. Full orders are as follows: To Admiral William T. Riker, commanding officer, *U.S.S Titan.* You are hereby requested and required to relinquish command of your vessel to Captain Christine Vale, commanding officer, *U.S.S Titan*, as of this date. Signed, Admiral Leonard James Akaar, Starfleet Command." From somewhere off in the distance, there was an answering beep as the ship's computer logged the order. "Computer, transfer all command codes to Christine Vale. Voice authorization: Riker Bering Yukon."

"*Transfer complete,*" said the ship's artificial female voice. "Titan *now under command of Captain Christine Vale.*"

Riker held out his hand to her, and in it there was a single gold pip. He leaned in to attach it to the line of three already at Christine's collar, and as he did, he spoke in a low tone so that only she could hear him. "You told me a while back you wanted the ship. Now you've got it."

Blood rumbled in her ears. "Sir." It was all she could manage. *Captain*, said a voice in the back of her thoughts. *Captain Vale. For real this time.* In that second, she felt the world turning around her, as if a phase-state change had occurred that only she was capable of seeing. She heard people applauding, but the sound seemed to come from very far away. "I . . . relieve you, sir."

"I stand relieved. You're in command now, Christine," he told her. "I'm just along for the ride."

"Sir," she repeated, still trying to gather her wits. All of this had blindsided her, and it was hard to react evenly. A laugh threatened to break loose, and she pushed it down and away. That wouldn't be the best way to begin her first command, even as she knew her friends and colleagues around her would think it right.

Vale was still forming the correct words when the dark-haired Efrosian officer came forward, offering her a padd as if it was the most important thing that had happened so far. "Commander Dalit Sarai reporting for duty, Captain," she began.

Sarai? The name rang a warning bell in Vale's thoughts. She searched her memory for the reasons why. *Something about being connected to Ishan Anjar and the Bacco crisis, something about Admiral Akaar, and none of it good . . .*

"I'm your new executive officer," concluded the woman.

Even through the deck of the turbolift, Kyzak could sense the brief, subtle motion as *Titan* was impelled forward and away from Mars orbit. It was a gift—something in Skagaran brain structure, so he had been told, an innate sense like the kind some folks had for feeling the approach of a storm cell. It made him want to be up there on the bridge of the big *Luna*-class starship, his hands on the helm console with the power to break the light barrier burning under his fingertips.

All at once he realized how much he missed being on a ship. Two tours on orbital installations had dulled his edge, he realized. Now he was so close to getting back on the horse, he could barely keep himself in check.

His preoccupation with that was almost enough to distract him from the frosty looks he was getting from the other crew members as they passed them by. Well, to be more accurate, the looks his *companion* was getting.

Commander Sarai stood across the lift car from him, steady as a statue, her regulation luggage hanging from her shoulder and a dead, empty gaze in her eyes that never once left a point on the wall near the floor indicator. Kyzak didn't know any Efrosians personally, but he knew that they weren't Vulcans. None of that stoic, silent stuff for them, apparently. The opposite, in fact: Efrosians were supposed to be quite emotional when circumstances required it. He wondered what it was about Sarai that made her an exception.

Sensing his attention, her gaze moved a fraction to fix

on Kyzak, then down to look at the gear he was hauling with him. "Why do you have that?" She jutted her chin at the saddle.

"It's mine," he said lamely. Wasn't that explanation enough? "My pa . . . my father made it for me. He's dead now. Don't have a lot else from him."

She gave a slow nod. "A keepsake."

"A little. Important piece of kit too. I need it to ride."

"Ride what? The only equine beings on this vessel are sentients with free will, and I doubt they would be happy to let you saddle them."

Kyzak jerked a thumb at the walls. "They got a holodeck here, don't they? Holodeck's got horses." He raised the saddle off the ground. "Not as good as the real thing, but I'll make allowances."

Sarai watched him in silence for a moment. The turbolift entered a horizontal traverse, and she spoke again: "Do you have something to say to me, Lieutenant?"

He covered his reaction with a casual shrug. "Uh, well, Commander . . . now that you mention it . . ." Kyzak thought about the other people that had passed them in *Titan*'s corridors, the ones here or there who looked at Sarai like she was someone who had crossed them. Kyzak had seen one Bolian ensign turn to a Syhaari petty officer and whisper something about the commander that he hadn't caught. "What's up with the stink-eye and all?" The moment he said the words, he realized he could have phrased it better.

He was about to backpedal and say something that wasn't quite so tactless, but Sarai was already answering. When she spoke, it was with the weariness of someone who had already accepted an unpleasant truth. "You have no idea who I am or why I am on this ship, do you?"

He decided to go with honesty. "Uh. No."

"A few months ago, I made a mistake that could have cost me my career. My second such mistake, in point of fact." Her gaze turned inward for a moment, and Kyzak thought he saw sorrow in her eyes. Then it was gone, like a light going off, and the woman was all business again. "To put it in a parlance you'll be familiar with, *I backed the wrong horse*."

A chill washed over his scales. "Are you . . . talking about the assassination?" He had been on the Delta 1 station when President Bacco was killed, one of the smallest and most remote listening posts at the far edge of Romulan space. The event, as terrible as it was, had seemed very distant to him. Not for the first time, he tried to imagine how it might have been in the heart of the Federation when that awful news had broken. He remembered the tearful message his mother had sent him over subspace.

"I did my duty," she told him, but in a way it was like Sarai wasn't really noticing Kyzak, more as if she were saying these things for herself. "There was a breach in Starfleet security and I took it to the only person who was willing to listen to me. Ishan Anjar."

That name, the lieutenant knew. Everyone in the Alpha Quadrant did. Ishan had been an ambitious Bajoran politician with his eyes on that nice big office in the Palais de Concorde. His ruthless drive, to remake what he saw as an ineffectual Federation of victimhood and appeasement into a militaristic one fit to be feared, had ultimately led to a conspiracy that almost brought down the pillars of government.

Off his look, Sarai's eyes narrowed in annoyance. "I didn't know what he was doing. I believed in what he said about strength . . . But I do not condone his methods." She looked away. "Because of my choices, I have become an outcast. And now, to make matters worse, I have been sent *here*."

"With all due respect, Commander . . . why are you telling me this?" The turbolift began to slow as it neared the crew quarters.

"You asked," said Sarai. "You deserve to know. And I would like at least one person on board this ship to have heard my side of the story before they judge me. Tell me, what did you do wrong to get posted to the *Titan*?"

The question caught him off-guard. "I, uh, wanted to come here."

A humorless smirk creased her lips. "Ah. For me this assignment is a punishment. For you, it's a reward." The lift halted, and the doors were barely open before Sarai was through them and into the corridor. "In that case, you should probably keep your distance from me, Lieutenant Kyzak. I'm . . . *tainted*."

Three

The next few days were a blur.

Dock departure and the kickoff for an extended duration mission were always an involved business for a senior starship officer, with a hundred little tasks that required attention and almost as many subordinates needing the same. Christine Vale thought she had a handle on all that, though, that she had gotten the whole "executive officer thing" down to a fine art. Even her apprehension at taking the center seat had been eased by the intense—albeit brief—time she spent captaining the *U.S.S. Lionheart* during the Bacco crisis. Privately, she had told herself that she was now ready to do it for real, and that when the moment came, it would be right. As she had dressed for the day in her quarters, she studied her own reflection in the mirror over her dresser. *I've got this,* she told herself.

I don't have this. Captain Vale kept her eyes on the bridge viewscreen in front of her, seeing only the warp-distorted lines of stars as they raced across the void. *Am I ready? Or was I just kidding myself?* Now that she stood atop the mountain, Vale had to admit that the view was making her a bit giddy. Perhaps if she had gotten even a hint of Starfleet's and Riker's intentions, she might have been able to prepare for the sudden change in her circumstances. But having new rank and status sprung on her from out of nowhere . . . It put Vale off-balance, and she didn't like it.

At her side, Commander Deanna Troi was quietly working through a series of crew fitness reports on her padd, and she didn't look up even though Vale knew the Betazoid had to sense her feelings. She was quietly thankful for that. Deanna was a good friend who understood Vale well enough to know that if she wanted support, it would be asked for. *Not just yet. I've got to navigate this myself.*

If Riker thought she was ready, if Akaar thought so, then Vale *was ready*. Maybe the circumstances of the promotion hadn't come in the way she wanted. That didn't matter. She was starting to realize that this mission was going to be different than what had gone before. A page had been turned over; ahead of them was a new chapter in *Titan*'s ongoing endeavors. *So embrace it, Chris*, she told herself.

Of course, if Troi radiated emotional warmth, then the woman to her right was quite literally the polar opposite. Sarai, like Deanna, was also busy with a report, but the commander was absorbed in it almost to the point of seeming disinterested in everything else going on around the bridge. Vale had served on other ships where arriving officers would give a brief speech and introduce themselves before they took on the role . . . There was something about it being good practice in the manual, she remembered. Sarai didn't bother with any of that, simply repeating word for word the terse introduction she had given in the shuttlebay and taking the XO's chair like she was impatient to get started.

So far, all attempts at small talk made Vale feel as if she were tossing her words into a black hole. Sarai did her job very well. In fact, she was pinpoint perfect about it. But unless circumstances required her to converse with another being, she interacted with no one. As far as Vale was aware, nobody had seen Sarai outside of her quarters when off-duty, either.

For now, it wasn't an issue . . . but it could become one. Vale had read Sarai's personnel file, noting the unsettling number of redacted sections within its pages where the commander's work for Starfleet Intelligence had been classified secret. And as for the parts that were visible, there were two notable black marks. The first, a Captain's Mast investigation over a friendly fire incident in her past that had seen her absolved of all charges but perhaps not the guilt; the second, the commander's more recent insubordination and circumvention of the chain of command with regard to Doctor Julian Bashir's actions in the Andorian reproductive crisis. It troubled Vale that Starfleet had given her a first officer who had disobeyed her former commanders when the mood took her. Perhaps someone higher up was giving Vale a taste of her own medicine, as payback for her own bucking of the regs. Or was it that Sarai was here because she was being granted a second . . . no, a *third* chance?

Vale sighed. *One problem at a time.*

Sarai suddenly looked up. "Yes, Captain?"

"Any update on our mission status?"

"No, Captain."

"Thank you, Number One." She tried the phrase out for size, but all it got her was a questioning scowl from Sarai. "It's, ah, an informal term for a first officer," she explained.

The Efrosian's eyes narrowed. "I see."

"At this speed, we should reach Dinac space in the next day or so," offered Troi, attempting to draw open the conversation. "Are you familiar with their species, Commander Sarai?"

"I contributed to the security evaluation of their civilization following the formal first contact in 2378." The reply was flat and without weight. "I have never met one of them." Sarai went back to her padd.

Christine and Deanna exchanged glances. "I hear that Casroc is a world of outstanding natural beauty," Troi went on, referring to the Dinac home planet. "Perhaps we might have the chance to look around when we get there."

Vale nodded, forgetting about Sarai's tight-lipped manner for the moment, and her thoughts returned to the mission at hand.

Titan's route out to the frontier passed close to Dinac territory, and it was a matter of course that they were to make contact with the Starfleet ship assigned to that area. The *Whitetree* was now thirty-one hours overdue for its last check-in with Starfleet Command, and that was enough to set the higher ranks worrying about her. Once they were in range, *Titan*'s powerful sensor suites would be able to sweep the zone and hopefully find the wayward ship. It might be something as simple as disruption from an ion storm blocking communications, or some minor malfunction. Vale hoped so. She wanted very much for her first task as *Titan*'s captain to be something positive.

Thinking that made her look around the bridge, and there she saw—with the notable exception of

Commander Sarai—a dozen faces who all looked back at her with expectant expressions. Keru at the security station, Pazlar at sciences, McCreedy at engineering, even in a small way Tuvok at tactical, they all seemed to be waiting for her to say something. They had been so since *Titan* left the Sol system.

They want a speech, thought Vale. *Something stirring, like Will gave us. But I'm no good at that. It's not what I do.*

She glanced back at Sarai, with her fixed, sullen manner. *Maybe it's what I do* now. *I don't really want to follow my new first officer's example.* Vale took a breath and got up out of the chair. All eyes immediately turned to her, and she found herself unconsciously tugging the hem of her uniform tunic to straighten it.

"Okay," she began. "Look, I know that a newly minted captain is supposed to stride on to the bridge and come up with something spontaneously rousing, but I've never really been one to rely on words when deeds are what count." Vale felt a change in the air as her crew listened to her speak; suddenly, distinctly, she felt like she was *in command.* "So I'm going to—"

The strident chime of an intercom cut through the air and snapped her concentration in two. Lieutenant Ssura's voice issued out of hidden speakers. *"Bridge? Admiral Riker requests Captain Vale's presence in his office at her first opportunity."*

"—to let everyone continue to do their jobs as well as I know you will," Vale concluded, the words coming in a rush. "Carry on." Without waiting to see how her comments had settled, she walked away toward the turbolift.

"Good pitch, Captain," said Troi, as she passed her.

The admiral's office—or, to give it the correct designation, the sector command hub—had previously been an observation gallery on the dorsal surface of *Titan*'s primary hull, a couple of decks down from the bridge cupola. Part of the refits completed at Utopia Planatia, the rectangular compartment was now a combination of briefing room, operations center and workplace from which Riker could keep a weather eye on the situation over dozens of star systems.

The hub was dominated by a large oval holotable. Dozens of virtual panes hung suspended in the air above it, and Lieutenant Ssura was up to his shoulders in them, leaning right into the holographic displays to manipulate the gesture-sensitive interface. He came to attention as Vale entered and pointed toward an office area behind glass walls at the far end of the room. "Go right in, Captain."

Riker was standing in front of a replicator as she entered. It was the first time they had been able to talk privately since leaving Mars. "Chris!" He pointed to a padd on the table. "Take a look. I've been thinking about what Melora said, looking at some sites of scientific interest along our projected cruise." A cup materialized in front of him, and Vale smelled Bajoran *cela* tea. "Can I get you something?"

"How about the comm code for your speechwriter?"

An easy smile bloomed. "Ah. I'm sorry, did I interrupt something?"

"Something," she repeated. "You know me. I like to *act* instead of *talk*."

He took his seat. "You can always go back up there and do the sermon again if you didn't like it the first time around. You're the captain now. They have to listen to you." When the humor didn't work, he nodded toward an empty chair and Vale took it. "Chris," he began again, becoming serious, "I know this was sudden—"

She didn't let him finish. "You know, Admiral, sir, there's a part of me wondering if you sprang this on me because of what Akaar did to you. He never warned you that a promotion was coming. You had to deal with it on the fly."

Riker's manner cooled. "I did. I made . . . I am *making* my peace with it. Akaar told me later that he hadn't given me anything I couldn't handle. And now I'm doing the same with you." He sipped his drink and nodded at the bulkheads. "Don't you want this?"

"Not fair," she shot back. "You know that I do. I just would have liked some time . . . to brace myself."

Riker waved away the comment. "No need for that. I saw what you did on *Lionheart*, and before that every mission on this ship when I wasn't on the bridge and you were. You're a captain, Christine. And I didn't want you to make the same mistakes I did when I was an exec." He paused. "We all have our doubts. That's what makes us human. It's also what keeps us grounded."

Vale leaned forward. "All right. If we're putting our cards on the table . . . What about Sarai? Why assign her as my XO?"

The admiral sat back in his chair and put down his cup. "As much as I'd like it to be so, the rank doesn't make me all powerful."

"You didn't choose her." It wasn't a question. "So. Akaar, then?"

"He had a hand in it. But even the admiral of the fleet

answers to somebody. Dalit Sarai is here because she's not one of us. Because of the choices she made in the past, she's an outsider."

Vale connected the dots. "She's here to keep watch?"

"That's the trade-off, I think. For us and for her. After the business with the Cytherians, there are people who would happily ship me off to some faraway Gamma Quadrant outpost for the rest of my career."

She nodded. "You and me both, sir. I did break a whole bunch of regulations when I went looking for Bashir."

"Not forgotten," said Riker. "If it hadn't been Sarai . . ." He let the sentence hang.

She didn't need him to fill in the rest. *If it hadn't been Sarai, Starfleet would have probably made someone else captain of this ship and I . . . who knows where I would be?*

He leaned in again. "This is not a problem for us, Chris. It's an opportunity. Our mission and our circumstances may have changed, but we haven't."

There was more she wanted to say, but then Ssura appeared at the doorway, his paw kneading a padd. "Pardon me, sir and ma'am, but Commander Tuvok has passed on a message of some import. We have received subspace contact from the Dinac, sent directly from their homeworld."

Vale quickly did the math in her head. "They'd need to put a whole lot of power behind it to reach us out here."

"What kind of contact?" said Riker.

Ssura's ears bowed. "A distress signal, sir."

Melora Pazlar tapped a glassy rectangle on the surface of the briefing room table and the screen on the wall shifted to an image of a planet from orbit, all ocher tones, green strips of ocean and fluffy white clouds. "Casroc," she explained. "A fairly typical Class-M world orbiting a white F-type main sequence star, home to—"

The briefing room door hissed open and Lieutenant Kyzak entered in a rush. He saw Pazlar and gave her a winning smile. "Great. *Finally*. This ship has a *lot* of briefing rooms." He straightened. "I'm sorry I'm late, Commander. I think it's going to be a while before I get the ship's layout straight in my head."

"You didn't miss much, Mister Kyzak," she said, and Pazlar found herself returning the smile. "Just be on time in the future."

He nodded and slipped into the one vacant seat next to Zurin Dakal. "Howdy," he said to the other officer, looking him up and down. "Cardassian, right?"

"Lieutenant Dakal," said Zurin, nodding and offering his hand. "Very observant," he said with a wry smirk.

"Sorry, I don't mean to gawk, but I never met one of you before." Kyzak blew out a breath and shook his hand. "Truth be told, I'm gonna need a guidebook to identify all the species on this ship, I reckon."

"It gets easier, sir," said Ensign Fell. The Deltan leaned closer, as if offering a confidence to the new crewman. "Just make sure you don't confuse the Kasheeta with the Pahkwa-thanh. They really hate that."

"Or the Kazarites with the Thymerae," added Y'lira Modan, *Titan*'s Selenean cryptolinguist. The other officers in the room began to offer their own warnings, one after another.

"The Chelons and the Rigellians too," Dakal picked up the thread. "It can be troublesome."

Kyzak frowned. "Why do I feel like I should be taking

notes?" He glanced at the Deltan. "What were those first two again?"

Pazlar tapped her finger on the table, halting the conversation. "Interpersonal advice can be doled out later," she insisted. "Mission brief comes first." She reiterated her description of the planet Casroc before moving to the next image; this one was of a representative male and female of the Dinac species. "Native sentients are a canine-humanoid biotype, usually ranging from one-point-five to two meters in height. Life span is slightly below the standard human average because of environmental issues, but that's something we'll be able to help them with if and when they become members of the UFP. Current population is around seven billion beings, with a democratic socialist world government and a technology level of grade nine on the Jackson metric. They discovered warp drive theory in the last decade or so, and they're very fast learners." Ensign Fell raised a hand. "Peya, you have a question?"

"What are the environmental issues you mentioned?"

"Casroc is quite arid, and livable land is at a premium there. The Federation Science Council estimates that within the next four generations, the Dinac will reach a critical population size that will adversely affect their civilization. They need to leave the cradle and start finding other worlds to colonize if they want to continue to grow." Pazlar advanced to another image, this one of a rocky desert captured on the planet's surface. Tall, orange-red stone buttes sculpted by wind reached into the sky, and the plains around them seemed to go on forever.

"Huh," said Kyzak. "Reminds me of home."

Dakal eyed the Skagaran. "I feel the same."

Kyzak shot him a look. "They have prairies on Cardassia Prime? Who knew . . ."

"The Dinac have proven to be an open and friendly people," continued Pazlar. "They want to become part of the galaxy at large, and they have reached out to us to help them make that happen. Currently, the Corps of Engineers and Starfleet Academy are working with the ruling council on Casroc as part of a cultural and technological exchange program."

Y'lira's smooth golden features shifted as she took that in. "So there are no major Prime Directive issues at hand, but at the same time we have to let them find their way out here."

"They're quite rich in topaline." Dakal looked down at the padd in front of him, reading off the results of a geological survey. "There are many races who would trade an alliance for that mineral."

"The Dinac want to do things on their own terms," said Pazlar. "They're adamant about it. No shortcuts."

Kyzak nodded approvingly. "Gotta respect that."

"We also have the astropolitical situation to consider." The science officer tapped another key and the image was replaced by a tactical plot of the sector surrounding the Dinac home star system. "Look here." Pazlar highlighted a zone of space several light-years away that was marked by a triangular red icon. "The Tholian Assembly is just over the stellar horizon."

"That'd be on the wrong side of too close for comfort," muttered Kyzak.

"Succinctly put, Lieutenant." She nodded. "For now, they're ignoring the fact that the Dinac even exist, but that may not last forever. And when the Tholians and their friends in the Typhon Pact eventually *do* decide to turn their attention in Casroc's direction, it would be better for the Federation to have another friend out here."

"So what's the purpose of our visit?" asked Fell. "Show the flag?"

"Something like that," said Pazlar. "*Titan* will rendezvous with *Whitetree* and offer any assistance if it is required. The *Whitetree* and her crew, most of whom are cadets, are working with the Dinac on their first long-range explorer vessel."

"And it will not be a bad idea for the Dinac to see one of Starfleet's most advanced vessels in action," noted Modan.

Pazlar gave a nod, recalling Admiral Riker's speech in the shuttlebay about setting examples. "We can show them what they can achieve. And we will learn something from them along the way. Their take on warp drive technology is very unique, and a lot of the senior scientists at the Corps of Engineers want to know more about it."

The discussion continued for another ten minutes, with the science officer fielding questions about the alien civilization they would soon encounter until at last she brought the orientation briefing to a close.

"There's a full background report package in your data queues," she told them. "Any other questions you may have about the Dinac should be covered there. Otherwise, contact me directly. If all goes well, this will be a smooth start to the cruise and an opportunity to come face-to-face with a new civilization. Dismissed."

After the others had left, Kyzak loitered by the briefing room door, and Pazlar shot him a look as she gathered up her padd.

"Commander . . ." he began, "I, uh, wanted to apologize again about my late arrival."

She smiled. "You can call me Melora. And don't worry, I'm not going to be filing a report because you were two minutes late to a meeting."

"Thanks. The last assignment I had, the base commander ran a very tight ship, and that kind of thing was pretty much the rule. And I'm Ethan, by the way."

"*Titan*'s a bit more relaxed than some fleet postings," she admitted. "Admiral Riker and Commander . . . I mean, *Captain* Vale tend to give their crew some leeway, as long as we do our jobs."

"Good to know. Next time I'll get directions *first*." He frowned slightly. "But to be honest, I wasn't kidding about that whole guidebook thing. I mean, I passed my xeno culture classes at the Academy like everyone else, but I saw beings on my way here that are totally, well, *alien* to me." Kyzak gave a rueful grin. "I shared a turbolift with an arthropod the size of a pony and someone that looked like a glow-lamp made of crystals. It's a little outside my experience."

"That would have been Chaka and Se'al Cethente Qas, our resident computer sciences and astrophysics specialists." Pazlar's smile grew. There was something almost endearing about Kyzak's manner.

"You're Elaysian, is that right? From Gemworld?" Off her nod, he blew out a breath. "Okay, good. I got that one right."

"Only three hundred and forty-nine more to go."

He took a breath. "Melora . . . if it's not out of line for me to ask . . . I'd appreciate it if I could take some of your time, maybe help me get up to speed on who and what I'm going to be working with on this mission?"

Her first reaction was to shut him down and refuse. Kyzak's request could be exactly what it was on the surface, or it might be an attempt to look for something else . . . something more personal. She opened her mouth to speak, then halted. Things between her and Xin Ra-Havreii had been cooling since before that business with the Cytherians, and just that morning the chief engineer had left her a message canceling a dinner meeting planned for the end of alpha shift, with no more than a cursory explanation. Her relationship with Xin could be enjoyable, but it could also be hard work, and right now it was at the wrong end of that equation. Suddenly, the idea of having a drink with someone new seemed very appealing to her.

"Tell me, do you have dinner plans?"

"No, sir."

"You do now, Lieutenant."

Kyzak's crooked smile told her that she'd been right about him; but then in the next second the door to the briefing room hissed open and Admiral Riker entered, a grim cast to his face.

"Melora! Good, you're here." He shot a nod at the Skagaran. "Mister Kyzak."

"Sir." Both officers immediately came to attention.

Riker held out a padd to her. "You need to see this." As she took it and began to read, the color drained from her face. "I know you're heading off-duty," he continued, "but I'm afraid I'm going to have to ask you to deal with this first."

"Of course, sir," she replied, putting aside her reaction and focusing on the job at hand.

Kyzak's head twitched and he glanced out the briefing room windows at the warp-distorted starlight beyond. "We just increased speed. Sir, what's wrong?"

Riker nodded toward the padd. "That's a message from the capital city on Casroc, by way of the Dinac

Expeditionary Initiative. They're reporting that they have lost all contact with the explorer ship they dispatched on its maiden voyage. The *Whitetree* was flying with them."

"I'll assemble all the astro-science department heads, and get to work on reconfiguring *Titan*'s long-range sensors for a full-spectrum search protocol," said Pazlar, all trace of other concerns now shuttered away in the face of this new emergency. "The Dinac are saying that they can't raise the *Whitetree* either."

"What can I do, sir?" said Kyzak.

"Get up to the bridge and take ops, mister. Commander Rager will need to be briefed by Captain Vale." Riker's frown deepened. "I'm afraid this mission has just become a search-and-rescue operation."

The wreck was alone in the blackness and the silence, the gossamer wing-vanes broken and shredded by the shock waves that had battered them, the hull cracked and scorched. A thin comet tail of frozen breathing gasses and water vapor streamed out behind the ovoid craft as it tumbled on its uncontrolled course, drawing a faint, shimmering line down toward the ruined vessel. Pieces of hull had sloughed off as the internal atmosphere boiled away into the vacuum, great splinters of carefully carved wood now cast to space, lingering millions of kilometers away from the world where the trees they had once been had grown.

The pinnace was a sorry sight. Its unusual alien beauty had been stripped from it by stellar fires and subspace particle bombardment. What had once been a sculpted marvel of engineering and artistry was now a burned figure, its metal endoskeleton peeking out from the places where the fuselage had been brutally ripped away.

Titan reverted from warp velocity a light-minute away from the wreck, the powerful scanners in the *Luna*-class ship's upper sensor dome finally picking out the derelict against the endless range of night.

It had taken days to find the explorer, with crews working around the clock to scour the sector surrounding the last known coordinates of the *Whitetree* and her Dinac companion. Of the Federation starship, there was no trace, but careful sifting of ion traces across the spectrum had at last brought *Titan* to the bones of the pinnace.

Closing to a respectful distance, targeted searchlight beams from the bigger ship cast forth to illuminate the alien explorer, as a repeating comm signal went out calling to anyone who might have survived the pinnace's ordeal.

No voice returned. Sensors played over the fractured hull and penetrated deeper, looking for energy sources, life signs, anything that might indicate that the Dinac vessel was not completely dead.

Aside from the faintest trace of stored power in the ceramic battery cores buried deep in the vessel's spine, every scan returned a negative result. Cold and dark and broken, the explorer tumbled onward, drifting on a slow course that would take it hundreds of thousands of years to reach the nearest star system.

With delicacy, *Titan* reached out with glittering tractor beams and halted the pinnace's endless fall.

"We arrived too late." It was the first time Tuvok had seen Commander Sarai display anything close to emotion. The first officer shook her head, a bleak manner to her words. "There are no life-forms detected aboard the alien craft."

Tuvok glanced at the repeater screen on his tactical console, where the same sensor readings Sarai was consulting were scrolling down the panel. He set about tapping in a string of commands, shunting the scan data to a subroutine that would compare the damage done to the pinnace with known weapons-fire patterns.

Captain Vale leaned forward in her chair. "Any biological traces?" She was reticent to say *bodies*, Tuvok thought, as if to utter the word would somehow cement the reality that the pinnace carried no survivors. There would have been no such squeamishness among a Vulcan crew, only the bare logic of the tragedy stripped of all emotive content; but Tuvok had served with non-Vulcan crews long enough to know that they required such emotional props in order to function efficiently. In a small way, he felt regret for Vale, Sarai and the others, that they could not come to this dilemma with the same clarity that he did. He glanced toward Counselor Troi; the Betazoid empath would feel it more than all of them.

"None," reported Sarai. "The hull has a large organic component, and that may be affecting scans, but I doubt it."

Troi asked the question that all of them were thinking: "The ship is empty? A vessel of that class carries a crew of eighty-four Dinac. Is it possible they all could have been lost . . ." She trailed off, wondering at the fate of the missing.

Vale gave a terse shake of the head. "Even catastrophic explosive decompression wouldn't take everyone."

Sarai looked up from her console. "Captain, with

your permission, I've already prepared a protocol for an away team deployment to the wreck. We need to take a look at it firsthand."

"Agreed. But I want a full sensor work-up on the ship before anyone sets foot on it." Vale turned to look back at Tuvok. "Commander, your evaluation?"

The security chief read aloud the results of his damage report. "Patterns of destruction across the hull and superstructure of the pinnace do not appear to be the result of a conventional directed energy attack. There are no matches with known phaser, disruptor or particle beam weapons. Given the density of delta-type radiation decay in the fuselage, I believe that this was the result of exposure to a subspace phenomenon and not offensive action."

"I concur," Pazlar spoke up from the science station.

"Which immediately begs the question," said Troi: "If the *Whitetree* was somehow destroyed, was the Dinac ship caught in the same effect?"

Sarai frowned. "Anything capable of obliterating a *Saber*-class starship before it could send out a Mayday would have left traces. We have found nothing. No wreckage, no escape pods, no log buoy." She pointed toward the main viewscreen and the image of the wreck. "This is the first evidence we have of any kind of misadventure."

Vale rose out of her chair, and Tuvok watched her hands come together behind her back. "Bridge to Hub. Admiral, are you seeing this?"

Riker's voice issued out of the air. *"That I am, Captain. Mister Ssura's preparing a data packet on our discovery to transmit to Casroc as we speak. I'll address the members of the Dinac council myself."* Tuvok heard the sorrow in his voice. *"How do you intend to proceed?"*

"We need to be certain that no one survived and do whatever we can to recover any records that may be intact. Right now, that wreck is the only indication we have as to the fate of the explorers and the crew of the *Whitetree*."

"Agreed. Keep me in the loop. Riker out."

A moment of silence followed, and it was Commander Lavena who broke it, her soft-spoken question hanging in the air. "Ships don't just vanish. There has to be something left behind, some ripple in the water . . ." The Selkie officer stopped, as if she hadn't been aware she was thinking aloud.

Unbidden, Tuvok found his thoughts spinning back to his experiences aboard the *Starship Voyager*, which, like the *Whitetree*, had disappeared without a trace in the area of space known as the Badlands, catapulted across the galaxy to the Delta Quadrant by an alien intelligence. For many years the question of *Voyager*'s loss had gone unresolved. Tuvok wondered if a similar conversation to this one had unfolded aboard the ships sent to find Kathryn Janeway's lost command. *How to cope with a mystery that has no clues?* he asked himself. *An incorrect assumption; the absence of evidence is itself evidence.*

"There are two hundred souls out here who need us to find them," Vale told the bridge crew. "Our fellow officers. Some of them our friends. And people who counted us to be their allies. This doesn't end until we know their fate. We owe them nothing less."

Captain Vale nodded toward Sarai. "Let's go to work."

Four

"*This is hard news, Admiral Riker.*" There was a distinct growl in the alien voice coming over the static-laced comm channel, and he couldn't be sure if it was just an artifact of Dinac speech passing through the universal translator, or a valid emotional cue. "*We hoped for success, but you bring us only ill omens and sorrow.*"

Riker sat at his desk, watching the holographic screen in front of him as a subspace radio waveform flexed with each word spoken. "It gives me no pleasure to be the bearer of this information, Lord Council." Light-years away, the admiral's words were being broadcast to a great meeting hall on the central continent of Casroc. The Dinac's interstellar communications were not advanced, with no visual component to their transmissions and none of the counter-interference technologies employed by the Federation. Still, he could hear the mutter of voices in the background as the other members of the Dinac ruling body absorbed his report. "I can only tell you what we have discovered so far. Your ship endures, but so far my crew have found no survivors."

"You are certain of this?"

"Our sensors scanned the pinnace thoroughly. A team is preparing to board the wreck now to make a physical search, but I regret to say the likelihood of them finding anything is low."

A different voice rose, another of the council members speaking up. *"Admiral, we must make it clear to your kind that there can be no . . .* interference *with the bodies of our people, do you understand? The funerary rites of the Dinac are very precious to us. You will cause great distress if your crew do not adhere to that instruction."*

Riker glanced up at Ssura, who stood silently at the doorway to his office. Had the council not grasped the meaning of the data *Titan* had streamed back to their planet? The Caitian offered no explanation. "Forgive me," he began again, "perhaps I was not clear in my earlier words. Honored members of the council, as far as we can determine, there are *no* bodies aboard your ship."

"You . . . will please repeat that."

"No physical remains of any kind. Whatever fate befell them, all trace of their forms was swept away by it."

Silence answered him, and as a few seconds stretched to ten, then twenty, he began to wonder if the communications link had been lost. He gave Ssura a questioning look, but the lieutenant shook his head and extended a paw toward the holographic screen. The waveform was still moving, albeit very slightly, indicating that the channel remained open.

"Lord Council? Are you there? Do you understand?"

"Your meaning has been made clear to us, Admiral

Riker." When the reply came, he sensed a shift in tone from the Dinac leader. *"Is it possible for your ship to recover our explorer and return it to us?"*

He nodded, thinking it through. "The craft is too large to be carried in our shuttlebay, but *Titan* can bring it to Casroc under tow, if you wish."

"We do." The reply was firm. *"This must be done immediately, Admiral. How soon can you be in orbit above our homeworld?"*

"A few days, perhaps . . ." He ran a quick estimate in his head. "But, sir, there is also the matter of our sister ship, the *Whitetree*. The whereabouts of that vessel are still unknown, and—"

"Immediately," insisted the Dinac leader, becoming more forceful with each word. *"The articles of the agreement between the United Federation of Planets and our species promise that you will lend all possible assistance to our exploration project! This must be done without delay! Or will it be required that we contact your superiors to see it done?"*

"That won't be necessary," Riker replied, inwardly bristling at the implied threat. "I empathize with your distress over this matter. We'll bring your ship home."

"That is all we ask." There was a crackle, as the signal died and the waveform shifted back to a flat line.

"What was that?" Riker asked the question to the air.

"The nature of Dinac postmortem customs is known, sir," began Ssura. "A file is included in the general report on their species."

"I'm aware of that, I read it." Riker shook his head. "Not what I meant. No, when I told them about the missing bodies. Their reaction . . . It seemed off."

Ssura's whiskers twitched. "Possibly. It is difficult to

be certain with only an audio feed to draw conversational cues from. I personally have always found it hard to parse the intentions of canine-humanoid beings."

Riker resisted the opportunity to suggest that might be a *cat-and-dog* thing. "Could they be hiding something from us?" He scowled. "I should have asked Deanna to join us for this."

"I could forward a recording of the conversation to Counselor Troi. She may be able to glean something from it after the fact."

"Do that. Maybe I'm reading too much into it, but an expert opinion wouldn't go amiss."

Ssura tapped the screen of the ever-present padd clasped in his paw. "Done." He looked up. "Admiral, a suggestion? Regarding the *Whitetree* search?"

Riker frowned. It went against the grain to turn around and leave after *Titan* had just found their first lead as to the fate of the other Starfleet vessel, but the demands of diplomacy had to take precedence in this matter. A year or two ago, if an officer of flag rank had told *Captain* Riker to break off a search for his lost comrades in order to tow a derelict home, he would have resisted—maybe even found a way to buck the command. But things were different now that he was on this side of the desk. *Admiral* Riker had a bigger picture to consider: not just the fate of the *Whitetree* or even that of the *Titan*, but of a whole sector. He did not have the luxury of a captain's view anymore. "I'm thinking we deploy a few shuttles, keep them out here while we take the pinnace home . . ."

"That may not be required. Our guest White-Blue recently submitted a series of advanced sensor probe modifications for review. With the increased range and acuity he proposes, *Titan* could deploy a group of upgraded probes in this region to search autonomously while we fulfill the Dinac request."

"And it wouldn't put any more lives at risk . . ." Riker nodded. "Two good ideas in a row, Lieutenant. Keep it up."

"I have many more."

"I don't doubt it."

A sharp beep sounded from Ssura's padd before he could go on. "Advisory from the bridge," he explained, reading the screen. "Commander Sarai and the away team have just deployed to the wreck."

After the bright light of the transporter effect dissipated, for a moment, there was only darkness; then the lights on the helmets of eight EVA suits came on at once, and Zurin Dakal blinked as his eyes adjusted to the sudden flood of illumination.

"Sarai to *Titan*," said the commander, standing to his right. "Down and safe. Proceeding with initial survey. Reporting interval will be every fifteen minutes, standard." She didn't wait for the ship to acknowledge her message and instead cast a measuring look over the rest of the away team. "Pazlar. Fell. Dakal. Sortollo: You are team one. Find the biocomputer core and ascertain status." Sarai beckoned to the three other members of the group. "Team two: Denken. Torvig. Keyexisi. You will come with me. We will access the pinnace's power plant and make it safe. Clear?"

Like all the others, Zurin gave a shallow bow, the best equivalent of a nod inside the bulky environmental gear of the suits. Sarai didn't say any more, and with a jerk of her arm she started moving away down the airless corridor, bouncing off the frost-rimed wooden deck in small loping jumps.

"You heard the XO," said Pazlar. "Move out."

Lieutenant Sortollo had a phaser in one hand and a tricorder in the other. The latter projected a three-dimensional image of the interior of the Dinac explorer ship, relayed in real-time from *Titan*'s sensors. "That-away," he said, pointing. "I'll take point."

Peya Fell eyed the security officer and the weapon in his hand. "Gian . . . You really think there's any threat in here with us?"

"You want to take the chance?" Sortollo asked, his helmet lights casting a cold radiance over the curved walls.

"I suppose not," said the Deltan.

Zurin tried to step across the deck and he skipped off, bumping against the low overhead. "The mag-lock plates in our boots will not work here. Wooden floors."

"Plenty of handholds though," noted Pazlar, moving arm over arm down the narrow passage. "Gravity probably went off-line the same time as life support."

"Getting a big hole punched in your ship will do that for you," said Fell. The glow of her tricorder screen lit her pale face. "I'm getting the same kind of readings we took from the ship. Heavy subspace particle decay products."

"An isolytic weapon discharge?" suggested the security guard.

"Negative," said Pazlar. "The pattern is too diffuse for that. If I had to make a guess, I'd say a graviton collapsar effect . . . Only that would have crushed this ship to a supercompacted dot in a nanosecond."

An uncomfortable silence descended, and they moved on in a group without speaking. It was finally Zurin who felt compelled to say what all were thinking. "Could that have happened to the *Whitetree*?"

"I don't think so." The science officer blew out a breath. "Something so small, even if we couldn't see it, it would be so hyperdense it would register on *Titan*'s sensor grid as a gravitational anomaly."

The group paused at an airlock iris that was jammed half-shut, and together they pushed the leaves open to proceed forward. In the next corridor section, small pieces of debris were floating everywhere: oddly shaped Dinac eating utensils, oval booklets made of actual paper, cups and other bric-a-brac. Sortollo moved through it, parting the drifting remnants with the flat of one hand.

"Look, I know you science guys are the smart ones and all," said the lieutenant. "But has anyone actually considered that maybe the *Whitetree* isn't around because it *got away* from whatever went down out here?"

Zurin considered the question. He didn't doubt for a moment that there was anyone on the *Titan* who didn't want Sortollo's solution to be the right one. Nothing would be better than the cadet ship suddenly appearing on the edge of sensor range, intact and undamaged. *But fate never listens to hope*, he thought, recalling something that his grandmother had once said. "If the ship had warped away, there would be an ion trail. If it was destroyed, wreckage. But there is literally no trace out there." Saying it out loud made a melancholy mood settle in Zurin's thoughts. "Apart from this hulk, we have nothing but some free hydrogen and a lot of questions."

"Like space just opened up and took them," Fell said quietly. She realized the others were looking at her, and she shook it off. "Sorry. It's this place." The Deltan gestured around at the gloomy corridor. "It's bringing out the worst in me."

Zurin couldn't deny that Peya was right. The dim, cold emptiness of the derelict ship was faintly repellant to the Cardassian in a way he couldn't quite articulate. Whatever vitality and warmth had once coursed through the spaces of the Dinac explorer ship had been torn away, and now the vessel felt lifeless and hollow. He wasn't one to believe in such things as phantoms and realms of the dead, but this place made him come close. It was almost as if space was somehow *different* here. *Alien*, he thought, although that word wasn't enough to encompass the unsettling sense of abnormality plucking at his senses.

"*Focus*," Pazlar said firmly. "There are answers, and we're going to find them."

"Yes, sir," Zurin replied, pushing some floating orb-shaped object out of the way. He heard a click over the comm channel as Commander Sarai came on-line.

"All teams, brace yourselves. We have battery power here. Gravity coming back in three, two, one."

The four-fifths standard *g* that was Dinac-normal pulled at Dakal's legs, and he dropped easily to the deck into a ready stance. The others did the same, and as the drifting debris fell to the floor around them, a series of electrofluorescent emergency lamps flicked to life, throwing soft illumination across the passage.

The Cardassian's gaze was immediately caught by a familiar shape as it clattered off the curved wall and along the deck to land at his feet. He nudged it with his boot. "Tricorder," he said aloud.

"Say again?" Pazlar turned to look his way as Zurin

went to his haunches and picked the device out of the mix of debris.

He held up a standard-issue Starfleet engineering tricorder, the model that was usually issued to members of the Corps of Engineers. "The power cell is damaged, but this is definitely one of ours." He turned it over and saw the code label identifying the device as being issued from *Whitetree*'s stores. "If the memory module is intact . . ."

The lieutenant commander nodded. "Good find, Zurin. We'll take it back to *Titan* and upload the contents."

"If that's here," said Sortollo, "then it means there had to be Starfleet crew on board this barge as well."

Pazlar moved to the next hatch, unwilling to dwell on the security officer's comment. "Let's get this open. The compartment beyond this one should be the cradle for the primary biocomputer."

With some power restored, it was easier to open the iris, and one by one the members of the away team entered the chamber. Zurin grimaced as his boots sucked at the deck. He looked down and saw that the floor of the compartment was one large puddle of milky green fluid, perhaps two centimeters deep. The thick, oily liquid was leaking from a large ovoid suspended on a wooden frame in the middle of the chamber, oozing out of fractures that webbed the surface of the egg-shaped capsule. The emergency lighting in this room was malfunctioning, flickering in random bursts of cold blue.

"This is not a good sign," said Fell, scanning the ovoid. "Battery power is very weak in here. There's contamination in the operator fluids. It's decaying rapidly."

Sortollo made a face, as if he had seen something

disgusting. "What is that inside that pod? Looks like . . . *brains*."

"Close, but not quite," offered Pazlar. "The Dinac use cultured organo-processors for high-level computing. Similar to our bioneural gel packs, but on a larger scale." She moved closer, frowning. "We're not going to have time to run a bypass and download the data chains stored in this thing. It's damaged."

"It's not really alive," explained Fell, off the security officer's growing dismay. "Well, no more than a plant or a fungus."

"Right." Sortollo didn't seem convinced. He turned to the science officer. "What do we do, Commander?"

"We need to stop the decay. We can't take the bio-computer back to *Titan*, it would die on the way."

"Didn't you just say it wasn't alive?" Sortollo shot Fell a look.

Pazlar ignored the comment. "Have to keep it active . . ." She folded up her tricorder and drew her phaser, dialing down the beam setting so it would be the width of a needle. "I'm going to need a hand here."

Peya followed suit. "I didn't think we would be doing surgery today. Where is a doctor when you need one?"

"Take it slow," ordered Pazlar, and together the two women got to work cutting open the ovoid capsule.

The casing of the pod was unpleasantly soft, and it peeled back like folds of flesh as the phasers did their work. Zurin noted Sortollo's lips thin, and he forced a smile. "I didn't think you'd be squeamish, Lieutenant."

"I'm not," said the security officer. "But all of a sudden I can't stop thinking about that plate of greasy Ktarian eggs I had for breakfast." He looked away and swallowed.

"Here we go." Melora reached into the cut and took hold of a thick section of the biomass. Fell produced a small portable power module from a pouch on the thigh of her EVA suit and used a universal probe to connect it to the "brain." The biocomputer quivered, and presently a soft glow spread through the fleshy pod.

"That should keep it stable for a while," said the Deltan, "but we'll need to bring a stand-alone generator over from *Titan* as soon as possible. We should be able to set up a data connection."

From the corner of his eye, Zurin saw a shimmer of light as the lamps on Sortollo's suit suddenly shifted position, as if the security officer had jerked backward. He turned and found the lieutenant standing stiffly, the phaser in his hand raised. "What's wrong?"

"Did you see that?" Sortollo took a wary step forward, panning his weapon back and forth over the rippling surface of the spilled fluid. Dakal saw more pieces of debris floating in the liquid, bits of splintered wood, loose tools and another of the orb objects like the one he had seen in the corridor. "Something moved," insisted the lieutenant.

Zurin peered at the milky slick. "Are you sure, Gian? It could have been a trick of the light."

The tension in Sortollo's stance lessened. "Yeah. You're right. The gravity on this wreck has been off for days . . . It must have been the debris settling." He gave a weak chuckle. "Peya's not the only one this ghost ship has got spooked."

"I know what you mean," agreed the Cardassian. "I have felt like something has been watching us ever since we arrived." He dismissed his own words with a wave of the hand. "The mind plays tricks."

"We're need to bring more teams over," said Pazlar, halting the conversation before it could go further. "The captain and the admiral will want a detailed investigation."

Fell examined the biomodule through its translucent membrane. "I think we may have caught it in time. If there's any data to be recovered, it will be in here."

Pazlar's head bobbed behind her visor, and she tapped the comm on her cuff. "Team One to Team Two, *Titan*. We've stabilized the computer core. Stand by." She shot Zurin and Sortollo a wry look. "It seems we will be sticking around on this ghost ship for a while, gentlemen."

"Great," said the security officer, with feeling.

With the exacting, thoughtful precision that only a four-year-old child could exhibit, Natasha climbed the back of the sofa until she was standing on the cushions and staring out of the tall ports and into the depths of space. Deanna watched her daughter lean forward, putting her small hands on the transparent panel, almost pressing her nose to it.

"I don't like that," declared the girl.

"What do you mean, little one?" Deanna crossed to the window so she could see what her daughter was looking at.

"That," repeated the girl. She pointed at the shape of the Dinac pinnace, moving off the stern to the port, shrouded in a twinkling aura projected from one of *Titan*'s tractor beam emitters. At low warp velocity, the starship moved in formation with the stricken wreck, the pair looking like two cetaceans sharing a slipstream current. "It's not right," insisted the child.

Deanna paused, uncertain of how to respond. Being one-quarter Betazed, Tasha had doubtless inherited some measure of her mother's empathic senses; Deanna wasn't certain as to how developed they were. But some of the away team returning from work over on the alien derelict had reported a negative emotional reaction to being on the vessel, and for the first time the counselor began to wonder if the ship's gloomy influence was more than just psychological. Could such sudden loss of life actually leave a mark, in a telepathic sense? If such a "shadow" had tainted the pinnace, why would Tasha feel it?

Deanna looked at the alien vessel for a long moment, thinking about extending her own empathic senses toward it, or perhaps even requesting permission to go aboard. *Are there really ghosts over there?*

Then the door chimed and Tasha's momentary bout of sullen mood vanished instantly. "Daddy!" she piped, and she threw herself off the sofa in a wild rush, dashing across the cabin to greet Will as he entered.

"Oof!" Breath blew out of Will as Tasha collided with her father, and he swept her off her feet, hoisting her high. "Hello, ladies," he said, with a wan smile. "Whose turn is it to choose dinner?"

"Mine!" insisted Tasha. She scrambled down to the floor and ran to the replicator alcove. The girl took a deep breath and began a conversation with the food synthesizer.

Deanna came to her husband and greeted him with a kiss. "You did have that talk with her about last time, yes?" she said quietly.

"I did," he replied. On the previous occasion they had allowed Tasha to pick the Riker-Troi family meal; it had largely been a selection of Bajoran sweet pastries and flavored ice cream. "But she gets that chocolate habit from you, *imzadi*." Will shrugged off his uniform jacket and tossed it on a chair.

Deanna smiled. "It's a genetic predisposition."

Will attempted to return the smile, but despite both their efforts, the mood didn't lighten. "Tough day," he admitted to her. "No good choices from start to finish."

She gave a nod. "For all of us."

He paused, considering. "How is Christine handling it?"

Deanna hesitated. "Are you asking as my husband or as a flag officer?"

"Both. Neither." He blew out a breath and tried again. "As a friend."

"I think it would be fair to say that Captain Vale had a hell of a first day. And a second day, and a third, fourth, fifth . . . Any expectation of an easy start to our new mission is long gone."

"Easy isn't what we do, Deanna. Chris understands that."

"All the same, you don't need to be an empath to know that this situation has cast a pall over the crew. We lose the Vela Sector mission, then our first encounter out here is . . . that." She nodded toward the port and the towed wreck. "Some of our people had friends on board the *Whitetree*."

"I know. Do you remember Lieutenant Ythiss? One of Xin's warp propulsion engineers?"

"Yes. He transferred back to Starfleet Academy a couple of years ago, became an instructor. He was on the *Whitetree*?"

Will nodded. "And now missing in action, like all the others. Cadets and teachers, that's all they were. Out here to learn. And something took them away."

"We'll find them." Deanna sounded more certain than she felt.

"I want to believe that." He glanced up to see Tasha carefully removing plates from the replicator alcove. "Our young blood is too precious to be lost . . . But the report Commander Sarai brought back from the wreck was not encouraging."

"*Encouraging* doesn't seem to be a word in Dalit Sarai's dictionary," Deanna noted, changing the subject. "Along with *sociable*. Or *smile*. I've met Medusans who were more open."

"She's carrying a lot of baggage," Will said, after a moment. "And she's not here out of choice. Anyone's choice."

"Not true. Someone made sure she was assigned to this ship."

Her husband nodded. "I'd like to know who that was."

"All the same, she needs to earn the trust of the crew if she expects to serve as first officer. You know that job, Will. You can't do it from behind a rulebook."

"You're right. But Sarai has to come halfway. She's good at what she does, that's indisputable. That's not enough. All the crew know about her are rumors about planting her flag next to Ishan Anjar's during the presidential crisis, and that is something that only Sarai can change. If she even wants to."

"If you tell someone they're a pariah enough times, they'll start to believe it." Deanna sighed. "She deserves a chance to prove otherwise."

Will got up as Tasha beckoned to her parents from

the dining table. "Again, what you say is right. But now Sarai has got that opportunity; what happens next is up to her."

A few hours of sleep, an invigorating sonic shower and a freshly replicated uniform was usually all it took to make Melora Pazlar feel rested and ready for duty, but today it didn't seem like quite enough. The problem of the missing ship, the missing crews, had grown to consume her every waking thought. She felt it pulling on her everywhere she went, like a tidal drag.

Pazlar frowned as she walked the length of cargo bay four, inspecting the items of free-floating wreckage and damaged equipment that *Titan*'s engineering crew had transported across from the Dinac explorer ship. Some of the largest items were parts of the fuselage, tractored in from the trail of debris following the derelict. Others were pieces of hardware beamed from the interior spaces of the pinnace for closer inspection. Pazlar shared a glance with Torvig as she passed him working at a curved section of a broken intercooler matrix, using a phaser to burn off accreted carbonization.

They didn't speak; for the moment, they had nothing more to discuss. The slow and unpleasant process of picking through the remains of the alien vessel had thrown up only more questions, and nothing that moved them any closer toward an understanding of what mishap had befallen the two ships.

Pazlar peered at the screen of the portable scanner she carried in her hand, panning a sensor wand over the pieces of the pinnace. *The same readings here,* she thought. There was a very distinct radiation fingerprint that only the ultrasensitive wand was able to pick up, and so far she couldn't interpret what it augured.

She heard someone approaching but didn't turn to look at them. "Torvig," she began, "this reading on the deep subspace band . . ."

"You forgot my name already? And here was me thinking I'd made a memorable impression on you." She turned and saw Lieutenant Kyzak standing nearby, his arms folded across his chest.

"Oh, Ethan. Hello again." She covered her mistake with a smile. "I'm sorry. We spoke about getting some lunch, didn't we? I apologize, I meant to get back to you, but the Dinac ship . . . It's taking up all my time."

"Good excuse," he said. "As long as it's not because I made a fool of myself in the O-club."

"It's not that," she replied, and he drew another smile out of her. The impromptu dinner the two officers had shared a few days earlier had actually been very enjoyable, having turned into a long evening of good conversation.

Pazlar didn't know much about Kyzak's homeworld, the colony that called itself North Star, and Ethan had been entertaining company as he rectified that shortfall. With great enthusiasm, he explained how civilization on his planet had first come to resemble the Ancient West of Earth's nineteenth century, thanks to the original—and somewhat less friendly—Skagaran colonists who founded North Star bulking out their populace with humans kidnapped from that era. Centuries later, after slave revolts and major socio-political changes, North Star's human and Skagaran peoples lived and worked alongside one another in relative harmony. Kyzak was charming in his own way, and his disarming grin helped Melora to dismiss the concerns she might usually have had about fraternizing with an officer of lower rank. For his part, Ethan had been fascinated by her descriptions of life growing up on Gemworld and her planet's unique microgravity environment.

"As much as I'd like to be here to pass the time, I came down for work reasons," he explained. "Commander Rager wants me to join the next away team sortie over to the pinnace. I've got orders to study the ship's flight controls and navigation data, maybe get a feel for what attitude the Dinac had her in when . . ." He paused. "Whatever it was happened. I came to ask if you had anything new to add to the report, but I'm guessing that's a no."

Pazlar gave a weary shake of the head. "We have a lot of puzzle pieces but no picture. And the frustrating thing is, each time I think we have found the right kind of approach for the problem, something arises to prove me wrong." She sighed. "If I didn't know better, I would think some higher power is playing games with us."

"Never been one to court fate or such." Kyzak dropped into a crouch, looking at the debris. "I have every confidence in you, Melora . . ." He stopped abruptly, realizing that he was on the bounds of overfamiliarity. "*Commander,* I mean." With care, he picked up one of the items of miscellaneous wreckage taken from the corridors of the pinnace. "I have no idea what this is for."

"Which makes two of us." The object in Kyzak's hands was a spherical construct that, like the biocomputer on board the explorer ship, used both organic neural circuits as well as more conventional mechanical systems. "The first away team came across a few of them scattered around the vessel. I think they may be a kind of remote monitoring device, possibly something the Dinac deployed in the moments before the . . . event. But we've had no luck activating it. If we could, we might be able to get a better picture of the moments before . . ."

"Huh." Kyzak rolled the orb between his hands, considering the shape and the mass of it. "Maybe I'm off-base here, but this doesn't look like the other Dinac tech I've read about." He frowned and put it back where he found it.

"It's difficult to be certain," she told him. "The most up-to-date information about the Dinac systems would be on board the *Whitetree*, and . . ." She let the sentence hang.

A grim cast came over Kyzak's face. "Right."

For the moment, Pazlar didn't want to dwell on the matter of the missing Starfleet ship. "Our investigations have turned up strong concentrations of tetryon radiation present in the hull of the wreck, but to be honest that indicator just throws up a whole lot of new questions on top of the ones we already have." She showed him the scanner screen, and he moved closer to her to peer at the display.

"Tetryon," said Kyzak, sounding out the word in his native drawl. "That's a high-density subspace energy form," he went on, "and a mighty rare one, if I recall."

"Very rare," said another voice, this one with a waspish tone. Pazlar looked up to Xin Ra-Havreii threading his way through the lines of debris laid out in a careful grid. His attention was fixed on Melora and Kyzak, and he virtually ignored Torvig's presence. Xin made the comment sound like an accusation, and the Skagaran immediately picked up on it, his friendly manner dropping away to become more formal.

"Sir," he said to the chief engineer.

Ra-Havreii spared the Skagaran the briefest of withering looks and then turned his attention on Pazlar. "I want to speak with you. Privately."

Kyzak got the message and made his excuses. "Right. I'll, uh, carry on."

Pazlar willed herself not to react. Xin was predictable, she had to give him that. Weeks of broken dates and poor justifications, all forgotten the moment she showed any interest in someone else. She refused to allow herself to feel awkward about the situation. Xin was Efrosian, and his species had what many other cultures considered to be a lax approach to the maintenance of a relationship. Despite his attempts to grow beyond that, Xin kept falling back into ingrained habits, and Melora had grown tired of being stood up at the ship's replimat or the officers' club. She had her fill of waiting for him to put in the work, and now Melora let that show in her expression. "What is your concern, Commander Ra-Havreii?"

He blinked, and his eyes narrowed. When he spoke again, it was quietly enough so his voice would not carry. "'Lora, I realize that, recently, things between us have not been—"

"Stop." Her hand came up and the word left her mouth before she was even aware of it. "Just *stop.* Stop pretending that you and I have anything approaching an actual relationship, Xin. I'm done with it." There was no malice in her words, only weariness. Perhaps the drain she felt from striking dead end after dead end in the fruitless search for the missing had also bled out all her annoyance into the bargain. She found she could not be angry at him. "You're not here when I need you. You're only here when you remember."

"I have a ship to run!" he snapped, then caught himself. "I'm sorry."

"You think you are. You're not." She turned away. "I think it would be best if we kept things on a professional basis between us from now on, Commander."

"You'd prefer to spend your time with that lieutenant, the Skagaran?"

"I just met him," said Melora. "We shared a table for dinner. That doesn't mean we're betrothed."

"This is a mistake," insisted Ra-Havreii.

"Yes," she agreed, "one we both made."

Peya Fell attached the optical data network cable to the flank of the computer lab's isolated server unit and looked up, her eyebrows rising in anticipation. "I believe the correct term is 'Good to go,' gentlemen." She took a wary look at the battered engineering tricorder resting on a sample cradle nearby, the other end of the glowing ODN cable extending out from a port in its casing.

Zurin Dakal exchanged glances with Holor Sethe, one of *Titan*'s computing systems specialists. The milk-pale Cygnian lieutenant tapped a command into a keyboard and nodded his assent. "Download commencing."

A screen on the far wall immediately filled with a torrent of complex symbols, the visual manifestation of the data spooling out from the damaged tricorder. But rather than the well-ordered code base typical to Starfleet's LCARS operating system, there was nothing but a jumble of corrupted files. Jagged fragments of unusable source data tumbled down the screen, and Dakal gave Sethe an odd look.

"Did you actually just cringe?" he asked.

The Cygnian nodded. "To see that? Oh yes. It's horrible. You're looking at a major corruption event there, right down to the kernel."

"Can you recover anything?" Peya knew the answer before she asked the question but wanted to hear the answer nonetheless.

"Unlikely." Sethe puffed out his narrow chest. "Imagine breaking a cup. With some molecular adhesive, patience and a bit of time, you might be able to reassemble something resembling a drinking vessel. Now imagine that same cup ground to powder! Ensign, I wouldn't know where to start with this . . ."

Zurin said something under his breath, and Peya guessed it was some Cardassian gutter oath. It surprised her to see him react like that—but then he wasn't the only one she had recently witnessed exhibiting signs of a short temper. Zurin realized his lapse, and his gray skin darkened a little. "Forgive me. I have had some trouble sleeping." He took a breath. "All right, the main data core is worthless. But what about the buffer?"

Peya nodded. "Yes. Even if we lose the majority of the data on the device, the digital patterns of the last input might still be in the isolinear circuits."

"That . . ." began Sethe, suddenly animated by the idea, "that is a very real possibility!" Fingers moving in a blur, the lieutenant programmed a new macro to search for the buffer data, and the corrupted information on the wallscreen vanished, to be replaced by something more coherent.

"Success!" said Zurin. "Good call, Peya."

"It's an audio recording," noted Sethe. "The parity has degraded, but I think we can recover it."

The three of them went to their panels and set to work. Within a few minutes, they had pulled enough material from the damaged tricorder to risk a playback.

"Here we go," said Zurin quietly. Peya felt an odd chill fall over her as the lab went silent, as hushed as the mourning watches held for the dead back home on Delta IV. Then a voice spoke—sibilant, scratchy and broken with interference.

"*Managed to escape the lower decks,*" came the words. "*Three of us, out of eight survivors that we were aware of.*" There was a hollow resonance to the voice, and Peya recognized the odd acoustics of the interior of the Dinac pinnace. "*We are being stalked now. There are several of them on board the explorer. I cannot fathom how they were able to board, there was no ship—*"

The words cut out, and Zurin's expression turned stony. "I know who that is." He shot a look at the Deltan. "Peya, don't you recognize him? It's Ythiss."

"Oh . . ." She felt color drain from her face. "Yes. It is." Suddenly, she didn't want to hear anything else, for fear of what would come next.

There was a crackle of sound and the Selayan's voice returned; now it was hushed, as if he were hiding from something. "*—to see. I am going to be found, like the others were. Each of them, taken when we were separated, or resting. Tried sleeping in shifts, that did not work . . .*" He trailed off, and in the distance the recording picked up a sharp noise. Like bones snapping.

Then there was only silence. Sethe's hands dropped away from his keyboard, his tail drooping. "I'm afraid . . . that's all there is."

Five

"Run it again," said Captain Vale, staring at the featureless surface of the briefing room table.

Off a nod from Commander Pazlar, Ensign Fell tapped a control on the padd before her and the partial recording started over. No one spoke as what might have been the last words of Lieutenant Ythiss crackled from hidden speakers. For a brief moment, it was as if the ghost of the former *Titan* officer was in the room with them, calling out to warn them of his fate.

"We are being stalked now. There are several of them on board the explorer."

"Hold." Admiral Riker held up a hand, and Fell halted the playback. "*Stalked*. Strange that he would use that word."

"I remember Ythiss," said Vale. "He was the matter-of-fact type. If he said that, he meant it."

"We are certain it is him speaking?" Troi asked.

"Yes, Counselor," said Dakal. "I triple-checked the

voice pattern against Starfleet personnel records. It's a ninety-seven percent match."

"Were you able to learn anything else from the tricorder?" said Riker.

Pazlar shook her head. "Nothing of use. The device's casing did exhibit the same tetryon particle fingerprint we've seen elsewhere on the Dinac pinnace." She gestured to the ports, where the bow of the alien ship was just visible at the end of a tractor beam tether. "Density is highest on the port side of the derelict, which means they were side-on to whatever energy effect generated the radiation surge."

The recording went on, with the Selayan's weary, fearful words playing out toward their sudden conclusion.

"It is our estimation that someone boarded the Dinac ship after whatever event occurred to put it out of action," Fell offered. "Based on Ythiss's observations, they may have come from a cloaked ship."

"Romulans?" Even as Troi said the word, she shook her head. "What reason would the Star Empire have to be out here?"

"It's not likely to be them," Dakal said firmly. "We would have picked up the trace neutrino emissions common to Romulan cloaking systems long before now. It appears we're dealing with something else."

"Something capable of ghosting through space," said Riker. "Something capable of making a *Saber*-class starship disappear."

Vale frowned, running a hand over her forehead. "Whoever did this went after *Whitetree*, and the crew of the explorer, but they left the Dinac ship behind. Why? Perhaps if we can figure out what was . . . discarded, we can find a clue toward what was taken."

"The pinnace is barely spaceworthy," noted Riker. "Perhaps it was too damaged."

Fell nodded. "In addition, the *Whitetree*'s technology is more advanced than that aboard the Dinac ship."

"Are we considering this an act of piracy?" Troi glanced at her husband. "Not a disaster?"

"I think right now we're considering *everything*. That's our problem: narrowing it down." Vale got up from her chair and crossed to the ports, propelled by a sudden burst of irritable energy. "Keep at it, Melora. Any shipboard resources you need, you have my permission to use them."

Whatever reply *Titan*'s science officer was about to make was never voiced. From out of nowhere, a bass shudder resonated through the framework of the starship, and abruptly the warp-distorted stars flashing past outside contracted back into pinpricks of light. The deck vibrated as the starship dropped out of warp velocity and back into normal space.

"What the—" Vale grabbed at a support pillar to keep her balance as a yellow alert warning sounded over the intercom. She slapped at the combadge on her chest. "Vale to Bridge, report!"

Tuvok answered her. *"Stand by, Captain. Commander Sarai is in contact with main engineering. We registered a momentary particle surge six milliseconds before the warp matrix collapsed."*

"Reports coming in from all decks . . ." Troi was already checking her own panel. "Several minor injuries . . ."

"Tuvok," Riker broke in, "what was the nature of the particle surge?"

"Source unknown at this time, Admiral," reported the

Vulcan, *"but it appears to be a broad-spectrum burst of tetryons."*

"Oh, hell no." As the curse left the captain's lips, she saw the blackness of space beyond the bow of her starship defy rationality and distort. Behaving as if it were some kind of ephemeral membrane, the fabric of the interstellar void flexed. Something moved behind space, pushing, searching for a weak point. Vale had the sudden, horrible sense that whatever it was had come looking for *Titan*.

Then, with a blinding burst of exotic radiation, a ragged-edged rip sliced across the dark and opened wide. Great sickle-shaped arcs of lightning in grotesque, alien hues emerged from the fissure, lashing out in all directions. Wild pulses of uncontrolled gravitation swept out from the newborn anomaly and slammed into the starship, spinning it like a dinghy in a stormswell.

Briefly overwhelmed, *Titan*'s inertial dampeners failed, and Vale felt the deck fall away from her as the briefing room inverted.

Dalit Sarai's knuckles went white as her hands tightly gripped the arms of the command chair, and she felt the momentary swooping sensation in the pit of her stomach as the *Titan*'s internal gravity envelope shuddered. "Maximum shields!" she barked, the command sounding across thc bridge like a whip-crack. The Efrosian shot a look toward the conn and ops stations before her. "Lavena, Rager! I want a gravitation plot on that anomaly, this instant! Impulse power to full and astern, pull us away!"

The two officers sounded off as they followed her commands, but Sarai had already forgotten about them, moving instantly to the next order. "Sensors. Give me multi-spectral imagery on that thing, main viewscreen, now!"

"Working on it, XO," called Ensign Polan, from what would normally have been Commander Pazlar's station. "Wait one."

Sarai scowled. The junior officer was wasting time they didn't have. In a situation like this, every fraction of a second was vital. "Now!" she repeated.

"Onscreen!" Polan slapped at the console, and the ugly maw of radiant energy on the viewer became a chaotic riot of color upon color, with multiple templates showing the anomaly's footprint in infrared, ultraviolet, magnetic, quantum, even temporal energy ranges. However, it mattered little through which lens the thing was being viewed; it was horrific across all spectra, a brutal mutilation of the laws of nature.

Are we looking at whatever took our sister ship? Sarai couldn't help but see the thing like a lamprey mouth, opening wide to consume the starship. The first officer shook off the fanciful image; this was no time for such things. She had to focus on the tangible, the factual. One error of judgment now, and the *Titan* would follow the *Whitetree* into whatever terrible unknown lurked beyond the throat of the rippling maw. There was no doubt in her mind that she was staring into the face of the thing that had swallowed the other vessel.

"Energy shock," reported Rager. "Incoming . . . Can't outrun it!"

She nodded. Coils of lightning filled the void around them, writhing toward the *Titan*. No matter what choice they made, they were going to be hit. "Activate restraints," Sarai added, as an afterthought, and automatic safety belts snapped out from hidden ports on each chair to secure the occupants in place.

Ever since they had come upon the Dinac derelict, Sarai had been poring over the data coming in from the teams aboard the wreck, at once formulating theories on what had transpired out here while keeping her own counsel. Now all those possibilities threatened to crowd in on her thoughts if she allowed them. The key to control, she reminded herself, is to isolate oneself from distractions. Know the problem and work on it to the exclusion of all else. Sarai dismissed the faint glimmers of terror pulling at the edges of her attention and gave her all to the moment.

"Shields are at full power," reported Tuvok from the tactical console. "However, the Dinac ship is not protected."

"There are still away teams over there," said Lavena. "Can we cycle the deflectors, beam them back?"

Sarai knew the answer without needing to check. "No." They had seconds before the leading edges of the energy-lightning struck. In all likelihood, the unprotected derelict would be destroyed.

In the past, she had served with officers of severe nature and cold intent, beings who might have been willing to let the wreck absorb the brunt of the shock effect, sacrificing it and the handful of people on board for the greater number of crew and civilians aboard the *Titan*. Some faraway part of Dalit Sarai wondered if she could make a call like that—or if the officers standing around her already believed that she would.

"Power from weapons and life support to boost

shields, reinforce structural integrity field." She called out the command to Lieutenant McCreedy at the engineering station. "Give me direct shield modulation and tractor control at my station."

Sarai could not help but notice the brief instant as the engineer shot Tuvok a questioning look, and in turn the Vulcan gave a brief nod. *Asking him for permission to obey. They do not trust me.*

It didn't matter. The panel under her right hand lit up with the required control link for the shield matrix, the one under her left repeating the targeting systems for the tractor beam holding the Dinac pinnace in tow.

Ambidexterity had its advantages; working both panels at once, Sarai simultaneously altered the gain and intensity of the tractor beam to bring the wreck dangerously close to the *Titan* while also pushing out part of the shield envelope to extend its protection to the derelict.

It was done in the same moment that the outer surges of rogue energy kissed the starship's deflectors. *Titan* rang like a bell, and Sarai saw all the structural field gauges briefly peak into the red as it was stressed beyond all reasonable tolerances; but the ship rebounded and punched through the buffeting wave force.

"We made it," reported Rager. "Derelict is still with us." There was disbelief in her voice.

Sarai cut dead through any moment of self-congratulation. "That was just the first surge. We are not in the clear yet." Behind the command chair, a turbolift door hissed open and Captain Vale emerged, with Admiral Riker and Commander Pazlar at her heels. Vale seemed to be unaware she was bleeding from a cut on her cheekbone.

"What in the black hells is that?" Vale demanded,

glaring at the anomaly on the screen as if it were personally spiting her.

"Increasing tetryon particle emission source," replied Pazlar, taking the place of a relieved-looking Polan. "I've never seen a subspace effect like this before. We're looking at a spontaneously generated spatial anomaly far beyond normal magnitudes for something of this nature."

"Where did it come from?" said Vale. "Artificial source, or something else?"

"Can't tell at this range. We would have to maneuver closer."

Lavena twisted in her chair to look back at them, a mask of frustration on the Selkie's delicate features. "That's going to happen if we want it to or not, Captain. We're losing ground to this thing. Shearing effect. Traction from the impulse drive is dropping."

"And with the warp matrix collapse, we have no faster-than-light power," Sarai added.

Riker slipped into the seat that his wife would usually have taken on the bridge, peering at a console there. "Quick thinking with the wreck, Commander."

Sarai nodded an acknowledgment. "It will count for nothing if we can't pull away from this rift."

"Gravity shear is increasing," said Tuvok. The sensor profile on the main screen showed the shift in absolutes as a color change from cold blue to hot orange-red. At the event horizon of the subspace rift, the laws of physics that governed the universe began to break down, becoming malleable as the unreal subdimension beyond spilled over into ours. Constants such as the force of gravity, the speed of light, even the power that bonded atoms to one another, all immutable and unchangeable, came undone at the barrier between dimensional spaces. Caught in the bleed of such effects, *Titan* was losing ground, unable to find purchase against the fabric of space-time.

Sarai felt a chill run through her. "This is what happened to the *Whitetree*. This is why there is no trace of them." The first officer stared into the bottomless pit that the rift gave entry to and wondered if anything could survive in there. Unlikely. If fate was kind to those poor souls, they had perished quickly and without suffering.

Vale leaned forward over Lavena's station, one hand on the back of the flight controller's chair. "Can you bring us about, Aili?"

"Trying, Captain." There was clear frustration in her tone. "But it's like swimming through mud. Impulse power is dissipating away into nothing."

"We could try a forced restart of the warp drive," suggested the admiral. "Xin would hate me for it, and we'd blow out half the circuits, but it might be enough to stop us sliding into that singularity."

"That would see us dead, sir," Sarai said flatly. From behind her, the engineering officer gave a glum nod of agreement. "A second matrix collapse would take the ship down with it. It's too risky."

Riker fixed the first officer with a hard gaze. "If you have a better solution, now is not the time to keep it to yourself."

Sarai opened her mouth to speak and hesitated. *They will not trust me. I will say the words and they will not trust my judgment*. "If I give the order, it must be done immediately. No hesitation." She glanced up at Tuvok, then to Vale. "Captain, with your permission?"

She expected Vale to repeat what had happened before, to look to Riker for some kind of accord over the request, but to Sarai's surprise Vale never broke her gaze. "All hands," said the captain, after a moment. "Commander Sarai has the conn. Give her exactly what she wants."

Once more, she didn't waste time with a nod of thanks. Sarai took a breath, and when she spoke again it was with strength and direction, drawn from somewhere deep. "Cut power to the impulse engines." If she was wrong, none of them would live long enough to chastise her for her error. "Divert all power to deflector shields."

"The rift has us," said Rager. "We are in an uncontrolled approach toward the event horizon. Contact in fifty-one seconds."

"Sound collision alarm," said Sarai. It seemed odd to her how calm she sounded. "Tactical: Prepare two quantum torpedoes for point-blank firing procedures."

Tuvok's hands flew across his panel, making the weapons ready. "Target, Commander?"

"None," she told him. "Set to proximity detonation." Sarai calculated the math in her head. "Five light-seconds from the event horizon. Stand by to launch."

Ahead of the starship, new wreathes of monstrous electro-energy discharges crackled through the vacuum, leaving bright lines of distortion as they disrupted the sensor feeds. *Titan* began to tremble as the forces acting on it grew in intensity.

"Deflectors are buckling," said Riker, reading off the data from his screen. "If we lose them—"

"We will be vapor and free atoms long before that happens, sir," Sarai snapped. "Launch torpedoes."

"Quantum torpedoes away. Running." Tuvok eyed her. "Commander, the detonation of these weapons at this range and their interaction with the event horizon will be highly volatile."

"Yes, it will." She took a breath, one that could be her last. "All power to forward shields and SIF. Absolutely *everything*."

"Diverting . . . *everything*," said McCreedy. Lights dimmed as the power to the bridge fell to emergency levels.

"Detonation," reported Tuvok.

Sarai shouted out the last order: "Brace for impact!"

The soundless explosions caused a wash of white to flash over the viewscreen, and for a moment two spheres of energy discharge bloomed into being. The quantum warheads, like the rift effect, relied on the ability to briefly deform the structure of local space-time. Liberating such energy at so close a range caused a backlash that rippled out and caught the falling starship in its wake.

The vessel moaned as stresses as great as those in the heart of a sun were briefly imposed upon it, but the deflectors absorbed and redirected the forces, even as multiple power distribution routers below decks blew in the aftershock. The gravitational distortions holding *Titan* in their grasp were momentarily swamped—and in that instant, the ship had its freedom once more.

But only for seconds. "Full impulse, escape course!" shouted Sarai.

Lavena and Rager had been waiting for the word, and now the two officers worked in tandem to blast the starship away from the grasp of the anomaly before it could reach out for them anew.

Sarai felt giddy as the motion of the vessel translated through the decks. She gritted her teeth and counted off the seconds. If she made it past ten, they would not die today.

At the mark of twelve, she stopped and blew out a breath. "Viewer ahead," she ordered, and the main screen snapped back to the blackness of space.

"Reading a sudden drop-off in the power levels of the rift," said Pazlar. Her tone made it clear that was unexpected. "It's closing! It might be some additional effect from the torpedo detonation. Ambient tetryon levels still above the red line, though."

"Helm, put some distance between us and that thing," ordered Vale, crossing back to the command stations. "Commander, well done. I wonder if I might have my chair back now?"

Sarai disengaged the restraints and stood up, taking care not to show the momentary weakness she felt in her legs from the adrenaline rush. "Thank you, Captain, for trusting me."

Vale regarded her. "You're my XO. You get that as a matter of course. Is there any reason that should change?"

Sarai shook her head and said nothing more.

Afterward, all Peya Fell wanted to do was go home and hug her parents, but the reality was that they were half a quadrant away on Dhei and all that waited for in her cabin was her roommate, Ensign Venoss. She was a pleasant sort, but talkative, and Peya knew that if she went back to the junior officers' quarters, Venoss would want to pick apart the events of the day in minute detail. All Peya wanted was some quiet.

And so she returned to the computer lab to work on trying to pull more data out of the damaged tricorder and the Dinac bioprocessor, losing herself in work even to the point that she was still busy when Lieutenant Sethe called it a night. She waved to the Cygnian, promising to finish up within the next twenty minutes.

Two hours later Fell was still there, still working at decompiling the data. She wasn't really aware of her eyelids starting to droop until her chin slipped off the heel of her hand, and the Deltan realized that she had fallen into a momentary microsleep. She stretched in the chair and sighed. According to her chronometer, *Titan* was well into its Gamma Shift, and that meant she had been up for nearly eighteen hours.

But the work wasn't done, and she couldn't escape the feeling that something important was being missed. Peya didn't want to go back to her rack, not yet.

She eyed the replicator across the room and toyed with the idea of ordering up a mug of *raktajino* but then rejected the thought immediately. The heavy Klingon coffee-substitute was too acidic for her palate, and even a small amount tended to keep her up for uncomfortably too long. Instead, she had some water and walked a circuit of the room before taking her seat in front of the analysis console once again.

Peya considered the subroutines running before her. The current rebuild process string was nearing completion, and with a bone-weary sigh she saw that it too was probably going to turn out inconclusive. The combination of the idiosyncratic Dinac bioprogramming language and the damage to the pinnace's systems made it hard for Starfleet's software to grasp what data was still intact over on the alien explorer.

The ensign's head lolled forward, and this time she didn't notice the screen blurring as her fatigue took control. In a matter of seconds, Peya Fell was snoring gently, balanced upright in her chair. She began to dream of home.

Shenti Yisec Eres Ree let the door to his cabin hiss shut and peeled off his uniform as he padded deeper into his quarters. Fully disrobed, he tossed the used clothing aside with a desultory flick of his talon, landing it in a pile near the bin in the corner of the compartment. He would recycle it later. For now, Ree wanted rest.

The mister nozzles in his refreshment cubicle coated his leathery skin with a fine layer of fresh water—a luxury that the Pahkwa-thanh always enjoyed—and he loped back across his cabin toward the large flat rock that dominated the rearmost section of his quarters. Replicated from a molecular model taken from the actual sleep-stone he had cut for himself as a youth on Pahkwa Majoris, it was a small touch of home for the doctor, one that today he badly needed. Infrared lamps tuned to the same heat-light spectrum as his homeworld's sun kept the wedge-shaped piece of rock at a perfect temperature for his repose, and with a rattling yawn that showed all his arrow-point teeth, Ree climbed onto the tan-colored rock and curled up, tucking his head forward, bringing his tail up and around.

Dealing with the aftermath of the spatial anomaly had eaten up his entire shift and more besides. Along with treating dozens of minor injuries and shock effects from the hard ride *Titan* had taken getting free of the subspace rift, he had worked up a crash program of antiradiation treatments for all the species on board who were particularly sensitive to such energy wavebands. With so many different physiologies to deal with, so many drug types and dosage amounts, even something as relatively straightforward as a program of booster shots became a major undertaking. But it was done now, and Ree had left Nurse Ogawa to keep things moving as her shift began with the ending of his. Sickbay was in good hands. No one had died. The injured had been healed. He decided to call today a good day.

Ree felt the warmth of sun-baked stone seeping into his pores and surrendered himself to sleep.

In Peya's dreamscape, at first it was welcoming and cool, a good strong breeze that made her skin sing as she walked across the grass. The rain falling around her was refreshing, and she realized how much she missed it, lush and strong and just like home. The tall grass whispered under her boots, parting with each footfall, her legs sinking to the ankles as she advanced.

Peya looked up, expecting to see a clear sky and the distant glow of the sun—but something was amiss. There was only blackness above, a starless void that wasn't even night. The dark was too deep, too wide, and something about it touched a deep-seated sense of wrongness. She felt the first stirrings of a primal, animalistic kind of fear, the sort of panic that was buried down deep in her hindbrain.

Up in the fathomless dark, Peya thought she saw something moving. A ship, perhaps, very far away. Silver-blue and hurtful in aspect, like a thrown dagger. She flinched away, unwilling to gaze upon it for too long.

Beneath her feet, the grass was wilting. No longer the firm, green blades she knew from the hills near where she had grown up, but a powdery, shifting mass of brown fronds and dust. She could not plant her boots, and she stumbled. The ground moved, refusing to give her purchase.

Light reflected off metal danced about her, but Peya resisted the urge to look up. If she did, she would see the knife-ship up there, looming large, coming to cut open her world. Panic rose, burning hot, and what little footing there was beneath her suddenly vanished. She stumbled into a yawning sinkhole, a deathly dark mirror of the void-sky above her.

Peya tried to open her mouth to scream, but the rain was falling hard, dragging away her words and the breath from her lungs.

At first the heat was like an old friend, welcoming Ree and cradling him in his slumber. It reminded him of the days of his youth, before adulthood, before responsibility, when he had been free to run and hunt across the sands and the rocky scrubland. The heat made him feel alive, as if the energy from his homeworld's sun was being transferred directly to him. Ree felt it warming his blood, banishing all trace of torpor. He *basked*.

Strange, though, how the sunlight seemed to be coming not from one fixed point in the sky but from all around him. From the very air itself, excited until it began to shimmer before his lidded gaze, and from the stone on which he lay, growing hotter by the second. The heat pulled on him with a force like high gravity, and the first note of warning sounded in his mind.

Too much. Even for a saurian such as he, with great tolerance for high temperatures, it was becoming too much. The solar radiance shifted away from a welcoming caress upon his reptilian skin toward something oppressive. The light made his eyesight blur. It was causing him pain.

With effort, Ree pulled himself off the rock, slipping to the sand beneath. The punishing glare of the sun made it hard to see far, but he sensed he was not alone in the clearing. He tried to call out to the blurs that might have been other Pahkwa-thahn, but all that escaped his dry lips was a low croak.

This is not right. The thought pushed itself to the front of Ree's mind. On the hottest days of his world, it had never been as punishing as it was now. An irrational fear gripped him, a sudden terror as the impulse to look up twitched through him. He was afraid to raise his head, afraid that he would have only a moment to gaze upon a swollen, murderous sun in the sky before it burned his sight from him.

On instinct, Ree loped across the burning ground, ignoring the pain as it seared the pads of his feet, letting his nostrils find the scent of the low trees and skeletal scrub that surrounded the settlement. Shadows with sharp, angular edges fell across him, and he saw wilted branches bending low under the pressure of the day as he passed beneath them. The twisted trees glittered as if they were coated in chrome, turning toward him, grasping through the heavy air like questing talons.

Ree spun around, realizing his mistake, trying to find the path he had taken into the cover of the scrub; but there were only shadows there now.

The grass moved like it was alive, dragging her down and smothering her. Peya felt almost betrayed, as if her world itself had turned against her. She was powerless to stop it pulling her under, the ceaseless pressure projecting her into a gloomy space that felt cavernous and claustrophobic all at the same time. Bright lights—hard, silver blades of illumination—stabbed out at her, and she tried to scramble away. A crag of ancient stone cut at her fingers, her palms. Peya fought to beat back the panic that resonated through her. The fear was going to engulf her, and she could hear her heart hammering in her ears, feel the crackling tingle along her nerves to the very tips of her fingers.

Something grabbed her. Hands clasped around her wrists, her legs, hot and clammy and unnatural to the touch, but in the ice-dark she saw nothing. They pulled her, dragging Peya toward the light and the promise of the pain it held.

She screamed—

He shrank to the burning, sandy earth and brought up his claws in a defensive posture, but Ree was overwhelmed. The blazing sun blinded him, making everything a watery blur of color and form, and the spindly branches of the dead trees were everywhere, their thorns plucking at his thick skin, their dusty vines snaking around him. He snapped at nothing, tasting a rotten-meat foulness in his throat that made him gag and choke.

The quality of the light was hard, raking him with its rays, and in the sparse place where the shadows fell, Ree thought he glimpsed shining fronds glittering like knives. Struggling did nothing, the ground sucking at his legs. He reached out, trying to find something to grab on to, but his claws only struck at air.

A fathomless terror ran through Ree's mind, primal and powerful, robbing him of his control. He moaned as panic surged in him. Something was holding him down. He was certain of it, feeling the ghost of heavy restraints preventing him from escape. Ree's muscles bunched as he tried to pull free, but nothing moved. Trapped now, he was pinned like a prey animal in the jaws of a predator.

Then, against reason, the burning sun behind the web of metallic branches began to *move*, growing larger as it came closer. The heat flooded over him, and Ree felt his flesh begin to smolder.

He tried to cry out—

She was instantly, shatteringly awake.

Peya lay on the floor of the computer lab, the stool she had been sitting on upended nearby. She felt dizzy and sick.

Did I fall? Was that it? I dozed off and overbalanced?

She got to her feet and massaged the hand she had landed on, unable to stop herself casting furtive glances into the darker corners of the room. Suddenly the empty computer lab felt oppressive and isolated, and that primitive impulse in Fell's mind pushed her out into the corridor.

A chilling thought ghosted though her: *I am alone.*

While I slept, everyone else vanished, just like the other crews.

She shook her head, trying to banish the foolish notion—but the passageway, dimly lit during ship's night, was totally devoid of life. Peya found herself holding her breath, listening for the slightest sound of someone, anyone. With each step she took down the silent corridor, the irrational terror buried its claws in her a little deeper.

Then, rounding a corner into a junction where two more radial passages connected, Peya came across a pair of noncommissioned officers standing near a replicator alcove. The fear drained away and was gone.

One of the noncoms gave her a wary look. "Are you all right, Ensign?"

She pushed past him and gave her answer to the replicator instead. "*Raktajino*," demanded Fell. "Double strong, double sweet."

He awoke with a shock.

Claws scraping uselessly over the warm surface of the sleep-stone, Ree slipped off the angled rock and staggered away a step or two, blinking furiously. He gasped and drew in a lungful of air.

Loping to the refresher cubicle, he let the mister run longer than usual, absorbing the cool water, letting it bead and run over his flesh. It did not banish the phantom of the nightmare, however. The remnants of the imagery and the emotions it left behind clung to Ree like gossamer.

"A dream," he said aloud, as if speaking the words would fix the event in the unreal and banish it from the room. "Merely a dream."

It did not help. Ree's flesh prickled with the very real sensation that he was not alone in his quarters. He reached for a control tab on the wall and tapped it with one extended claw. The lighting level immediately rose from the low ambient illumination of ship's night to something like Terran-standard daylight. Ree tensed, his body still reacting to the sense-memory of the solar heat, but no punishing burn came with the brightness.

He stalked about the compartment, taking a deep breath as he moved, sifting it for scent markers. But all Ree found were traces of his own danger-response pheromones. No one was there.

A low growl escaped the saurian's lips. He was annoyed at such a foolish lapse of rationality. He had allowed himself to be unsettled by what was nothing more than his mind's attempt to parse the stressors of his day and settle itself for a deeper, restful sleep. With a sigh, he dropped the lighting level back down to night mode and wandered back toward the sleep-stone.

His gaze flicked to the chronometer on a nearby nightstand and he stopped. *How long was I asleep?*

To Ree, it felt like only moments had passed, but according to the clock, the unpleasant dream had robbed him of almost an entire night. Gamma Shift was in its last watch phase, and the doctor would be required for duty in just a few hours. His lips drew back in a toothy scowl, and unconsciously Ree kneaded the muscles of his wrist, in the same place where the illusory restraints had held him trapped.

He turned over his manus to examine the spot, and his eyes widened. A precise strip of dermal bruising, like one might see from a strap pulled too tightly, discolored the Pahkwa-thanh's flesh.

Six

Riker stepped out of the turbolift and set off toward sickbay, with Lieutenant Ssura keeping perfect pace at his side. The Caitian's presence was becoming second nature to the admiral, as commonplace as his shadow. In all his years as a command-level officer, Riker had never felt the need for a yeoman to serve as an assistant, but with a rise to the admiralty the sheer amount of reports he had to sign off on made it something he could no longer do without.

The downside was that, even when he was out of the office, Admiral Riker was never really out of the office. Ssura walked and talked, eyes never leaving his ever-present padd, and still he moved without bumping into the other crew members that they passed.

"I have taken the liberty of compiling a first draft of the threat report regarding the subspace phenomenon we encountered, sir," Ssura was saying. "I will transmit it to Admiral Akaar after you have reviewed it."

He nodded absently. "I'll get to that. But first I want to know what's got my wife so concerned."

"There is no doubt Commander Troi would not have requested your presence if it was not of import."

"That's what I'm afraid of." He hadn't seen Deanna since that morning, sparing her and Tasha a quick kiss before he set off for the hub to get an early start. The agenda for the day had involved taking a look at *Whitetree*'s crew manifest and addressing the possibility that there would need to be hundreds of condolence communiqués to send out. Riker's jaw set. He didn't want to go down that road, not until they were sure.

Pushing that thought aside, he strode through the door into the ship's sickbay and found a group of his officers waiting by the main medical imaging panel on the far wall. His wife was there, along with Vale and Sarai, Ree and Ogawa, security chief Ranul Keru, and Sariel Rager from ops. A frown threatened to form on his face; this grouping meant that whatever had compelled Deanna to call the meeting was of serious import indeed.

"Admiral, thanks for coming," said Vale. That fact that Christine used his rank also underlined the gravity of the situation. She glanced at Deanna. "Now we're all here, Counselor, tell them what you told me."

Riker experienced a brief flicker of surprise at the thought of his wife going to Vale before him with something significant, but then he dismissed it. Vale was *Titan*'s captain, and that was the chain of command.

Troi wasted no time with preamble. "I believe that *Titan*'s security has been breached in a clandestine manner, and that we are facing an ongoing threat. Very likely the same threat responsible for the loss of the *Whitetree* and the crew of the Dinac explorer."

Keru eyed her. "My people have registered no security issues since we entered the sector, Counselor. Can you be more specific?"

There was a curious moment when Troi's gaze flicked between Riker and Commander Rager before she went on. "Over the past few days, since we made contact with the Dinac ship and took it under tow, there has been a gradual increase in crew members reporting incidents of sleep disruption. At first, it was difficult to map because of the widely differing circadian cycles of the various races aboard ship, but after Huilan came to me this morning with some concerns, I realized that a pattern is forming."

Riker nodded. Huilan Sen'kara was Deanna's direct subordinate on the ship's counseling staff and an accomplished psychoanalyst.

Ree cleared his throat, as if a little uncomfortable to admit something. "I, ah, spoke with Doctor Sen'kara after experiencing a particularly troubling dream last night. I thought it was merely the product of stress, but the doctor became concerned by the similarity it exhibited to other sleep disturbances he had become aware of."

"Peya Fell came to me today with the same issue. And she and Doctor Ree are just the latest. Eighteen crew members across ten different species have all reported disturbed dreams or requested sleep aids since we found the pinnace."

"Are we looking at some kind of telepathic assault?" said Sarai.

Troi shook her head. "No. I've felt nothing, and just to be certain I spoke with the other psionically sensitive members of the crew. No trace of any mental disturbances felt by any of them either."

Keru scowled. "Forgive me, but how do some nightmares correlate to a danger to the ship and the crew?" The burly Trill was very much a man who believed in things that he could grasp, and the idea of something so ephemeral as a potential threat did not sit well with him. "Are these things being caused by something else, like a viral infection or a neurotoxic agent?"

"We're running deep analysis now," offered Ree. "Food, water, atmospherics. The first thing we checked was if something had been brought back on the materials recovered from the wreck, but we've come up clean there. And there's only partial commonality between these dreamers and the crew who have been aboard the Dinac ship."

Slowly, a creeping chill spread through Riker's blood as a horrible familiarity came upon him. A memory of something he had worked hard to put behind him emerged like a knife drawn from a sheath. He instinctively glanced at Sariel Rager and found his expression mirrored in hers. *Cold, ominous dread.*

Suddenly, he knew why Deanna had specifically asked that he and the ops officer be present for this discussion. "Is it *them*?" he asked her. "Have they found their way back to us?"

"I think it is a very strong possibility." Deanna sighed.

"You're talking about . . ." Rager became ashen, unable to say the words. She swallowed hard and tried again. "What happened aboard the *Enterprise*?"

Vale answered for Deanna: "I reviewed Captain Picard's and Doctor Crusher's logs of those events. It all fits the profile."

Sarai raised an eyebrow. "What profile?" She shot a look at Riker. "Who are *they*, Admiral?"

All at once he wanted to sit down, the bleak certainty of it all draining him of energy. But instead, Riker took a breath and reached for the memory—and the anguish that came with it. "We were in the Amargosa Diaspora," he began. "It was nearly two decades ago. The *Enterprise*-D was on a survey mission in that region, mapping a globular cluster."

"We caught the attention of something . . ." said Rager. "A species living in a tertiary subspace manifold. And they didn't have good intentions."

"Subspace?" echoed Keru. "Is it possible for intelligent life to actually exist in that kind of realm?"

Ree's head bobbed. "The laws of nature might differ there to what we are familiar with, but yes, in theory life could evolve to sentience in such a space."

Riker continued: "Our chief engineer was using a new warp power algorithm to boost the acuity of the *Enterprise*'s sensor array. Afterward, we realized that the energy signature reached into the deeper regions of subspace. Like Sariel said, we disturbed something, and they came looking. A race of beings with a solanagen-based cellular structure deliberately caused a spatial rupture on board our ship, and through it they began to . . . take people."

"They abducted us against our will!" Rager said hotly. "*Did things to us*. They killed a man. Replaced his blood with a polymer fluid, and then tossed him back like a failed experiment when they were done!"

Riker unconsciously rubbed his arm. "Sariel and I were among the people that they took. While we slept, they stole us away for a few hours, returned us when it was over. We never found out what they wanted. They never made any attempts to communicate with us, but it was clear their intentions were not benign. In the end, we sealed off the rupture they created with a graviton pulse, but not before they released some kind of matter-energy probe into our universe."

Vale nodded. "Picard's report noted that the *Enterprise* was unable to track it once it got into our space."

"Yes," said Troi. "These abductions were highly traumatic for everyone affected . . . And I believe that cycle is occurring again, here and now."

Keru stiffened. "Doctor, this happened to you? And Ensign Fell, and all the others?"

The saurian's snout dipped. "It would seem so. I had a full bioscan of my body to determine if anything was amiss. There is microscopic evidence that samples of my blood, spinal fluid and lung tissue were taken without my knowledge."

"It is the same pattern of behavior as before," said Deanna. "Abduction. Experimentation. Return."

"If these beings are looking for a diverse sample base," Sarai noted, "then *Titan* is the perfect resource."

"We're checking everyone who reported the same symptoms for other indicators," Ogawa added. "There may be more people who haven't even realized they were . . . taken."

"But we're light-years away from Amargosa," insisted Keru. "And *Titan* hasn't done anything like that warp power tap you mentioned, Admiral."

"It's not a matter of physical distance," said Sarai, thinking it through. "Connections between *n*-dimensional and *s*-dimensional spaces don't have to be co-terminus. And as for the energy that first attracted these beings . . . What if the origin was the Dinac ship?"

"Possible," said Rager. "Dinac warp systems are

unusual. They could have a level of subspace bleed that we're unaware of, enough to attract the . . ."

"The Solanae." Vale supplied the name. "That's the designation that Starfleet Xenobiology gave to those beings."

Loathing simmered in Riker's thoughts. "If they're trying to access our space again, we have to do everything we can to prevent it." He shook his head. It all fit. The strange tetryon traces, the remnants of a particle that should have been highly unstable in normal space. And suddenly the absence of the explorer's crew made sense, as did the seemingly random appearance of the spatial rift that had threatened the *Titan* only hours before.

Vale's thoughts paralleled Riker's. "Whatever these Solanae want, I think it's safe to say they've upped their game. They're not just abducting individuals. They're taking entire *starships*. It's the only explanation that makes sense regarding the vanishing of the *Whitetree*."

"They want this vessel too." Troi's words were grim.

"They can try." Keru sniffed. "They couldn't take *Titan* because the *Luna*-class is a more advanced design. Better deflectors. Advanced quantum torpedoes. *Saber*-class ships don't have any of that." He shook his head. "Okay. I'm coming around on this. Clearly, we need to act, and quickly. The Solanae might have failed to drag our ship to who-knows-where, but if they can take people without us knowing it, they can send things here as well."

"That's uncertain," said Ogawa. "The difference in cellular energy states between our universe and subspace are extreme, certainly for a life-form that originated there. They wouldn't easily be able to cross from one to another."

Ree nodded at his colleague. "Yes. A carbon-based organic form sharing *our* quantum signature. Something that originated in this universe . . . would be able to survive for days, perhaps weeks, in a subspace manifold. But the reverse would not be so. An unprotected solanagen-based being here would have a survival margin of *minutes*, or less."

"Are you absolutely sure of that? There was that tricorder audio from the pinnace. Lieutenant Ythiss mentioned intruders aboard the vessel," said the Trill. "Are you willing to risk that happening on our ship, Doctor?"

"No one is," Riker said firmly, tapping his combadge. "Riker to Tuvok, respond."

The Vulcan's crisp answer was immediate. "*Go ahead, Admiral.*"

"Raise the deflectors and modify the waveband distribution to include a coherent graviton pulse, full spectrum compression. Keep them active until otherwise ordered, is that clear?"

"Aye, sir. Shall I also extend the field to encompass the derelict?"

"Tuvok, who's over there?" said Vale.

"Commander Pazlar, Ensign Fell, Lieutenants Kyzak and Dakal."

"Do it," Riker ordered. "And contact Melora, let her know what's going on."

"Understood."

He took a breath. "Hopefully that'll halt any further attempts to take our people. But it's a stopgap at best."

Vale met his gaze, frowning. "Admiral, with all due respect, are we cutting off our only avenue of contact with these beings? You said before, with the incident aboard the *Enterprise* they returned the people they took. It might be the only way to recover the crew of the explorer and the *Whitetree*."

"You propose we wait and hope these aliens are willing to return the abductees?" Sarai scowled. "It would also leave us open to further abductions and, as Mister Keru said, the possibility of sabotage."

"I know the risks, XO," Vale said firmly. "We have to consider all the options."

But the admiral was already shaking his head, the shadow of the traumatic events all those years before weighing heavily upon him. "I'm making this an order, Captain. Nobody else gets taken."

Vale's lips thinned, but she nodded. "Aye, sir."

"Shield harmonics macro is programmed and ready," reported Lieutenant McCreedy. "Deflectors at your command, sir."

Tuvok nodded, without turning to look at the engineer. "Activate." The Vulcan glanced down at the repeater screen at his right, watching the haloes of invisible projected energy as they radiated out from the *Titan*, erecting what he hoped would be an impenetrable barrier to any further attacks on the ship—as long as the shields could be supplied with power, that was.

On the display, the normally ovoid shape of the projection was slightly lopsided, with additional energy applied to extend the defensive membrane out around the wreck of the Dinac explorer. Despite the asymmetrical configuration, McCreedy's calculations were sound and the deflectors set in place.

"Tactical," Tuvok began, inclining his head toward

the station that he himself would usually have occupied, had the captain and first officer been on the bridge. "Mister Kuu'iut, commence a level-three security scan of the surrounding zone of space. If Admiral Riker suspects a threat is imminent, we would do well to find some trace of it before another assault occurs."

"Assault?" repeated the Betelgeusian. "Commander, are you saying that rift we encountered was a *weapon*?" The young officer seemed amazed by the possibility.

"I suspect that may be the case." He halted as a warning tone sounded from behind him, pinging softly at McCreedy's console. "Lieutenant? Is there a problem?"

"I'm not sure . . ." Her brow furrowed. "When the modified shields went up, there was a momentary power fluctuation."

"Location?"

"Inside the ship. Cargo bay four, sir. It looks like some kind of activation spike. As if something just came on-line. The wavelength doesn't correlate with Starfleet-issue technology."

Ensign Polan spoke up from his post at the science station, his eyes widening. "Bay four is where the wreckage from the pinnace is being held."

"Do you think it is possible," said the Chelon ensign, "for objects to retain an empathic imprint of events that took place around them?" Kekil had an odd habit of inserting pauses into his speech when he was deep in thought about something. The biologist was usually easy company, but Torvig found that the reptilian being could become obsessed with one train of thought and follow it almost to the point of no return. Lieutenant Commander Pazlar had called it "going down the rabbit hole," a Terran aphorism that Torvig had never quite been able to grasp.

Kekil was holding a long, bowed section of the decking from the Dinac ship, the vacuum-burned texture of the wooden plank giving it an old, decaying appearance. His large eyes blinked slowly as he turned the thought over in his mind.

"I believe not." Along with the two Rossini ensigns, Torvig and Kekil were the only ones in the cargo bay, each person having their own section of the recovered wreckage to analyze; but Kekil insisted on doing his analysis out loud, and it had the effect of interrupting Torvig's line of reasoning each time he uttered something in that breathy, slightly labored voice of his.

"Some beings are able to read psychometric energies from inert objects," Kekil insisted. "I once met an Orion empath who touch-sensed a lodestone from my home on Chelon. She knew much about me." He nodded sagely.

Torvig sniffed the air and thought about turning down the gain in his audial implants. "Would that be the same Orion who stole your combadge when we were on Zofor Beta?"

"Larcenous intent does not preclude parapsychic ability," said the Chelon defensively, putting down the piece of wood.

"What would you expect to find if you could see into the past of an object?" said Torvig. "To quantify such a subjective—" The tricorder grasped by the manipulator claw at the tip of the Choblik's tail interrupted him with a discordant beep, and Torvig brought it up to his face to study the display. "Odd . . ."

"Something wrong?" Paolo Rossini looked up from across the bay, seeing his change in manner. At Paolo's side, his sibling, Koasa, continued to work at scanning a broken bulkhead section.

"A power fluctuation," said Torvig, his tongue flicking out to wet his lips. "In this compartment. But there are no devices here drawing energy other than the tools we brought with us."

A low, dull click sounded behind Ensign Kekil, and he turned to look in the direction of the sound. The cybernetic augmentations in Torvig's ears boosted the acuity of his hearing twentyfold, and he immediately triangulated the source of the noise. He pointed with his free hand.

Kekil dropped to his knees, the broad-shouldered form of his shelled back sinking to the deck. Torvig heard his bony beak clack thoughtfully. "One of those orbs," he explained. "It must have rolled off from the rest of the debris samples." He reached for it, and the sphere seemed to twitch, rolling a little farther away, just out of Kekil's grasp.

An abrupt wariness made Torvig's neck whip around, as he shot glances back and forth, searching for others of the distinctive orb-shaped objects among the wreckage. There were several of the spheroids, all identical, all yet to be cataloged.

The Chelon snatched at the orb before him with one thick-fingered claw and held it up. "What are these things, anyway?" He removed a thin protoplaser tool from a pocket on the overjacket he wore. "I wonder, has anyone thought about opening one up?" The red nib of the tool glowed brightly as Kekil applied it to the rubbery skin covering the sphere.

"Maybe you shouldn't do that," called Paolo, holding up a hand. "Not outside of a lab environment, anyway."

"Scans say they are inert," Kekil retorted, as his laser burned into the orb.

It *screamed.*

What happened next was a blur, almost too fast for Torvig's artificially enhanced neural pathways to fully process. There was the odor, an acrid mixture of cooking meat and burning polymers, and then a shimmer of yellow-white as the orb released a discharge of fluid at the Chelon. Reeling backward, a thin wail issued out of Kekil's open beak.

Seams that hadn't been there before opened down the sides of the orb, cut by an invisible blade. Inside was something glistening and damp, halfway between the tissue of a ripe fruit and the marbled texture of raw meat. The sphere split into a form with eight fleshy flukes, and it exploded out of Kekil's grip toward the ensign's wide-eyed, openmouthed face.

Torvig let out a bark of shock as the orb-thing enveloped the Chelon's head with enough force to send him stumbling to the ground. Dry, clacking sounds came from all across the cargo bay as the other orbs—three more of them—underwent the same grotesque transformation.

He was aware of a voice calling out over the intercom, the stoic tones of Commander Tuvok. A warning.

Too late, thought Torvig.

Tossing aside his tricorder, the Choblik bounded across the short distance to the Chelon ensign, even as Kekil managed to get back some control of his limbs. Torvig saw him clawing at the opened orb-thing, trying and failing to peel it off his face. All around, other pallets of samples and temporary benches were crashing to the deck as the alien spheroids burst into motion. He heard Paolo calling out for security and medical help.

Torvig gritted his teeth and grabbed the orb smothering Kekil with both hands, pulling at it. The creature—if it was right to think of it as that—writhed and squirmed in his grip, spitting a second, less potent discharge of acid into the air. Torvig jerked back and reflexively let go.

With a glutinous tearing sound, the orb-thing unwrapped from Kekil's face and flicked itself away with a twitch of powerful musculature. It moved, half-spinning, half-bouncing, in a form midway between its fully opened petal shape and the neutral spherical aspect.

Torvig dropped to his knees next to the big Chelon, and his fur rippled with a sudden chill. Kekil gasped, struggling to say something, but his mouthparts would not work. His beak scraped together and then was still. Sorrow gripped Torvig as he heard the last breath escape the Chelon's lungs.

Another crash of falling debris made his deer-like head snap up and around, and he caught sight of Koasa Rossini swinging a sensor wand like a baton, using it to strike back at a swift gray-white blur as it shot past him.

"There!" Paolo was pointing across the compartment at a service bay near the main doors of the cargo bay. "What the hell are they doing?"

As he watched, Torvig saw the orb-things gathering near the base of the wall. One of them opened into its octopoidal form and flung its mass against the middle of the removable panel across the bay. Powerful secreted acidic fluids burned into the tripolymers, and in seconds, the creature had melted a ragged hole through the panel. It detached and undulated through the opening it had made.

Inside that bay was a circuitry bus for the environmental and computer system, along with power regulators for the cargo transporter. The other orbs opened and followed the first, their muscular flukes curling back burn-distorted sections of metal as they squeezed through.

Torvig broke into a sprint. He hurdled a collapsed bench and landed with a grunt as the last orb slid through the gap in the plate. With a jerk of his wiry body, Torvig grabbed the edges of the safety panel and shoved it aside, magnetic connecters clicking as they disengaged.

Inside, the equipment bay was a mass of glowing isolinear circuits and power conduits. A narrow crawlspace, barely wide enough to admit an adult human, extended away from him. Torvig saw a wet trail of fluid catch the light and heard movement deeper down the passageway.

If these things get into the spaces between the decks, if they attack an EPS conduit or a phaser coolant line . . . The thought of what could result was too horrible to consider.

For one brief moment, Torvig hesitated; then he dove forward into the service tunnel, bunching up his limbs along the line of his body, lowering his head and long neck. Choblik anatomy, even in its cybernetically augmented form, was highly flexible, and in a pinch the ensign was capable of squeezing into very small spaces.

Such confinement made Torvig distressed, and it

wasn't something he would have volunteered for—but this was an emergency, and there was only time to *react*, not *deliberate*.

The metal claws on the tips of his manipulators scraped at the walls of the tunnel as he wriggled through, pulling himself after the fleeing alien orbs. He could see them just ahead, beyond his reach. The spade-like muscular flukes they used as limbs twitched, and through their translucent flesh, Torvig saw what looked like tracks of flexible circuitry embedded in the tough skin. *What are these things? Machine or living creature? Or perhaps they are like me, a mixture of both?*

That acrid burn-stink filled his nostrils once again as the orb-things ejected more acid spittle into the walls, causing the bulkhead to pucker and melt. Sparks flew as the alien creatures flocked to the new tear in the *Titan*'s structure, compressing their forms to push through the rough-edged puncture. The hole was far too small for Torvig to fit through

Desperately, the ensign snatched at the last of the orb-things as it crawled into the gap, and the creature reacted, lashing out with another aerosol of venom. Inside the confined space of the access tunnel, there was nowhere else for the full force of the discharge to go other than onto Torvig, and he moaned in great pain. His body jerked uncontrollably, and the Choblik's head banged hard into the tunnel's low ceiling.

Stifled by the stench of acid-burned metal and seared flesh, Torvig gasped as his vision dimmed. Distantly, from somewhere far behind him, he heard voices calling his name, heard the rising-falling wail of an alert siren.

Then nothing.

"What now?" Xin Ra-Havreii rose angrily to his feet and stormed out of the small alcove that served as his office in main engineering. The pulsing glow from *Titan*'s dual refracting intermix chamber normally cast a steady, throbbing light over the compartment, but with the clarions of red alert sounding, the entire space was bathed with a hellish crimson glow. The Efrosian chief engineer glared at his crew, as if it were the fault of one of them that he had been disturbed. "Anyone?" he demanded.

Meldok, the blue-skinned Benzite ensign at the intercooler control panel, gave him a worried look over his breather rig. "Is it that rift effect again?"

Xin ignored his question. The answer was obviously *no*; last time, *Titan* had been thrown off its axis immediately and the ship's attitude was still stable. "Somebody get me the bridge! I want to know what in the nine suns is going on up there, and I want to know it five minutes ago!"

As Xin said the words, the doors to the main radial corridor on the engineering deck hissed open and three security guards ran in, led by a burly Orion. The Orion started snapping out orders to his team—Boslic and Catullan females, a Bajoran male—who sprinted out to take up stations all around the engine core.

Xin had made little effort to remember the names of the security staff, but he did recall that the Orion was a chief petty officer named Dennisar. He strode up to the barrel-chested noncom and prodded him with a finger. "You. Explain."

"Intruder alert," Dennisar shot back, scanning the compartment. "Details are still coming in, but we believe the ship's security has been compromised."

"You *believe*?" Xin retorted. "You don't know for sure?"

"There was that power spike a few minutes ago." Crandall, another one of Xin's team working at the dilithium monitoring stage, offered up an unasked-for opinion. "Was that something to do with this?"

"I'm going to need a better explanation than that," snapped the chief engineer. "You can't just barge in here!"

"Actually, I can." Dennisar finally turned his gaze on him. The Orion was almost as wide as he was tall, and he had a full head of height on Xin, who wasn't a small man himself. "Sir," he added, as an afterthought. "In fact, that's pretty much my whole job description."

"Chief," called the Bajoran, and by force of habit both Xin and Dennisar turned, thinking that the security guard was addressing them. The dark-skinned man was serious, one hand gripping a phaser rifle, the other with a security tricorder module connected to a cuff rig. He was aiming at the deck near the secondary fusion initiators. "Got an unusual energy reading."

"You cooking anything in here you shouldn't be, sir?" Dennisar asked, brandishing his own weapon. "Off-spec modifications, that kind of thing?"

Xin almost snorted with laughter. "Chief Petty Officer, there's barely a square meter of tritanium in this whole engine room that hasn't been modified off specification." As he spoke, the Bajoran approached the suspect area of the deck warily. "Tell your man to back off."

"Blay, what do you have?" said Dennisar.

"It's moving," came the dour reply.

That brought Xin up short. "What did you say?" He blinked, belatedly catching up to the danger at hand. "Where did this intruder come from? What's the nature of it?" Suddenly he was thinking of the Dinac ship. Melora was over there right now. *Was she in jeopardy?* He didn't like the abrupt sense of vulnerability that possibility raised in him. He pushed the fear away and glared at the Orion. "I asked you a question!"

There was a loud screech of twisting metal, and the deck plates beneath the feet of Crewman Blay unexpectedly collapsed, slumping in on themselves to drop the Bajoran into the spaces beneath. He yelled in surprise and disappeared down to his waist; in the same instant, Xin saw things moving in the glow of the warp core. Blay cried out again, and this time it was a scream of pain.

"Stay clear!" Xin shouted at Meldok, who had come closer. Dennisar and the other security guards came running in, and the chief engineer found himself among them as the shifting shapes under the deck burst into motion.

He had only the vaguest impression of the object that struck him. As large as a soccer ball, and fast, like it had been shot from a cannon. It clipped Xin's cheek with a glancing blow as he flinched away from its motion, but even that near-hit was like taking a punch. His teeth rattled in his jaw and he stumbled, tasting blood. Other things, spheres or fleshy flower shapes, similarly ejected themselves from the crawl spaces beneath the decking. They left melted support frames and snarls of torn ODN cables behind them.

"Fire!" Dennisar shouted the command, and his people

started shooting—even Blay, who was still dragging himself back out of the sinkhole that had formed in the middle of Xin's precious engine room. Yellow-orange beams of phaser light stabbed out, cutting at the fast-moving orbs. One might have been hit, but Xin could not be sure. He was dazed and his cheek felt like it was on fire.

The engineer wiped at his face and the burning transferred to his fingers. An oily, searing residue came away with them. *Some kind of venom?* His stomach knotted.

He staggered and felt hands grab his arm, his shoulder. "I've got you, sir," said Meldok.

With an angry grunt, Xin shrugged off the ensign's help and pushed away. Ignoring the pain across his face and his hand, he shouted to attract Dennisar's attention. "Look there! Moving toward the command panel!"

Xin gaped as the strange hybrid flicked into a spinning motion that landed it, splayed open, across the broad curve of the glassy black console. There was a sizzling crackle of noise as the pulsing octopoidal form emitted a gush of semi-fluid gel that melted into the tri-polymer surface. Plastics liquefied instantly and the orb fell into the nest of complex isolinear circuits within the console, sparking with unspent power. In the heart of the main control panel, spills of acid ate through vital circuits, severing critical connections faster than *Titan*'s computer core could reroute them.

Behind him, Xin heard more shrieks of phaser fire and the wet hiss of venom discharges, but he ignored them, breaking into a run to get to the controls before . . .

The constant pulse of the warp core flickered as its regulatory systems were interrupted. Xin turned in place just in time to see the glowing intermix conduits stutter and go silent, forced into an emergency shutdown by built-in safety protocols. Unlike the tetryon disruption that had briefly shut down the warp drive a day earlier, this attack had gone straight to the heart, like a poisoned dagger.

Seconds later the entire compartment was plunged into near darkness, and Xin was knocked down, falling with a crash to the deck.

There was little that remained intact of the explorer ship's command center. The damage suffered by the pinnace had buckled many of the support frame elements holding up the domed ceiling, dropping great segments of carved hardwood onto the control panels below. Situated at the end of the long corridor that ran almost the entire length of the vessel, the compartment looked like the contents of a scrap yard squeezed into an impossibly small space. The temporary lighting rigs that had been beamed over from the *Titan* threw hard white light over everything, casting sharp-edged shadows everywhere else.

Zurin Dakal coughed slightly and scowled. Atmosphere, gravity and some heating had been restored to this part of the vessel, but it was still damp and cold, enough to remind him of how much he missed the dry warmth of Cardassia Prime. He glanced down the corridor, catching sight of the glittering transparent barrier holding in the weak atmosphere. The far section of the corridor—in fact, all of the ship beyond the nineteenth bulkhead—had sheared off in the incident that had set the pinnace adrift, and only the mobile field emitter deployed down there was keeping the weak envelope of environment in place. It was better than having to work for hours from behind a helmet, he reflected. *But not by much.*

Nearby, Commander Pazlar and Peya Fell were trying to bring a dead control podium back to life, and at what remained of the navigator's station Lieutenant Kyzak was grumbling a steady, low stream of monosyllabic curse words as he tried and failed to access the system. The Skagaran had managed to bring an interface on-line, but it had only the most basic data about the alien ship's movements.

He looked up and caught Zurin's eye. "No success?" asked the Cardassian.

"Not an inch of it," Kyzak confirmed, getting up from the console. "I'm about ready to quit and go back to the barn." He sighed. "It would be a real boon if I had a Dinac pilot here to help me read this stuff."

"Do what you can," called Melora, without looking up from her task. "When we get this ship back to Casroc, I doubt we'll see it again."

"The Dinac have complex rituals about venerating their dead," added Peya. "They'll probably burn this vessel when they're done with it."

Zurin nodded absently as something caught his eye. A glitter of light through one of the oval viewports in the hull wall. Unlike Starfleet ship designers, the Dinac liked having lots of ports in the fuselage of their craft, projecting data directly onto the artificial mineral-glass hybrid instead of screens. The port displays were inert on this side of the vessel, which meant what Zurin saw was something outside. Something on *Titan*.

He peered through the portal. Close by and rising

high over the small mass of the derelict, the downswept engine pylons of the starship arched over the Dinac craft like the wings of some great bird. From a spot on the stern at the end of the runway leading to *Titan*'s shuttlebay, a bright emitter node cast a sparkling net of counter-gravitational tractor beam energy that held the wreck steady.

As Zurin looked, the blink of light he had seen before occurred again, and this time he saw it for what it was: an uncontrolled pulse crackling through the glowing intercoolers of *Titan*'s portside nacelle.

That's wrong. The warning thought was still forming in his brain when another flash—this time from the tractor emitter—washed out his vision for a moment. Pazlar, Kyzak and Fell all reacted, but only Zurin was in the right place to see the shocking moment as the warp engines went dark.

The core's dead. It was the only explanation for such a sudden loss of power.

Like a fast-forward image of ink spreading over paper, the darkness reached out from the dead warp nacelles and covered *Titan*, blacking out ports and running lights in the time it took Zurin to suck in a chill breath of stale air. All around them, speed-distended starlight snapped back into bright points of illumination as both vessels were unceremoniously dumped back out of warp space for the second time in as many days.

The last thing to die was the tractor emitter tethering the explorer ship to *Titan*, and it did not go without incident. A random surge of energy, perhaps something forced through the beam matrix by whatever overload had doused the warp core, rippled out from the emitter as the tractor field dissipated, swatting the little ship aside. Stunned silent by what he saw, by the time Zurin realized he should have shouted a warning, there was no time to do so.

The pinnace rolled sharply, the deck canting at a steep angle. Zurin grabbed a support pillar, while Pazlar and Fell grabbed on to the control podium. But Kyzak was out of arm's reach of anything, so when the impact knocked away the power cables to the temporary force field generator and the membrane winked out, the force of decompression that followed grabbed the Skagaran and yanked him away down the long corridor. His arms and legs windmilling, unable to stop his headlong flight, Kyzak raced away from Zurin toward the endless void.

Seven

In his last year at Starfleet Academy, during survival training on the frozen surface of the Jovian moon Europa, there had been a moment when Ethan Kyzak had lost his footing on a ridge. He remembered it clearly, the ice crumbling beneath his boots and the sudden giddy rush as he fell. He hit the snow pack and started sliding, faster and faster. For the first few seconds, he had been terrified, afraid that he might smash his EVA helmet on some hidden rocky outcrop or vanish into a bottomless crevasse. But then, as the slope started to even out and the sliding, rushing motion became less chaotic, he found himself leaning into it, like it was his own personal luge. By the time he reached the bottom, he was laughing, and aside from some abrasion on his suit, a few bruises and a demerit from his instructor, he came though it unscathed. He did learn a lesson that day, although it wasn't the one the survival course was meant to instill. The lesson: *Know when the danger is real, and when it's not.*

It was very real now.

Europan ice flashed through his mind's eye in the scant few seconds as Kyzak was blown backward toward open space by the force of explosive decompression. He was caught in a hurricane, battered by the outgassing atmosphere and a torrent of debris following him out toward open vacuum and certain death. The air in Kyzak's lungs was pulled from him and his hands flailed as he tried to grab at the slick floor, or his helmet still mag-locked to the tool pad on his thigh. He slammed off the wall and tumbled. It seemed to take forever, as he watched the command compartment recede away, with the horrified faces of Pazlar, Fell and Dakal all watching him go, powerless to stop it. What terrified him was that he was falling backward. He wouldn't know it was too late until he saw the Dinac ship tumbling away from him, as the cold of space froze him solid.

How long would he live out there? Would it be quick? Or would he feel every millisecond of an agonizing end?

Kyzak thought he saw Lieutenant Dakal making a move, almost as if the damn fool Cardassian was going to leap off and come after him. *Can't die with that on me,* he wanted to shout, if he had been able. *Can't let him perish because he was dumb enough to try and save me.*

But Dakal was doing something else back there in the screaming wind and the crashing of the wreckage; he was grabbing at a piece of Starfleet tech, something they'd brought over from *Titan* and—

The hurricane dragging Kyzak to his end ceased as abruptly as it had begun, and he had a moment of gut-twisting shock to assimilate before he collided with the restored force field membrane in a shower of sparks. The energy barrier flexed alarmingly and then dumped the lieutenant in a heap on the frost-covered wooden deck.

The polar cold and dangerously thin air made his chest feel like it was stuffed with rocks when he tried to breathe, but he couldn't stop himself from giving in to an understandable reaction.

When Dakal came pounding down the corridor toward him, Kyzak managed to roll over onto his back. He was shaking, almost convulsing.

"Is he all right?" Pazlar's voice echoed along the passageway.

"He thinks something is funny," Dakal said, panting out the words.

Kyzak was laughing silently, and so much that it hurt his ribs. "Zurin . . ." He finally managed, forcing the word out. "My new best friend."

"You are welcome," said the Cardassian, helping him to his feet. Dakal's gray features were paler than usual. "For a moment there, I thought I was too slow . . ."

"Just . . ." Kyzak was finding it hard to breathe. "Just fast *enough*." He fumbled for his helmet and dragged it up and into place. There was the welcome hiss of the seal and then the merciful rush of oxygen from his suit's internal reserves. He could hear a high-pitched ringing in his ears, but he ignored it.

Dakal was doing the same thing. "We lost a lot of atmosphere just then," he said, his own helmet display lighting up as it went active. "Better stay on suit air for now."

"I concur," said Pazlar, lending him a hand up. "What happened to us?"

Fell was at one of the viewports. "We're out of warp, in a tumble . . . And I don't see *Titan*."

"There." Pazlar raised an arm to point back down the

broken corridor, and Kyzak instinctively turned to see. He felt sick as he saw exactly how close he had come to death. The force field Dakal had managed to reactivate in those vital seconds was less than half a meter from the torn open end of the passageway, and beyond it there were only twisted fingers of superstructure, and emptiness. He blinked, raising a hand to rub his eyes before he realized how useless a gesture that was and let it fall away again. He let Dakal help him stay standing.

Out past the broken spars of space-hardened woods, across a chasm of nothing, the shadow-wreathed shape of the *Titan* was moving away from them at a steady rate. Her lights all blinded, the vessel was a colossal piece of dead metal, the internal glow that usually illuminated the hull doused so only the faint rays of distant stars gave it shape.

"*Titan*, this is Commander Pazlar," Melora spoke into her helmet's comm relay. "Do you read? This is the away team . . . Please respond."

No voice acknowledged them. Fell tried her communicator as well, and the result was the same. "We're sending," said the Deltan. "But they're not replying."

"A massive power outage." Dakal's conclusion was bleak. "If the mains went off-line, that could kill warp drive, primary systems, everything . . ."

"Emergency . . . standby . . ." managed Kyzak. "Should activate."

"It should," agreed Melora. "But it hasn't." She sighed. "We have to get back over there. They'll need our help."

"Not likely, unless anyone brought a thruster pack with them," said Fell. "No power on *Titan* means no transporting back, ma'am."

Kyzak gathered enough of himself to stand on his own two feet, and Dakal gently let him go. The blurring in front of his face wasn't going away, so the lieutenant raised his hands again, blinking as he tried to focus. He still had that damned ringing in his ears too. Thin and reedy, giving him a headache.

Dakal squinted at the diminishing form of the other starship. "Every second that passes, we're getting farther apart. I saw a feedback shock come down the tractor beam just as *Titan* went dark. It kicked us away from them."

"Melora, what do we do?" In the moment, Fell forgot all formality of rank as the fear brimmed beneath her words.

Kyzak didn't listen to whatever answer she gave, however. His gloved fingers probed at the flat, see-through visor of his helmet; or at least the visor that was *supposed* to be see-through. The blurring wasn't in his vision; it was the helmet itself, the faceplate badly cracked where it had struck the wall in his near-death tumble. Self-repair gel bubbled away to nothing as the jagged splits in the plate crept slowly across it, growing an ugly spiderweb from one side to the other.

And the ringing—that wasn't in his ears. The high-pitched whistle was air escaping, the precious breaths of Kyzak's oxygen outgassing faster than the EVA suit's built-in microreplicator could replace it.

Lights came on in fits and starts, as the sickbay's dedicated backup struggled to come on-line. Alyssa Ogawa found her way to an equipment rack and handed out a few wrist-mounted SIMs beacons. The combined effect was to turn the usually neutral environment of the sickbay into a cavern-like space full of jumping shadows and gloom.

Vale sucked in a breath and steeled herself. They would all be looking to her for strength and direction. "Is anyone hurt?"

"It would appear not, at least in here." In the dimness, Doctor Ree's hunched saurian form seemed almost threatening.

"It's *them*," said Sariel Rager, in a wary voice.

Vale didn't answer her. "All right, we need to work the problem here. Our people are trained for this kind of thing. We have to take the initiative."

She heard the dull click of a communicator. "Keru to Bridge," said the security chief. "Commander Tuvok, respond." Silence answered him.

"We are out of warp again," said Sarai. "And this time, whatever caused it has taken down mains as well."

Vale nodded, bumping into the admiral as she turned around, feeling her way through the shadows. "If the warp field didn't collapse evenly, there'll be neutrino particle discharges all through the ship . . . That'll interfere with the EPS conduits, comms . . ." She shook her head. "What a damned mess."

Riker's face caught the torchlight, and at his side Vale saw Deanna. Both of them covered their concerns with a mask of professionalism, but the captain knew they had to be thinking of their daughter. "Is this my fault?" said the admiral quietly. "I tell Tuvok to activate that graviton pulse, then this happens?"

"Fix the problem, not the blame," Vale responded, then she spoke louder, so everyone could hear her. "All right, listen up. Alyssa, Shenti, Deanna: Assemble crisis teams and prepare for an influx of patients. Dalit, take Ssura and make your way to auxiliary control, check to see if it's operable just in case we need it." She turned toward Riker. "Admiral, I need you and Ranul to head down to—"

"Engineering?" he said, finishing her thought for her.

"As quick as you can, sir. We need power back, and we need it now."

"Captain, we should treat this as an attack until we're sure what took place." Keru's statement gave everyone pause. "If that rift reappears, there will be nothing we can do to stop it from pulling us in."

"All the more reason to proceed with rapidity," offered Ssura.

"Sariel," she went on, turning to Rager, "you and I will head up to the bridge, determine the situation there." The woman gave her a shallow nod. It was clear that the situation had shaken Vale's first officer, but she was keeping it under control.

Riker took a moment to share some private words of comfort with his wife, and then he was gone, with Keru keeping pace. Ssura helped himself to an emergency kit from a locker as Sarai took a tricorder, tapping at the device to set a scanning program running.

Vale beckoned her over, out of earshot of the others. "Commander, before you go, a word?"

"Captain." Sarai approached, her arms folded. "You have other orders for me?"

"No." Irritation flared in her at the Efrosian's terse manner. "I want to know exactly what you think you're doing."

Sarai's lips thinned. "You will need to be more specific."

"You haven't held the post of first officer before, Commander. Perhaps you need to review the part about supporting your captain's decisions." Vale leaned closer. "You disagreed with me in front of the command crew."

"About raising the deflectors?" Sarai met her gaze. "Yes, I did. You were in error. Leaving *Titan* unprotected was the wrong call."

Vale's jaw hardened. "Because we're so much better off now."

"At the time, Admiral Riker's order was sound." The XO glanced at the dimmed room around them. "There was no way to know that this . . . effect would occur."

"The admiral is not in command of *Titan*. I am." Vale held the other woman's gaze. "And your job is to follow my orders, not question them. If you have a problem with something I say, you bring it to me in private." She took a breath, moderating her tone. "Before, when the rift had us in its teeth, *I* supported *you*, Commander. I expect the same in return."

"In that situation, you did the right thing," Sarai replied flatly. "But disagreeing with Riker was incorrect." Vale was going to say more, but the woman went on. "Captain, understand that I don't care what you or the rest of the crew may think of me. But know that I will always do what is best for the safety and security of this ship, and the United Federation of Planets. If that means disagreeing with you, or anyone else for that matter, then so be it."

"I appreciate your candor," Vale shot back. "But as someone who narrowly avoided being cashiered for bucking the chain of command once before, you ought to think seriously about your conduct from this point on."

Sarai's expression softened for a moment. "Ah. Of course. That is what we are really talking about, is it not? *Ishan Anjar*?"

During the sixty days of turmoil that had followed the assassination of Federation President Nan Bacco, Dalit Sarai had been serving as an administrative liaison officer for Starfleet Intelligence to the admiralty. When she discovered a suspected security breach regarding data on the highly volatile Shedai Meta-Genome—an alien technology with great destructive potential—her concerns were dismissed by Admiral Akaar and his staff.

Sarai determined—*correctly*, as it later became clear—that Doctor Julian Bashir of Deep Space 9 had illegally accessed the Shedai data as part of a clandestine plan. The Andorian race were suffering with an ongoing reproductive crisis that threatened the survival of their species, and while the Meta-Genome contained elements of a cure, it also held the potential for something far worse. Any unsanctioned access to it, even for the most altruistic of reasons, could not be permitted.

It was now a matter of record that in her frustration with Akaar's unwillingness to give credence to her concerns, Sarai went directly to Ishan Anjar. The ambitious Bajoran senator who had stepped into the role of president pro tem was currently serving a sentence in a Federation penal colony for his part in engineering the assassination. Sarai's actions had tainted the commander's reputation after the fact, possibly beyond all hope of recovery.

"I know what is said about me," Sarai explained. "People believe that I went to Ishan because I was one of his 'chosen few,' one of the officers who bought into his rhetoric about a stronger, more assertive Federation.

And perhaps I *did* believe in some of the things he said. But I *never* went to him because I wanted a promotion or a ship of my own. I was never a part of his treasonous, dishonorable conspiracy." For the first time since they had met, Vale saw real emotion from the other woman: a flash of deep anger and disgust. "I went over Admiral Akaar's head to Ishan because no one else would listen. Because of what happened in my past, I wasn't considered credible." She looked away, the moment fading. "Ishan Anjar *listened*."

"And look what that got you," said Vale.

Sarai gave a sharp nod, a jut of the chin. "Indeed. Had I known what Ishan was doing, I would have dragged him from the Palais de la Concorde myself. I only care about what is right, about the rules we live by and the ideals we took an oath to uphold. If you and I disagree over those things, Captain Vale, I will not be silent about it." She paused. "Is there anything else you wish to say to me, sir? Or do I have permission to proceed?"

Vale held her gaze for a long moment, then nodded. "Carry on, Number One."

Keru accessed a weapons locker on the next deck down from sickbay, arming himself with a hand phaser and providing one to the admiral. "Set for heavy stun," Riker told him, as they moved on. "Just in case."

"These . . . Solanae," Keru began. "What can you tell me about them? Strengths, weaknesses?"

Riker didn't meet the Trill's gaze right away. A glimmer of vulnerability passed over his face, caught in the glow from Keru's wrist beacon. It wasn't something the security chief was used to seeing on the admiral's face. Riker often seemed unshakable, fearless even, and the fact that the threat of these invaders could give him pause made Keru wonder exactly what traumatic ordeal Riker had experienced at their hands.

"Can't be sure of either," he admitted, after a moment. Riker threw him a sideways glance as the two of them advanced down the darkened corridor. "When they took me the last time, when they had Sariel . . . Doctor Crusher had dosed me with a neurostimulant to counteract whatever they were using to keep our people docile. I had a phaser . . . I remember firing as Rager and I escaped. I think I hit one of them, but it's hard to be certain. The weapon didn't function correctly in their dimensional space."

"Can you describe them?"

"Tall. They were covered by hooded, metallic robes, almost monastic. Clawed manipulators. I only got glimpses of their faces. Like something halfway between a desert lizard and a deep ocean predator." He grimaced. "Trust me, if you see one, you'll know it. They're very memorable."

Keru took this in. "Why attack us now, after all this time?"

"Maybe Sarai was right: Perhaps the Dinac did something to catch the eye of the Solanae."

"If that's true, then we're not the only ones at risk."

"Agreed." Riker gave a nod. They reached an emergency bulkhead and together worked the manual latch to open it. The passage ahead was barely lit by the feeble glow of battery lights, and their wrist beacons cast long, pale beams into the darkness.

Keru froze. "Do you hear that?" At the edge of his

hearing, the Trill picked out a sound like the hissing of a snake. The warning signs that presaged a loss of atmosphere were drilled into every member of Starfleet in their first weeks, and for a second Keru thought he was listening to air outgassing through a microscopic breach in the hull. But then he remembered where they were, deep in the mid-deck and a good distance from the nearest exterior bulkhead. Even as he strained to guess at the sound, it changed. The hissing became fluid, and now it was joined by an acrid stink of burning polymer.

"There!" Riker's light trailed up the wall of the corridor to find a service nexus fitted to the ceiling—essentially a switching and relay device wired into the *Titan*'s complex web of internal circuitry. Globules of thick liquid were running off the edges of the casing, dripping off to hit the deck, where they made the carpet smolder underfoot.

Then with a crash, the base of the panel unexpectedly fell open and something gray, slimy and above all *fast* ejected itself from inside the service module. Torn strips of glowing ODN cable trailed after it, ragged edged as if they had been chewed.

Keru got the impression of a spinning shape, something more like a plant than a living creature, as it bounced off the wall, arresting its fall with a deposit of sticky mucus before flicking away again toward the deck. It was almost a ball, almost a nest of tentacle-flukes, and Keru was sure it was gripping something as it moved. A piece of broken circuitry.

"What the hell is that?" said Riker, aiming his phaser. "It's not one of them?"

"I've never seen anything like it," the admiral shot back.

The thing slid across the deck, reacting in a way that was too twitchy to be artificial. It moved like a trapped animal, spinning about as it seemed to realize that Riker and Keru were between it and the only route of escape. It had to be *alive*.

The orb-thing spat out the precious piece of hardware it had been carrying and attacked. Keru saw it reel back and eject a thin stream of acidic fluid, a liquid whip that burned the carpet in a black line where the fat droplets fell. Both men dodged away, and he heard Riker curse under his breath as a dot of the venom caught his arm and burned away the material in an instant.

Whatever the creature was made of, it had to be mostly musculature. With a twitching flex of its form, it shot off the deck, rebounding off the low overhead to aim itself directly at Keru's chest. He saw the blink of a massive, symmetrical mouth filled with pointed teeth, concealed in the middle of the nest of tentacles.

He fired and caught the life-form as it came at him. Phaser energy flashed, and for a split second the whole corridor was lit with fire-glow amber. Keru's aim was dead-on, and it blasted the creature back and down. A buzzing, spitting noise issued from it, becoming a dying wail that cut off after a moment. The twitching limbs bent back in on themselves, and the thing curled up, the sphere-shape's epidermis scorched red-black and torn open like a rotten fruit.

Riker gave the orb a kick with the tip of his boot. "I think you killed it."

"With a stun blast?"

"It seems so." The admiral eyed the creature, then turned his attention to the gutted service nexus. "What was it doing in there?"

"The optical data network cables in there, they run through this deck. All through the ship, from main engineering to the computer core, holodecks and replicator banks . . ." He frowned. "If something gets in there, it would be like a rodent in the walls of a house."

Riker crouched and gingerly picked up the piece of circuit the creature had been carrying. "This is a power regulator. What was it doing with this? It must have ripped it right out of the switching module."

Keru had no answer. Instead, he scanned the dead form with a tricorder, letting the sensors probe the interior structure of the thing. "Getting confused readings here. Organic *and* mechanical elements." He hesitated as a new readout scrolled down the screen. "Sir, the molecular scan shows a large amount of solanagen-based material in its composition."

"Now we know for sure," said Riker.

"Does that help, Lieutenant?" Peya Fell stepped back and looked down at Kyzak as he sat disconsolately on the chilly deck of the derelict. The front of his helmet was obscured by a couple of flexible suit patches she had pulled from her EVA gear's emergency pack, effectively blotting out most of the man's vision but preventing the loss of more air via the cracks in his faceplate.

Kyzak nodded, the motion exaggerated by the bulky suit. "I guess so. Someone's gonna have to lead me by the hand, though."

"None of us are going anywhere for now," Fell told him.

"I'm not sure staying put is a good idea," said Dakal,

crouching by the force field generator, examining the power pack. "The longer we remain on board this wreck, the greater the distance becomes between us and the *Titan*."

Commander Pazlar stood a few meters away, holding on to a hull brace, staring down the corridor toward a ragged disk of open space. Every seventy-six seconds, the shape of the other starship would become visible through the gap in the hull, rising into and then out of view as the derelict continued its tumble.

Seventy-six. Fell had counted the interval exactly, and there were other numbers swirling around in her thoughts as well. *Eight*: hours of breathable air remaining for each member of the away team. *Ninety-one*: minutes of breathable air remaining for Lieutenant Kyzak, thanks to the damage to his helmet. *Fifty-two*: number of hours overdue *Titan* would need to be for her next check-in before Starfleet raised an alert. *Four*: number of days before the nearest starship would reach this sector.

Fell knew that if she thought hard enough about it, she would be able to come up with another number: a percentage chance of her own survival. She shuddered and pushed away the notion, looking back toward Dakal. "Zurin, we have no way off this vessel. We should just stay put and wait. *Titan* will come back for us."

"If they can." The Cardassian's reply was forbidding. "Look out there, Peya. They're in the same situation we are. A power outage strong enough to knock out a *Luna*-class starship is no small thing. Captain Vale and everyone else over there are dealing with their own problems right now. We can't count on them to rescue us. We have to do something to save ourselves."

"Dinac don't have transporter tech, do they?" Kyzak waved his hand at the air. "No shuttles either."

Dakal gave a slow nod. "The pinnace had escape pods . . . but they were in the section of the vessel that sheared off. All we have right now is a little air and some gravity. And that won't last forever."

Pazlar turned to look at him. "You wouldn't be saying this if you didn't have a suggestion, Mister Dakal. So let's hear it."

He blew out a breath. "We re-create what happened to Lieutenant Kyzak. Except this time, we do it by design."

Kyzak snorted with derision. "I'm not about to go through that again. Being blown out into space—well, almost—one time was enough."

Dakal pointed with both hands. "I think we can do it. If we time things correctly, we can switch off the force field and let the decompression propel us into space. It's a matter of calculation." Out past the hole in the hull, *Titan* waxed and waned once again. It was shrinking a little more with each new pass. "We aim ourselves at the ship and let physics do the rest. Tether us all together, trigger the mag-locks in our boots at full power. The odds are, one of us will skim the hull close enough to make a connection."

Fell's jaw dropped open. "You're serious."

"That's insane," Kyzak said flatly. "I'm a navigator. I'm trained in spatial mechanics. And I'm telling you, if you're off by so much as a degree, you'll slide right past *Titan* and zoom off into the black."

"It can be done," Dakal insisted.

"So can shooting an arrow blindfolded at bats in a pitch-dark sky! Doesn't mean you're actually gonna hit one of them!"

As Fell watched, Commander Pazlar detached from the stanchion and drifted across to the power unit generating the barrier still holding the last gasps of atmosphere inside the Dinac pinnace. "Zurin, I know you well enough to know that you've thought over all the angles. I know you wouldn't suggest something that was hopeless. But answer me this." She tapped the control pad on the generator. "The remote relay here is damaged. So who is going to stand back and manually deactivate the force field so the others can get off this wreck?"

"It doesn't matter," said Kyzak, from behind his blinded helmet. "Either way, it's a death sentence."

"On three," said the captain, and when the count dropped, she and Rager put their effort into forcing open the doors to the turbolift shaft.

Vale peered warily over the lip of the doorway and frowned into the darkness within. She cast about with a wrist beacon, aiming the light downward. "There's a car just below. See it?"

Sariel craned her neck to look. Yes, there it was: The hemispheric dome was visible a meter below the level of the deck.

"No life signs within." Vale checked her tricorder. "Must have stalled there when the power went out."

Rager looked up and saw a black tunnel extending away from them, lit by tiny pinpricks of light from bioluminescent glow strips. The ladder that followed the wall of the turbolift shaft disappeared into the shadows, and she had the unpleasant mental image of an open throat, waiting to consume them. She shuddered and looked away.

The captain must have caught her expression. "Don't

worry, I'm not going to insist we climb it. There's a quicker way."

She nodded absently, glancing back down the corridor at the ragged group of crew members and civilians working to help one another through the crisis.

Climbing up to this deck from the sickbay level, through service hatches in the floor, Rager and Captain Vale had encountered several groups of *Titan*'s crew dealing with their own distinct problems. Leakage from the aquatic environment pods spilling seawater into a storage compartment. A jammed emergency bulkhead that had pinned two crewmen to the deck. Some broken limbs from shock effects. Methane-breathers trapped in a lab where the atmosphere was filling up with dangerously toxic levels of oxygen; and more. They had done what they could to help, but the bridge was their main objective, and the continued silence from the ship's command deck made Rager's concerns grow the closer they got to it.

She thought about her friend and colleague Aili Lavena, Rager's constant companion at the conn next to Sariel's ops station. *What if we get up there and they're all dead? Or, worse, all* gone*?* The thought made her skin crawl, and a particular kind of fear that she had thought long buried rose up in her mind, cold to the touch and ghostly like smoke.

"Here we go," Vale was saying. "Watch your step." The captain eased herself over the lip and dropped the short distance to the top of the stalled cab. Rager took a breath to steady herself and then followed her down. The turbolift beneath their feet made a low groan of stressed metal as it took their weight, but it didn't move.

"Get that open, Commander." Vale pointed to a

circular hatch in the dome, before dropping to her haunches to work at a small panel off to one side.

The egress hatch had a manual lever that Rager could pump to work it open, and in short order she had it done. She shone her torch down into the empty turbolift car and saw nothing. Still, she couldn't stop herself from flinching when the beam reflected off a glassy wall panel in a distinct way, and her mind filled in the gaps with the image of a shiny, jagged blade.

"You all right?" said the captain, after they dropped down into the lift car.

"Fine, sir." The reply was automatic and utterly untruthful. Rager lowered herself into a seated position. "No, I'm not. That was a lie." She blew out a breath.

"I'm sorry," Vale continued. "I'm sorry I brought all this back up for you, Sariel. But you and Admiral Riker . . . you're the only two with direct experience."

"That's one way to put it, Captain."

Vale took her SIMs beacon and opened a flap on the back of its casing, quickly running a thin cable from the device to a slot inside the other hatch. "Power circuit for the turbolift," she explained. "If I transfer some battery power from the beacon to the module, it should be enough to reactivate the car. We can ride it up to the bridge."

Rager nodded, and her hand strayed to the phaser she had picked up along the way. "Good."

The captain sat back, waiting for the process to complete. "I know this must be hard. But I need you to focus."

"You don't know," Rager replied, without thinking. "You *can't* know what it was like. And focus is the problem. I thought it had all gone away, Captain, I thought I had gotten rid of it . . . But no. It's still there." She tapped her chest. "Just buried."

Vale sighed. "Yes. You're right, I don't know what it was like for you and Will and the others. But we have to do whatever we can to make sure the same thing doesn't happen to anyone else."

Slowly, beyond her control, the gates of memory were opening, and Rager's mind cruelly played back her experiences during that mission aboard the *Enterprise*. The nightmarish half-dream of being taken. The wicked blade poised over her face. The creeping paralysis, and that unnerving bone-snap clicking as her abductors spoke among themselves in their strange, alien language. "Years ago, and suddenly it's like it happened yesterday. I thought I was over it. Guess not." She closed her eyes for a moment and tried to blot it out. "You wouldn't know this, but there were bad dreams afterward. They went on for months. Deanna . . . Counselor Troi, she helped me with it." Other things came back to her now, not just the event itself, but the aftermath. The shadow it had cast over her life, that creeping fear that it could happen again, anywhere and at any time. Rager looked at Vale. "I felt like I had been marked, somehow. Like I couldn't be safe anymore. I mean, when we join up we know there are risks, right, Captain?" Off Vale's nod, she went on. "But you don't ever think it would be something like this. Stolen right out of your bed, like something out of a fairy tale."

"Sariel," began Vale, her tone softening, "if you don't think you're up to it: When *Titan* is back up and running, if you want to stand down—"

"That's not it." Rager shook her head. "Do you know, afterward I was going to resign my commission?

So many things had happened to us aboard *Enterprise* that year, not just the abduction but the incident with a Tyken's Rift . . ." She suppressed another shiver. "I went home, back to Earth. My tour was up. I was ready to quit."

Vale gave her a measuring look. "What made you stay?"

Rager sighed as another memory took hold. She seized on it, using it like a lifeline to pull her from the depths of her fears. "My grandfather told me a story. A piece of family history I'd never heard, from a long way back. About a great-great-great-aunt of mine. She was an aerospace fighter pilot during Earth's Third World War, served with distinction. I knew all that. She was part of the inspiration that made me join Starfleet in the first place. You could say it ran in the family." Vale nodded, listening intently. "But not a lot of us knew that she had been shot down during the war and captured by the enemy. What she went through . . . I understood it."

"And she survived?"

"Yes. Matter of fact, she escaped with the rest of her flight and climbed right back in the cockpit. Fought to the end of hostilities, and went on to live a good long life. I figured if Great-Aunt Vanessa could face her fears, then so could I." She managed a weak smile. "I just needed to remember that."

The wrist beacon chimed and Vale looked down at it. "Transfer complete. Let's get moving." She gestured at the hatch. "After you, Commander."

"Aye, Captain." Rager drew herself up, putting her doubts aside for the moment, and she tapped the turbolift control panel experimentally.

Dull lights flickered on and the roof hatch snapped shut. "Here we go." Valc leaned closer to the panel. "*Bridge*," she told it.

The magnetic locks released, and, with a lurch, the turbolift began to ascend.

Eight

A group of Keru's security officers had come to the same conclusions as Riker and the security chief. They found them at the doors to main engineering, working on the manual latches to draw open the big drop-hatch that had sealed it off from the rest of the ship.

"Report," said Keru as they approached.

Ensign Hriss sketched a salute. "Sirs. We've had no luck contacting the bridge . . . And there have been sightings of strange animals in the deck spaces."

Riker halted the Caitian with his raised hand. "We know, Ensign. But right now, our priority is getting the mains back on-line."

"Last contact from Chief Dennisar said he was in there, but that was a while ago." Hriss nodded toward the hatch. "We could use some extra hands."

Ignoring the pain from the venom-burn on his arm, the admiral took a place alongside the *Titan* crew and put his back into lifting the heavy door off the deck. Smoke curled out from inside as they eased it up, and within a few moments the hatch was far enough off the deck to scramble under. Keru led the way, and Riker pulled his phaser once again, dreading what they might find.

In the semi-darkness, the black tower of the dead warp core reminded the admiral of some great sculpture of volcanic glass, glittering with reflected light. The core sat in the middle of the multi-story chamber, the support decks and service gantries around it visible as meshes of shadow caught by the beams of the lights. Riker imagined the place as some sinister cathedral space, lost and buried in antiquity.

Riker shook off the image. "Who's in charge here?" he shouted, his voice booming off the walls.

"As ever," a familiar, waspish reply came from somewhere out in the gloom, "I am."

A flood of illumination returned to the chamber with sparks of static discharge and a dull rumble of power. Service lamps reactivated in sequence, and Riker saw a stuttering glow pass along the length of the warp core, before settling back into the familiar throb that was *Titan*'s heartbeat. A wave of relief washed over him.

Xin Ra-Havreii, looking somewhat worse for wear, turned away from a mess of opened consoles, strewn cables and discarded tools before the matter-antimatter intermix chamber. He threw Riker an arch nod, as if he resented the other man's intrusion. "Perfect timing, Admiral. As you can see, main power is restored."

Riker saw engineering and security crew alike blinking as illumination was restored. He glanced at a systems display panel. "Restored to *this* compartment, not to the whole ship. You're going to need to do better than that, Commander."

"We'll get there," Xin retorted, pushing past Hriss and two other security guards. "But in the meantime, I'll tell you what I told the Orion." He jerked his thumb in the direction of Dennisar. "If these people you brought down here aren't going to help me fix the problem, then kindly order them to get out of my way." He turned and shouted a command to one of the other junior engineers working at an opened equipment bay. "Torvig! Stop gawping at that and get our EPS governors back on-line."

"I was just making sure White-Blue's holomatrix—"

"That freeloader has his own power module, he'll be fine. Do your job, now!" Xin turned his attention back to Riker. "Still here?"

Usually, Riker's tolerance for the chief engineer's abrasive—often downright *rude*—manner ran long, in part as a matter of respect for the Efrosian's undeniable skills. But today was a different day, and the admiral wasn't in the mood. He fixed Ra-Havreii with a cold-eyed glare. "Explain what happened down here." Xin opened his mouth to speak, but Riker wasn't done. "And *don't* tell me you're too busy."

The engineer seemed to realize that he had overstepped the mark, and he gave another nod. "Torvig was there when it started," he began, "in the cargo bay. Devices from the Dinac pinnace, these orbs among the items Melora brought back for analysis, they became active."

"*Alive*," piped Torvig, catching the conversation. "That would be a more accurate description."

"We had a close encounter with one of them," said Keru, gesturing with his phaser.

"Us too," said Dennisar, as he approached.

"Yes." Xin pointed at a ruined control console. "As far as I can determine, they got into the service spaces between decks, started severing vital power and systems connections." Then he pointed at a ruined section of flooring just in front of the warp core. "They attacked through here. I conjecture they are attracted to high levels of ambient energy."

"How many?" said Riker.

"Four," offered Torvig. "There were four in the cargo bay."

"I dealt with one," noted Keru.

"Another sacrificed itself to destroy the mains console," added the Orion. "The others escaped before we could stop them. Used that acidic bile of theirs to burn through the wall panels."

"Did they take anything with them?"

"Yes." Xin raised an eyebrow. "How did you know that? Yes, they ripped out sections of a monitoring console, dragged it away."

"The one we saw had a power regulator circuit," said the Trill.

"Now these things are stealing pieces of technology, and we have no idea why." Riker frowned. "Those are not the actions of an animal acting on base instinct. I don't want to find out what they're up to the hard way. We have to locate those last two orb-creatures and stop them before they can do more damage."

"Then there's the external threat: How far are we from getting our shields back up?" demanded Keru.

"*Far*," Xin shot back. "Gravity, life support and around forty percent of computer systems remain unaffected by whatever mayhem those things have been wreaking. But shields, transporters, warp and impulse, weapons? Those are going to take longer to bring back to life. More so if you don't let me do my job."

"Commander!" Ensign Meldok called down from a service gantry over their heads. "I've managed to restore some internal communications, but the combadge network is still off-line. I think we may be able to contact the bridge now."

Riker turned and found an intercom panel on a nearby wall. "Engineering to Bridge, are you hearing us? This is Riker. Can you respond?"

The reply that came back was distorted and broken but still recognizable as the voice of Christine Vale. *"Admiral? We're on battery power up here. No crew casualties, but the ship is deaf, dumb and blind."*

Vale leaned over the center seat but didn't take it, her brow furrowing as she listened to the garbled words coming back to her from belowdecks.

"Commander Ra-Havreii's team is working on that right now." Riker's voice became a blare of static, then returned. *"Chris, I can confirm we have intruders on board. Not Solanae . . . At least, not anything like they were the last time we crossed paths. Something else. They're inside the service ducts."*

Vale exchanged glances with Tuvok. "Go on, sir," she said. The bridge fell silent as Riker described the unusual life-forms that they had encountered.

"We didn't see anything like that on our way up here," noted Rager. "Maybe they are some kind of animal from that subspace dimension?"

"A weaponized creature." Tuvok raised an eyebrow, considering the possibility. "Intriguing."

"Keru's mobilizing a security detail to find and

isolate the last of these things. As long as they remain at large, we're in danger."

"No argument there," said Vale.

"In the meantime, how do things look from where you are?"

She sighed. "Not good." The short turbolift journey up to the bridge had seemed to take an age, with the car's reduced power slowing its progress to a crawl, but whatever fears had crowded in the back of the captain's mind were put to rest when she and Rager arrived to find that the damage to the command deck was largely cosmetic. Tuvok, McCreedy and Polan had already rewired a cluster of emergency lamps to provide some heat and light, while Lavena worked on trying to restore functionality to the helm. So far, the Pacifican had not been successful. Vale gave Riker a brisk evaluation. "No sensors, internal or external. Inertial monitors indicate that we're adrift, but attitude and heading are unknown. Communications are down. We have some computer access but it's sporadic. Lieutenant McCreedy's on that right now. Tuvok says the last scans taken before we went dark indicated the disruptive effect was being generated internally, not from an outside source. Most likely your 'intruder' creatures, sir."

"I agree." She could hear the tightness in his words. Even though he had stepped out from the role of commanding officer, Vale knew that on some level, Riker still thought of *Titan* as *his* ship, and it pained him to see her so crippled. *"What about the Dinac explorer? We still have people over there, what's their status?"*

"Unknown," she replied. "Aili believes that the tractor beam pitched them away from us when the power went out. But until we get sensors back, they're on their own." Her lips thinned. "Frankly, Admiral . . . at this point, someone looking out of the damn window would have a better handle on what's going on."

"It's your call, Captain," he continued. *"How do you want to proceed?"*

Vale hesitated, her thoughts racing. Perhaps it would be possible to get a shuttlebay door open, deploy an auxiliary craft and send it off to find the derelict . . . But the away team was just four people, and on board *Titan* there were almost ninety lives for every *one* of Lieutenant Commander Pazlar's group. She went on: "Admiral, if we can get someone down to the shuttlebay, we can use the computers and reactors on board them to backstop our systems until *Titan*'s fully operable again. Odds are, they were isolated from whatever sabotage those creatures performed."

"I'll send someone over there . . ." Riker paused as another thought occurred to him. *"Have you had any contact from Commander Sarai? She should have made it to the auxiliary command center by now."*

Vale looked up at Tuvok. "Anything?"

The Vulcan tapped at his half-dead console. "Intercom reads as active, Captain, but there's no reply from that compartment."

"Try again," she ordered.

The auxiliary control room was a throwback to another era of starship design, to a time when Starfleet vessels went into harm's way on a regular basis, and when the threat of ship-to-ship battle was almost a constant. A legacy of vessels built in the first hundred or so years of the Federation's expansion, the need for an emergency manual monitor—essentially, a second bridge—came out of fears that, in combat, a hit that took out the main command deck would effectively cripple a starship.

Improvements in shield technology and hull plating, along with adaptable, configurable consoles in all parts of Starfleet ships had for a time made the concept of the auxiliary control room seem like overkill. But the idea had returned in the wake of the Dominion War, after the effects of massed starship engagements had left many Starfleet vessels unable to fight effectively after losing their first-line command systems. The *Luna*-class had reinstated it.

Titan's secondary control center was a small, cramped affair in the mid-deck of the vessel, low on the primary hull just above the main deflector dish array, and on the majority. It was inactive, at best manned by a couple of standby duty officers whose work was to ghost the actions of the command crew on the main bridge.

Those two officers—a Haliian ensign on his first tour at the ops console and a junior-grade lieutenant from Paradas serving her duty at the conn—were both dead. Sarai could see them from where she was in cover behind the free-standing tactical podium, each one slumped in their seats. The cloying stench of acid-burned flesh had made her gag when she entered the compartment, and she couldn't help but wonder: *Had they known what was going to kill them, in those last seconds? Or did it happen in the dark, suddenly and without mercy?*

Sarai shook off the morose thought and kneaded the grip of her phaser. "Do you have the intruders?" she hissed, calling out toward the shadow that was all she could see of Lieutenant Ssura.

"My tricorder can't lock on to them," he replied.

"Use your eyes!" she shot back. "Your species evolved from predators, didn't they?"

"Well, yes," said Ssura, almost conversationally, even as he was whispering. "But we don't really have those instincts—" He cut off in the middle of a sentence, and Sarai saw the Caitian's feline head jerk as he caught sight of something. Riker's aide aimed and fired his phaser, sending a pulse of orange fire across the room. In the jumping shadows and the brief surge of backlight, she glimpsed a rolling shape vanish behind the engineering panel and saw the melt-edged rip in the wall where the creatures must have entered the compartment.

"*Bridge to Auxiliary Control.*" Commander Tuvok's steady voice crackled out from an intercom panel five meters away. His tone was calm, and Sarai found it infuriating. "*Commander Sarai, Lieutenant Ssura, please acknowledge this message.*"

The first time she had moved toward the intercom, an aerosol of acid spittle had gushed out of the shadows at her, and Sarai was not willing to risk being blinded.

"There are two of them," Ssura offered. "One is near the replicator module." He paused. "I think."

Sarai chanced a look, over in the direction of the replicator unit, which flickered, still drawing some small amount of power even as other more vital systems were dark. The shimmer cast by the replicator's half-dead display silhouetted a smooth-sided form near the floor, but she could not be certain of its nature. Still, she took careful aim.

The silhouette moved, undulating up the wall toward the replicator's control panel. It oozed more than it walked, less something arachnid, more like a tentacled cephalopod. *Was there an intelligence in there?* she wondered. *If this isn't one of the Solanae, then what is it?* The orb-things had to be more than just simple fauna. They were reacting with purpose and, Sarai suspected, with a greater design in mind.

Her thumb hesitated over the phaser's firing stud. *If only we could take it intact . . .*

A thick glob of liquid fell from the darkness above her head and splashed on the console, making Sarai flinch. Instantly, polymers began to melt and run like heated wax. She reeled back, her target forgotten, and saw movement among the shadows.

From across the way, a gangly, furred figure came at her, colliding with the commander to knock her aside as the second orb-thing made its attack. She caught a glimpse of it, a spinning cluster of gray flukes glistening with venom, a ring of snapping fangs.

"Apologies," Ssura grunted, as he pushed her to the deck. "I saw it . . ."

Sarai saw the creature bounce off the tactical console and scuttle toward them. She fired at it, her aim hindered by the Caitian, and the beam cut at the air, hitting nothing.

Ssura uttered a low yowl that seemed part annoyance, part fear, and slashed at the air with one skinny paw. Claws that until now Sarai had never seen flashed as Ssura swatted the creature away. The orb was knocked back and fell into a rolling motion that carried it under another console.

She heard more hissing and smelled the chemical tang of burning plastics.

"I think I wounded it . . ." Ssura sniffed experimentally at his paw, then retched. "Such foulness . . ."

"It's eating its way into that control unit," said the XO. "Where's the other one?"

"There!" Ssura pointed toward the replicator alcove; the front of it was now a mess of slagged, molten matter. The writhing limbs of the other orb-creature jerked as it forced itself inside the mechanism.

Grim-faced, Sarai pushed the lieutenant aside, ignoring for the moment that his actions had saved her from injury, and fired at the base of the control unit. If she could damage the thing, interfere with whatever it was doing . . .

Phaser light crackled through the air, and Sarai was rewarded with a high-pitched keening sound. "I hit it," she snapped, all thought of making a live capture now put aside. "They feel pain."

"Not machines," Ssura insisted. "I believe their coming to this compartment was deliberate, not instinctual."

"I concur." Sarai felt a tightness in her throat and coughed. The chemical smell in her nostrils was growing stronger every second, and she realized that it was more than just the odor of acid-burned polymers in the air. From above, thin streams of white vapor were falling from tiny vents concealed in the auxiliary control room's ceiling. She jerked back, bringing a hand up to cover her mouth and nose. "Ssura, above! We have to get out, quickly!"

"The fire suppressors . . ." The Caitian understood. "Yes, by your leave, Commander!"

The streams were now a torrent, and the vapor swirled around them in a thickening fog. Sarai lurched away from cover and made for the doorway, trying not to breathe.

A conflagration aboard a starship was one of the most

dangerous occurrences to deal with, capable of wreaking massive damage in moments. Starfleet vessels used a series of miniature field projectors tied to heat sensor modules that would, on detection of flames, surround the fire in a globe of force and starve it of air before it could spread. But such systems required a steady power supply, and in the event of a mains disruption, a secondary, more conventional method of fire suppression was utilized. An inert halogen mist could smother any flames in moments; but, unlike the force-bubble, it was toxic to every oxygen-breathing life-form in the same area.

The orb: It triggered the halogen. Sarai was certain of it. *The creature is trying to turn our ship against us.* The certainty lodged in her mind, and she held on to it as it became harder and harder to breathe. The white mist was everywhere now, and Sarai's vision was turning gray.

She was dimly aware of the lieutenant holding her up, of the distant hiss of the doors sliding open—then suddenly her starved lungs were burning and Sarai stumbled against the corridor wall, gasping for breath.

Ssura closed the doors to the control room and then seemed to deflate, sagging. He dropped to the floor and the Caitian panted, his thin shoulders trembling. "That," he managed, "was a very unpleasant experience."

She lurched back toward the door, but the effort made her head swim. "We have to get back in there! Those things are inside the control grids—" Her voice turned into a strangled wheeze. Sarai forced out more words: "Have to warn the captain."

The dimness in the corridor began to fade, and it was a welcome sight as power started at long last to flow back into this section of the ship. The XO tapped at a wall panel, feeling relief as she summoned a communications tab. "Bridge? Respond."

"*Commander?*" Tuvok replied immediately. "*What is your situation?*"

Each word she spoke made her chest feel like fire. "Tell Vale . . . they're working . . . to a plan."

"So, how do we do this?" said Kyzak, peering up at Zurin from where he sat on the wooden deck. "Who gets to decide?" He glanced at Commander Pazlar, whose eyes widened as the unspoken addendum to that question hung in the silence that followed. As the ranking officer aboard the derelict, each of them knew that it was up to her to order one of them to stay behind.

But Zurin Dakal also knew that the thought of doing such a thing appalled Melora Pazlar. To give a command knowing full well that whomever obeyed it was going to their death was something few officers wanted to face, despite whatever their training had prepared them for. And yet it was something that any one of them might have to do if no other choice was at hand.

"I'm not going to ask for a volunteer," said the Elaysian, after a moment.

"So you're fine with Dakal's approach?" Fell broke in. "We should wait. *Titan* could have things licked any second now."

"And if they don't?" Pazlar retorted. "If we wait and wait, until our air runs out?" The Deltan looked away. "A slim chance is better than none. Zurin's figures are solid, we all checked them ourselves." She sighed. "I will stay."

"No!" Zurin shook his head. He held up a hand, and in it were four short twists of wire, their lengths concealed in the curl of his fingers. "We will draw lots. Let fate decide."

"Fine." Kyzak reached forward and pulled out a wire. "That's one." He grimaced and tossed it away.

Pazlar went next, taking another of the same length. "Two."

"Peya?" Zurin offered his hand to the Deltan, and she gingerly reached for one of the remaining wires. Closing her eyes, she picked the one on the right.

The Cardassian couldn't help but gasp as Fell revealed the short lot between her fingers. "Oh," she said, in a small voice. "Right."

"Ah, to hell with this!" Kyzak burst into motion, springing up from the deck to knock Zurin's hand aside. "No. This is not how we're doing this. Peya doesn't stay! Not you or you either!" He stabbed at the air with his finger. "*I stay.* You all go."

"Ethan . . ." began Pazlar, "you don't have to do that."

"Yeah, I do." He tapped the front of his cracked helmet. "Because you know what? I lied about how much air I have left."

Zurin felt for the emergency bleed connector on the hip of his EVA suit. "We can each give you some of ours," he insisted. "Enough for a few hours."

"No." Kyzak shook his head. "You'll just be wasting it." He moved across to the power module, casting a look up at the barrier holding in the thin membrane of atmosphere. "Tether up, you three. I'm going to do this."

Warily, Zurin extended a retracting cable out to Peya, who took it and snapped the connector to a D-ring on her own suit. The Deltan did the same thing, offering a cable to Pazlar, but Melora wasn't looking at her.

"Is this some kind of misplaced male bravado, Lieutenant?" she demanded, glaring at the other officer. "If you're looking for a glorious death, then you should have joined the Klingon Defense Force. We don't believe in sacrificing our people!"

"Believe me," he shot back, "I'm not pleased about how things are shaking out either! But this is logical, Commander. Needs of the many, and all that."

"I have never liked that quote," she told him.

Peya reached forward and connected Pazlar's D-ring herself. "We need to be closer to the break in the hull," she said quietly. The three of them moved in a careful line, stepping away from the support pillars and deck sections that Kyzak had struck on his near-fatal ejection.

"We'll get to *Titan*," Zurin told Kyzak. "Set your suit to survival mode the moment we're gone, go to low power and trigger your locator beacon. We'll get them to beam you back." He wanted to believe it would be possible.

The lieutenant didn't acknowledge his words. Instead, he found a place to wedge himself behind a console where the power generator was within arm's reach. "Get ready," he said, without meeting their gazes. "Take it from me, what happens next is a real kick in the pants." He peered at numbers clocking over on his wrist display as the optimum moment of departure approached.

Zurin wanted to find a way to thank him, but then Kyzak was pressing the keypad and the tornado of decompression was on them. The blast of the derelict's final, thin gasp of atmosphere was still enough to pull the three officers off their feet and expel them out of the wreck.

He spun about and went into a tumble as the derelict ship's corridor blurred past him and then vanished. Darkness enveloped them, and Zurin let his spin push him around.

The broken Dinac pinnace receded, resembling a shattered tree branch now more than any kind of spaceworthy vessel. Then it slid out of his view, and the Cardassian saw something else in the distance. A steel-white shape, adrift ahead of them. The *Titan*, slowly growing larger.

Vale listened with growing concern as Sarai explained what she had seen inside the auxiliary control room. The first officer's dour, matter-of-fact words made clear the suspicion they all shared: The orbs were acting in concert.

The captain tried to see it from the point of view of their assailants. Their attempt to trigger the spatial rift and drag *Titan* into a nowhere-space void had failed, so it was likely the orb-things were some sort of secondary attack vector. Vale guessed that the creatures had been lying dormant on board the explorer ever since the Dinac crew and the *U.S.S. Whitetree* had been taken, waiting for the right kind of stimulus to reactivate them. It seemed that Admiral Riker had unwittingly given it to them, awakening the things by attempting to seal off the *Titan* from further assault. It was clever, she had to admit. These Solanae had learned the nature of the defenses that were ranged against them and prepared accordingly.

Vale glanced toward the main viewscreen, which was

now active. Empty space looked back at her. She was afraid that any second a new spatial rift would form and engulf her crippled ship, but it had yet to happen. Was it possible that the Solanae couldn't just create such a tear in space-time at will? Perhaps it needed great power, or time to recharge the capacity. That seemed likely; sundering the barriers between layers of interdimensional space required incredible amounts of energy. *But they did it twice before that we know of,* said a voice in the back of her mind. *And we have no way of knowing when they will be ready to do it again.*

Vale crossed to Ensign Polan at the bridge's main science station. "Klace. Bring up the sensor recordings of the rift before we escaped. Look for precursor effects. The second we get our external sensors back on-line, I want you watching for those."

"Aye, Captain," said the Catullan, setting to work.

"Commander Sarai," Vale called out so her voice would be picked up by the intership system. "Hold position where you are. I'm sending security to you now."

"Acknowledged," grated the XO.

"Admiral, are you still there?" The channel was cross-connected so that Riker could hear all that was being discussed.

"I'm here, Captain. Xin's people are ready to begin a staged restart of our power network. But if we go back on-line and those creatures are still buried in our ship, we have no idea what effect that might have."

"Ticks on a dog," said McCreedy, almost to herself. "We could end up *feeding* them."

"Those spheres, live or dead or something in between, are weapons of terror," Vale said flatly. "I've seen the same pattern before, during the Dominion War.

Devices scattered by the enemy in the wake of an attack, designed to stay inert until first responders are on the scene. Then they trigger and start the whole cycle all over again." She shook her head. "Every second we let these things run uncontrolled through *Titan* is a second closer we are to following the *Whitetree* into oblivion. We have to get ahead of them. We cannot keep *reacting* to their attacks." Vale let out a long breath. "Admiral, tell Xin to get started."

"I already have," said another voice, joining the conversation with a gruff snarl. The chief engineer seemed irritated, and Vale guessed that he blamed the bridge crew for whatever damage the vessel had suffered. *"Emergency lighting is restored, turbolifts and hatch control coming on-stream now."*

Nearby, McCreedy nodded as her display board lit up, layer by layer. Piece by piece, *Titan* reawakened. "Confirming that. Now reading power restored to holomatrices, replicator subsystems—"

"Wait!" Sarai shouted, her smoke-scarred throat making the cry sound like the bark of a vixen. *"No, the replicators, do not activate them!"*

"What are you saying?" Xin shot back.

The same question was on Vale's lips, but she never had the opportunity to voice it. Instead, the answer as to *why* came with immediate and shocking force.

Across the bridge from where the captain was standing, in an alcove on the starboard side of the compartment, there was a small beverage replicator unit that was available for the crew to use during long shifts. It activated itself without any outside interaction, and Vale heard the familiar musical tone as the built-in fabrication grid set to work creating something.

But what materialized on the tray was not a mug of the strong black Izarian tea that Vale liked to drink to calm her thoughts. Instead, an ovoid mass of slick, gray-pallor flesh squeezed itself out of the receptacle and slid down the wall to the deck. Even as it fell to the carpet with a damp thud, the replicator was cycling again, making another of the same form from the ship's stocks of raw matter.

Aili Lavena was closest to the thing as it distended into a nest of wet flukes and snapping fangs. The Selkie helmsman recoiled from the creature, cursing in her native language.

"Karen, kill power to the replicators!" Vale shouted, but the engineer's answer was writ large across her face. The connection had locked open, and her console gave off sour beeps as it refused commands to sever the newly reforged power linkage.

More of the things were coming out of the slot, bursts of them emerging in gouts of acrid fluid.

"Captain!" She turned as Tuvok pulled something from a concealed panel beneath the tactical station and tossed it in her direction. She caught the small palm phaser instinctively, seeing the shape of another already in the Vulcan's grip.

"Get down!" shouted Vale, and her crew obeyed without hesitation, Lavena and Rager and the other bridge officers dropping out of the line of fire.

She fired, thumbing a wide-beam setting that Tuvok followed, catching the rolling mass of the newly created orb-creatures before they could gather momentum and attack the crew. As the tactical officer followed her down the length of the bridge, Vale switched back to a narrow beam and speared a rogue that had slipped out from beneath the others. Tuvok took out another, and she grimaced as the beam made it sizzle and shrivel. Before the replicator could begin the process again, Vale drew a beam across the face of the device in a downward diagonal motion, then again, burning a blackened X through the circuits.

"Commander!" McCreedy was calling into the intercom. "Shut down the replicator grid, now! Those things are inside the command pathways, they're using the system to create more of themselves!"

"I can't!" Xin shouted back, and Vale heard the sound of phaser fire in the background. *"Blasted infernal things have control of the override!"*

"H-how many replicator units are there on board this ship?" said Lavena, her voice breathy with bubbles from her drysuit.

Vale's blood ran cold as McCreedy gave the answer. "Hundreds of them. On every deck. In every cabin."

Nine

Sickbay was in chaos.

Titan's infirmary had a total of four different replicator units in various parts of the compartment, some of them simple modules designed for refreshments, others more advanced models designed to synthesize complex drugs or medical supplies. Each had become a gateway for a flood of the orb-things, as dozens of identical duplicates crawled from the glowing grids and set about wreaking havoc.

"Back!" Ree pushed Troi away as a pair of the octopoid-form creatures came up over a biobed to attack them. The saurian used his muscular tail to lash out and slam the orbs aside, battering them against the wall with ugly crunches of meat and bone. "Ach. The replicators are not responding to vocal commands. They won't shut off!"

The counselor had grabbed the first thing that came to hand to defend herself, a narrow-gauge protoplaser scalpel, and she held it before her, shooting off pulses of coherent light at any of the orbs that dared to come closer.

She heard a cry of pain and turned to see Alyssa Ogawa shrink back from a mass of the creatures. The arm of Ogawa's uniform jacket was melting off her arm, and she was trying to rip the material away before the acid burning into it got through to her flesh. Kershul, Ree's tripedal Edosian nurse, used all three of her hands to tear the tunic off her back and fling it away.

Too late, Troi realized that the creatures were herding them into a corner, rolling across the deck, propelling themselves up and over the walls, working as one to block off their escape route.

Ree bared his teeth. "So many . . . We can't get past them."

"We need . . ." Ogawa said, panting, "we need some help in here!"

As she brandished the protoplaser against the encroaching tide of the orb-things, an impulsive notion came to Troi. "Holosystems are active now, yes?"

"I believe so," said Ree, "but how will that help us?"

"Watch and learn." She cleared her throat. "Computer? Initiate Emergency Medical Hologram. Maximum number of iterations, contiguous. Activate now!"

At once, eight human females wearing the uniform of a medical officer materialized around the infirmary. They shared the same pleasant face framed by short blonde hair, and they all sported an identical look of slight surprise, each speaking at once.

"Please state the nature of the . . . oh . . ."

"State the nature of the medical emergency . . ."

"What is going on here?"

"Please state . . . Wait, what are those creatures doing in my sickbay?"

"I never made much use of these things," Ree admitted. "This Mark IX upgrade was a new addition after the refit."

"Outbreak in progress!" shouted Troi. "We are your patients, protect us from these . . . *macrophages*!"

There was an odd second when eight matching faces turned to give Troi a quizzical look; then with one voice they responded: "Complying."

With no flesh to fall victim to the caustic venom of the orb-creatures, the EMHs' hard-light forms were able to physically block the replicated invaders, coming shoulder to shoulder to form a wall of bodies between the creatures and their targets.

"This life-form does not exist in my data banks," said one of the Mark IXs.

"Solanagen-based atomic structure detected," offered another.

"Curious," agreed a third.

"Just keep them back!" barked Ree.

"There has to be some way to neutralize these things," said Kershul. "They just keep on coming."

Troi felt a pang of fear as a troubling thought caught up with her. *If this is happening here . . . is it happening* everywhere *on board?*

Ree seemed to sense her grim train of thought. "If we cannot turn them back, they'll swarm through the entire vessel."

"Calculating," offered the nearest of the EMHs, her tone inappropriately sunny for the situation they were in. "Based on rate of replication, matter stocks and extant fabricator units, current infestation comprises approximately six hundred and seventy-two discreet creatures, plus or minus eight percent, increasing by one new generation every forty-four point one seconds."

Troi closed her eyes. *Will. Tasha. Be safe.*

Riker fired off quick pulses from his phaser with barely a breath taken between them, knocking back two of the creatures as they half-ran, half-spun up across the surface of the engine room's main systems display table.

Off to his side, he saw Ranul Keru pause to readjust his weapons setting, just as another of the aliens scrambled up a control bank, clearly intending to hurl itself at the Trill security chief.

"Keru, on your right!" he shouted.

The officer turned, bringing up his arm to batter the creature back as it tried to curl its tentacles about him. With a snarl of pain, the Trill struck the orb with the mass of his drawn phaser, clubbing it back. "Drown all these bloody things," he spat. "How many are there?"

"Too many," Riker shot back, firing another brace of rounds. The strange Solanae proxies were coming at the engineering crew in waves, attacking with force and then dispersing, trying to keep them off-balance. "Not animals," the admiral said to himself, giving voice to the thought, "not by a long way."

Someone cried out in agony from one of the upper gantries, and Riker's gut twisted as a figure toppled over a balcony rail and fell two stories to the deck, struggling with a gray mass at his throat all the way down. The crewman landed with an ugly crunch of broken bone.

Behind Riker, Ensign Torvig braved the melee enough

to poke his head up over a smoldering console. "The invader creatures have inserted their gene-code into our replicator subsystems and taken control of the power matrix." He winced. "It's insidious *and* ingenious."

"They're using our own technology against us," Keru grated. "And we can't shut it down, not without plunging *Titan* into darkness all over again."

"If we do that, the ship may never recover," Torvig added.

Riker bit back a furious curse. "There must be *some* way to even the odds before we're overrun! Some way to take out the replicators, at least!"

Torvig's gaze went inward for a second. "That could be done . . . A deliberate energy surge to burn out the grids. But it would only be localized. Just to main engineering, not the rest of the ship."

"Do it!" snapped Riker.

"The risk—"

The admiral underlined his order by firing off another brace of shots, this time blasting an orb into smoke and flecks of biomechanical tissue before it could spring at the Choblik ensign.

Sobered, Torvig vaulted past Riker, almost falling on a flickering control panel behind him. The metallic manipulators on his paws and the tip of his tail raced across the console, and a stream of red warning flags rose across nearby monitor screens.

"Who is interfering with my system now?" Riker heard Xin reacting to the ensign's actions, but he gestured with his weapon, urging Torvig on.

"In three," said the ensign. "Two. *One*." His tail-hand tapped a key, and at once there were a half-dozen explosive discharges in different sections of the engine room.

Overpowered replicator matrices—some large-scale units made to fabricate tools or parts, others simple drink dispensers—all were immediately fried in a surge of electroplasma that blew out isolinear conduits and circuitry.

Riker clapped Torvig on the shoulder. "That's put an end to their reinforcements."

"Until others come to join them," said the ensign, undercutting the moment with a frown.

"Look!" shouted Meldok, from one of the gantries. "They're drawing back. Regrouping!"

The Benzite was correct: The orb throng moved as one single organism, retreating as a tide would recede from a shoreline. The mass of gray, spherical forms cohered and shifted. Riker hesitated, watching them, trying to predict their next move.

Then he saw it, as the mass slithered and rolled back upon itself, making for the center of the compartment. "They're going for the warp core."

Flowing over support frames and the flanks of the intermix chamber, the orb-things swarmed up and down the length of the glowing column, blotting out the pulses of light as they wrapped themselves around it.

"They can't mean to destroy it . . ." Torvig shook his head. "It would obliterate the *Titan*, and all they have done until now has been to take this ship intact."

Keru hesitated, his phaser aimed but unfired. "We can't risk shooting at them. A single miss and we're atomized."

"I don't want to wait around to find out what their Plan B is. At this point," Riker said, his voice carrying, "I'm open to any suggestions."

Keru's eyes narrowed and he pulled the tricorder

clipped to his waist. "We don't have transporters back yet, right?"

"Sort of," Torvig replied. He inclined his head at the nearby screen. "Man-rated matter transport systems are all still off-line, but inert cargo transport . . . that's possible."

"That could be enough . . ." The Trill passed the tricorder to Riker, who peered at the small display there.

"Is this . . ."

"An internal bioscan of one of the creatures. I took it after we were attacked by that one in the corridor, sir. Not hard when you've blasted one of them open," Keru said darkly.

"Let me see that." Xin didn't wait for permission but snatched the tricorder from the admiral. "Looks biomechanical, all right. Organic muscles and nerves, bolstered with synthetic blood and bone."

"*Bone*," echoed Riker. "Enough to make a skeletal lock for a beam-out?"

Torvig's ears flattened against his head in alarm. "In theory. But, sir, with the coarse matter stream model of a cargo transporter, whatever was picked up would be . . ." He swallowed. "Not survivable."

Riker's jaw hardened. "I'm not asking you because I want to take these things alive, Ensign. I'm asking because I want them *off this ship*."

"We can do it," Xin answered for his officer. "But at best the range will be limited. This compartment and a few close by. It won't be a clean sweep."

The admiral glanced back at the warp core, now covered with the mass of writhing alien forms. "Better than what we have now. Make it so."

"Assist me," Xin demanded of Torvig, and together

the two engineers reconfigured the console to slave control of the nearest cargo transporter to their command.

Keru frowned. "Why do I feel like we're just plugging one hole in the dam?"

"Because we are," said Riker. "This is a long way from being over."

Torvig's head bobbed. "Program ready."

Xin gave Riker an arch look. "You realize of course, sir, that if this doesn't work, I'll beam out pieces of the intermix chamber along with those things and we'll all be dead." He went on, without giving him time to reply. "Which would be a pity, because I wouldn't have the opportunity to say '*I told you so.*' " The Efrosian slid his hand up the slider-control interface. "Energizing."

The sparkling haze of the transporter effect seemed to blink in and out of phase with the orbs as the lock-on program struggled to capture the matter stream of the alien creatures. Seconds seemed to lengthen into hours, and it was only as the mass finally faded away that Riker realized he had been holding his breath. The orbs disintegrated into nothing and were gone.

The warp core's familiar heartbeat glow washed over the chamber and a ragged cheer went up from the engineering crew, but Xin scowled them back into silence. "Stop congratulating yourselves, the work's not done yet!"

"Main engineering is clear of . . . invaders," Torvig added. "For the moment. They were beamed out into space at maximum dispersal."

Xin nodded. "They won't come back from that. Now, if I can finish what I started, we can power up all of the *Titan*'s systems and repeat that trick shipwide."

Torvig peered at his screen. "I do not think the creatures will allow that."

Riker looked over his shoulder. "Explain, mister."

The ensign brought up a cutaway side-view graphic of the *Titan* on his panel. Patches of blue and red showed starkly where the vessel's internal systems had been badly disrupted. "A craft as complicated as a *Luna*-class starship has many nexus points for power distribution . . . This reading shows that one of them is being actively corrupted on a moment-to-moment basis." Torvig met his gaze. "Admiral, just like the ones in the replicators, there are others *inside* our system. If we can't root them out, then this is just a temporary victory."

"We need to find where they're hiding," said Riker, taking it in.

"Not hiding," Keru corrected, a flash of understanding in his eyes. "*Nesting*. They're half-animals, remember? And I think I know where they are."

"Take whomever you need," Riker told him.

"Torvig, you're with me," Keru beckoned the ensign sharply.

"Oh," said the Choblik, with no enthusiasm of any kind. "Good."

"Don't get him killed," shouted Xin, as Keru and Torvig moved off. "He's one of the few on this ship with any actual competence!"

"Admiral, I'll need you to contact the first officer through the intercom," Keru threw the words over his shoulder as he reopened the emergency hatch. "Tell Sarai we're coming to her."

The bioscan sensors built into Melora Pazlar's spacesuit kept up a steady stream of telemetry, projecting their readings on the inside of her helmet. The Elaysian's oxygen intake was elevated and her heartbeat was racing, a nagging alert chime sounding in her ears every few seconds warning that she should try to calm herself.

Not the easiest thing to do when hurtling through space like a missile. If she turned her head away and looked out into the blackness of interstellar space, she could almost believe she wasn't in motion. Relative to the distant stars, she and the two other people tethered to her were hardly moving at all. But looking out there made her feel hopeless and insignificant. It showed her how lost out here they were.

Pazlar couldn't see the wreck of the Dinac pinnace. That was behind her somewhere, swallowed up by the dark. She thought about Ethan Kyzak and her breath caught in her throat. *I liked him.* The admission came out of nowhere, and now that any control of the situation had been taken from her, it was easier for her to admit that she had wanted to *like him more*. There had been some kind of spark between them over dinner, hadn't there? Had she been mistaken? Melora felt sick inside as she realized she would never know for certain. Ethan had given away that possibility in exchange for a risky plan that might still see an end to everyone on the away team.

From the corner of her vision, Pazlar could see Peya Fell strung out ahead of her along the tether cable, and Zurin Dakal ahead of the Deltan. Dakal's back was toward her, but Peya was turned in her direction. The young ensign's pale, hairless head was visible through her transparent helmet. Her eyes were closed and her lips were moving, as if in some kind of prayer.

Then the science officer caught sight of the *Titan*, and it made her giddy. The starship was growing in size as they closed in on it, and like them, the vessel was adrift. She saw that whole sections of the ship were in darkness. Both engine nacelles were aglow with faint, pale orange, resembling distant candlelight, but the running lights were dead and many of the exterior ports were black pits in the hull. She thought she saw a blink of bright white, perhaps someone on board momentarily turning a beam outward, but it was gone in an instant.

She took a deep breath and tried to maintain a clinical, professional single-mindedness. They had all been prepared for this—zero-gravity survival and EVA operations were a core part of everyone's training—but Pazlar had to admit that there was nothing in the *Starfleet Survival Guide* about being shot out of one vessel in the vain hope of being able to land on the hull of another.

She could see that the *Titan* was in a slow, turning roll on an axis approximately thirty degrees off the vessel's centerline. The oval primary hull's saucer profile was turning toward them, its ventral surface becoming an arc of inky shadow as it blotted out the radiance of the starscape. Melora raised her arm, glancing at the built-in tricorder unit mounted just above her wrist, and tapped a tab to dismiss the medical alert display on her visor. It blinked into a different graphic, this one an estimate of the path the three were taking through space.

A glowing strip extended away from Melora's point of view, curving up and away, bisecting the hull of the *Titan* somewhere above the main deflector dish; but the motion of the starship was slower than they had expected. She ran the numbers in her mind and came up short.

If she was correct, the three of them would pass within fifty meters of *Titan*'s hull. Too far to reach, too far for the mag-locks in their boots to gain purchase. They would sail close enough to see the faces of anyone staring out of the ports at them, and then drift on into the eternal dàrk until they ran out of breathable air.

The hatch above him slid back and Keru looked up to see a black-furred face with wide, nervous eyes looking down at him. A paw extended out. "Sir?"

"Thanks, Lieutenant." He accepted Ssura's offer of a hand up and hauled himself out of the accessway. Torvig bounded up behind him, closely followed by crewmen Krotine and Cel.

"Report, Mister Keru," said Commander Sarai, stepping forward to meet the security chief. As the Trill was learning, the Efrosian XO wasted no time on niceties. She faced him with her arms folded in front of her, demanding his attention. "Admiral Riker says you have a theory about these intruders."

He nodded. "That's correct, sir. I put it together after we started to see different behaviors from the orb-creatures. Not just attacking the crew and knocking out our systems, but stealing pieces of tech."

"You think you know why?"

Keru nodded again, and he beckoned Torvig. "Ensign, tell the Commander."

"Aye, sir." Torvig bobbed on his feet, blinking at the ill-lit corridor. "The invaders are concentrating their assaults on nexus points throughout the ship. That is, nodes where *Titan*'s main data nodes converge." He waved his tail around at the walls. "We are right on top of one of them."

"More than sixty percent of this ship's data bandwidth

goes through ODN conduits on this level," added Keru. "Under normal circumstances, we'd reroute if the ship's security was compromised, but—"

"Yes, yes. I get the picture." Sarai made a terse *go-on* motion with her hand.

"We're one deck above the main computer core." He pointed at the sealed door before them. "The auxiliary manual monitor compartment is through there. This is the best point of infestation for anything that wants to leech off *Titan*'s data network."

"*Infect* would be a better analogy," offered Ssura.

"They were doing something in there," Sarai allowed. "Before they triggered the halogen gas, drove us out. Something beneath the deck."

"And that's what we need to stop." Keru summoned Krotine with a jut of the chin. The burly Boslic female dropped a carryall to the deck and opened it, revealing phaser rifles and a set of portable rebreather masks. "I took the liberty of picking up some extra hardware along the way."

Sarai helped herself to a mask and one of the rifles. "All right. I want everyone in for this. Lieutenant Ssura, you hold at the door and make sure nothing gets out." She slapped her hand phaser into Torvig's palm. "Ensign, help him."

"I'm not really trained for—"

The XO ignored him and turned away, sizing up Cel, Krotine and Keru. "Plan of attack?" she asked.

"Locate the highest concentration of the orbs and neutralize it."

"With phasers?" Sarai's eyes narrowed. "That won't be enough."

Keru pulled a cylindrical device from his belt, and the

danger trefoil on the casing caught the light. "No, Commander. But this will be."

Kyzak panted as his lungs tried to squeeze the last breaths of air out of the dregs of atmosphere still remaining in his damaged suit. The shadows all about him seemed to grow deeper with every passing moment. His chest ached and his vision was blurry. A constant, prickling ache had taken up residence behind his eyes, and it made every motion of his head a labor. Lying against the curved flank of a Dinac control dais, the lieutenant was just about able to watch the slow motion of puddles of starlight coming through the ports in the ship's hull.

The only noises were his own ragged breathing and the whine of fading air. *That's the sound of my life ending*, he told himself, listening to the thin, endless drone. He wanted to laugh, but he couldn't find that in himself anymore. There was only the bleak certainty that soon this would be over.

He hoped that Melora and the others would make it. *At least then, what I did will have had some purpose.*

"They're all going to die out here, just the same as you." The voice had a woolly, unreal quality to it. Kyzak blinked and tried to focus.

Her appearance blurred and distorted through the damaged visor, Commander Sarai crouched down next to the Skagaran and eyed him without pity. She had no suit, and the airless conditions didn't seem to affect her or the words she spoke. *You're not real,* he wanted to say, but all that escaped his lips was a dry croak. *Hallucinating. Oxygen deprivation.*

"Remember your training?" the first officer said coldly. "This is severe cerebral hypoxia, Ethan. Mental deterioration. Loss of motor control. You're slipping toward a coma. Very soon you're going to be dead."

He gritted his teeth and forced out the words: "Why . . . last thing I see . . . is you?"

"Because you lied to me when you told me why you were on the *Titan*. We both know why you're really here. What you're running from. But don't worry. When it ends, you'll be safe. You won't have to run anymore."

"I . . . I didn't come out here . . . to die." The shadows were closing in, leeching the color from his vision. His body felt heavy and disconnected.

"Are you sure?" The question followed him into nothingness.

Torvig retracted the control panel and rewired the circuits to open the doors to auxiliary control, tapping the keypad as Commander Keru threw him a nod.

The Trill took a deep breath of plastic-tasting air through the rebreather over his nose and mouth, then rocked forward off his heels as the doors slid back and jammed, half-open and half-closed.

"Go!" he ordered.

A fog of lingering white vapor from the fire suppression system flooded out as the squad rushed in, weapons raised high. Keru took point, with Sarai right behind him, and and the security team of Krotine and Cel at their back.

There was a distinct, vivid memory Keru had of his

childhood on Trillius Prime, of a day in the woods with his family, climbing trees and investigating the wildlife all around them. Little Ranul had accidentally stepped on a rotting log, and he had sunk to his ankle in the crumbling mass. Beneath it was a writhing swarm of cutter termites, busily turning the log into splinters, suddenly disturbed and turning to scuttle all over his bare legs. He remembered that moment now, his gaze falling on the accumulation of gray-fleshed spheroids that were caught in the process of dismantling the auxiliary bridge, the same sense of horror and surprise he had felt as a child rising in him.

"Take out the replicators!" Sarai snapped, bringing up her rifle to blast a food slot on the far wall. Keru did the same, finding a second slot along the back bulkhead and blasting it into fragments.

"They're everywhere!" shouted Cel, the Catullan woman's cry muffled by her mask. She swung her weapon to fire upward. Flash-burned octopoids dropped to the deck, trailing smoke and fluid.

Every flat surface, from the floor to the control panels and the low ceiling above their heads, was crawling with the alien creatures. Like the termites, they seemed to be eating their way into the *Titan*'s structure, repurposing what they found to some other design.

Reacting as antibodies would to the arrival of outside vectors, the orb-things went on the offensive, spitting stringy globs of acid phlegm or making their leaping attacks at the team's faces. Krotine took a hit from a cluster of the creatures and screamed in pain, fighting to tear them off before they could bring her down.

"Keep moving!" Keru used wide-beam bursts to cut a path across the auxiliary bridge, seeing the invaders fall and deflate just like the one that had first attacked him and Riker in the corridor.

Sarai was with him all the way, and the first officer's efficiency with the phaser rifle was impressive. He got the sense that the Efrosian woman had far better firearms training than most officers; what that meant, he wasn't certain, but he decided to file the thought away for later consideration.

"There!" she called. "On the deck!"

Keru pivoted, firing again. They were holding the creatures back, but he could feel the momentum of the firefight slipping away. The invaders had been caught by surprise, but that advantage was almost spent. He looked in the direction Sarai indicated.

A control podium had been uprooted from the deck, half of its surface melted to blackened slurry by toxic secretions. All around it, in the place where the communications officer would have sat if it were active, the deck panels had been ripped up to expose the Jefferies tubes below. Bunches of torn ODN cable bled sharp blue light into the rough-edged pit, and Keru glimpsed pieces of mismatched circuitry and isolinear chips held together by melted polymer. But it was impossible to get closer, as a hissing torrent of crawling forms reformed to block his path, dozens of them crowded atop one another, fangs wet and snapping.

"Is this what you expected?" said Sarai.

"More or less," admitted Keru. "Fall back!" He shouldered his rifle and pulled the cylinder from his belt. As he thumbed the activation pad, the photon grenade switched from "safe" mode to "armed," immediately charging the tiny electromagnetic generator at the weapon's core. At full discharge, the grenade had enough power to blow a hole in the side of the ship; at lower settings the blast could wreak havoc with electrical circuits or even act as a wide-spectrum stun attack. Keru dialed down the yield to a setting he hoped would be the right one. Too high, and he risked damaging *Titan*'s spaceframe. Too low, and it would have no effect.

He hit the activator. "Grenade out!" he bellowed, and he gave Sarai a shove back toward the doors.

They both fired blindly as they ran, avoiding the creatures that lashed out and snapped at them. Ahead, Cel was supporting the injured Krotine, even as the Boslic woman continued to pick off scuttling attackers that tried to come after them. Behind him, Keru heard the building whine of the photon grenade reaching detonation potentiality, and he picked up the pace. The four of them went back through the jammed doors, and Keru was the last man out, burning a line of orange fire across the floor to discourage any pursuit.

He pushed back out into the corridor and went for the deck. "Cover!"

Keru lost his rebreather as he hit the floor. There was a flash of light and a brief, sudden thunderclap from the compartment behind them, as if a storm had been born and died in the space of a few milliseconds. Overpressure made his ears pop, and he blinked away the moment of disorientation.

Rolling onto his side, Keru aimed his phaser carbine along the line of the deck at the open door, waiting for the flood of creatures to come after them—but there was nothing, only the fizz and crackle of overloaded circuits.

"Did it work?" asked Torvig, crouching low by his side. "I think it worked."

"Only one way to be sure," said Sarai, bringing her

rifle to her shoulder. Without waiting for anyone else, the first officer pushed back into the auxiliary control room, her expression somber.

Keru went after her and caught a gust of foul air from inside the compartment: the harsh, acrid stink of ozone and other odors that recalled spoiled fat.

He found Sarai aiming her weapon at a heap of twitching orb-creatures. They were very clearly dead or dying, and the Trill felt a sense of relief at having succeeded, even as part of him detested the destruction of life. "They were just acting out of programmed instinct," he said, thinking aloud.

"So does a virus," Sarai snapped.

Keru felt a faint vibration from the combadge on his chest, a subtle signal that the internal communications system was active again. He tapped it. "Keru to Riker . . ."

"We read you," replied the admiral. *"What's the situation, Ranul?"*

"Target neutralized. But, sir, there's still hundreds of those orbs loose throughout the ship."

"Commander Ra-Havreii tells me that's covered," said Riker. *"Whatever you did in there, it was the right call. Systems are coming back all over."* As he spoke, lights in the corridor outside brightened from subsistence levels to full power. *"We're feeding the results of your tricorder scan to the transporter network right now. All decks, stand by for shipwide transporter sweep!"*

Keru and Sarai stepped back as a familiar golden glitter effect wreathed the corpses of the alien creatures. Elsewhere on the *Titan*, a networked series of transporters was gathering up everything that correlated to the invader's biotype and dematerializing it. In moments, they were all gone, leaving behind the destruction they had wreaked.

Sarai blew out a breath and turned to Torvig, who was gingerly padding into the compartment with Cel at his side. "Ensign, secure all systems and make certain there's nothing still here that can put us at further risk." Then she tapped her own combadge. "Engineering. I don't have to remind you that our next priority must be our shields."

"Yes, Admiral Riker has made me well aware of the urgency of the matter," Ra-Havreii's reply was caustic. *"Repeatedly, in fact! But contrary to the image popularized by other chief engineers, I am not a miracle worker! Meldok and Crandall will have the shields up in a few minutes. That's the best we can do. It may have escaped your notice, but we also have an away team to recover!"*

"Sirs," Torvig was peering into the rip in the deck plates. "There's something here I think you ought to see."

The Choblik's tone sent a warning tension through Keru's hands, and he gripped his weapon tighter, moving up to take a look. "What have you got?"

"It seems we have found where they were taking their . . . spoils." Torvig was shining a light down into the ragged-edged pit torn into the lower service ducts. The strange mass of material Keru had glimpsed earlier was now fully revealed. Jury-rigged feeds from the ship's EPS system were providing dangerously unregulated power to a clot of melted and reformed polymers. Embedded in the congealed mound were recognizable pieces of Starfleet hardware, everything from a viewscreen from someone's quarters to a gutted medical tricorder.

Keru heard Sarai's sharp intake of breath behind him.

"After the admiral and I came across that one in the corridor," he began, thinking it through, "I wondered if it was some kind of magpie effect. The theft of the hardware, I mean. But now I'm not so sure."

"What is a 'magpie'?" said Sarai.

"An Earth reference," explained Torvig. "A Terran species of avian, genus *Pica*, known for being attracted to shiny objects and stealing them for placement in their nests. A purely reflexive response based on the need to attract mating partners."

Keru nodded. "Like he said. But the orb-creatures were actually building something."

Sarai fingered her weapon, and Keru knew her first impulse was to destroy their discovery. Then she frowned. "I want this analyzed. Find out what they were doing."

Torvig's head bobbed. "I think parts of it may actually be organic, like the orbs themselves . . ."

"Then kill it first," Sarai said firmly. "And be certain. We've already seen what happens when we mistake *dormant* for *dead*."

It was torture.

Titan sailed lazily past them, and for all its proximity, the starship could have been in the Delta Quadrant for all it mattered. They tried to shift their course, using momentum against each other, but all it did was make things worse.

Pazlar watched as Peya struggled toward the hull, fright momentarily robbing her of reason as her arms snatched at nothing. Her reflex action was to grab at what she could never reach, her body reacting as if she were floating in a sea instead of the void of space. Against water, with something to push at, it might have been enough, but out here all the Deltan was doing was spending precious oxygen. In her panic, Peya had deactivated her communications link, so Melora could neither call out to calm her down nor hear her crying out inside the prison of her own helmet.

"Ah." Dakal's voice sounded close, even though he was at the other end of the tether line. "It appears my mathematics were not as sound as I thought. This is my fault. I'm sorry, Commander. I've let us all down."

"Zurin, no . . ." Pazlar felt fear flutter and then fade in her chest. She was so tired, enough that it smothered the terror that should have been filling her.

Instead, there was sorrow. Sorrow at the waste of it all, sorrow at the fact that she would never be able to find a solution to the conundrum of her own life. "I've never really fit," she said, the words coming from deep inside of their own accord. "I wanted to know why."

The curve of the starship drifted by, silent and stately. The darkness draping over the hull made it look as if it were cut from dull, matte obsidian. *Was anyone alive over there?* Suddenly the worst thing she could think of was that Peya, Zurin and she were the only ones still drawing breath. The horrible image of *Titan* as a floating tomb made her heart seize in her chest, and she closed her eyes.

"Melora!" Dakal's cry brought her back, dispelling the bleak thought. "Look!" He was pointing, and as she followed his outstretched hand, she saw the slow crawl of lights coming on all across the hull of the starship. Deck by deck, cabin by cabin, the vessel was returning to life. "There's still a chance!"

"Away Team to *Titan*," she called, her voice catching. "Please say you read me."

"I see you there, sir." The voice of Lieutenant Radowski, the ship's senior transporter chief, was like music to her ears. *"Let's get you in out of the cold."*

A grin formed on Bowan's face as he watched three columns of shimmering white light reshape themselves into figures clad in Starfleet EVA suits. As the transporter cycle closed out, he allowed himself a moment to savor the victory. All through the crisis, Radowski had done what he always did, holding his post in transporter room three even though the power cut had rendered the system inert, ready for that moment when he would be needed to reach out and rescue his crewmates.

He liked his job. The lieutenant knew that he was often the last chance that anyone in harm's way had, the only lifeline that could snatch them away from danger before it claimed them. Every person he brought home, no matter if it was a crash recovery from an imploding asteroid or just a simple point-to-point transit, was a win for Radowski. That look on their faces when they knew they were safe was all he needed to appreciate that he was making a difference out here.

"Commander, I have them!" he called into the intercom, before sprinting from behind his console to the group stumbling off the transporter platform.

"On my way!"

He didn't acknowledge the chief engineer's words, grabbing a medical kit from a wall alcove as he ran. Dakal was already helping Ensign Fell get her helmet off, and as Radowski approached, he saw that Commander Pazlar was having trouble with the latches of her own.

Pazlar's hands were shaking, and through the suit's thick gloves that was a recipe for panic. He'd seen it before, officers with plenty of spacewalk experience losing their cool when adrenaline aftershock kicked in and suddenly they couldn't work the latches, *couldn't get the damn helmet off*.

"Easy there," he told her, dropping the medkit so he could put both hands on the neck ring. "Let me help you." She was talking but he could only hear the dull buzz of her words through the helmet. Pazlar's head was darting around like she was looking for something that wasn't there. Then the latches disengaged and the helmet popped off with a hiss of displaced air.

"Where is Ethan?" she shouted at him.

"Who?"

"Lieutenant Kyzak," gasped Fell, wiping sweat from her pale face. "You didn't bring him back with us!"

Radowski shook his head. "There were only three of you out there—"

"Not in space!" cried the science officer. "On the derelict!"

"Oh crap." In his haste to bring his transporter system on-line, the lieutenant had used close range sensors to lock on to the first targets it could find: the drifting trio of the Elaysian, Cardassian and Deltan. But he hadn't stopped to look farther out once he had begun the beaming cycle. Radowski scrambled to his feet and practically hurled himself back at the control console. He registered Dakal saying something about *no air, damaged suit*, but it didn't matter. One look at the fear in Pazlar's eyes told him that Kyzak was in very serious trouble.

The sensors swept space and found the drifting hulk of the wrecked explorer several hundred kilometers off the port aft quarter. Life signs showed a faint, near-zero return, but there was a clean lock as he found a ping on the Starfleet emergency beacon frequency.

"Got him!" Radowski worked the controls and reeled in his new target. "Energizing."

A fourth figure hazed into solidity on the pad, this one slumped forward and motionless. All the lieutenant could make out was a damaged faceplate webbed with countless cracks, patched with makeshift suit seals. Pazlar was at the man's side in a moment, wrenching off the leaking helmet. The whiff of sweat and stale air was strong, and Radowski saw a humanoid face with lines of scales that was bloodless and ashen.

"He's not breathing," said Pazlar, the words like a death sentence.

At her side, Dakal cracked open the medkit and loaded a hypospray, slapping it into Pazlar's open hand. "Tri-Ox compound," he explained.

She pressed the nozzle of the hypo to Kyzak's neck and there was an immediate reaction. The Skagaran's body arched and he let out a whooping gasp, clutching at nothing.

"It's okay," said the science officer. "Ethan, just breathe normally. You're okay. We're safe."

"Safe . . ." Kyzak pushed out the word, as if the effort took everything he had.

Radowski felt a wave of relief wash over him, and he tapped his combadge. "Sickbay? Transporter room three. I need a medical team." Behind him, he heard the door hiss open.

"Not dead, then," Kyzak rasped, reaching up to

touch Pazlar's cheek with a shaky hand, smiling faintly. "Reckon no . . . angels like you."

"You're alive." Radowski looked around to see Commander Ra-Havreii standing in the doorway, conflicting emotions warring across his face. Even though there were four other people in the room, he was asking the question only of Commander Pazlar. "That's . . . good." Before anyone could respond, he turned away. "Carry on." Ra-Havreii left the room again without looking back.

Ten

Seen from orbit, Casroc was a mix of umber shades and wide swathes of yellow savannah that covered continents. Not the blue-white vista of Earth, Riker reflected, but the homeworld of the Dinac had a kind of raw beauty to it that was undeniable. High above, the planet's environmental issues were less noticeable, but he knew that down on the surface, life was hard.

It saddened him that he had to make things harder still for these people with the news that *Titan* brought them. Looking away, the admiral's gaze slipped over the curved walls and floor of the space station around him to a wide oval screen hanging from the ceiling. It showed an image captured by a sensor on the outer ring of the toroidal orbital platform.

In the background, the floating shape of the *Titan* filled most of the screen, but the activity in the foreground was where all attention was focused. There was a hush over the assembled beings standing on the bowed deck of ornate woods and inlaid marquetry before him, and again, Riker wished he could have been there under better circumstances.

On the screen, Dinac astronauts in bulky orange excursion suits completed the work of fitting a net-like sheath over the hull of the ruined explorer ship. In keeping with the nautical nomenclature used to describe their vessels—some peculiarity of the universal translator's software, he guessed—the four smaller craft surrounding the pinnace were identified as "sloops." Each had a tether cable attached to the rig about the derelict, and as somber, funereal tones played over the station's internal communications channel, Riker watched the quartet fire their sublight engines as one and pull the wreck away. Powerful lights in the belly of the sloops activated to illuminate the explorer with a dazzling glow.

As if anticipating his question, the tall engineer-commander standing to his right glanced down at Riker. "It will be taken on a journey around our planet to the night side, Admiral. There, it will circle Casroc in low orbit for several of our days as farewell rites are performed for the crew. This is done so that those on the surface may look up after sunset and find this craft and see it with their own eyes." She had a lilting tone to her voice, at odds with the lupine nature of her features. "This we do in the names of our vanished host-brothers and host-sisters, crèche-sons and crèche-daughters."

He nodded. "Our sorrows are shared." Riker shot his wife a look. Deanna said nothing, letting him take the lead. "But I would suggest that our lost comrades are only that. *Lost*. We have no definite confirmation of their deaths as yet."

"But neither can you offer more than words that they

still live." The Dinac leader standing in front of the screen turned to give the *Titan*'s landing party an unforgiving glare. He was the lord council, the same being Riker had spoken to over subspace after their first encounter with the wreck, and in the time it had taken them to reach Casroc, the leader's mood had hardened. "These stories you tell us of strange pocket universes lying beneath ours like caves in the earth, and denizens within them that come in the dark hours to steal our people and yours . . ." He shook his head. "It reminds me of the myths we tell our youngest whelps to keep them entertained."

"They are true," said Troi. "We wish it were not so, Lord Council. Know that hundreds of families within our Federation share the anguish of those on Casroc today."

The engineer-commander, who wore a bright blue ribbon about her arm that seemed to designate some kind of honorific, cocked her head, and her ears twitched. "Admiral Riker and Commander Troi, you have done the Dinac people a great service by bringing our ship home. On behalf of my fellow captains, I thank you. Guoapa was a mate-partner of mine, in years past." She paused. "And I will say, I believe your story."

The admission was unexpected, but Riker took it nonetheless. "May I ask why?"

Some of the other council members began whispering to one another in low tones, but the commander paid them no mind. "You are aware that we have been working to facilitate space travel beyond the bounds of our star system for some time. During our test flights there were . . ." She paused, groping for the right term. "*Phenomena*. Events that occurred in our zone of space that could not be adequately explained."

The lord council stepped forward. "Discovery is a dangerous endeavor. Lives and craft were lost as our pioneers set forth, nothing more. It is expected."

"That is so," agreed the commander. "But there have been vessels that vanished without trace, and craft found adrift and empty. We have always attributed it to misfortune, to the dangers of exploration. But what if we were mistaken?" Shc looked at Riker and Troi. "What if these . . . *Solanae* have been preying on us?"

Riker hesitated. He had already seen some of the theories Commander Pazlar had put together about the subspace incursion, including the possibility that some effect generated by the idiosyncratic technology of Dinac warp drives had been responsible for attracting the attention of the Solanae, just as a chance interaction of energies had started the chain of events aboard the *Enterprise* years earlier. It was very possible that the engineer-commander was right.

But the last thing he wanted to do was fuel the fears of an entire civilization by suggesting they might be abducted from their beds. "We can't be certain," Riker said carefully. "But it might be best for the Dinac Expeditionary Initiative to shut down their warp drive systems for the time being. Until we have a better picture of things."

A ripple of consternation went through the aliens. "You want us to halt our interstellar program?" said another of the council members. "For how long?"

"How do we know they haven't done this themselves?" hissed another. "A ruse, because they want to pen us in on a dying planet!"

"Nothing could be further from the truth," Troi insisted, her tone shifting. "We have an accord built on mutual trust and friendship. Casroc and the Dinac species want to join the galactic community, and the United Federation of Planets wish to help you do that. But this dilemma threatens both our societies. We have all been wounded by this."

Riker drew himself up. "I will make this promise to you, here and now: On my authority as a Starfleet officer, I and the crew of the *Titan* will not allow the Solanae to continue to threaten *any of us*. On the lives of my missing comrades, I swear this."

"Words of strength, Admiral Riker," said the lord council, with a grateful nod. "But I fear you will not be able to back them with deeds after the assault on your ships. If you could not stop them taking your *Whitetree*, then what hope is there?"

And in that moment, Riker found he had no good answer for him.

Sickbay's number two operating theater had been temporarily repurposed as a virtual autopsy lab, and on the worktables a series of portable holographic projectors were providing three-dimensional models of the alien orb-creatures. The simulated life-forms were built using detailed computer models, based on data gathered by Commander Keru's tricorder and the scans captured by *Titan*'s transporter system in the brief moments the invaders had been rendered down to a matter stream.

Doctor Ree put his blunt snout into the ghostly shape of an opened, octopoid-mode image of an orb, turning it in the air with small gestures of his talons. "Remarkable," he muttered. "I have not come across such an efficient synthesis of organic tissue and mechanical components since the Borg."

At his side, Commander Pazlar gave him a wary look. "There are no commonalities between Borg tech and these . . . creations."

"Of course." He agreed quickly. "The orbs are not nanoprobe-based artifacts. But on a gross level, the degree of flesh-to-mechanism integration is high." The doctor highlighted a section of what appeared to be brain matter. "Look here. This enlarged zone of neural tissue has an organ that resembles the telepathic center in a Cairn cerebral cortex. Possibly a gene-engineered communication nexus. And the areas common to instinctual behavior are enlarged, while those that usually govern creative or individual thought are atrophied . . ." He paused, forming a hypothesis. "Melora, I believe these orb-creatures are remote drones, of a sort. Part machine, part life-form, designed by the Solanae specifically to exist in our spatial realm."

"Because the Solanae themselves cannot," the science officer said, picking up the thread. "At least, not for very long. Their cellular energy states are incompatible with our reality, but somehow they were able to create these things to be their proxies."

Ree showed his teeth as an expression of agreement. "Looking through the transporter data, I found some interesting anomalies. A large percentage of the orbs we beamed out were *already* dead. And more were in the process of accelerated cellular decay. These drones, even if they were made to live in our dimension, do a poor job of it. Their life span is short. They are disposable scouts, and little more."

"Hence their desire to reproduce through the replicators." Pazlar nodded. "It wasn't just a swarming reaction, then. It was . . ." She blinked and seemed to lose focus for a moment. "It was self-preservation."

The doctor put down the stylus he was toying with and gave the Elaysian a measuring look. "Melora, are you all right? Your skin temperature is elevated. Perhaps you ought to stand down for a few hours."

She shook her head. "I've been cleared for duty. I'll carry on."

He persisted, despite her refusal. "Far be it from me to contradict Alyssa's opinion. But you have just suffered a traumatic experience, and been exposed to a prolonged deep space—"

"I'm a Gemworld native," she shot back, perhaps a little more sharply than she intended. "Microgravity is second nature to me."

"That's not what I meant."

"I'm fine," insisted the Elaysian. "I want to stay here, to be—" Melora looked out across the corridor, in the direction of the recovery ward, and caught herself before she said any more. "I'm fine," she repeated, with finality.

"Very well," said Ree, after a moment. It was well within his powers as chief medical officer to order her to rest if he thought it necessary; but then he recalled that across the corridor, Lieutenant Ethan Kyzak was lying on a biobed under sedation while his treatment did its work. Ree wondered how much of Melora's wish to stay in sickbay was connected to her responsibilities for the injured man. He decided not to press the matter, and he concentrated on the work before them.

"There's nothing to indicate the orbs could send or receive messages from subspace, only to and from one another," said Pazlar. "So if the Solanae deposited them in our dimension, did they plan to retrieve them at a later time?"

"Unlikely, given the decay rate of the organisms," Ree replied. "Which brings us to the secondary imperative." He turned to look at a clear tank resting on another table close by. Ensigns Meldok and Evesh were busy with micromanipulator waldoes, using them to cut into and pry open the odd, pupae-like mass that had been found where the orbs had "nested" in auxiliary control. "That," he concluded, pointing at the construct.

"What were they making?" Pazlar continued Ree's line of thought.

Meldok looked up as they approached, and the Benzite's azure brow furrowed. "This is unusual, sirs, to say the least." He swallowed a puff of breathing gas from the atmospheric supplementer on his chest and went on. "What we have here is a patchwork unit, jury-rigged from a number of disparate components taken from Starfleet and civilian technology."

Ree caught an unpleasantly loamy scent from the alien construct that made his nostril slits close reflexively. It smelled like rot and decay.

"And not just our tech," piped Evesh, peering out at them from behind a pair of magnifying goggles across her face. "Their own. The spheres cannibalized *themselves* to make this." The Tellarite tapped the side of the tank with a thick finger.

Pazlar eyed the object. "Can I assume that the fact you haven't already blown it out an airlock means this is not a weapon of some sort?"

"It's not a munition, no," agreed Meldok. "But it is dangerous. *Was* dangerous," he corrected.

"We cut off any power supply," Evesh added briskly.

"It wasn't complete when Torvig found it. Which is lucky for us."

"So what is it for?" Ree demanded, becoming impatient.

"*It's a signaling device,*" said Pazlar. "*The orb-creatures were building a subspace interplexing beacon.*"

Standing by the bridge's engineering console, Vale couldn't help but let her hand drift to the panel, the fingers drumming out a beat as she processed this new piece of information. She glanced away from the screen and looked to where Commander Sarai and Admiral Riker stood listening to the science officer's report.

Riker's expression was stony, and Vale saw the edges of old, deep anger there as well. "Are you able to determine the quantum frequency the beacon was designed to broadcast on?" she asked.

"*We were,*" came the reply. "*But for the record, the signal was never sent. Ranul and the XO got to it in time to prevent that from happening.*" There was a pause as the science officer checked her notes. "*According to Meldok's findings, the beacon was set to transmit a coherent subspace pulse at an energy level of sixteen—*"

"Sixteen-point-two keV," the admiral answered, seemingly before he was even aware of it.

"*That . . . that's correct, sir.*"

Riker looked away, and that grim shadow that Vale had glimpsed fell deeper across him.

"The same subspace frequency as the Solanae domain," offered Tuvok, from the tactical station. "We appear to have confirmed the identity of our aggressors."

"As if there was a doubt." Vale heard Sariel Rager's *sotto voce* comment but let it pass.

"Melora," Vale pitched up her voice for the intercom, "keep working at it. Forward everything you have to my data queue and Tuvok's."

"Aye, Captain. Sickbay out."

She shot a look at the Vulcan. "Commander, sift those reports for anything of tactical value. We're going to need it. And maintain our shields at full power until I tell you otherwise."

Tuvok nodded. "My evaluation is already under way, Captain."

Her arms folded, her gaze lost in the middle distance, Sarai spoke without preamble: "So. This is an invasion."

Vale frowned. "That's one possibility." She wanted to believe that there were others, but it was difficult to hold on to a different evaluation. Still, she had to try. With all the trials that Starfleet and the Federation had suffered in the past few years, it had become too easy to reach for the aggressive, bellicose answer to any challenge.

"They want to take us all," said Riker. "They tried once, probably using the same approach they took to snare the *Whitetree*. But when we resisted, those drones used a different tactic."

"Possible," offered Tuvok, without looking up from his station. "Theoretically, an active beacon of sufficient power might allow the Solanae to specifically program an artificial spatial rift at a quantum frequency that would overwhelm *Titan*'s deflector array. We would not be able to escape it."

"Captain." Sarai looked to Vale, then to Riker and back again. "What we have endured here can be considered an act of war. Based on the past incident aboard the *Enterprise*-D, and now the abduction of the *Whitetree* and the attacks on the *Titan*, there is little room for any alternate interpretation. After nearly two decades of silence, the Solanae have chosen Dinac space as their beachhead into our universe."

When Riker didn't add his voice to the debate, Vale's frown deepened, and she turned a firm glare on her first officer. "We say the word *invasion*, and we can't un-ring that bell, Commander. That means priority action messages to Starfleet Command. It means the raising of alert levels all across this sector. Ships and starbases going to a war footing." Every word the captain spoke was exactly what Riker should have been voicing, but still he said nothing.

"And if we don't?" said Sarai. "These . . . abductions . . . may be happening in other sectors. They may have happened *already* and we're just not aware of it."

"Our priority is finding the missing," Vale said, her tone turning brittle. "Not starting hostilities."

"That ship has sailed," said the admiral, at last breaking his silence. "We're the only vessel in this area. We have to get our people back, that's a given. But we need to stop the Solanae. The entire sector is at risk until the threat is neutralized."

Was that an order? Vale hesitated to ask the question. "I don't think anyone disagrees with that, Admiral," she began, framing her words carefully. "But we're back to square one here. We don't know for sure where the missing crews are. We don't have a next move."

"Incorrect," said Tuvok. He looked up from his panel. "Captain, I may have a lead."

"Let's hear it," said Riker.

The Vulcan went on. "As Captain Vale ordered, I

programmed a search subroutine to sift the data from Commander Pazlar and Doctor Ree's findings. The data shows that the biomechanical drones have a modified cellular energy state that allows them to exist in our universe, albeit for a limited time period."

"That much we know," Sarai broke in. "How do we use that information to our advantage?"

"I believe that it is possible to calibrate sensors to scan for traces of that same energy state. A high enough concentration would register as a detectable fingerprint on the surrounding environment. However, there would need to be a substantial number of Solanae-origin forms to enable detection. In addition, scan range would be relatively small."

"Uh, sirs?" Commander Lavena spoke up from the conn. "We already have something on board that could boost *Titan*'s scanner range." She gestured at her panel. "The modified sensor probes we released before we turned back for Casroc. White-Blue reprogrammed them for much higher acuity."

"Of course." Riker sat down in the seat to the right of the captain's chair and tapped a panel in the armrest. "Computer, connect me to White-Blue. Ask him to manifest on the bridge."

The admiral had barely finished speaking when the holographic rendition of the Sentry AI-hybrid flickered into being before them.

"Greetings, William-Riker," said the multi-limbed humanoid figure. "Interrogative: How may I assist you?"

Vale watched the AI as Riker quickly explained the situation. Very different from the physical drone form that they had first encountered on their entry into Sentry Coalition territory out past the Vela Pulsar, the synthetic being now more closely resembled the strange virtual forms of its kindred that Vale had seen "face-to-face" when she had briefly interfaced with their digital mind-space. She rubbed her scalp in the place where the neural jack had been inserted all that time ago, recalling how she had felt in that moment, as discussions that could lead to open warfare took place around her. The similarity of her current circumstances was not lost on *Titan*'s captain.

"Understood," White-Blue was saying. "Ex-loading data from Commander Tuvok's console now. Accessing sensor probes." He paused, and Vale saw the ripple of raw data shimmer over the AI's virtual form.

"What is it doing?" Sarai said warily.

"Connecting to our communications array," answered Rager. "Talking to the probes. If Aili's right, we'll be able to scan the whole sector in a few minutes."

"Detection," announced White-Blue.

"Or maybe faster," added Lavena.

Sarai's eyes widened. "How is it possible for it to process data so quickly?"

White-Blue's plain, near-featureless head swiveled to study the first officer with its triad of optical receptors. "It is preferable to I/We that you refer to this construct as 'he' and not 'it,' Dalit-Sarai. This construct has become comfortable with that socio-linguistic form." Vale thought she detected an air of mild reproach in the words. "In reply to your interrogative, this construct's clock speed is considerably faster than that of most organic beings. The process I/We have just completed would have taken four Standard hours, plus or minus twelve minutes, at your rate of cognition."

"He is useful to have around," Sarai said cautiously.

"What have you found?" Vale asked.

"Accessing tactical display." White-Blue pointed a limb at the main viewscreen, and the image shifted to a three-dimensional map view of local space.

Bright blue indicators picked out the locations of *Titan*'s sensor probes and their scanner ranges. Networked together through the wonder of advanced Sentry programming, Vale could see how they had been able to sweep a whole sector of space in a matter of moments, for what might otherwise have been the subspace equivalent of a needle in a haystack.

The detection return lit up in yellow and the tactical plot zoomed in, revealing a hazy ovoid shape. Vale recognized the low-definition appearance of an object captured at the very edge of sensor range. She could just about pick out craters and dark striations across the object's surface. "Doesn't look like a ship."

"It appears to be a cometary mass," offered Ensign Polan, speaking up for the first time. "Tracking indicates it is on a very long orbit around a Class-K supergiant star. Distance . . . two-point-seven light-years from our current coordinates."

"We've got them," said Sarai.

"We've got *something*," Vale corrected; but even as she said it, she could feel the situation pulling away from her.

Riker got to his feet. "Helm, set an intercept course. Maximum warp. The sooner we get there, the sooner we end this."

Vale found Lavena and Rager looking her way, waiting for the affirmation to commit. Her lips thinned, and at length, she gave a terse nod.

"Engaging," reported Rager, and the main screen snapped back to a view of deep space as the stars distorted around them.

The captain pressed her hands flat against her thighs to stop them from bunching, and she looked across to Riker. "Admiral?" she said quietly, inclining her head toward the door of her ready room. "Let's talk."

Will Riker hadn't been in the small office since the *Titan* had left the Sol system, but Riker noted that Vale had added her own personal touches. A framed photo of her parents. A plaque in Izarian script surrounding a police officer's shield. A digital painting of a spring landscape that shifted as it moved through an accelerated day-night cycle.

But Christine hadn't asked him—no, *summoned* him—in here to discuss choices in décor. *Titan*'s captain walked to the ready room's desk and sat on the edge.

She gestured around. "You want this back already?"

"I'm not sure I follow you, Chris." But that wasn't entirely true. He had a fair idea of where this conversation was headed before she drew breath.

"Things are going to be different now," said Vale. "I get that. A lot has changed since you came back from that meeting with Admiral Akaar. Hell, since we came back from the Vela Sector. So I want to be sure that we know where we stand."

His throat felt dry and he turned toward the replicator, intending to order up a glass of water—but the system was still off-line after the attack, each unit going through a painstaking purge regimen devised by Commander Ra-Havreii. He frowned and turned back. "Haven't we been through this already? You got the ship."

"Kinda," said Vale, with the hint of a frown.

"What do you mean?"

She met his gaze. "With all due respect, Will, *you're still here*. And you cast a pretty long shadow."

Riker didn't know how to answer that at first, so he deflected it. He made a contrite face and pulled at his tunic. "It's the uniform. These big belt buckles? They're not flattering."

The attempt at humor failed. Vale's expression didn't change. "You know what I mean. You're not the commanding officer of this ship anymore. Technically, you're a *passenger*."

He actually winced at the word, like it was an insult. "I think I'm a little more than that."

She let out a slow breath. "There are a handful of people whom I would say I look up to, and in Starfleet that list narrows down to just two or three. Jean-Luc Picard is one. You're another."

"I'm honored you think so."

Vale's eyes narrowed. "But that doesn't give you license to captain this ship for me. Not unless you want to relieve me and take *Titan* back."

"I was not—" The words came out before Riker's thoughts caught up to them, and he fell silent. Even as he considered it, he knew she was right. Out there, on the bridge and during the attack, he had been acting like it was *his* authority that was the ultimate one—when in fact Christine Vale was *Titan*'s captain, and hers was the final word. It didn't matter that Riker outranked her, or that this ship carried his flag. As Starfleet regulations stipulated, the captain was in charge of the vessel and everyone aboard it.

At length, he nodded. "I'm sorry, Chris. I overstepped. I guess I'm still getting used to the changes."

"We all are," she conceded. "I just want to make sure that the chain of command is clear." Vale gestured toward the ready room door and the bridge beyond. "They're my crew now. Not yours. That's not to say that I don't want your input, your guidance. I value it, more than you know."

"But I can't go back to the center seat." He sighed. "Old habits die hard, I guess." Riker forced a smile. "I think I'm starting to see the whole other side to that debate we used to have at the Academy, about flag officers throwing their weight around. What is it that Boothby used to call them? Badmirals."

Vale's expression softened. "I can't know what you and Rager went through with the Solanae, back on the *Enterprise*. But I know *you*, Will. And I know that experience is reaching up out of the past and coloring the choices you're making right now." She paused. "All I'm asking is that you take a step back, Admiral. I'm not saying anything that hasn't already occurred to you."

He broke her gaze and looked out of the ready room's port at the racing stars. "It's not easy," Riker admitted, pushing away old, dark memories.

"No," she agreed, "but then that's always been the job, right?"

Eleven

She sensed him before he entered the room.

Deanna turned as the doors hissed open and Will crossed the threshold. His smile was genuine, if somewhat frayed, and with an unspoken agreement the two of them came together and their hands found each other. Usually, the husband and wife kept open displays of affection to an absolute minimum while on duty, but there was something about this moment that made both Will and Deanna want to affirm the presence of the other.

"Shouldn't you be on the bridge?" she asked, looking up.

He nodded at the compartment around them. "This was on my way." They both knew that was a lie, but that was all right.

Titan's day school was just as species-diverse as its crew, and their daughter, Tasha, was nearby playing with a pair of Lieutenant Keyexisi's immature budlings. Too young to have names as yet, the small nonhumanoids had yet to open their eyes, so their daughter was helping them navigate the playroom by touch and smell.

The scene was so ordinary, so *normal*, it was hard to believe that half a day ago the school had been plunged into darkness and danger along with the rest of the ship. Tasha and her friends had suffered through the same terrors as everyone else in the crew and seemingly come through unscathed. *But then the young are more resilient than we give them credit for*, she thought.

Tasha seemed to sense the presence of her parents, and she turned to give them a wide smile and a wave of the hand. Will and Deanna returned the gesture.

"We're closing in on the Solanae outpost," said her husband. "It may get unpleasant. I wanted to warn you."

"Do you want me with you?" Deanna looked into his eyes, searching his surface thoughts. She could sense the tension he was keeping hidden, and the lurking shadow of old, half-forgotten fear.

"No. Somehow, I don't think diplomacy is going to be part of this day's action."

Deanna frowned. "It sounds like you've already made up your mind."

"You know me better than that."

"I know you'll do whatever you have to do to protect us." Deanna meant the crew of the *Titan* as much as herself and Tasha.

Behind them, T'Pel clapped her hands together three times, a signal to the children that their break time was over and lessons were about to resume. Tuvok's wife found a place to sit among the gathering of youngsters and began to read from a padd.

"Sometimes . . ." Will said quietly, "sometimes I just want to scoop up all of those kids and drop them off on a pastoral colony world where nothing could hurt them."

"And then spend every waking hour worrying that your daughter would forget your face?" Deanna replied.

"I'm not sure the trade-off is worth it." He released her hand. "In the past couple of days, I've been remembering how precious certain things are to me."

Deanna nodded. "The more we age, the easier it is to become afraid. What each of us has becomes more precious as time passes. We fear we'll lose what we love."

He grinned at his wife's insight, in spite of himself. "Am I made of glass?"

Before she could answer, Commander Sarai's brusque tones cut through the air. "*Admiral Riker, your presence is required urgently on the bridge.*"

"Duty calls." Will leaned in and gave her a light kiss on the cheek. "Keep safe," he said, turning back toward the door.

"Keep *us* safe," she said after him.

Once, hundreds of thousands of years ago, the object had been part of a colossal shoal of ice fragments, pieces of matter too far from the orbit of their parent star to be drawn in to form worlds. Chance interactions of gravity had caused collisions that gradually knocked this particular ovoid lump of frozen gasses and rock out of its safe state of grace in the depths of an Oort cloud and set it on a slow parabola down into the gravity well of the bright supergiant star many light-days distant.

Inexorable forces of mass and motion had gathered the object in, cosmic winds brushing its surface as it orbited closer to the blue-white star. A tail of dust and liberated gas extended behind the main mass, and the nameless comet entered into a ballet that would go on for millennia. Unremarkable, undisturbed, the craggy egg of stone, water ice, frozen methane and ammonia was one of millions just like it throughout the galaxy.

The comet's dull commonality drew no attention—a factor that was key to the beings who concealed themselves within it.

Commander Tuvok's tactical plot showed him the entire elliptical orbit of the celestial body, while a subdisplay provided a closer analysis of the comet's head. The compact nucleus was deep space cold and heavy with dense metals, his readings blurred slightly by the haze of the coma—the cloud of dust haloing the leading mass. Behind it, a glowing tail of particles cut a line through the void. As the comet drew closer to the star and the point of perihelion, the tail would grow and take on greater definition.

"Curious," muttered the Vulcan. *Titan*'s standard sensor pallets read little that would make one think that this object was anything other than a conventional, unexceptional comet. But the modified sweep he had programmed to search for the distinctive Solanae energy fingerprint glowed brightly when overlaid on the nucleus.

That led him to only one conclusion: The comet outpost had been constructed with total stealth in mind. Those within it wished to go unseen by the universe at large. Tuvok explained as much to Captain Vale and Commander Sarai as Admiral Riker and his aide arrived on the bridge.

"It's a remote place to have a secret base," Sarai

noted. "No space-capable cultures within several light-years, except for the Dinac. Coincidence?"

Vale didn't pick up the question. "Can we determine the number of individual life-forms from this distance?" On the screen, the comet loomed large, but in reality they were still several thousand kilometers from it.

Melora Pazlar was now back at her science station, and she looked up from her console. "It's difficult to separate them out, Captain. We could be reading another nest of the orb-creatures or other, more advanced entities."

"Hundreds?" asked Lavena from the conn.

Pazlar shook her head. "More like tens of thousands."

"If it's the . . . humanoids," began Rager, "then how can they actually *be* here? They can't live in our space, we know that."

Tuvok nodded. "Commander La Forge's report of the incident aboard the *Enterprise*-D suggested that the Solanae might be capable of generating a pocket of their dimensional space inside ours. But something on a scale large enough to accommodate the reading would require a very potent power source. I see nothing to indicate that here."

"Could it be cloaked in some way?" said Sarai, studying the comet.

"There would be a neutrino signature," Tuvok explained. "There is none."

"They have had a long time to learn and adapt," Riker said. "So, they're here. What about our people and the Dinac? Any trace of the *Whitetree*?"

"Negative," said Pazlar. "But I'm picking up unusual readings from the surface of the cometary nucleus. A high degree of reflectivity. I'm not sure what's causing it, but it wasn't visible on our long-range scans. If we move closer, I might be able to interpret the return."

"Shield status?" Vale looked over her shoulder at Tuvok.

"Optimal," he told her. "Graviton pulse modulation is active."

"Take them up to full power, Commander, and sound yellow alert. Prepare phasers and photon torpedoes in case this goes sideways."

He nodded, entering the captain's commands. "Ready." Warning icons snapped on across the bridge, mirrored on every deck below them.

Vale exchanged looks with Riker and Sarai. "Here we go." The captain gestured to Rager and Lavena. "One-quarter impulse. Take us to five thousand kilometers off the starboard side, parallel course with the comet."

"Aye, Captain," chorused the officers, and *Titan* shifted position.

The image of the great chunk of ice and rock centered itself on the screen, slowly growing larger. "Mass analysis confirms that the target is lighter than expected," Pazlar reported. "That would suggest there are hollows beneath the surface. Tunnels, a network of caverns."

"Artificial?" said Riker.

"Unknown. But if the Solanae are anywhere, that's the place. The nucleus has an extremely flimsy atmosphere. The exterior is not somewhere you would want to take a stroll." The science officer broke off, the twin ridges on her forehead stiffening. "I'm getting more anomalous readings from the surface of the comet. Sporadic pulses of energy, but I can't lock down a locus."

The admiral met the captain's gaze. "They have to know we're out here."

Vale nodded. "They're keeping the lights off and pretending no one is home." She took a breath. "Let's not play games. Mister Tuvok, hail them on all frequencies. Basic linguacode."

"Aye." He glanced down and activated the subroutine that would transmit the universal "handshake" message. No response was forthcoming.

"You really believe they will have a dialogue with us?" Tuvok clearly heard the doubt in Sarai's voice. "The Solanae have shown no interest in opening any avenue of communication other than violence."

"No matter what has happened," Vale said firmly, "I am not giving the order to shoot first."

"Energy readings increasing . . ." called Pazlar. "We're being targeted!"

"They clearly don't see it the same way," said Sarai. "Helm! Evasive maneuvers!"

Tuvok saw the same surge of power on his station, as the *Titan* lurched away on a random vector from the comet. The composition was a kind of plasma-energy matrix that resembled weapons used by the Romulan Star Empire in decades past but with an unusual decay pattern.

The cool, analytical part of Tuvok's tactical mind examined the assault as it swept out to meet them, registering it all in a split second, already beginning to form options for counterattack.

Then it hit the *Titan* squarely amidships, and he watched the deflector shields in that quadrant drop by almost forty percent power in an instant. Tuvok reported the damage, and Vale snapped out new orders to keep the starship on an irregular course, even as new bolts of power leapt from the shiny surface of the comet and burned through the coma toward them.

"You knew it would come to this," Riker said quietly to himself, not in reproof but with a grim certainty.

Vale didn't respond to the admiral. Instead, she turned to Tuvok. "Target their weapons arrays and return fire."

The Vulcan hesitated, a quizzical cast to his features. The data filling his tactical display was not in error, and yet it was difficult to make sense of it. "I cannot."

Two more plasma surges were emitted from points across the shimmering surface of the cometary mass, the first cutting wide of the mark, the second slamming hard into the forward deflectors.

Tuvok gripped the edges of his console to remain standing and explained what he saw before him. "There are no weapons arrays down there, Captain." The sensors looked and saw no emitter muzzles, no focal crystals or lasing tubes.

"Then what is shooting at us?" Sarai demanded. "Those plasma bursts are no illusion!"

"Correct," he said, his voice calm and level.

It was in moments like this, Tuvok reflected, that the self-control of emotional species was tested. For all the frosty demeanor she exhibited under normal circumstances, the Efrosian hid a kernel of slow-burning anger that now showed itself. Stress brought Sarai's aggression to the surface, and Tuvok wondered how deep it might go.

But for the moment, such questions were not relevant. "It appears that almost the entire surface area of the cometary mass is acting as an offensive energy grid. In some manner, the outer skin of ice has been coated with a medium allowing the generation and projection of"—*Titan* trembled as another blast caressed the shields—"plasma bolts."

Riker studied the tactical plot on the chair's secondary screen. "That makes the entire comet one gigantic, omni-directional weapon! There's no blind side to it, no way we can maneuver out of its firing arc."

Tuvok nodded his assent. "We can only withdraw, Admiral, to beyond weapons range."

"Incoming!" called Pazlar. "Multiple surges this time! They're unloading it all on us!"

Brilliant yellow-white energy rose off the surface of the comet in a crackling haze, and for a moment it seemed to envelop the *Titan*. The starship rocked under the punishing impact, and Tuvok held on as the gravity compensators tried to keep up with changing states in the aftermath of the impact. Across the bridge, a panel blew out in a shower of sparks, and the tactical officer's console lit up with a dozen advisory warnings about power drains and diminishing deflectors.

"Phasers!" barked Vale. "Return fire, full spread!"

Tuvok nodded and set the ship's weapons to answer the alien attack. Rods of orange fire lanced out from the dorsal and ventral phaser rings on *Titan*'s primary hull, crossing each other as they aimed for the center mass of the comet.

But something was awry, and Tuvok saw it immediately. Where the beams should have connected with the surface of the comet nucleus, they twisted inexplicably and shed energy, dissipating most of their power into halos of repulsed radiation.

"Phaser effectiveness is down to thirteen percent," reported the Vulcan. "Damage to the target is minor."

At the science station, Pazlar was seeing the same unusual result. "It appears to be some kind of localized effect, perhaps from the membrane shrouding the comet.

It's warping space close to the surface of the nucleus. It's like the laws of physics are being distorted."

"Photon torpedo," Vale ordered. "Single shot, medium yield. Let's see if that works."

"Torpedo away," Tuvok replied, releasing the weapon into the void. The bright orange starlight shot straight toward the comet, but at the last moment it seemed to balk from its path and spin into a wild roll. The glowing warhead spiraled away into the darkness and exploded harmlessly.

"Same thing," said Pazlar. "The torpedo's guidance system suddenly lost all ability to control itself. The inputs went wild as it came close to the target—" She cut off and then spoke again. "Another surge. They're going to fire!"

"All power to impulse and shields," said the captain. "Damn it. Back us off!"

The next impact was the worst yet, enough that it pitched the unwary Lieutenant Ssura to the deck and caused the bridge's power to fade out for a few seconds. When power came back, the readouts were unpromising. "We have lost shields in three quadrants," Tuvok said aloud. "Remaining deflectors are failing." Even as he spoke, he was still searching for another line of attack, of some way to strike at the enemy before them.

Lieutenant McCreedy spoke up from the engineering console. "Captain, I've got the chief screaming blue murder. Those hits blew out most of the shield generators we just spent the last few hours repairing. It's going to take time to get them up and running again. The next plasma strike we take will go right to the bare metal." The engineer's matter-of-fact evaluation was sobering.

Against an unprotected hull, a plasma bolt would burn through tritanium like a blowtorch.

"I have an option," said Tuvok. "Scans of the comet nucleus show no diffraction fields or transporter countermeasures."

Riker seized on his words. "We never saw any evidence that the Solanae had transporter technology. Is it possible they don't have a defense against it?"

"No transporters could be something to do with the different physical laws in their origin dimension," Pazlar said quickly, picking up on the line of reasoning. "They may never have developed that science."

Tuvok went on: "It may be possible to transport a timed antimatter warhead directly into the interior of the comet."

The bridge fell silent. Tuvok was well aware that Starfleet's operational rules of engagement frowned on the use of so-called "transporter bombs," forbidding them from deployment in all but the most extreme of circumstances, and only then under authorization from a flag officer. When used, it was an indiscriminate weapon that struck without warning, an attack of last resort.

All eyes turned to Riker. At length, the admiral gave a grave nod. "Prepare a warhead, Mister Tuvok. If we have to exercise that option, I'll sanction it."

Christine Vale's expression darkened. It was immediately clear she was uncomfortable with escalating the engagement to that level—but with *Titan* virtually unprotected against further attacks, her offensive choices were diminishing rapidly.

It fell to Ranul Keru to present another approach. "Sirs, there's another way we can do this. If they have nothing that can stop us beaming in, let me take a security team over there. *Titan* can fall back beyond weapons range and sweep back in to get us out."

"Power surge," reported Pazlar. "Same as before. They're getting ready to fire again!"

"A sound approach," Tuvok noted. "It would require additional energy to the transporters to penetrate the localized field effect, however. There would be a greater level of physical risk to those involved. If the confinement beam fails—"

"I'll take the chance," Keru said, without hesitation.

"Do it," Vale told him. "Take whoever and whatever you need."

"Aye-aye, Captain." Keru stepped away from his console and beckoned to Lieutenant Dakal at the secondary sensors panel. "I'll need a science officer. Zurin, you're with me." The Cardassian covered a moment of apprehension with a nod, and the two men rushed from the bridge.

"Helm, get us out of their reach before they decide to swing at us again," Vale ordered.

Tuvok watched the comet lurch away as the ship pulled clear of the combat zone.

The transition took too long, and it made Ranul Keru feel like vomiting when it was over. A sickly sensation crawled over his flesh as the buzzing, crackling hum of the transporter beam faded away, and he had to steady himself on the nearest thing to him—which happened to be Crewman Blay, one of his best security men. The stocky, dark-skinned Bajoran gave him a look that let Keru know he felt the same way.

"Ugh." Lieutenant Sortollo bent forward and coughed. He looked up and caught the eye of Dennisar, gesturing toward the big Orion petty officer. "Chief," he gasped. "I think that beam-in temporarily mixed up my guts with yours."

Dennisar just grunted. If he felt any discomfort, he didn't show it. The Orion panned around with the heavy phaser compression rifle in his hand, peering right and left.

Along with Zurin Dakal and another security crewman, the terse Napean named Jaq, Keru and his team had materialized inside a sharp-sided corridor that appeared to have been cut through the stone-hard ice of the comet. They were quite alone in the gloomy alien space, and a braying, atonal noise was sounding at regular intervals from somewhere nearby. The security chief guessed it was some kind of alert siren.

"Is that for us?" said Jaq.

Zurin pulled his tricorder and started scanning. He was the only one of them not carrying a rifle, and his hand phaser remained holstered, much to Keru's irritation. They were behind enemy lines now, and they had to act like it. "I don't read anyone approaching this location," said the Cardassian. "I think. The tricorder is glitching. Must be the warp effect."

Keru nodded. Before they had beamed out, Doctor Ree had dosed all of the away team with a theragen derivative compound to help their bodies deal with the low-level radiation that shrouded the comet nucleus. It didn't help with the slight queasiness that came with it, though.

There was something about this place that seemed . . . *off*. Keru would have been hard pressed to put his finger on it, but if he were forced to explain it, he would have said the effect reminded him of how he felt when woken abruptly from a deep sleep. He blinked, shaking off the sensation, and tapped his combadge. "*Titan*, this is Keru. Transport complete. We're moving in."

The reply was heavy with static but clear enough to understand. "*Proceed with caution, Mister Keru,*" said Commander Sarai.

"Never would have thought of that. Good advice." Blay sneered under his breath. Keru had overheard the Bajoran making disparaging comments about the new first officer, and he shot the man a glare to stop him doing so again. Whatever any of them thought about the Efrosian, now was not the time to air it.

"Look sharp," he told them all. "Dennisar, Jaq, take point. Zurin, stay close to me. Blay, Sortollo, watch our backs. Standard spacing, combat overwatch." He glanced at Dakal. "Which way?"

Zurin peered at the tricorder, then gestured ahead. "This corridor extends for fifty-three meters, then splits at a junction. I have faint thermal readings to the left."

"Moving," said Dennisar, and he led the way. For a man his size, he was surprisingly quiet.

"It's warm in here," Sortollo ventured. "Thought it would be cooler."

"They've got some kind of climate control system," explained Dakal. "Atmospheric composition and ambient temperature are close to those recorded by the *Enterprise* in the subspace domain."

"Look for anything that might be a power core," said Keru. In the quick pre-mission briefing he had conducted in the transporter room, the Trill had made it clear that they were here to fulfill two objectives. One: neutralize the Solanae plasma array. Two: determine the disposition and strengths of the enemy.

Although distrust was, on some level, a key part of his duty as a security officer, Keru had still hoped that there would be a peaceable solution to the disappearance of the *Whitetree*—right up until the moment the *Titan* had been invaded by the orb-like drones. Now he found himself coming to Commander Sarai's take on the situation: *This could be the start of an invasion from subspace*.

Dakal's attention was still on his tricorder. "There's a larger area off the end of the corridor . . . a cavern? I can't read the full dimensions—" He broke off as the device emitted a beeping tone. "Life-form detected. It's close."

He had barely said the words before a being emerged around the corner up ahead, moving at a swift jog. Keru had an impression of a monastic figure in silver-gray robes woven from metallic thread, and peering out from the depths of a wide hood was a face that seemed more suitable to a deep sea environment: bulbous eyes, heavy reptilian scales and a beaked mouth, the latter releasing a staccato string of loud clicks as it saw the intruders. Claw-hands came up and the alien was shocked into motion, flinging itself at a control panel on the far wall.

Jaq fired his phaser, but the sound of the weapon's discharge was wrong, as if it were being strangled. The beam hit the robed alien and knocked it down—but just as quickly, it was back on its feet and scrambling for the control panel.

With two long, loping steps, Dennisar closed the distance and planted a green fist in the alien's face, putting it down once more. This time, it didn't stir again.

The Napean glared at his weapon. "What happened there? That was heavy stun!"

"That warping effect again? We should recalibrate our emitters," said Sortollo.

Dakal went to the fallen alien and scanned it. "Alive, but unconscious. Quick thinking, Chief."

"It's a Solanae?" said the Orion.

The science officer nodded. "Biosignature is a match for the *Enterprise* files from seventeen years ago."

"Let's not wait for him to wake up," said Keru. He paused for a moment, examining a creature that had lived in the nightmares of his crewmates William Riker and Sariel Rager for nearly two decades. A shiver passed down his spine, and he looked away. "Onward."

Lurin's tricorder struggled to make sense of the space it detected at the end of the corridor, and when they finally got there, he understood why.

"Whoa," whispered Sortollo. "It's like being inside a cored apple."

It was an apt description. Before the away team was a vast, open inner space that was just one of dozens of similar caverns beneath the surface of the comet. The walls rose up and met high over their heads, and the empty void between them had been filled by a webway of cables and sail-like pieces of some kind of fabric. Objects—some of them as large as a Starfleet runabout—were suspended up there, and he could make out the silver motes of Solanae moving between them on rope bridges. "They're cabins," he guessed. "Rooms cut loose, as it were."

Sortollo and Keru were close, peering over the same low ice-rock ridge the away team were using to stay concealed. "You think someone lives in them?" asked the lieutenant. "Like a tree house, or something?"

"Except there's no tree," noted Keru. "Look closer at the walls."

The Trill indicated where there were hundreds of cell-like chambers cut into the curving structure, reminiscent of the way that certain insect forms made hives for themselves in the soft coastal sandstone near where Zurin had grown up on Cardassia Prime. According to the tricorder, many of the chambers were teeming with life, a fact he quietly reported to Keru.

Titan's security chief frowned. "If those are soldiers, then we may have just found their forward operating base. The bridgehead."

"Commander," Blay called out in a low growl. The Bajoran had followed a sloping path leading to the nearest tier of cell-compartments and was now beckoning Keru to him. "You need to see this."

Zurin followed, with Dennisar at his heels. The Cardassian's throat went dry, and at last he drew his phaser. The tricorder in his other hand was vibrating at regular intervals now, spooling out report after report about the numerous Solanae life signs crowding around them. If they decided to attack en masse, there would be no chance that the away team could fight them off.

Blay pointed to an open, asymmetrical doorway. "Movement inside," he whispered. "And that clicking sound."

"It's how they communicate," noted Dennisar.

Zurin's scans were ominous. "A lot of life-forms in there, and the surrounding cells. Smaller masses than the one we saw in the corridor."

"More of those bloody spheres?" Blay raised his rifle.

"No." The readings didn't match the drones, he explained. They were more biologically complex. "A more advanced evolution, perhaps?"

"Take a look," ordered Keru, and they slipped into the dim space.

Inside, the air was humid and cloying, not the pleasant dry heat of Zurin's native Cardassia, but an oily, overpowering warmth. He heard a sudden torrent of high-pitched clicking from close by and spun in place, just as lights atop Keru's and Blay's rifles flashed on. A stark glow poured across the shiny walls and illuminated a space filled with moving bodies and silvery cloth.

Three Solanae reared up in front of them and went into a panicked chorus of click-speech, wavering between threatening gestures and leaning back to drape themselves protectively over the other moving forms behind them.

What Zurin saw there were not the biomechanical drones that invaded *Titan*. The rest of the compartment was filled with more Solanae, but of various sizes and stages of growth. He automatically scanned them with the tricorder. "Children," he said, reading off the data. "These are the immature form of the adult Solanae." The scans synched up with the readings he had already taken, and a picture began to form. The full-grown aliens—and now the scanner was picking out the biological differences between discreet gender types—were much older in many cases, some even exhibiting what were likely signs of physical infirmity. "These are their elderly and their young."

"Haven't seen anything that looks like a weapon," added Blay. What the Bajoran said next was exactly what Zurin was thinking. "Commander, I don't think this is a military base. It's some kind of colony. Look at them. These are *civilians*, not soldiers."

Before them, the Solanae adults huddled with the children, shivering in what appeared to be abject terror.

The interference across the communications channel made it hard for Riker to follow every word of Keru's report, but he got the sense of it very quickly. Of all the things he had expected to hear the security officer say, this had not been one of them.

The admiral asked Keru to repeat himself one more time to be certain of it. The report did not alter: They had found only unarmed Solanae in the caverns beneath the surface of the comet. Riker sat back in his chair, his hand straying to his beard, processing what he had heard.

"Is it possible the away team beamed in to a habitat for noncombatants only?" said Sarai, pacing slowly across the middle of *Titan*'s bridge. "We have no concept of how Solanae society operates. The soldiers could be in a different area."

"I don't know." At her console, Melora Pazlar was shaking her head. "I'm cross-linking the short-range readings from Lieutenant Dakal's tricorder right now with the data *Titan*'s sensors were able to get. We detected a lot of life signs inside the nucleus, and it's looking like most of them correlate to the biopatterns of these civilians."

"And yet they were giving us a beating a few minutes ago," Vale snapped. Riker could hear the tension in the new captain's voice, and he resisted the urge to say something. She went on: "Maybe that's the reason why.

Every species has the urge to protect its young. It could be why the Solanae lashed out at us with everything they had. They were trying to drive us off."

"A logical hypothesis," offered Tuvok. "However, a purely territorial defensive reaction does not account for the loss of the *Whitetree*, the drones on the Dinac explorer, nor does it correlate with their subsequent assault on this vessel prior to our arrival here."

Vale nodded. "Agreed. We're missing something." She sat forward in the command chair and tapped her combadge. "Commander Keru, this is the captain. I am ordering an immediate halt to any offensive actions. You and your away team are not—repeat, *not*—to fire on anyone without my express command. No matter what the circumstances. Understood?"

There was a momentary pause as the Trill took that in. *"Understood, Captain. Weapons hold."*

"Chris, what's your thinking?" asked Riker, looking across at her. Like Vale, he too had the strong sense that an important part of the puzzle had yet to be revealed to them. But at the same time, the old scars of anger and fear left over from his first encounter with the Solanae threatened to pull him into a more confrontational direction.

"I'm calling a ceasefire until we can clarify this situation," she told him. "It's not like *Titan* is in any shape for combat operations." Vale turned away to address Keru once more. "Ranul, I need you and Zurin to open a line of communication with these beings. Find someone in authority, tell them we want to parley."

"We'll try, sir," Keru replied, the buzz of static growing louder with each word. *"But I don't know if we will—"* His voice finally dissolved into a howling gale of interference.

"Can you get him back?" Sarai was asking, but any reply the XO might have received was lost in the strident sound of an alert tone from Pazlar's console.

Riker's hands tightened on the arms of his chair, anticipating another vicious salvo of plasma fire from the comet; but the threat to come was something far worse.

"Internal sensors warning!" called Melora. "Multiple spatial rupture events are opening and closing on all decks! Tetryon particle surges . . ."

Without warning, a gauzy shimmer of eerie light crackled into existence near the starboard bulkhead of the bridge, growing quickly into a jagged-edged tear. A ripple of invisible force poured out of the fast-forming rift and resonated across the compartment, knocking the unwary off their feet. Static charge crackled over the glossy black surfaces of the ship's multi-function panels, and there was a sickening lurch, as if *Titan*'s gravity matrix had been turned by ninety degrees.

Riker's body shifted; suddenly the starboard wall was the floor and the deck under his feet felt like a steep, sheer cliff face. The automatic restraints in his chair snaked over his torso to hold him in place.

Alien luminosity, a color of warped light that he remembered all too clearly, bled out of the rift as it grew into a defined opening ringed by cloudy streaks of energy. For all its presence, the phenomena was strangely quiet. *Almost dream-like.*

It was the same portal that years before had dragged him from his cabin on the *Enterprise*-D. He remembered it opening at the foot of his bed, the strange pull on his body as ghostly lines of intensity picked him up and stole him away. The memory was vivid, so powerful that it robbed him of his breath.

Then the moment was gone and time was moving again for Riker. He heard Vale cry out as a figure stumbled off the floor and tumbled head over heels toward the yawning rift.

Sarai. With nothing to grab on to, the first officer lost her footing, and the portal took her. Riker instinctively bolted forward to reach out for her, but the autorestraints snagged him and forced him firmly back into the chair.

Dalit Sarai did not scream as she was taken, did not even speak. One second she was there, less than a meter from Riker's outstretched fingertips; and the next she was swallowed up by the rift. Like a light switching off, the phenomenon vanished with a fizz of displaced energy, and the disorienting effects went with it.

A chilling silence swept across the bridge as the crew struggled to process what had just taken place. But Will Riker's thoughts were dragged away to a dark place deep in his own mind. A place of echoing horror.

The exact manner in which Betazoid psionic ability operated was a mystery to him, as it was to most who studied the unique talents of Deanna Troi's people. But what Riker did know was that years of being connected to her on intimate emotional and physical planes had given them both a kind of ephemeral bond that he neither doubted nor tried too hard to understand.

And so Riker's breath caught in his throat as he realized that he could no longer feel the steady empathic presence of his wife aboard the ship.

Twelve

"All spatial rifts have closed." Pazlar was ashen as she reported the ship's status. "Without the shields or the graviton pulse to deflect any incursion, the Solanae were free to launch a direct assault on us. Instead of taking the whole ship, they employed the same methods of abduction they had in the past, just on a different scale." She paused, letting that sink in. "For the record, I confirmed the quantum signature of the portals. A subspace energy level of sixteen-point-two keV."

"How . . ." Vale's throat went dry, and she had to swallow hard before she could ask the question. "How many did they take?"

"Thirty-seven beings." The answer came from Ranul Keru's deputy, Ensign Kuu'iut, who stood at the security station. The Betelgeusian's expression was sorrowful. "They were all abducted in the same manner as Commander Sarai."

When Admiral Riker spoke, it was in a dead voice

that Vale had never heard from him before. "How many civilians?"

Kuu'iut couldn't meet Riker's eyes, and he shot a troubled look toward Tuvok before returning to the inventory of names before him. "Nine. Most of them were children from one of the ship's schools." Vale heard Aili Lavena choke off a sob as the ensign forced himself to go on. "Admiral Riker, sir, your wife and daughter are among those listed as missing. Commander Tuvok, your partner also is on the list. I'm very sorry."

"I understand." In that moment, Tuvok was more controlled than the captain had ever seen him to be. Riker, by contrast, was on the verge of open fury.

Before Vale could say anything to him, the admiral turned to the tactical officer. "I am immediately authorizing the activation and deployment of four photon torpedoes, to be transported aboard the comet nucleus as static weapons. I want the Solanae to see them, Tuvok. I want them to know that they've pushed us to this—"

"Admiral," Vale began, speaking over him, "we do not want to escalate this any further."

Riker's eyes flashed as he turned to her, and for one moment she thought he was going to explode with anger. But the admiral's voice stayed level and firm, even as his gaze bored into her. If anything, that seemed worse. "Escalate?" he repeated. "So far, all we have done is take hit after hit from these beings. And now they're kidnapping our people right in front of us! If they won't talk to us, the threat of force may be the only tool we can use!"

"Four torpedoes detonated inside the comet nucleus would be enough to crack it open like an egg," she replied. "You want to operate on a policy of mutually assured destruction?"

"If it gets us results, I won't flinch from it."

Those words did not sound like the Will Riker that Christine Vale knew, and she almost said that out loud, catching herself before she did. Mentally, she took a step back. *What is he feeling right now?* She could barely grasp the notion of what emotional turmoil the admiral was experiencing: a terror from the man's past coming back to haunt him in the worst possible way, by stealing the people he held most precious.

She could tell him to stand down. Cite regulations, tell Riker that he was clearly emotionally compromised by the events unfolding around them. But Vale knew that if that statement left her mouth, she might never be able to call it back. To do so would run the risk of breaking something fundamental in the relationship they shared, as officers, as crewmates . . . and as friends.

She took a breath and chose a different path. "Mister Tuvok, belay that order. We will *not* deploy any munitions to the comet. That is a tactic of desperation."

"This seems like a desperate hour to me!" Riker's voice was low and cold, and now she knew they were on the edges of it.

The moment, she told herself, *where he will push back.* Riker had only to invoke the power his flag rank granted him, and Vale would be reduced to the role she had served as his executive over the past few years, captain's rank or not.

"I am *Titan*'s commanding officer," she stated firmly, "and the decision is mine. Unless you wish to contest that, sir?"

He wanted to. Vale could see it in him, and at the end it was only the strength of the trust between the two of them that prevented Riker from challenging her. "You had better be right about this, Chris," he said quietly, so only she could hear him.

But the truth was, she wasn't sure that she *was* right, and the cold rush that thought brought to her was sobering. *This is command,* said a voice in the back of her mind. *This is what it means to sit in the big seat. Do what you think is right. But be ready to accept that you could be wrong.*

Vale turned away, schooling her expression as she glanced at the woman at the engineering station. "McCreedy, if we can't have shields, at least find us a way to maintain a graviton envelope around the ship to prevent any more portals from forming." She looked away. "And someone reestablish contact with the away team. I want to talk to Keru, right now."

When the nightmares had been the worst, in the weeks after that first encounter with the Solanae aboard the *Enterprise*, Troi had listened to those affected by the abductions as part of her duties as ship's counselor. Sariel Rager, Geordi La Forge, Worf and Will—she had listened to them all and helped them as best she could to banish the terrors the experience left behind. It had not been a complete success. The mind was hard to predict, and the behavior of those touched deeply by something traumatic could not be precisely mapped. Poor Angelina Kaminer, one of *Enterprise*'s contingent of civilians, had not been able to deal with the dreams that followed. Troi recalled that the woman had broken off an engagement with the engineering officer who had brought her to the starship and returned home to Deneva for more intensive psychiatric treatment.

Empathy made Deanna Troi a superlative counselor, but it also made her part of the dilemma. The half-Betazoid experienced echoes of the emotions of all the people she supported, and sometimes it was hard to disengage. On some level, her husband had never truly been able to let go of that incident, instead making it part of himself. He dealt with it in his own way, assimilating the trauma without letting it dominate his life like Kaminer had. But ever since they had learned that the Solanae were returning, Troi had been afraid that Will's old scars would reopen. More than anything, she wanted to be with him, together with Tasha.

She held her daughter tight, sensing the girl's directionless panic bubbling away beneath the surface, and did her best to project a feeling of safety. There was fear all around them, an ocean of it made up of different currents spilling from different minds. Some dark and deep, others cold and shallow.

Troi opened her eyes and looked around. A chamber made out of shadows ranged away from walls and ceiling invisible in the half-dark, but still oppressively close. The wide space was similar in size to *Titan*'s shuttlebay, and it was filled with frightened people. She saw rangy Dinac in shipsuits huddling together in hushed gatherings and dozens of people in the gray-shouldered black tunics of Starfleet uniforms. *Survivors,* she thought. *Prisoners.* One did not need to be a telepath to make that determination. The oppressive air of desperation in the chamber made it clear to all.

Tasha was half-asleep and fretful, so Troi moved carefully until she was in a sitting position, without disturbing her child. She took a breath of stale air and tried to remember how she had gotten here. There was no recall of the actual moment of transition, only a cold-hot shock that had rippled over her flesh. Her skin prickled with sense-memory.

I was in the day school when the alert sounded. The children were afraid. T'Pel had attempted to calm them with a simple rhyme-song, but it didn't work. She had entered the room, intent on offering a helping hand. *And then the rift opened. The deck seemed to tip up and away from me.*

There had been screaming from the children, first as they watched their Vulcan tutor stumble and fall headlong into the widening fissure cut through the air; and then worse as the young ones themselves lost their grip and went after her in ones and twos. *I had Tasha's hand. She was being pulled from me, and I felt her slipping.* Troi had tried to hold on, gripping the leg of a mounted table as a support.

It was not enough. With a cry so heartrending it seemed to cut Troi to the core, Tasha was pulled away and she fell into the hissing, crackling rift. *I didn't think. I just released my grip on the table. I could not let her go alone.*

The portal drew her in and then there had been blackness. Until now.

"Commander Troi," said a soft voice, and she turned to see T'Pel crouching beside her. The Vulcan spoke in a whisper. "How do you feel? I will fetch Doctor Shull if you require medical attention."

"No . . . I'm all right." Troi blinked. "How did I get here? How long was I unconscious? Where are the others?" She caught sight of another familiar face as Ensign Waen walked past, her gaze locked on some unseen faraway place. A cold chill settled on Troi. "How many of us are there here?"

T'Pel answered her questions one after the other, without emphasis or embellishment. "You were deposited in this chamber through an energy annulus, as was I and the children. They are close by; I have gathered them and kept them as comfortable as possible. You have been unconscious for approximately two-point-three hours. I decided to place you and Tasha together until you awoke. Along with the three of us, Commander Sarai has located thirty-three other abductees from the *Titan*."

"She's here too?" There were a lot more people in Starfleet uniforms in the chamber, and now Troi's thoughts were catching up with her. "Wait. You said a name: Shull? The doctor from the *Whitetree*?" The counselor had scrutinized the other ship's crew manifest as part of her preparations for any rescue operations, and now she was looking at the strangers around her, trying to place them.

"Correct, Commander," said T'Pel. "We have been incarcerated alongside the people *Titan* was searching for. The explorer crew from Casroc are also here."

Troi paused, taking that in. "Who is the ranking officer present?"

A faint frown crossed the teacher's face. "There have been several deaths since the *Whitetree* crew arrived. Their command staff are either missing or dead. You and Commander Sarai currently represent the most senior Starfleet representatives in this group."

"Missing?" She eyed T'Pel. "So some of the *Whitetree*'s crew were not brought here?"

"No," T'Pel said gravely. "I am saying that they were all brought here, and some of them have been killed by our captors in the interim." She looked away. "You should speak to Lieutenant Ythiss. He can explain in greater detail."

Troi nodded, turning over that grim fact in her mind. "All right. Just let me wake my daughter first. I don't want her to come round and think that she's alone here."

They materialized between a trio of pattern enhancers set up on the rough-hewn floor of the cavern. Dakal had set them up to assist in bringing Vale and Riker across from the *Titan* without the same ill effects the away team had experienced on their arrival, but still the transport effect seemed to take longer than usual to deposit them inside the cometary nucleus.

At Vale's side, Lieutenant Ssura paused and took a panting breath. He seemed a little woozy but quickly shook it off. Vale felt the same slight sense of dislocation, of upset to her senses.

The fourth person in the group of new arrivals was tactical officer Lieutenant Pava Ek'Noor sh'Aqabaa, who had joined them on the insistence of Commander Tuvok. The Vulcan was now in command of the *Titan* while Vale and Riker were off-ship, and he had argued firmly against allowing two high-ranking officers to depart the vessel at the same time. With Sarai missing, Tuvok stated flatly that it was foolish to put both the captain and the admiral in harm's way.

But this was not a situation where logic or regulations were going to win the day. Christine had absolutely no doubt that Will would have demoted her on the spot if she tried to force him to remain behind; and she would react with similar ire if he had done the same.

After the conversation on the bridge, the tension between the two of them had not lessened. It was something new for the pair of them to be on either side of a situation and, most important, to be in opposing positions of power over it. Vale reluctantly admitted to herself that she could not predict how things were going to unfold from here. She could only trust in her own instincts, and in the hope the good man that she knew Will Riker to be would not get lost in the stresses he was under.

Pava glanced around. She was the only one of them carrying a phaser, and on Vale's orders it remained holstered. "Look at this place. It's huge."

"This is just one cavern," said Keru, beckoning them from the transport site. "There's a dozen more just like it."

Riker glanced at the Trill and then toward Lieutenant Dakal. "You've seen them?"

The Cardassian nodded. "We visited a couple of other chambers. The interior layouts are much the same as this one, mostly living spaces and life support mechanisms."

"But no weapons?" pressed the admiral. "No offensive systems?"

"I didn't see anything like that, sir," Dakal replied.

"It might all be on the surface," offered Ssura. "Part of that unusual skin-material coating the nucleus."

"How are they even *here*?" Riker wondered aloud. "They shouldn't be able to survive."

"Here they come." Pava forestalled any more conversation with a jut of her chin. The Andorian's antennae lowered as a group of figures approached.

Sortollo and Dennisar led a trio of hooded beings up the shallow rise to the transport site. Like Keru, the two security men had their rifles on straps across their shoulders, but Vale knew that they could have them drawn and firing in an instant. She hoped that wouldn't have to happen.

Vale sensed Riker stiffen as the aliens approached, each of them reaching up to roll back their hoods and reveal their scaled faces. The Solanae's aspects suggested some odd mixture of aquatic or insect ancestry in their genetic makeup, and the fusion of traits was just one more piece of *wrongness* about the whole environment around them.

"I've calibrated the universal translator as well as I can," Dakal explained. "It was difficult at first to convince them to speak to us. I think they thought we had come to kill their young." That idea clearly troubled the Cardassian.

One of the aliens spoke, and the peculiar snap-clicking of its speech made the hairs on the back of Vale's neck stand up. Looking them in the eye, she suddenly had a much better understanding of what Riker and Rager had been carrying around with them for the last decade and a half.

The translator picked up the words and rendered them into broken English. "We will not surrender to you. We will make battle until we are all the dead and the ash."

Vale shot Keru a look, then back to the aliens. "We did not come here for battle. We came to find our people, who have gone missing."

"What have you done with them?" Riker snapped. "You took prisoners, abducted them without warning or provocation. Return them to us now, and we can end this peacefully."

The aliens exchanged quick-fire bursts of clicks that the translator couldn't parse, then the one that had spoken before went on. "You think you know who we are. You are not correct. We do not have anything that belongs to you. We want you to go away. Leave us alone."

"That's not going to happen," Vale told them. "Not until we have some answers." She advanced a step, and the aliens huddled closer together, as if they expected an attack. She gestured around at the ice-rock walls, careful not to make any sudden movements. "This is not your home. You have come to our space, our universe, from your own. That might be seen as an invasion. A prelude to battle."

"No," clicked the creature. "No no no. We are not invaders. We are—" The translator dropped out for a split second as the device struggled to find the relevant term to explain the alien concept. "We are exiles. We are escapees. Fled here. To this place."

"Fled *what*?" Keru said, under his breath.

Riker was shaking his head. "I do not believe you. Your kind have reached into our universe before, you've taken people and deliberately hurt them. Killed them, even. I witnessed that firsthand. Now you've brought countless numbers of your kind here, for reasons we can only guess at! How can we take you at your word?"

The Solanae fell silent for a long moment, then one of the others cocked its head and clacked its stubby, beak-like mouth. "We do not have your people here. We have taken no one." The translator gave this one a more feminine tone, picking up on the fact that it was nominally a different gender from the other two.

"Then why did you attack our ship?" demanded the admiral.

"You came to us in mode of war," she retorted. "Weapons engorged with power. Energy armor at strength.

We know your kind hate and fear us. What were we to think?"

"You ignored our attempts to communicate," Riker went on.

"Untruth!" snapped the first Solanae. "No words were spoken, none were heard."

"Admiral, if I may?" Dakal held up a hand. "Like transporter technology, I don't think the Solanae have subspace communications. It's entirely possible they use a completely different system from us."

"They never heard us," Vale reflected. "Just saw us coming, ready to throw down." She fixed the aliens with a firm gaze. "We don't want warfare, but we will give battle if we are forced to it. We do not want that to be what happens here. No one has to die today. I believe that is what you want as well."

"It is," said the female. "But how can we reach that end without mutual trust?"

Riker folded his arms. "Your defensive technology creates a warping effect all through this comet mass. It's blocking the full range of our sensors. Allow our ship to conduct a deep scan of this nucleus, and we will know for certain in moments if any of our missing people are being held prisoner."

"You would have us lower the protective membrane around the Refuge?" The Solanae who had been silent now spoke up. "Without it we have no shelter! Your vessel will be able to attack us with impunity!"

"Believe me," Pava added, "if we wanted to destroy this place, we could do so as easily as we transported ourselves here."

There was another burst of rapid-fire snaps and clicks from the Solanae, and it was immediately clear to Vale by the animated jerks of their heads and the motions of their claws that they were in disagreement over what was being discussed. And then, in what seemed like a very human gesture, the smaller alien male grabbed the arm of the other male to stop him but was shrugged off.

"You give us no choice," said the first Solanae. He pulled at the collar of his gunmetal-colored robe, and Vale saw a rod-like device there—some kind of communicator. He spoke a string of clicks into it, and an alarm tone sounded across the interior of the cavern. "Conduct your scan," continued the alien, "but do it swiftly."

An atonal alarm—no doubt a warning that the defensive system was off-line—echoed all around them. "They did it." Dakal blinked at his tricorder. "They shut down the membrane field."

"*Titan*, scan for life signs," Riker snapped.

A strange hissing sound rose up from all around, setting Vale's teeth on edge. For a moment, she couldn't be sure of what it was she was hearing; but then she realized the three Solanae were all making the same noise. It was an utterance of raw fear, some shared cry of terror among all the aliens as they waited for what they thought would be their end. It horrified her to think that the sound around them was the collective voices of all the Solanae in this cavern, all suffering at once. "Stop," she demanded. "*Stop it!* Restore the membrane!"

The lead Solanae managed a few words into his communicator, and then the barrier was restored.

Vale blinked and shot a look at Riker. "Was that enough?" she said, unable to keep an accusatory tone from her words.

Keru answered for the admiral: "We'll soon see."

"*Tuvok to Away Team.*" The answer came quickly.

"*Commander Pazlar reports that a deep-penetration scan of the nucleus was completed. Aside from crew members dispatched after* Titan*'s arrival here, we detect no non-Solanae beings on or in the vicinity of the comet.*"

Riker's poker face remained unchanged. "What about technology capable of generating subspace portals, like the ones that appeared on our ship?"

"*Such technology would be difficult to conceal, Admiral. There is no evidence of anything matching that profile.*"

Pava's hand was close to her phaser. She didn't seem happy with what she was hearing. "Then maybe they sent our people somewhere else." She glared at the Solanae. "Is that what you did? Took children, like yours, and sent them into subspace?"

"No!" clicked the female Solanae. "That idea is abhorrent!"

"What else must we do to convince you?" The first of the alien group, who seemed weaker after the momentary loss of the protective field, gestured at them. "We have only defended ourselves. We have not attacked you without provocation."

"I am willing to accept that *you*"—Riker pointed at the aliens—"that you may have had no hand in taking our people. But your species, what we call the Solanae: They *did*."

"Yes," said the female, her head bowed in what could only be regret. "On that matter, we finally find something to agree upon."

The aliens took them to an open space, an arena-like place built into a wide platform that extended out from the inner wall of the great cavern. It reminded Zurin of ruins he had seen in his youth, of Cardassia's ancient Hebitan amphitheaters where long-lost plays had been performed before live audiences. *Do these beings have something similar in their culture?* he wondered. But the more he saw of this so-called Refuge, the more Zurin was getting the impression that this place was not a colony that had been built with care and attention to detail. No, it had the air of something that had been thrown together using whatever was at hand. The alien settlement had a make-do-and-mend quality to it that suggested it had been established in a hurry. *They said they came here because they were fleeing from something.* He reflected on what that might mean.

Keru and the security team formed a discreet but nonetheless threatening perimeter around the amphitheater, while Zurin joined Ssura, Pava, Captain Vale and Admiral Riker. More small groups of wary Solanae gathered on the stepped terraces surrounding the open area in the middle, clearly there to see with their own eyes what fate was going to unfold for them.

The three beings that had come to the transport site sat across from them on ice-stone blocks. The nominal leader was the male whose name most closely translated to Kikkir. The female was called Tokiz, and the other male, smaller in stature and possibly the eldest of the group, was Xikkix.

"We call ourselves the Ciari," said the female. "We use this name to divorce ourselves from the actions and designs of others of our species, which you name as Solanae."

"The word means '*they who are sorrowful*' in our speech," explained the elder male. "It is our penance."

"You feel guilt," said Admiral Riker. His expression was rigid, unreadable. "Is this because of the harm your species has caused?"

"Yes," said Kikkir. "Understand that we are not warriors. Most of us are scientists and thinkers. We are not the invasion force that you fear. We have come to this place to live out our lives in peace and trouble no others. This choice was put upon us. Many of our number perished in our escape, many more in the time it took to perfect our Refuge and our solution."

"What does that mean, 'solution'?" said Captain Vale.

Xikkix gestured to a device he wore, mounted on an armband. On closer examination, Zurin saw that the apparatus had a reservoir half-full of a dark, oily liquid and an injector head to deliver regular doses of the fluid into the elder's flesh. "This: a biomimetic compound that moderates the decay effect of your space on our cells. Without it, we could not exist here."

"That is how they can survive the cellular energy differential," said Ssura. "A chemical supplement."

"We perfected this," Xikkix continued. "Those we left behind did not."

Zurin took a moment to scan the fluid with his tricorder. "There were similar chemical markers in the flesh of the orb-drones," he noted. "But a very crude form. Nowhere near as stable as this compound."

Riker considered that for a moment, then produced a padd on which was encoded a basic visual representation of the relationship between subspace regions, highlighting the differential zones of this universe and the realm that was the origin place of the Solanae. The admiral offered it to Kikkir, who took it gingerly. "You understand what this displays?"

"We do." Tokiz peered at the screen. "That is where we are from. This is where we fled to."

"Why did your species abduct our people?" Captain Vale leaned forward. "Not just the ones taken recently, but in the past?"

"We know well of those events," Xikkix noted. "The *experiments*." The alien's odd eyes moved strangely, each one focusing on a different member of the away team in turn. "Beings of your species profile were sampled." He indicated Vale, then swung his claw to point at Pava and then Zurin in turn. "Yours and yours also. And others."

"They took Andorians. And Cardassians?" Riker shot Dakal a questioning look.

"It's possible, sir," he admitted. "But I imagine Central Command would have buried any logs of missing ships for fear of causing a panic."

"What others?" said Vale.

"Samples from all major galactic collectives in this spatial zone," continued Xikkix. "I recall some were of a brutal warrior race, others of a species with copper-based biochemistry. Many were taken for evaluation."

"He could be talking about Klingons and Romulans," Pava said quietly.

"You did this?" Vale looked directly at the elder Solanae. "You *personally* were there when this happened?"

"I was." Xikkix cocked his head and studied Riker intently. "I recall you now. The escapee. You broke out of capture with a female sample."

"We are living, thinking beings. We were not your *samples*," Riker said, putting icy emphasis on the word.

The Solanae looked away. "Yes. Forgive me. I came

to understand that what we were doing was wrong. Too late. For that, I will forever be ashamed."

"And the reason?" Vale prompted, for the moment pushing the conversation away from the past.

"Our leaders ordered the experiments to ascertain if this dimensional space was capable of supporting our existence," continued Kikkir. "Other realms were scouted and determined to be unsuitable. Fluidic domains, even those of antimaterial structures. But this was determined to be the closest to our own, of all those our science was capable of reaching."

"How did you find us?" Riker asked, in a low voice.

"We knew of you long before we began our sampling," said Xikkix. "We had been observing you for some time." The alien glanced at Vale. "You ask *why*? Why would a species ignore all morality and do the terrible things that we did to your kind? Because we wanted to *survive*. At any cost."

Tokiz spoke again. "The subspace domain where the Solanae evolved is in a process of accelerated entropic decay. By your methods of time measurement, it will reach a point of critical collapse in less than three hundred years. The remaining energy of our origin space will be absorbed into neighboring dimensional realms, and all that we are shall vanish."

"Apart from the Solanae, no other species in our dimension achieved sentience and extra-planetary evolutionary status. In order to preserve our unique civilization, the choice was made." Xikkix gestured at the air with his claw. "A mass migration."

Zurin found himself nodding. "But you knew you would need to alter your physiology in order to exist in our dimension. To permanently change your cellular energy states to be compatible with ours." He glanced at Riker and Vale. "That's why they took people: to learn how to make themselves more like us."

"And we did it with no regard to those we injured." The elder Solanae's tone became morose. "We became callous and cruel in the act. All in the name of survival, all to find the *solution*." Xikkix looked up, and Dakal saw him staring at Riker, almost imploring him. "But that is not the worst of our crimes." He looked away, to Kikkir. "Tell them. Tell them now. They must know it all if we are to have trust."

"Tell us *what*?" growled Pava, her hand snaking toward her weapon once again.

Vale raised her hand to warn off the Andorian before she did anything that they might all regret. "Answer the question," said the captain.

"The experiments were not only so we would learn how to biologically alter ourselves," began Kikkir. "But also we could build weapons that could operate in your realm."

"The orb-drones," sniffed Keru. "We've seen them."

"Those are only a means to an end," said Tokiz. "A hunting device."

"The true weapon . . ." Kikkir paused, and he seemed afraid to go on, knowing that what he said next might incur the wrath of the *Titan*, Starfleet, perhaps of every power in this galaxy. "Knowledge of the functioning of life like yours so that it could be destroyed by viral vectors. For depopulation of worlds that we wished to claim."

A deathly chill washed over Zurin's flesh. "You are describing biogenic weapons."

Xikkix suddenly stood up, animated by his anxiety. "When we learned the end goal, we opposed it! We resisted! Such malice. It was not who we are! But fear of death changed us, made us hateful and jealous. And when we who called for sanity spoke out, we were isolated. *Terminated.*"

"We are a sad minority," added Tokiz. "What you see around you is all that remains of that group. The dissidents and their families, who tried to turn our race from the genocidal path our leaders set upon."

"At first we tried to sabotage the experiments," Kikkir went on. "We halted the abductions, for a time. But it was not enough. The decision had been made, and the time of action was coming closer . . . And so, rather than perish, we committed one last act of defiance." The Solanae stood and placed a comforting talon on the shoulder of the elder alien. "We gathered, we stole all data and research on methods of altering Solanae cellular energies. We took the secrets of manufacturing the solution, and we went into hiding, in the only place that was beyond the reach of our enemies."

"*Here*," said Vale. "You came to our universe, and closed the door behind you."

"We did not close it well enough," Tokiz snapped. "It was our hope to begin again, to perfect the solution so that we might one day grow beyond the need for it and live here in isolation. But we were always afraid."

"Afraid of *you*," said the elder Solanae. "That you would find us and punish us. Afraid of *them*." Xikkix's head drooped. "That they would push through and discover the Refuge . . . and take what they so desperately need to *invade*."

Thirteen

It was hard to walk at first. Deanna found herself drifting off true as she made her way across the chamber, picking a path through groups of people who huddled together for warmth and the meager comfort of their crewmates. T'Pel had warned her that the unusual properties of the place where they found themselves had a deleterious effect on the balance sense of some humanoid species.

She looked up at the odd, sickly illumination coming from the glowing globes in the curved ceiling above. Even that seemed strange, as if the light itself was coming to her through a filter shifting it into some unnatural wavelength.

"Commander Troi?" She heard a familiar voice and turned to find Lieutenant Ythiss beckoning her from a shadowed corner. "It *is* you! Please, over here."

"I'm glad you're alive," she told him. "When the *Whitetree* went missing, Starfleet feared the worst." Troi paused. "We found the recording you made, the tricorder."

"I am sorry we have to meet again under these circumstances." The Selayan's hooded head drooped, and he limped toward her. "I should have told you to leave us and get away. This place . . ." He paused to stifle a wet gasp. "Commander, this place is death."

He seemed fatigued, so Troi followed him down to the floor in a cross-legged settle. "T'Pel said some of your crew have died."

"I didn't know until I got here." He nodded toward one of the Dinac. "Guoapa and I were among the last to be brought through. The aliens sent their proxies to the pinnace after they had damaged it and systematically searched the craft. They wanted to make sure there were no witnesses left behind, I think."

On hearing her name spoken, the Dinac engineer-commander came over and joined them, placing her paw flat on Troi's chest in her race's manner of greeting. Troi returned the gesture.

"Ythiss speaks the truth. These monsters scooped us up like driftwood on a storm-wracked shore."

"We know these aliens as Solanae," Troi noted. "And I am afraid to say this is not the first time the Federation have encountered them." She quickly explained the incident aboard the *Enterprise*-D and the grim possibility that Solanae abductions had been taking place for years.

Guoapa made a spitting sound. "Dinac do not respond well to being cast as anyone's prey."

"None would," offered Troi. "Can you tell me more about what happened to you?"

Ythiss took his time. The events had clearly traumatized him more than he wanted to admit, his forked tongue flicking nervously in and out of his mouth as he spoke, tasting the dead air. His description of the

Whitetree's passage through the spatial rift mirrored what the *Titan* had almost been subjected to, and he went on to relay what the survivors of that ship's crew had experienced. "These Solanae . . . they herded the cadets and officers off the ship and killed anyone who showed the slightest sign of resistance. Put them all here. As I said, we were the last to arrive."

"We have tried to determine what happened to your Starfleet ship," Guoapa noted, "but no one knows. It is here, somewhere, but what these beings are doing with it . . ." She trailed off.

Troi considered that and all the troubling possibilities it represented. A Starfleet craft—even a relatively small vessel like a *Saber*-class ship—in enemy hands was a dangerous development.

"Whatever they have planned for it . . . and us . . ." Ythiss continued, "they cannot wait too long."

"What do you mean?"

Guoapa looked around suddenly, peering into the dimness, picking up on Ythiss's intentions. "I see nothing. Go. Show her."

Ythiss nodded and beckoned Troi again, this time deeper into the shadows. She followed him and saw a crumpled uniform jacket lying on the ground, which had been turned into a makeshift bundle. With care, the lieutenant unfolded the cloth and revealed a small pile of arrowhead-shaped communicator insignias and other lengths of flexible circuitry that she guessed were Dinac technology.

"The Solanae confiscated all our tools, tricorders and phasers, but they missed some of these. I've gathered as many as I can from all the survivors."

Immediately, Troi pulled her combadge and held it

in her hand, considering. "Normally, I'd say that *Titan* would be scanning for these, but if we're deep in a tertiary subspace manifold, they won't be able to track us." She handed the device to Ythiss. "You're an engineer, so I'm guessing you have a plan for these."

The Selayan managed a hiss, which was his equivalent of a chuckle. "Of course, Commander. Captain . . . I mean, *Admiral* Riker told me to always have an ace up my sleeve." He placed the combadge with the others, taking up a different one. "I have an idea. We may have enough of these to make it work, but we cannot waste time." Ythiss coughed again, putting a scaly hand to his mouth. His fingers came away marked with spots of dark fluid. "Look here," he said, covering.

As Troi watched, Ythiss took another combadge between his fingers and broke it in two with a dull snap. The metal flaked and crumbled, almost as if it were decayed.

"Molecular decoherence," announced Guoapa. "The atomic structure of the device is degrading with exposure to this subspace realm. Everything brought from our dimension to this one will eventually corrode in the same way, including your *Starship Whitetree* . . . and us."

Ythiss said nothing for a moment, but the reason for the spots of blood on his hand were suddenly clear. "The rate is not constant," he managed. "*Whitetree*'s doctor agrees with us. But eventually, we will all suffer an irreversible cellular breakdown."

"Then we had—" Troi's words turned to ash in her mouth as a sudden sense of cold, dusty *unlikeness* touched her thoughts. "I can sense something."

A moment later, a harsh alarm tone sounded through the air. "It's them!" Guoapa guided her away as Ythiss scrambled stiffly back into the gloom to hide his stock of gear.

The empathic pressure of the Solanae minds was like the draft of frigid air, and it rolled over Deanna Troi as a hexagonal panel in one of the chamber walls rumbled open.

Figures in hooded metallic robes pushed into the chamber, and groups of Starfleet cadets and Dinac techs alike scrambled to get out of their way. Some of the Solanae raised their taloned hands, and Troi saw the glow of wrist-mounted weapons there, the maws of plasma throwers crackling with ready threat. Others in the alien group came in and deposited bodies on the ground, with all the care and attention of someone tossing a piece of trash into a reclaimator. She didn't need to reach out with her empathic senses to know that the people being returned were quite dead.

One of the Solanae turned to study her, and Troi felt like a microbe being scrutinized by some aloof, indifferent scientist. She had the immediate and definite sense that these beings saw everyone in the chamber as disposable curiosities, as lesser forms of life that had little or no value. Not since she had touched the mind of a Borg drone had Troi felt such a complete and total disregard for another being. It was a kind of xenophobia, she realized, an acceptance that anything not-Solanae was inconsequential—and, thus, free to be tormented, tortured and experimented upon.

"Which of you is in command here?" She stepped forward, drawing herself up, slipping out of Guoapa's grasp before the Dinac could stop her. *The key is to make them see us as equals, not lessers,* Troi told herself. *To make them empathize.*

The nearest Solanae aimed its plasma weapon at her head, and she realized that her first attempt would not have the effect she wanted. The alien barked out a series of click-words that had the timber of a warning, but Troi stood her ground. *If we can just get them to* talk *to us . . .*

But the emotive response reflecting back at her was little more than disdain. The Solanae group exchanged more words, clacking their claws together, and then retreated back the way they had come.

The hatch slammed shut and Troi took a shaky breath, feeling sickened as the shadow of the alien minds ebbed away. "As they left . . ." she said, the words falling from her, "I think they were mocking me. Like you might laugh at an animal that tried to mimic sentient behavior."

The Dinac engineer-commander studied her. "How do you know that?" Guoapa peered closely at Troi. "And how did you know they were coming before the alarm sounded?"

"I'm part-Betazoid. An empath," she explained. "I can read the emotions of other beings, sometimes their intentions. There must be something about Solanae brain structure that makes that easier for me." Troi took a shaky breath. "Although now I wish dearly that wasn't the case."

"Do you think you could read them at a greater distance?" Ythiss asked as he approached.

"Must I?" She paused, swallowing her disgust, then nodded. "I think so. I would need to concentrate."

"Commander, that plan I spoke of? I think you could be the final element I need to make it work." He stifled another gasp and turned away.

Troi's gaze crossed the chamber, and she found T'Pel

and the children, huddling together against the horrors they had been put through.

"What do you need me to do?" she said.

"That could have gone . . . better." Vale didn't look in Riker's direction as she spoke. Instead, the captain stood with her back to the admiral, looking out of the hub's ports at the comet but not really seeing it.

Had anyone else been in the room, they might have caught the moment when Riker bristled at the other officer's tone. "We're playing the hand we've been dealt," he said. "That's all we can do."

"It's all we can do *now*," Vale replied, her tone flat. "Our options dried up pretty damn quickly when the photon torpedoes were rolled out."

Riker folded his arms. "If you're expecting me to express regret for an order I considered to be a proportional response, you're fishing in the wrong place, *Captain*."

"The key part of that statement is *your order*," Vale responded, and finally she turned around to meet Riker's gaze. "Given on *my* bridge, *Admiral*."

"An order you belayed, as I remember it." He chewed on that for a moment. "Correctly, as it turned out."

"If you think I'm going to thank you for admitting you were mistaken, it's you that's fishing wrong, or whatever the hell people do in Alaska." Vale's temper flared, and she tamped it down just as swiftly. "Bad enough I have Sarai challenging me, but you too? Is this how it is going to be from now on?"

Riker took a breath. "We've already discussed this—"

"Obviously, not to a conclusion!" she snapped back. "I

knew there was the potential for you and I to have differences of opinion after this promotion. We've been down that road before when I was your first officer, and every time we came to something like this, we found a way to meet in the middle. But things have changed now. I'll say it again: You gave me the ship. *So get out of the damn chair.*"

"Are you done?" he retorted. "Or is there more you want to get off your chest?"

"Plenty." Vale folded her arms. "I want to hear you say it. I want you to tell me the reason you almost turned some of this ship's most destructive weapons on a colony full of civilian refugees."

"They were firing on us. There was nothing to indicate they were anything other than aggressors."

"And so we meet that aggression with what? Greater force?" She stepped away from the window, toward the holotable. "Do I hear Ishan Anjar's voice echoing way out here?"

Riker's eyes narrowed. "That's a cheap shot, Captain, and you know it. You can't compare me to him. Ishan was a ruthless opportunist. I made what I thought was the right call."

"And so did Ishan, by going around the chain of command and using his authority to push through the choices he wanted. Sound familiar?"

"It's not the same!" The admiral's ire was rising now. "It's not remotely the same. If you can't see that, then you're not the woman I thought you were."

"I am the captain of this ship," Vale retorted. "When I was the first officer, I was shown respect. I'm not getting it now, sir."

He opened his mouth to say something more, then closed it again.

Vale saw it and pressed her point. "You have something to add? Go ahead. What was it you said to me when you made me XO? 'Consider yourself to have permission to speak freely at all times.' "

He opened his hands. "Are you deliberately trying to get a rise out of me? Is that what this is?"

"No." She glared at him. "This is me, pissed off with you. And pissed off with myself, because you're letting your fears about your family guide you, and I've allowed you to do it."

When Riker spoke again, ice formed on his words. "You want to think very carefully about what you say next, Captain Vale."

She gave a bitter laugh. "I'm not about to start now, Admiral Riker! The only reason that sticks in your craw is because you know I'm right."

Riker fell silent, and she knew that he was wrestling with the question she had set before him.

"I can't blame you," Vale went on. "Hell, I would be lying to you if I said I didn't feel that exact same thing myself. But I reeled it back in, and you didn't. I don't have a wife and a daughter lost out there." She pointed into the darkness beyond the ports. "Just my crew—who are the only real family I have."

"Those people on the comet . . ." Riker's voice was low and distant as he processed it all. "Would we have done the same if our roles were reversed?" He shook his head before Vale could frame a reply. "Don't bother responding to that. I know your answer. I know *my* answer." He shook his head. "Those esoteric warp drives the Dinac have built—they must have inadvertently duplicated some elements of the same effect Geordi La Forge registered on board the *Enterprise*. They drew the attention of the Solanae from subspace. We may have led the same people who took me and Sariel to the very thing they have been looking for: the Ciari dissidents, their Refuge and their damned solution." The admiral took a deep, solemn breath. "I know what we're into here. So don't second-guess me, Chris. It's beneath you. I know I overstepped."

"*Again*," she pressed, refusing to concede her point, even by a small margin. "If you're going to make a habit of it, then we are going to have a problem, Will."

"I felt them take her," he admitted. "Deanna and, somehow, Tasha too. After what I went through in the past . . . the nightmare of it . . . I don't want that for them, or for anyone else. Yes, I have a family, and it's not just my wife and my daughter, it's the one you share too."

"You had a human reaction," said the captain. "If a dog bites you, it's hard not to believe the next dog you meet won't do the same. But we have to look past that first reaction to know the difference. You taught me that."

Riker sighed. "Yes. I made a bad call and you were there to make it right. That's why you have that center seat. That's why you were my strong right arm for all the years before you earned that fourth pip on your collar."

"I don't take any pleasure in calling you on it," Vale said, her tone softening. "Believe me. There's something else you said, way back at the start when you offered me the job on *Titan*, before we kicked off with that whole business with the Romulans and Remans. You reminded me of that quote from Jonathan Archer's memoirs, the one the instructors at the Academy always trotted out: 'Being a captain is making the hard choices.' "

He nodded, automatically completing the quotation: " 'Not just once in a while, but every single day.' "

"That's where we are now. Hard choices. For you and for me." She paused. "Huh. I actually feel better after airing all that out." Then Vale eyed him. "So, are you going to pull rank on me now I've shot my mouth off?"

Despite the severity of their circumstances, a brief, wry smile pulled at the corner of Riker's lips. "You know me better than that." The tension that had clouded the air between them ebbed.

"Just checking," she noted. Vale came closer and put her hand on his arm. "We're in this together. Despite the new orders, this mission, all of it, despite all that has changed—"

"Nothing has changed," he replied. "Let's do better from here on." Riker drew himself up. "We're going to get our people home . . . and we're going to protect the ones on that colony."

The hatch to *Titan*'s sensor control compartment parted and Lieutenant Kyzak entered, tapping a padd against his thigh. He nodded to Ensign Evesh as the Tellarite female passed him on her way out. "Hey," he began, "I was told to report here by Commander Rager. Something about liaising with engineering on creating a subspace topographic plot?"

Evesh pointed a thick finger over her shoulder, into the depths of the chamber, where complex scanner rigs and control consoles sat in clusters. "Over there, sir," she told him and continued on her way.

Kyzak straightened and walked on. Thin ports ran the length of the walls, allowing him to look down on the saucer-shaped primary hull of the *Titan*. The ship's main sensor module was set above and to the aft of the saucer on thick pylons, separating it from the ship proper to cut down on interference from the vessel's other systems. "Hello there," he called. "Reporting for duty? Anyone here?" The compartment seemed empty.

Or so he thought. "Oh," said a withering voice. "Rager sent the Skagaran."

Chief Engineer Xin Ra-Havreii stood up from behind the panel he had been working at and gave Kyzak a scornful look that could have cut through sheet tritanium. The commander spoke as if he were addressing someone else, but the lieutenant had been correct in his earlier evaluation. They were quite alone.

"I'm—"

"I know why you're here," interrupted Ra-Havreii.

Kyzak held to attention for a moment, then let it slip away. "Where's everyone else?"

"On the comet, not that it's any of your business. Fell, Dakal, Torvig . . . and Commander Pazlar. They're working with the Solanae dissidents." Ra-Havreii looked him up and down and clearly didn't like what he saw. "It's important work, do you understand what that means? We're going to find a way to scan into the infinitely complicated layers of subspace and find the abductees."

Kyzak nodded. Despite the suspicion on both sides, the alien refugees had agreed to help a team from the *Titan* with their dilemma. He had no doubt it would not be easy for either group to find trust for the other, but the alternative was far worse. "And where do I come in?"

"You're a *pilot*, aren't you?" The engineer said the word like it rhymed with *moron*. "You know how to read an astrogation map."

"There's a little more to it than that."

Ra-Havreii carried on: "Captain Vale has ordered me to provide her with a detailed tactical plot of the hyper-spatial topography of this region, highlighting any zones congruent to subspace ruptures, isodynamic rifts or interphase points." He folded his arms across his chest. "Stop me if I'm getting too complicated for you to follow, or if you have trouble with the larger words."

A thin, humorless smile bloomed on Kyzak's face. "So. It's gonna be like that, is it?"

The Efrosian engineer's bushy white eyebrows rose. "Like what?"

"You're going to be a pill for this whole assignment because you decided to take a dislike to me."

To his surprise, Ra-Havreii nodded. "Then yes, it *is* going to be like that. And yes again, I *have* taken a dislike to you. I'm your superior officer. I'm allowed to do that kind of thing, Lieutenant." He took a step forward. "I'm willing to bet you get a long way on that homespun charisma of yours. It must be a shock when you come up against someone who finds the whole 'rustic North Star farmboy' routine thoroughly irritating."

"You got a problem with me, you can request someone else," Kyzak replied. "*Sir*. I'm sure I could deal with the rejection. And for the record, I grew up on a ranch, not a farm. Big difference."

"I don't like your tone," said the engineer, ignoring the suggestion. "Are you always this insubordinate to your superiors?"

Kyzak went to the console and started work, bringing up a sensor map. "Only when they are clearly a jackass."

Ra-Havreii blinked, confused for a moment. It was possible he didn't actually know what breed of animal a jackass actually was, but the inference made it clear enough. "I can have you put on report for speaking to me like that."

"Really, sir?" Kyzak didn't look up at him. "Because you've just said you already made your mind up about me, so why the heck should I make any attempt to be polite? Or, in fact, give one tinker's damn what you think of me?" He made a snorting noise. "Let's you and me just do our jobs and get this done."

"No." Ra-Havreii tapped on the keyboard, suspending the console's functions. "You're not in charge here, I am. And if I want to make you run laps around the warp nacelles, you'll do it!"

Kyzak took a breath and looked the other man in the eye. "I can see why she got tired of your attitude."

It was exactly, precisely the wrong thing to say to the Efrosian. Ra-Havreii's gold-toned cheeks darkened to coppery shades. "What do you mean?"

"That's what this is about, right?" Kyzak pressed. "Melora? She never talked about you either of the times we shared a meal, but starships are like small towns, you know? People talk. I found out pretty quick about you and the science officer."

"My relationship with Melora Pazlar is none of your business, *Lieutenant*!"

"The way I heard it? You don't *have* a relationship with Melora Pazlar. And that means you don't get to pass judgment on who she can and can't spend time with, *Commander*."

Ra-Havreii turned on that burning glare again. "So you and her, you are . . ." He lost the thread of his words.

Kyzak took a step back. "You really don't have any idea about Melora, do you? Or me, for that matter.

You're presuming a lot, sir. You think you know me, my intentions, my orientation?"

"I assumed—"

The Skagaran cut him off. "For your information, I don't limit my options, not that it's any of your business. And who I associate with off-duty has nothing to do with you!"

The engineer seemed at a rare loss for words, and Kyzak briefly felt sorry for him. After his conversation with Commander Sarai in the turbolift, he had gone back to his xeno-ethnology texts and read up on Efrosian culture. Their society wasn't big on commitments between males and females, with a casual and, some might say, off-hand approach to relationships. It was the very opposite of the way that Skagarans were raised, and Elaysians like Melora, if he read her right. Kyzak guessed that Ra-Havreii had a hard time adjusting to those differing expectations.

He picked up the padd. "You want to put me on report for speaking my mind, go ahead, it won't be the first time. But quit getting your personal life mixed up with the job. My advice to you? Move on." Kyzak gestured with the device in his hand. "I'm gonna go finish this in the aft relay bay, if that's all the same to you, sir."

Ra-Havreii waved him away, his expression stony and unreadable. "You're dismissed."

Fourteen

"Now?" Sarai eyed her, grasping the heavily modified combadge between her thumb and forefinger.

"Not yet," said Troi, leaning against the inside of the metal hatch. Another combadge, stripped and repurposed by Lieutenant Ythiss, was magnetically attached to the part of the wide door where the locking mechanism was located. "They're still close by."

She closed her eyes and made her own thoughts silent, quieting her mind. Blocking out the fear of the other prisoners, the first officer's cold focus and the steady, fretting worry of the Selayan engineer, Troi concentrated on making herself a lens for the emotions of the Solanae in the corridor outside.

That same icy contempt for us. She sensed it like black fog, swirling around her. *We are no better than animals to them. They've been conditioned to think of anything 'other' as insignificant.* Such a deep-seated disregard for life appalled her, but the counselor pushed her own reaction away. She had to *focus*. With no other way to know where their abductors were, Troi's empathic ability was the only advantage they had.

Commander Sarai did not like relying on something as ephemeral as psionic ability, and she had said so in no uncertain terms when Troi, Ythiss and Guoapa had brought the escape plan to her. But the Efrosian had to admit that they had few options open to them. To attack the Solanae when they entered the chamber, to try and overpower them and take their weapons, was a risky strategy. Some of the more hotheaded cadets from the *Whitetree* had already tried before the arrival of the *Titan* contingent, and it had not gone well. The fall-back plan—to cross-circuit some of Ythiss's salvaged gear to create an improvised energy-discharge device—was equally perilous.

Then slowly, like a tide drawing out, the unsettling sense of the Solanae presence faded, and Troi's last connection with the aliens was something like relief from them. *We disgust them. They're glad to be away from us.*

"Now?" repeated Sarai, seeing the shift in the counselor's expression.

"Now," Troi told her. "It must be a shift change in progress."

"We need to back away," Ythiss insisted. "Just in case it doesn't work."

Troi nodded and found engineer-commander Guoapa observing nearby. "I need you to keep everyone calm," she told her. "We'll be back within two hours. But if we do not—"

The Dinac held up a paw. "I understand, Commander Troi. Your bravery does you credit. I will hold the crews together. We are united in this."

"On three?" asked Ythiss, blinking his large slitted eyes.

"No," Sarai snapped, and she tapped the combadge in her hand.

There was an immediate skirl of high-pitched sound that came from the unit attached to the door, and Troi saw the metal surface vibrate. Fat sparks popped and fizzed as the modified communicator burned itself out in a controlled overload, generating a brief, powerful distortion field in the area of the hatch's magnetic lock.

Troi heard a hollow thud and the door mechanism released, sliding back a few centimeters. Quickly, Starfleet and Dinac crew members alike put their shoulders to the hatch to push it open, creating enough of a gap for a person to fit through.

Sarai was the first out, taking two of *Whitetree*'s security officers with her; Lieutenant Kelt was a Mazarite male with dark olive skin and a wolfish face, while his companion was a pale, bearded Borothan ensign named Hubose. Ythiss paused at the gap and made an exaggerated "after-you" gesture. Troi took a breath and followed the others into the corridor beyond.

Outside, she fought down the giddy shift in balance she had felt in the prison chamber and looked around, getting her bearings. The curving passageway had a low ceiling, but it was wide, broad enough that a cargo shuttle could have fit down it with room to spare. The surface had a smooth appearance, like a grown shell or a molded ceramic. Lights were sparse, set equidistant every hundred or so meters, and their illumination did not reach very far. Heavy black shadows fell between them, giving the place a peculiarly neglected feeling. Troi had a flash of childhood memory: her parents taking her to a "haunted house" at a fair. She remembered feeling small and vulnerable in those dark corridors, and the sensation returned before she could head it off.

Behind them, the hatch thudded closed again, and Sarai turned to face her. "It seems we were correct. The Solanae don't concern themselves with close surveillance of their prisoners."

"Because they think we're no threat," muttered Hubose.

"Which way, Commander?" said Ythiss.

Troi pointed to the right. "The ones guarding us went that way."

Sarai nodded to the left. "We'll go this way, then. Stay in the shadows."

Dropping into single file, the group of escapees moved on as quietly and as quickly as they dared. The corridors went on for kilometers, and without a way to reckon the passing of time, hours seemed to go by as they moved deeper into the structure.

"We should try to locate some weapons," whispered Kelt. "Find an armory."

"Find a map first," Ythiss countered. "I see very faint markings on the walls. Could be indicators, but I can't decipher them."

"Where?" Troi looked at the bare metal and saw nothing.

"The light frequency of the symbols is probably outside the register of humanoid optical acuity," continued the Selayan. "It's barely in range of mine."

"The ship is our first priority," Sarai spoke over them. "If we can find the *Whitetree*, we have a fighting chance."

Troi was about to answer when a cold chill made the skin on her arms turn to gooseflesh. "I have contact."

Sarai gestured sharply and they melted into the shadows. The commander shot Troi a look, and she in turn pointed toward another hatchway a few meters distant.

The hexagonal door was smaller than that of the holding area. After a couple of minutes, the hatch pulled back to allow a group of Solanae to exit. Some of them wore the metallic robes that seemed to be the common garb for the species, but others went bareheaded, clothed instead in heavier armor plates that resembled the same ceramic-shell material of the walls.

When the party of aliens disappeared around the curve of the corridor, Sarai gave a jerk of her hand. Troi jogged after the XO and the security officers, with Ythiss trying to keep pace, grimacing as he limped.

"Not locked," said the Selayan as he peered at the door control. Kelt tapped it with the heel of his hand and they slipped inside.

This compartment was much smaller than the holding chamber, and one whole wall was a series of slatted viewing windows. Troi instinctively drifted toward them, peering out.

Behind her, Sarai was taking in the room. Dozens of holographic screens floated at head height, each showing a different image, cycling from one to another at regular intervals. "This must be a monitoring center," she decided. "Hubose, stay close to the door in case we have company. Kelt, Ythiss, look for anything that could be useful to us."

"Do you see this?" said Troi, her eyes adjusting to the view outside.

Sarai came closer "Are we on a ship, or a planet?"

"Neither, Commander." Out past the thick viewports, black, porous rock curved away, the surface spiked with dull steel towers that projected out at all angles. Troi saw other clenched fists of dark stone connected to one another by thick brass pipes lit from within, floating in an asymmetrical sequence. "This appears to be some kind of asteroid . . ."

"More accurately, a chain of them," corrected Sarai. "Each of the rocky masses is linked to the others by those tubes. Accessways, perhaps. The overall size of this complex must be massive."

"Perhaps there are no planets as we know them in this domain?" offered Lieutenant Ythiss, catching their conversation.

Troi nodded but didn't answer. Her attention was taken not by scope of the Solanae facility but by the hue of the starscape it hung against. It was not the diamond-scattered darkness she was familiar with, not even the exotic colors of a glowing nebula or protosun nursery. The space in this domain was a lurid purple-yellow from horizon to horizon, an ill tone that reminded her of bruised skin. The unnaturalness of it stilled her voice, and if she needed proof that they had been drawn into a universe unlike their own, it was out there in that sickly, diseased sky.

"This is subspace . . ." breathed Sarai, sharing the same mix of awe and repulsion that Troi felt. "We might be the first of our kind to see this."

"Not the first," said Troi, thinking of all those the Solanae had taken for their experiments. It was an effort to pull herself away from the view.

Ythiss stood nearby, his cobra head flicking back and forth as he studied the holoscreens. "Look here." He pointed at one. It appeared to show a nightmarish rendition of an operating theater, with a cluster of hooded Solanae working at something. "What do they have?"

Troi felt Sarai's emotional aura ice over in an instant. "It would appear to be part of a human torso."

Ythiss made a crackling noise in his throat. "Oh no."

Then suddenly the image flicked away, to be replaced with a view of a sheer metal surface. Part of a familiar pennant was visible in the corner of the picture, and Troi realized that it was a Starfleet insignia. "Lieutenant, can you hold that image?"

"I'll try." Ythiss warily extended a claw into the holographic field, making it tremble. "I think it may be a gestural interface, similar to the ones we use." After a couple of false starts, the Selayan managed to draw back the focus to show a fuller view.

It was, as Troi hoped, the *U.S.S. Whitetree*—but the *Saber*-class ship was far from being intact.

Behind her, she heard Lieutenant Kelt curse under his breath. "What . . . what have they done to her?"

It seemed that the ship was sharing the same fate as her crew. The *Whitetree* had become something to be cut open, picked apart, experimented on. The basic spaceframe remained in one piece, but Troi saw where whole sections of the hull had been gouged out, leaving ragged wounds in the spade-shaped fuselage. *Whitetree*'s warp nacelles were still intact, and still aglow with low power, but the length of them was covered in a silvery mesh that resembled ivy growing over brickwork. The most visible damage to the craft was a huge hollow that had been made across the back of the ship's secondary hull. A nest of massive cables, each glowing red-orange with power, snaked out of the hole in the vessel's spine.

"They've cut right through into the engineering

spaces," Ythiss explained. "Exposed the warp core apparatus. Plugged into it."

"Plugged *what* into it?" asked Kelt.

"Expand the view," ordered Sarai, and Ythiss complied.

Drawing back the image still farther, it became clear that the captured ship was tethered inside a large crater, somewhere on one of the facility's asteroid nodes. Surrounding it in a broken halo were curved panels made of metallic fabric. The power cables cross-connected to them, and Troi got the very real sense that the energy being siphoned from the *Whitetree* was making them *grow*. "Are they solar sails?" she wondered.

"Why would they need those?" Kelt shook his head. "Can you even see any stars out there?"

"They're not for collecting energy, they're for projecting it," Sarai said, her brow furrowing. "I've seen something like this before, in intelligence documents we captured after the Dominion War . . ." She hesitated before continuing. "It is not widely known that during the conflict, the enemy attempted to construct an artificial wormhole to the Gamma Quadrant after being denied access to the Bajoran gateway . . ."

"The verteron collider," said Troi, nodding. "Yes. I was on the *Enterprise*-E when we undertook the mission to stop them."

"The Dominion considered several alternative methods before they chose the collider, Counselor," Sarai noted. "One was the controlled destabilization of a starship's warp core to force-create a subspace rift." She gestured at the panels. "Those sails are energy waveguides to shape the formation of a singularity. The configuration is almost identical."

"Oh." Ythiss nodded. "Yes. It is extremely dangerous, but, correctly focused, a warp field implosion could soften the barrier between dimensional realms. Enough to allow something from one side to push through to the other. Something very big."

A bleak thought occurred to Troi. "No. They can't survive in our space, we know that. They're not planning on coming to us, at least not yet. What if they want to bring something to them?"

"The comet colony *Titan* discovered—" began Sarai, but she never got to finish her words.

A black shadow rose in Troi's thoughts, flooding over her. "Outside!" She shouted the warning, but it was too late. She had been distracted by the portent of what they had discovered, her attention elsewhere for a moment too long.

The hatch snapped open and Hubose took a glancing plasma blast across the chest, falling with a strangled cry of pain. Five of the armor-clad Solanae boiled into the room, clattering and snapping in a vicious cacophony of noise.

Ythiss backed away from the holograph, shocked at the realization that it was probably his actions that had alerted the aliens to their presence.

The armed Solanae pointed their wrist-blasters at the Starfleet officers, with open threat in their postures and their strident tone. The nearest grabbed Kelt by the arm and yanked him hard, shoving him across the deck toward the doorway.

"Stop!" Troi held up her hands, pleading with them. "Please, just stop! If you will just—"

The Solanae that had shot Hubose made an angry rattling noise and turned its weapon on the injured

Borothan once again. The second blast was point-blank, and it killed the ensign outright. Troi felt the glow of his agony vanish like a snuffed-out candle.

Their situation was clear: *Surrender or die.*

Torvig looked up from behind the imaging device and cocked his head. "That's it. Ready to transmit."

Ranul Keru watched the interplay between the Choblik ensign and Lieutenant Dakal, who stood nearby with a tricorder. "Confirmed. It'll take a moment to prepare the holomatrix." The Cardassian tapped his combadge. "White-Blue, how are things at your end?"

"*System on-line and functioning*," came the AI's reply. Over on *Titan*'s primary holodeck, the Sentry was helping to coordinate the process.

Keru made eye contact with Dennisar and Sortollo. The two remaining members of his security detail down on the comet nucleus were silently reinforcing the orders he had given to them hours earlier. It was important to make the Solanae refugees—these "Ciari"—feel that Starfleet was not some kind of occupying army, and to that end Keru had deliberately reduced the number of boots on the ground to just three. Along with a four-person team of engineering and science specialists led by Commander Pazlar, they were all that remained of the Federation's footprint on the Refuge.

It wasn't an order Keru accepted easily, but he obeyed nonetheless. There was a part of him that looked at the Solanae dissidents and wondered how much of their story was true. If the *Titan* crew were being played in some kind of complex ruse, this could all go wrong very quickly, but more than anything, Ranul trusted in his commanding officer to make the right call. Christine Vale had told him to reel things in, and that was exactly what he had done. He hoped that the captain was right to have faith in these people. The alternative was something he didn't want to contemplate.

The deployment of the holo-imager kit was another attempt to make the Ciari feel more secure, and it had the added benefit of allowing face-to-face communication to take place without having to beam more people over. Slowly, the misgivings on both sides had given way to a wary acceptance, but it was fragile; Keru knew that the slightest misstep would throw them right back to square one. They had almost caused a panic when a few of the remote autonomous probes *Titan* had deployed days earlier returned to their mothership, coming together in a small flock to drift off the starship's port bow. Having only just granted *Titan* permission to approach the comet once more, the aliens reacted badly, fearing an attack. Ultimately, Pazlar had convinced the outspoken scientist Tokiz that no harm was meant, and both Keru and the science officer later agreed that the moment could have benefited greatly from Deanna Troi's diplomatic skills. Her absence, and that of all of the abductees, was keenly felt by everyone.

At last the cautious alliance seemed to be bearing fruit. Working side by side with Tokiz and the Ciari's nominal leader, Kikkir, Commander Pazlar's team had found a way to zero in on the zone deep in subspace where the Solanae originated from, and where all those who had been taken were now likely being held. Keru had only the basic understanding of subspace dynamics that was part of a Starfleet security officer's training, but he knew that the malleable, ever-changing structure of dimensional interfaces was difficult to map. The equivalent to finding a needle in an infinitely large haystack, to paraphrase the human saying. This shared success might be the thing that would grow the nascent trust between the two groups, if only they could turn it to their advantage.

He looked up as the Solanae trio approached. Beyond them, past the open sides of the temporary pergola set up for the away team, Keru saw more groups of refugees. Many of them were immature Solanae, huddling together, daring each other to observe this cluster of outsiders.

"They wonder why you have come," said Xikkix, the elder of the three noting the Trill's attention. "It is the way of the young. At first they were afraid. Now they are curious. We have done our best to educate them, to teach them more than our leaders wanted them to know."

"In what way?" he asked.

"The creed we were made to accept was no less than total xenophobia," he said flatly, his mouthparts clicking as the universal translator rendered them into Standard. "If a people can be made to hate that which is unlike, they can be distracted from the decay amid their own kind."

Keru found himself nodding. "A sad truth," he agreed, "one that is not limited to your civilization."

"We strive to be better," added Kikkir.

"As do the members of the United Federation of Planets." Torvig spoke up, his words at once earnest and honest.

Kikkir's eyes flicked. "I hope so."

"Let's get this under way," said Pazlar. She threw a nod to Dakal, who made an adjustment to something on his tricorder.

Suddenly, gossamer walls of light, translucent enough to see through, grew up around them. Keru recognized the structure of the inside of a holodeck. The Solanae scientists jerked in surprise, but their shock was short-lived, quickly replaced by curiosity.

"This is . . . a visual representation of the interior of your craft?" asked Tokiz.

"Part of it." Pazlar nodded. "As we see images of it, images of us are being simultaneously transmitted back to that compartment on board the *Titan*."

Hazy shapes took on solidity before them, resolving into Admiral Riker and Captain Vale. Riker gave a shallow bow. *"Hello again. I hope this form of communication is acceptable to you."*

Kikkir looked around, reaching out with one clawed hand to touch the hologram of Vale. His talon passed through her, momentarily disrupting the image. It had been Keru's suggestion to keep the holos as soft light only, to show the Ciari that the Federation was committed to keeping their presence minimal.

"An impressive technology," said the alien. "I would enjoy learning more about its functions at a future time."

"I hope we have that opportunity," said Vale. *"But for now, we have more pressing matters. Commander Pazlar informed us that you were able to isolate the dimensional spectra of your origin domain."*

"It is done," said Tokiz, with what seemed like regret. "We had hoped that we need never use our science to find that place again. On first our arrival in this space, we destroyed our transfer devices, cutting ourselves off from there. We hoped it would be forever."

"You burned your ships," Riker muttered under his breath.

"We had no intention of going back," Kikkir said firmly. "That has not changed."

"We're not asking you to do that." Peya Fell spoke up, breaking her silence. *"But we might have to."*

"Is that possible?" Riker's holo-image flickered as he turned to Pazlar. *"I know we don't have access to the same kind of 'portals' the Solanae can generate, but if we boost transporter power, can we beam someone into that dimensional space?"*

Pazlar and Dakal exchanged glances, and the Cardassian ventured the answer. "There's a reason why there's a time lag between the Solanae incursions into our space, sir." He held up his forearm at a forty-five degree angle. "There's a dimensional gradient between us and them. Energy moving from a lower-potentiality subspace realm such as the Solanae domain is like water flowing downhill. Easier to shift, but even that requires immense power output. They need a long recharge period before they can come at us again. But to go the other way . . . to go *uphill* . . ."

"From here to there," Pazlar picked up the thread. "To punch an annular confinement beam through that many dimensional layers would take more power than *Titan* could generate. And we have no way to know if a living being could even survive that journey."

Vale scowled *"So we know where our people are but we can't get to them? This is exactly what happened on board the* Enterprise." She shook her head. *"Not good enough. We've been reactive to this situation for too long. We have to take the initiative or we are lost."*

"We did destroy our dimensional transfer modules, as Tokiz stated," said Kikkir, "but we did not destroy the knowledge of their operation. We will impart this information to you. Use it to find your people and know in certainty that those who dwell on the Refuge are not your enemies."

"And of course, if we deal with the invaders, we'll be protecting your colony here as well," added Keru.

"Of course," Kikkir agreed. "Our intentions are toward self-preservation as well as altruism."

"Good that we can all be candid!" Torvig piped up hopefully.

"Admiral, Captain, I've examined the theory behind the Ciari transit," said Pazlar, "and I believe we can adapt it to our use. Ensign Torvig agrees, which means Xin will as well, if you lean on him."

"I'm sensing a 'however' coming up," Riker replied.

The Elasysian nodded. "*However*, because of the gradient effect that we mentioned, the energy we'll need to put behind a portal will be very high. We can't just tear open a doorway and push a smaller vessel through, like a shuttle or a runabout. *Titan* has to go. Only a ship of its mass and strength could possibly hope to survive the translation through the subspace layers."

Even via the ghostly hologram, Keru could see Vale visibly pale at the thought, and he shared her concerns. *"That's a big ask. How would we even initiate such a transition?"*

Pazlar looked at Torvig. "Tell them, Ensign."

The Choblik bobbed on his artificial claw-feet. "I believe the correct Terran vernacular is 'I will not coat this in sugar.'" He swallowed hard. "We would need to deliberately imbalance the warp engines to create a resonant wormhole effect in synchrony with the Ciari dimensional transfer equation. In theory, we could momentarily invert the gradient and cross the barriers between subspace realms."

Riker voiced the question they all were dreading: *"And if it goes wrong?"*

"There are a multiplicity of potential outcomes," Torvig offered. "The most likely is that the ship will be torn apart by spatial stresses. The next most likely is that it will become lost in *n*-dimensional space. The next—"

"Enough, Ensign, we get the idea," said Vale, silencing him with a wave. *"One last question, then: Are we sure this is the only way?"*

Keru looked around as each member of the science and engineering team gave a nod. Dennisar and Sortollo met the security chief's gaze, and while neither of them said a word, the question on the faces of the Orion and Terran was identical: *Are they crazy?*

"All right," said Vale. *"Then we do it. Pack up your stuff and get back to the ship. Start work on preparing the warp engines for . . . whatever it is you have to do to them."* The captain gave a shallow bow to the three aliens. *"You have our thanks."*

"There is one matter I would like to address before we conclude." The older of the Ciari dissidents stepped forward, approaching the hologram of Riker. "May I be granted permission to visit you on your craft before you set off?" Xikkix stared at the admiral, waiting expectantly for an answer.

"Why?" Riker's reply was blunt.

"I wish to converse with you, Admiral," Xikkix said flatly. "In private."

Keru couldn't read the other man's expression. *That bloody poker face of his,* he thought.

But at length, Riker gave a sharp nod. *"All right.*

Ensign Torvig, make it happen." The hologram faded before any more could be said.

He dismissed Lieutenant Ssura, and presently Admiral Riker waited alone in the hub, watching the motion of the Refuge through space. The spectacle of the gleaming, haloed comet mass and the ghostly pennant of its tail briefly took his mind off the present crisis. Riker let the wonder of it take him in, but the moment was brittle and soon fractured.

He heard the door whisper open and turned, bowing slightly in greeting as the elderly Solanae scientist was escorted into the room. Riker caught a questioning glance from Ensign Hriss, the Caitian security guard who had guided the alien up from the transporter room, and he shook his head, dismissing him.

"Your matter-transit device is a clever technology," said the alien, noting Riker's attention. "Like your image-communications system. You have many such machines. Yours is an advanced people."

"No more than the Solanae, I would guess," Riker replied. "After all, you came to our space across dimensions, not just spans of interstellar distance. That is very impressive."

Xikkix cocked his scaly head. "Shall we dispense with these diplomatic niceties, Admiral? I compliment you, you compliment me." His words were soft clatters of bone beneath the synthetic voice of the universal translator. "I have little time left. I am weary of such things."

"Very well. I too appreciate the value of directness."

The Solanae moved to the ports. "Such a vista. It is so unlike the sky beneath which I was hatched." Xikkix's black, depthless eyes studied him. "I did not think you would grant me this opportunity. To come here and speak with you."

Even as gentle as Xikkix's speech was, the irregular click-patterns of the words still put Riker's teeth on edge. He belatedly realized that, on some level, he was *afraid* of this wizened, aged being, even though the Solanae posed no physical threat to him. Once more, the ghost of old trauma pressed down upon him and it would not retreat. "So talk," said Riker.

"You suspect I came here to apologize to you," Xikkix went on. "You are wrong. I will do nothing of the sort." He raised a bony talon to point. "Am I guilty of doing terrible things to innocent beings? *Yes*. Do I deeply regret it? Does it live with me each day? *Yes* and *yes*." The Solanae leaned closer. "Would I do it all again? *Absolutely.* Because I believed it was the only way."

Riker fought off the compulsion to lean back as the alien's face hovered a few inches from his own. "Why are you telling me this?"

"You and I were there, Riker. You understand. You saw that room of horrors and you remember clearly what happened in that place. When we took you. What we did to you." Xikkix reached out and pinched the flesh of Riker's arm through his uniform tunic.

He willed himself not to react. "You severed my arm and then reattached it. What possible reason did you have to do that?" The question rolled out of him.

"We did it because we could!" Xikkix's eyes were unblinking and cold. "Because we wanted to see what would happen! We had only a basic grasp of your anatomy. It was how we learned if you felt pain, how long you would take to die, or how intelligent you were . . ."

Riker's lips thinned and he banished the dark churn of negative emotions inside him. "You could have asked us for help. If what you say is right, that your space is decaying, we would have listened to you."

"The Solanae would never accept charity from aliens!" Xikkix looked away. "We have always taken what we want. I learned too late that attribute was going to doom us. Now I am very old and my time is at an end. And all I wish for is to know that my species will not die away, disintegrated in some arbitrary cosmic shift that none will witness. I want a legacy for my people." He prodded Riker in the chest. "I am not here in atonement, do you see? I committed atrocities in the name of survival. I think you have also seen the edges of that great and consuming darkness as well, Riker."

He nodded. "There was a war, a few years ago—one in a line of several we endured over the past few decades—but the worst of them. Billions dead and planets burned to ash. If you're asking me what it means to wonder if your whole civilization might be ended, then yes, I understand."

Xikkix's head bobbed, and Riker saw that he was attempting the human gesture of a nod. "I am very old," he repeated, "and so tired. I have given all that I can, transferred my knowledge to Kikkir and the others. Now I want only to be certain that the Ciari are what will remain of the Solanae. They are the kernel of all that is good in my species. I want your oath that they will live, Riker. On the lives of your mate and your brood."

It came to Riker then, the meaning of this meeting.

The elder Solanae had come to him not because he was seeking forgiveness, but because he wanted to *confess*. And in some twisted way, Xikkix had never been able to find forgiveness with one of his own kind. He could only speak this truth to someone like Riker: a victim of all that he had done. "You have my word," said the admiral. "The refugees are under Starfleet's protection."

Xikkix released a long, low rattle. "I believe you," he said. "And so it is ended. Now I pay for what I have done." Before Riker realized what the alien was doing, the aged Solanae scientist reached up and pulled at the drug-injector armband he wore. It snapped off in his clawed grip and went dark, spilling out a jet of the fluid solution.

"No!" Riker went to grab him, but Xikkix was already falling to the deck, his body twitching in shock, his dark eyes turning milky white.

"Yes," managed the alien. "This is my choice. Yes."

The admiral shouted at the intercom. "Sickbay to the hub! Medical emergency!"

But even as the words left his mouth, Riker knew it would not matter. Xikkix had come to *Titan* because he wanted to do this, and the Solanae had known that to remove the armband would mean certain death.

Riker stepped back, angry and sorrowful at the waste of life behind the gesture, and found Ssura at the door following the medical team into the cabin. "What happened, sir?" said the Caitian, his eyes wide with shock.

"He asked me to make a promise," Riker replied.

Fifteen

"I expected them to kill us," said Sarai, her voice flat and without inflection.

Troi ignored the flicker of irritation that statement brought up in her and nodded toward the body wrapped in a donated uniform tunic. "They *did* kill one of us. Hubose."

Sarai shook her head and gestured around the holding area at the rest of the prisoners. "More than just one," she clarified. "Instead, they searched our prison, took away Lieutenant Ythiss's cache of equipment and left us untouched. Which, one could argue, may be a kind of death sentence."

The failure of their escape plan had frustrated Troi, and now the first officer's dour commentary was chafing on her. "Optimism doesn't feature very strongly in your lexicon, does it?"

Sarai gave her a strange look and actually allowed a humorless bark of laughter to escape her lips. "With all due respect, Counselor Troi, don't talk about me as if you know me." It was only the two of them here, standing some distance away from the rest of the group. After the escape party had been dragged back with poor Hubose's body, the scattered knots of Dinac, *Whitetree* and *Titan* crew members had been galvanized to come together in a gesture of unified self-protection. It was only Sarai who had insisted on standing alone.

"I really don't like your kind, it has to be said," offered the Efrosian woman.

"Betazoids?"

"Mind-readers," she corrected.

Troi clasped her hands together. "I'm familiar with that kind of reaction from some people. The fear that your personal thoughts are open to others. But I wouldn't expect it from you. Your species has telepathic potentiality. Efrosian females express operant empathic senses."

"My abilities are of poor focus and very limited range," Sarai shot back. Troi resisted the opportunity to make a barbed comment about the first officer's lack of empathy and said nothing. "That's why Lieutenant Ythiss wanted your help and not mine," Sarai continued, shaking her head. "But you're not following me. I was a field operative for Starfleet Intelligence before I went to liaison duties at Command, and now to *Titan*. Your kind—or, if you insist, *our kind*—are always trouble. It's hard to be a spy around those who can see through any legend you put up. But at least *I* could sense when they realized I was lying."

"A legend," Troi repeated. "That's what they call a cover identity in the espionage community, isn't it? Because it is a mythology about someone. A fiction interwoven with elements of truth."

"I know that look." Sarai studied her. "You're wondering how much of me is counterfeit, aren't you?"

"Now who is reading whom?" countered Troi. "I can't see your thoughts, Commander Sarai. Like you, I can only sense emotional states, and not much of yours at that. You've been trained to be highly guarded."

"I know what you are capable of, telepathically," Sarai noted. "I have a much higher security clearance than you, so I had access to almost all of your personal file." Troi couldn't help but show a moment of surprise at that, but Sarai was still speaking. "Don't worry, I didn't single you out. I read up on every member of the senior staff, as much as I could learn. Starfleet Intelligence has a lot to say about *Titan* and the beings aboard it." She paused. "I'm reading an emotion you're experiencing right now, Counselor. How does it feels when someone is prying into your life?"

Troi tried a different tack, her tone hardening. "You seem quite determined to be unlikable. That's a trait we could do without at this moment."

"How unfortunate for us." Sarai gestured around again, making it clear she meant "all of us here" with that statement. "I wasn't assigned to Vale's command to make friends or become a part of *Titan*'s extended family." Sarai couldn't hide the mocking emphasis she put on the last two words. "I was given this role because I am expected to do a job. I don't have to be everyone's boon companion to accomplish that."

"True," Troi allowed, "but it wouldn't hurt to be less detached from your crew."

"So enlightening," Sarai snapped, turning her back, clearly meaning none of it. "You've given me much to think about."

"I read a lot of your file too," Troi retorted.

Sarai made that dismissive snort again. "I rather doubt that."

"I know about the friendly fire incident on the colony. The Bolian child who died. The reason you were taken off active duty with SI."

The first officer stiffened. "Do you really think that this is an efficient use of your time at this moment, Troi? Why don't we just accept that we have seen some of the things each other would prefer not to discuss, and leave it at that? Unless of course you consider devising a method of escape for these people less important than your impromptu psychoanalysis of me."

"It would be very easy for me to make it an order." Troi matched the other woman's mordant tone. "I'm sure Captain Vale and Doctor Ree would accept my insistence that the first officer attend a mandatory counseling session each week. And as you are someone who so clearly has a *renewed* dedication to following regulations, you would be there." Troi sensed the last words hit home. Sarai's record was marred by the black marks of insubordinate conduct, most recently when she stepped outside the chain of command during the Bacco crisis. If the first officer wanted her career in Starfleet to continue, that was something she couldn't risk again.

When Sarai finally turned back to look at Troi, it was as if the mask had slipped for a moment and the counselor was getting a brief look at the person beneath, the conflict and the complexity therein. But before she could read deeper into that instant of vulnerability, it was gone, and Troi wondered if she had just imagined it.

"I want Ensign Hubose to be the last person to perish in this alien pit," Sarai said firmly. "And right now, anything that isn't a step toward making that happen is worthless to me. So help me or go look after your daughter, or do whatever will aid us. And when we are home safe, you and I can debate what we see in each other's heads until entropy."

She walked away, leaving Troi with more questions than she had begun with.

"We can do it," said Pazlar.

"Affirmative." Standing next to the science officer in the middle of the bridge, White-Blue's holographic form gestured with a virtual manipulator. "Digital modeling of the forced collapse event is within expected parameters. I/We have supplied the final warp matrix program to Chief Engineer Ra-Havreii."

"How did he take that?" said Vale, frowning.

"Not well," offered Lieutenant McCreedy. "I think he may have actually thrown something at me. I didn't stick around to find out." The engineering officer patted her console. "I've input the data. Along with the shield modulations programmed by Commander Tuvok, we should be able to make it."

"Should," echoed Vale.

At her side, Admiral Riker sat resting his chin on his hand, his gaze distant. He didn't add any comment of his own, and the captain guessed that he was still processing what had taken place in the hub. The suicide of the Solanae scientist had shaken them all.

Vale sighed. "Then we're doing this. Make no mistake, the order I am about to give will put this vessel and this crew in harm's way. We've gone to strange and distant places before now, seen things no one else had seen. But once that wormhole effect is triggered, *Titan* will go to somewhere that is truly alien to all of us. We will be entering a realm unlike anything ever encountered before. We have no certainty that we will make it back." She stood up. "I have faith in Melora and White-Blue's computations, but I won't speak for everyone. This will be a strictly volunteer mission. I won't think any less of anyone who wants to stand down."

"Captain, I . . ." There was a tremor in Ensign Polan's voice as he broke the silence that followed.

"It's all right, Klace." Vale shook her head. "You can remain behind."

"Thank you." The Catullan's face colored and he stepped away from the secondary science console and exited the bridge, unwilling to look the others in the eye.

"Anyone else?" Her gaze went around the room and finally alighted on Riker.

The admiral blinked as he realized she was looking at him. "I'm coming along."

"You really shouldn't," Vale told him. "Starfleet Command will have me in front of a board of inquiry for putting a flag officer in unnecessary jeopardy."

For a moment, it seemed as if Riker was going to pull rank on her, but then he shook his head. "Captain, this is your ship and your command. I'll remain behind if you think that is best. I will follow whatever orders you give."

"Thank you, Admiral. On reflection, I think it would be foolish for me not to have your experience and insight to call upon. I'd be honored if you'd take on Commander Sarai's bridge duties until we can recover her and the other abductees."

Riker smiled slightly. "I haven't served as a first officer for a while. I may be a little rusty."

"I'll make allowances . . . Number One." Vale looked up and saw the rest of her crew looking on expectantly.

No one else had followed Polan off the bridge. "I appreciate your support, all of you. Contact your divisions and pass on the order. Volunteers only. Prep the ship for skeleton crew operations."

"Interrogative," began White-Blue. "What of the civilians and nonessential crew? *Titan*'s auxiliary vessels will not be able to accommodate them all."

"We can launch the escape pods too," offered Rager. "Program them to gather in gaggle mode and cluster with the shuttles."

A chime from the tactical station sounded, and Tuvok spoke up. "Captain, that may not be required. I am receiving a message from the Refuge. The Ciari are hailing us with an offer of assistance."

Vale and Riker exchanged glances. The last contact between the ship and the dissidents on the comet had been somber, repatriating the body of the scientist Xikkix. Christine had been afraid that the aliens would blame Riker for the death of the elder, but they accepted it with a stoic calm, as if it had been expected. "Onscreen, Commander," she said.

The main viewscreen switched from an exterior view of space to an image of the Refuge's interior. Pazlar had left a portable subspace transceiver behind on the comet nucleus, so that any future communications could avoid the mistakes made on *Titan*'s first approach. Kikkir and Tokiz were visible through the crackles of interference. Having spent some time in their company, Vale was now able to clearly differentiate between the elements of Solanae facial structure, and she saw that both of them were now wearing lines of white coloration over their cheekridges. *Something to indicate mourning*? she wondered.

"On behalf of myself and my crew, let me once more

express my regret about these events." She addressed them both.

Tokiz gestured with a talon wrapped in cloth. *"Xikkix chose his manner of ending, as is his right. No fault lies with you."*

Kikkir rolled back his hood and looked directly into the monitor. *"And now, we watch as you, beings whom we feared would wish to end* us, *voyage forth to prevent that ending. It has been discussed, Captain Vale, and decided among us. We must do more than merely provide you with the path to follow. There is shelter here too, if you wish it for your kind."*

"We will understand if you refuse," added Tokiz. *"This trust between us is still not set."*

It seemed like it had been days since Vale had felt anything like hope, that emotion replaced in her by a dogged determination to win—but now it returned in the offer of sanctuary from a race of beings that by many lights should have been their enemies. "Your offer is very generous," she told them. "And we accept it with gratitude. Our people will come to the Refuge. Together, you can wait out the storm." Vale gave a smile. "Thank you. Commander Tuvok will arrange the details."

"Voyage well, Captain Vale," said Kikkir. *"We will await your safe return."*

The screen snapped back to the exterior view, and Keru took a step down to Vale's side. He spoke quietly. "We're trusting them? I should go over there with the civilians, just in case—"

Vale shook her head. "I want you here when we go toe to toe with the Solanae. Send Pava to keep watch. But I'm telling you and you're going to tell her: Those beings over there are not our adversaries. They're reaching out to us and we're not going to turn away from them. Clear?"

"Crystal, sir," he replied. "I had to ask."

Riker made a thoughtful noise in the back of his throat. "You might just have put us on the road to a peaceful resolution to something that's dogged Starfleet . . . and me . . . for decades."

"I hope so," Vale told him.

"Does your species believe in life after death?"

The question wasn't the one Torvig had been expecting. He was up to his snout in the complex strings of warp matrix equations being programmed into *Titan*'s engine subsystems, the two cybernetic hands on the ends of his paws and the additional one at the end of his tail all clattering back and forth over the master control console as he performed the final pre-initiation checks. He glanced over at Commander Ra-Havreii, who hovered nearby with an expectant look on his bearded face.

"Well?" prompted the Efrosian. "Do they?"

Torvig took a breath. "Um. Not as many species do. On my world, we revere Those Who Came Before, the beings who touched our species and uplifted us to true sentience in the Great Upgrade, but we do not believe in some kind of metaphysical afterlife." He nodded toward a stocky young Bajoran from the Valo II colony. "Crewman Yakoj has spoken to me in the past of his belief in the Prophets, perhaps you should ask him—"

"When you are dead, you are gone," Ra-Havreii said bluntly, and Torvig understood that the engineer wasn't really interested in the Bajoran's point of view, or the

Choblik's for that matter. "The important thing is to minimize the number of regrets you have when you get there."

It was not the first time that Torvig had found himself speaking to his commanding officer and experiencing a conversation that seemed to be utterly unrelated to what was actually being said. Ra-Havreii was idiosyncratic in that regard, the ensign reflected, and often difficult to read. "Good advice, sir," he offered. "Meanwhile, I just need to complete the input of this matrix segment, and—"

"You're not done yet?" Ra-Havreii cut him off again. "Less talking and more working!" He snorted and stalked away, barking out orders to the Rossinis.

"What was that about?" Torvig's colleague Mordecai Crandall paused in his own preparations nearby.

"I honestly do not know," Torvig told him. "I think that might have been what you humans call a 'pep talk.' "

"Really?" Crandall's eyes widened. "Well, then he's doing it wrong."

An alert chimed and the other engineer looked back at his panel. "Message from White-Blue. All but one of the transwarp probes have been brought back aboard. He's exloading his persona matrix from the holodeck buffers into the remaining unit."

Torvig's ears flicked back in concern. The Sentry had offered to take up position as a "pilot ship" to lead the *Titan* into the spatial rift they were about to create, on the assumption that his AI cortex would be able to process navigation data faster than Lavena and Rager on the bridge. In the past, large waterborne vessels would follow a small pilot craft as they approached a shoreline, with the latter helmed by someone intimately familiar with the hidden banks and currents of a shallow passage. White-Blue would fulfill the same role for the starship.

It was a sensible precaution—but Torvig could not help but be afraid for his friend's well-being. If anything went wrong, the probe carrying White-Blue's consciousness would be destroyed and there would be no way to recover him.

Of course, if that happened, it was likely the *Titan* would suffer the same fate a few seconds later, so there would be little time for Torvig to have the regrets that Ra-Havreii spoke of.

"Attention, all decks, all divisions. This is the captain speaking." Vale's crisp tones issued out of the intercom, and everyone paused to listen. The only other sound was the steady thrumming pulse of the warp core, so familiar to Torvig that he hardly even noticed it anymore. *"All nonessential personnel have now been put off the ship. We're clear of the comet and in open space. In the next few moments we will do something extremely risky, but we will come through it intact. I have the utmost faith in this crew, as you must have in one another."* She hesitated, and it was as if everyone on the ship held their breath. *"Let's bring our people home."*

The pulse of the core quickened as more power went to the engines, and on his screen Torvig saw the green indicator that showed a good telemetry connection between *Titan* and White-Blue's consciousness inside the pilot probe.

"Come on, then!" shouted Ra-Havreii, his voice carrying across the width of main engineering. "You heard the captain! Let's go ahead and deliberately break the bloody warp drive!"

"Triggering imbalance effect in five. Four. Three." Torvig's throat went dry, but he maintained the countdown. "Two. One. *Mark.*"

Out ahead of the starship, at the leading edge of the warp field effect bleeding out of *Titan*'s nacelles, the needle shape of the probe moved like an insect skating across the surface tension of a pond. It pressed into the boundaries of the reality-bending energy matrix that pushed starships beyond light velocity, finding the point of maximum dynamic resistance.

Data streamed through the probe's sensor grid, cascades of numbers passing into and out of White-Blue's complex neural net. He sifted them like grains of sand, feeding back vital information to the *Luna*-class ship at his stern, showing them the peaks and troughs of the warp effect as it began to slip away from true toward something far more chaotic.

It came on like the formation of a gargantuan hurricane in the skies of some gas giant. Space itself rippled as the warp field interacted with it, in a manner that was never meant to occur. Faster-than-light travel was always a war against the laws of physics, a brief match where clever science would overrule the nature of things for a time—but in the end, the unbreakable rules of reality would win out. Those rules could be bent but never broken.

But here and now, they came close to it. The warp field tore free of its controlled formation and the wormhole opened to swallow them whole. White-Blue felt a sensation across his probe-body's skin that he could not parse—if he were an organic, he might have said he was giddy, disoriented, bewildered—and then he was in the mouth of it, falling though space that was not-space. The probe dropped into the gap between realities and left the universe behind.

He remembered his mission and rode the pulsing waves of distortion as an avian might skate over thermals, sending back picosecond bursts of navigational data to the *Titan* as she followed him in. The Sentry upped his clock speed to near maximum, accelerating his perception of events so that time on human scales seemed glacially slow, but still it was a challenge to maintain control of his course. Behind the probe, the starship rose on waves of glittering, distorted radiation and the wormhole mouth irised shut. They were committed now, willingly projecting themselves out of synchrony with their own universe and into the infinite realms of subspace.

Interdimensional space was vast beyond reckoning, an unending foam of universes, pocket realms and cosms that could never be completely mapped. White-Blue's sensor grids tasted the impossibilities of them, sounding into the deeps in search of the origin place of the Solanae. It was out there somewhere, easily distant enough that he—and the ship he guided—could get lost along the way. He processed the concern over that outcome for a moment. A single vector estimate out of place, a decimal point miscalculated, and they could emerge in Fluidic Space, a Chaotic Void or worse, some vastly different quantum parallel where nature worked on different rules and life like them could simply not exist. For all the awe and wonder White-Blue experienced as he piloted them through the maelstrom, he processed a fear-analogue too. Somewhere in this unending array of layered universes large and small was also the domain that was home to the Null, the monstrous protomatter life-form his AI species had been created to defend against. The prospect of meeting that mindless force once again made the Sentry afraid.

He shunted the negative process behind that thought to a redundant buffer and concentrated on the matter before him. The shearing effect equation given to the *Titan* crew by the Ciari dissidents was working. The resistance against probe and starship was still strong, but not enough to stop them from making headway. Moment by moment, they dropped deeper into the tertiary manifolds of subspace, protected only by the hazed membranes of powerful deflector fields. *Titan* was moving with him, still on course, still holding steady.

White-Blue experienced satisfaction. It pleased the AI to have a way in which he could contribute to the mission. In his time on board the vessel, in all his forms, his neural pathways had configured to appreciate the presence of the organics who crewed the ship. He felt a kinship with them that surprised him, sharing the emotional response to the abduction of some of their number. The Sentry might not have been part of their Starfleet or even shared any similarity in nature to them, but he still considered these people his friends; and so he shared this danger with William-Riker, Christine-Vale and all the others.

The tunnel of distorted orange light rolled around them, the crackling input of data still threatening to overwhelm White-Blue's processors as it washed over him. He wished that he could read it and know it all, wondering what kind of secrets the cosmos hid down here, beneath the weave of the multiversal fabric. But it was all going by too fast, and he had more pressing issues to deal with. Ripples of unknown fire buffeted the probe and the starship, storms of particles so exotic and charmed it was impossible to observe them from outside this interspace. Dimensional membranes concealing other infinite layers of nested universes swept by, great bubbles that might have been home to entire civilizations. But those were not the reason they had come.

At 16.2 keV on the human scale of measurement, a macrodimensional cosm existed where the unstable compound called solanagen could fuse into proteins to create the building blocks of life. They were closing on it now, storming across a sea of unknowns and shrieking alien fire. Pressures beyond the tolerances of the probe's hull piled high upon it, and White-Blue registered exterior panels buckling, sensor clusters going dead. The transdimensional wormhole was constricting, trying to reject them. Arcs of golden lightning as wide as solar disks crossed the path of the probe and the starship. Telemetry feeding back from the *Titan* showed a similar story; the organics' ship was suffering the terrible bombardment just as White-Blue was. The hazardous passage was punishing them alike for daring to venture beyond their home realities.

16 keV. A monitor module threaded the information to the probe's memory core. 16.03 . . . 16.07 . . . 16.14 . . .

Close now. The far end of the projected wormhole was yawning open, presenting the first glimpses of a strange purple-yellow sky. White-Blue dialed down his clock speed, easing himself back toward a human-scale tempo. The entire journey had taken only seconds from their point of view, but for the AI it felt like eons.

16.20 keV. He reported the transition back to the *Titan* and with a blinding, shuddering, sickening shock, the travelers exploded out of the dying wormhole and came crashing into existence inside the realm of the Solanae.

Immediately, the probe's systems went into a kind of spasm as they fought to adjust to an alien reality where the laws of nature were slightly off true. Gravitation, light, matter, all were infinitesimally shifted in this place, and White-Blue's synthetic mind was confused. The probe reeled drunkenly, the microwarp engines sputtering and dying.

Titan seemed to be suffering the same malaise as well, but somebody on the bridge had the presence of mind to put out a tractor beam and reel White-Blue's machine-body in. Still, the ray of force kept losing coherence as it tried to operate in a realm for which it was not calibrated.

The automatic self-diagnostic White-Blue triggered on arrival here concluded with dozens of error readings, but his sensors were still active. And so, the AI's program registered the approach of a swarm of craft detaching themselves from what appeared to be a chain of asteroidal objects a few light-seconds distant.

The swarm was made of dense rocks, each moving with a fusion torch motor behind it. More asteroids, the Sentry surmised, likely hollowed out, pressurized and turned into spacefaring vessels. They drew nearer, and it became clear that their intent was not benign.

Streamers of fiery plasma spat from their irregular prows and lashed over *Titan*'s hull in whipping arcs. Black streaks of damage were left in their wake.

The tractor beam pulled him into the secondary shuttlebay along the leading edge of the starship's saucer. The last observation White-Blue made before vanishing inside was the disturbing manner in which return fire from *Titan*'s phasers dissipated into a harmless glittering haze before it got anywhere near the asteroid-craft.

Sixteen

For one brief instant, a wave of crippling nausea broke over the bridge crew, and Tuvok felt himself gripped by a crawling, prickly agony that reached deep into his flesh and bones.

It was the alien nature of the Solanae space, the altered physics of the subdimension reaching out to attack the *Titan* and her crew. Left unchecked, it would have eaten into them like a corrosive, breaking apart the molecular bonds of everything that had come from their home universe. But the moment had been prepared for: Within seconds of reverting from the wormhole transit, a preprogrammed macro on Tuvok's console activated a low-level dampening field that enveloped the ship, resisting the effects of the space around them.

Straightening, Tuvok heard Captain Vale curse under her breath. "Feels like my skin was boiling off me," she muttered. "That must be what it is like for an unprotected Solanae in our dimension . . ."

Lieutenant McCreedy called out, her urgent warning ending the discussion. "Captain, we've got a problem here. Warp power is failing. It's the interference effect disrupting the matrix."

"Getting the same readings from White-Blue's probe," added Rager at ops. "He's adrift."

Admiral Riker was getting to his feet, still a little unsteady from the transition. "Let's get him back here."

"I'm having difficulty locking on with a tractor beam," Lavena reported. "Give me a moment." She muttered something low and terse that was lost in the bubbling of her drysuit's water breather. "Wait, no. I've got him. Sir, the beam keeps fading in and out. It's hard to compensate."

"The subspace effect again," said Pazlar, turning from her console. "It's degrading all our systems. We'll have to work against it while we're here."

"Do your best, Aili," Riker told her.

"First things first: Program our escape course in case we have to blast out of subspace in a hurry." Vale snapped out the orders. "Then I want a high-intensity scan of the surrounding area."

"Already on it," Pazlar replied. "I'm reading what looks like the *Whitetree*'s transponder beacon inside an unidentified construct. We're close."

"Some luck, then," began Riker. "What do we have?"

"On-screen." Pazlar migrated the display to the bridge's main viewer, and the crew fell silent as the alien vista was revealed to them. Space unlike anything Tuvok had ever glimpsed—outside of an impressionist's surreal artwork—filled the screen.

He glanced down, looking at the repeater showing the same sensor readings the science officer was looking at.

"Contacts in quadrant two," he noted. "Congruent to the location of the *Whitetree*'s beacon. An artificial structure made up of large rock fragments and heavy-grade metals. Perhaps remnants of a small moon or other space body."

The Vulcan kept his mind on the matter at hand, but it was impossible for him not to ask the question that had been gnawing at him since the mass abduction that had taken place aboard the *Titan* several hours earlier: *Is T'Pel aboard that facility?* After losing his son and daughter-in-law in recent years, Tuvok had been forced to reevaluate the elements of his personal life and address the issue of what was most important to him.

He had left Starfleet behind in the past, but the choice had never sat well with him. Eventually, Tuvok had returned to the vocation that suited him best, what a human might have colloquially described as his "calling." Here, in his role as the *Starship Titan*'s second officer, he had found the same level of satisfaction that service under Captains Sulu and Janeway had given him. Vulcans did not believe in such illogical concepts as fate or destiny, but if there were such a force acting upon Tuvok, then it was served best by his being here, *now*. But that meant bringing his wife with him, for after all that had happened he could not again sacrifice his marriage on the altar of his duty. *Had that choice been the correct one to make*? he wondered. Now T'Pel's life was in grave danger, and he was partly responsible for putting her there. Tuvok wondered what his wife would say about that, if she could speak to him at this moment. She would not admonish him; T'Pel would tell him to do his duty. She would trust him. *She and the others trust us all to bring them home.*

"An asteroid outpost," Riker was gesturing at the construct on the main screen.

Tuvok returned to the moment at hand and nodded his agreement, but then the sensor sweep changed to an alert configuration. "New data," said the Vulcan. "I am now reading multiple targets leaving the outpost and proceeding on approach vectors toward the *Titan*."

On the main viewscreen, dots of glittering black obsidian moved, propelled on plumes of crimson fire. "Captain," warned Rager from ops, "that looks like an attack posture to me."

"I concur," said Tuvok.

Vale didn't need to hear any more. "Aili, get White-Blue's probe back on board right now! Tuvok, shields."

He nodded. "Deflectors active, but power levels are low. Once again, the subspace background effect is interfering with normal operations." He paused. "Weapons, Captain?"

Vale and Riker exchanged glances. "Hold on that, for the moment, Let's see what their intentions are first."

"Confirming three life signs aboard each craft. Solanagen-based physiology." Pazlar let that sink in. They were about to come face-to-face with the Solanae in their own territory. "Not conventional ships," she went on. "The hulls are irregular, made out of dense nickel-iron ore."

"They're throwing rocks at us?" Vale raised an eyebrow. "Can we make contact with them somehow? If our normal comms don't work, then—" She broke off as a sudden flare of light at the tip of the nearest asteroid-ship turned into a discharge of sun-hot plasma fire.

The first hit spent a good percentage of its power on the shields, but it was still potent enough to burn across the outer hull. *Titan* shuddered beneath the impact.

"I think that makes their purpose clear," said Riker. "They have to know who and what we are, Captain."

"And if so, that means they know why we're here." Vale clutched at the arms of her chair as another streak of plasma impacted the hull. "So much for talking." She looked up at Tuvok. "We'll give them one last chance to deescalate. Commander, I want a full phaser spread across their bows. Show them what they're dealing with."

"Aye, Captain." He tapped out the command, bringing *Titan*'s weapons array to bear. Even though there were a dozen of the small, irregular alien craft, the starship's firepower was more than enough to annihilate thc Solanae interceptors several times over. Captain Vale's tactics were sound: A show of force might get the aliens to stand down, perhaps even be enough to encourage them to turn over the abductees without more loss of life. "Firing *now*."

But the moment he tapped the activation pad on his console, the Vulcan knew something was wrong. The energy flow rates, the discharge pattern—they were all out of synchrony. Instead of a steady and coherent burst of phased energy, the shots fired from *Titan*'s emitters were feeble streaks of faltering color that barely made it a few thousand meters before they dissipated into harmless light.

"What the hell?" Riker saw it in the way the beams faded. "That was barely a shot at all!"

"Phaser collimation is not reacting as it should." Tuvok's hands flashed over his panel as he tried to remodulate the energy signature of the weapons. "Range is severely effected. Point-to-target discharge is significantly weakened."

"Can we compensate?" *Titan* shuddered again and again as Vale threw him the question.

His reply was terse. "Negative. The efficiency of our primary weapons has been greatly reduced, Captain. We will need to seek an alternative offensive strategy."

Vale's lips thinned. "Lavena, back us off." She paused. "All right, we'll go to torpedoes then."

"I would strongly urge you not to do that!" Pazlar called out. "The ambient spatial readings I'm seeing here are far more intense than I expected. If we fire a photon or quantum torpedo, the moment the warhead passes out beyond the effect of our protective disruption field, it will be affected by the subspace differential."

"And we don't know how that would play out," said Riker, grimacing. "It could detonate right on top of us!"

"Options, people," demanded Vale. "We didn't come here just to have our butts kicked the moment we arrived." She turned in her chair to look at her engineering officer. "Karen, can we rig portable field emitters to the torpedo casings? Make them stable enough to deploy?"

McCreedy hesitated, thinking it through. "That could work. I'll get on it, but it'll take some time."

"They're coming around for another pass," said Lavena. "A formation attack pattern."

Tuvok saw Riker's jaw set. "They think they've got the measure of us. And without our usual tactical advantages, they may be right."

"Then I guess we'll have to innovate." As Vale said the words, *Titan* shook as streaks of fire punched into the primary and secondary hulls.

"Major hull breaches on decks five, fourteen and fifteen," Tuvok reported. "Uncontrolled plasma discharge on deck eight, closing conduits. Structural integrity is holding. Vented sections are autosealing." He didn't need to add that had the ship's full complement been aboard, those breaches would have been immediately fatal to dozens of the crew. "Deflectors are below optimal strength but holding."

"For now," Riker added. "Captain, perhaps if we make a speed run in toward the asteroid outpost, we might be able to leave these interceptors in the dust."

"But not for long," she countered. "We've got maneuverability on them, but they have the numbers."

Tuvok listened to the exchange and studied his display, a plan forming in his mind. "Captain, I may have a possible solution. But it will require a large amount of ship's power."

"We can divert life support from all the unmanned areas of the ship," said Riker.

"I have factored that in," Tuvok continued. "It will also require the energy currently powering our deflectors as well."

Vale studied him, considering. "We barely have them now anyway. Let's hear it, Commander."

He took a breath. "It will necessitate simultaneous remote command of all cargo and man-rated transporter systems throughout the ship. Some assistance may be required."

The captain didn't hesitate. She tapped her combadge. "Bridge to Transporter Chief Radowski. Bowan, get up here on the double. We need you!"

The six Solanae craft descended once again on the intruder vessel in a turning flock. Passing around each other to confuse any targeting systems the Federation ship might be using, the rock-hulled interceptors pivoted on their fusion drives and spat more whips of plasmatic fire at the bigger vessel. Their orders were to punish the outworlders for daring to sully this domain with their presence, to harry the ship until it was worn out and broken. Destruction of the bigger craft was already approved by the Solanae command cadre, but that outcome would be bettered if they could beat the intruder into submission. If the ship could be hobbled and then *taken*—that would be a victory of great value.

The Solanae already had one outworlder craft in their possession. To have *two*, even if the second were badly damaged—that triumph could only serve to underline what the leaders had been telling their people all along: that these extradimensional beings were weak and fit only to be the quarry of the Solanae race.

Closing the distance, the interceptor crews each chose their next target. Data gathered by orb-drones and previous abductions had given them good intelligence on the design and structure of these Federation vessels. They would break into teams, two attacking the large drive nacelles slung under the hull of the intruder ship, and the third seeking out the wide cupola atop the vessel where the invaders housed their control center. They would at once cripple the ship and kill off its brain, making it a simple matter to board and occupy. The terminal phase of the attack began, weapons seething with power as the plasma projectors cycled up to fire.

Then, without warning, the interceptor pair on the outer edge of the formation were suddenly enveloped in a glittering haze of particles, a brilliant white glow that flared and faded, taking the stone ships with it. The interceptors were *gone*, wiped from existence as if they had never been.

Shock rippled through the crews of the other four craft and they hastily aborted their attack runs—but they were already being tracked, as sensors locked onto their mass and form. Two more craft went the same way as the first pair, caught in a shimmering effect that removed them from space. The last remaining duo broke formation and poured full power to their thrusters, cutting spiraling courses through the livid space in hopes of avoiding the same fate as their cohorts—and they failed, as the *Titan* turned on them, keeping pace. One by one, they were snared by the flicker of dematerialization and pulled out of solidity.

The Federation ship came about in a hard turn and headed in toward the chain of asteroids.

"Caught them all!" cried Radowski. "Fish in a barrel, yeah!" A grin split the engineer's face, but it slipped off when he saw the steady, unchanging expression of Commander Tuvok looking back at him. He swallowed, pulling back his enthusiasm a few notches. "Sorry. I'm just glad I could help."

Vale patted him on the shoulder. "Good work, Lieutenant."

The eyebrow Tuvok raised at Radowski's enthusiastic outburst settled back and he scanned his console. "No indication of other vessels being launched. Those six craft may have been their entire defensive force."

"Pattern buffers are operating normally," reported McCreedy. "The transporters are now locked in the interim beaming cycle. Which means we're not going to be able to use them until we release the interceptor ships."

Vale glanced at Radowski, inviting him to comment.

"Commander Tuvok's plan to use the transporters to dematerialize those alien ships was risky but inspired," he offered. "Now we've got them, we can hold their patterns in the system for maybe ten hours before they start to degrade, as long as shipboard power levels remain constant. But Lieutenant McCreedy's right, they're tying up the whole system. *Titan*'s transporters were not designed to handle so many objects of that mass at once."

"There is another option," said the Vulcan, and Vale knew what it was before he said it. "If we reverse the materialization cycle, we can set the patterns to wide-beam dispersal as we did when we removed the orb-drone infestation."

"Destroying those ships and their crews," Radowski broke in. "That seems too harsh."

"They *were* trying to kill us," said McCreedy. "In fact, they were trying *very* hard."

Vale met the transporter chief's gaze. "I'm sure they wouldn't extend us the same courtesy. But for now, keep them bottled up." She glanced at the main viewscreen and the asteroid complex. "They have our people, now we have some of theirs. Maybe we can work out an exchange of prisoners." But one look toward Admiral Riker told her he believed that the Solanae were unlikely to take up such an offer.

"Captain, we're being scanned by the outpost," called Pazlar. Vale turned and strode down from the aft of the bridge to the science station. "I'm detecting plasma nodes like the one we saw on the comet, but smaller. If we approach, they're going to fire on us."

"No surprise there," Vale replied. "What about the abductees? Anything?"

The science officer brought up a digital rendering of the oddly proportioned asteroid base. She highlighted an area on one of the large sections. "It's difficult to get consistent life sign readings at this range, but there's definitely a group in this section here with nonsolanagen biology. How many, I can't say. The scanners can't decide if there are ten or ten thousand."

"But that's most likely where our people are." Vale nodded to herself. "So we start there. Take them back by force if we have to."

"At this stage, that's pretty much a given," said Riker. "And the *Whitetree*? Is it in there, is it intact?"

"Not exactly." Pazlar shook her head. "White-Blue ran a correlation process on the scans from his probe's sensors and ours. There is what appears to be a large bay some distance away from the holding area, and that's where the transponder is located. White-Blue managed to get a partial scan that tallies with our detection of starship-grade hull metals." She brought up another image on her display. "Look at this."

Vale recognized a wire-frame graphic representation of a *Saber*-class starship, but festooned with strange pieces of machinery she couldn't identify. "They've done something to the *Whitetree*."

"A few of the readings coming from the asteroid facility were confusing me until I saw White-Blue's data. Captain, we're detecting decay particles and bleed effects from an active, unshielded warp core." Pazlar tapped the display. "*Whitetree*'s matter-antimatter stack has been exposed, and they're running it hot. I hesitate to guess at *why*, because every possible answer to that question is very unpleasant."

"And then some," said Vale, thinking it through. Attempting to dismantle a live warp core could lead to a matter-antimatter annihilation explosion at the very least; at worst, the creation of a subspace fissure. "We need to get in there and shut that down."

"So, two teams?" suggested Riker. "We take the largest cargo shuttle we have, strip it down to the bare metal and send it in to get as many abductees out as possible. At the same time, a smaller shuttle with a security and engineering detail to neutralize the *Whitetree*'s warp core."

"Do you believe the other ship can be recovered, Admiral?" asked Tuvok.

"We've got to try," said Riker.

"Good plan." Vale gave a sharp nod, turning back to Pazlar. "Melora, get below and have Commander Keru and Chief Dennisar meet you in the main shuttlebay. Prep the *Monk* for launch, bring our people home."

"Aye, Captain. We'll make as much room on board as we can." She turned and made for the lower turbolift.

Vale dropped back into the center seat and tapped the intercom panel. "This is the captain. Lieutenants Dakal, Kyzak and Sortollo, Ensign Bolaji, report to shuttlebay one for immediate deployment aboard the *Horne*. Commander Pazlar will have your orders. Vale out."

Riker took the seat next to her. "We take *Titan* in, draw the fire from the plasma nodes to cover the approach of the shuttles."

She nodded. "It's right out of the Will Riker playbook. Do you like it?"

"I'll like it a lot when it works."

"You said *when*, not *if*. That's a good sign."

He sighed. "Right now, optimism seems to be the only thing around here that is working properly."

The shuttlebay door opened to reveal the ill colors of the strange space surrounding the *Titan*. Pazlar hesitated, peering at it with part scientific curiosity, part discomfort.

"Coming through!" Chief Petty Officer Dennisar bumped her shoulder as he came down *Monk*'s rear ramp, effortlessly carrying three crew chairs in his broad arms. He dumped them to one side of the cargo shuttle, near a pile of other removable panels, and blew out a breath. "That's all we can strip out without pulling up deck plates, sir," he told her. "Commander Keru says we're ready to go."

"All right. Double-check the dampening field before we set off. We lose that out there and this mission will be over before it starts." She paused and looked over at the *Horne* as Dennisar moved away to follow her orders. The smaller *Flyer*-class ship was sleek and quick-looking in comparison to the big and bulky Type-9A shuttle, like an ancient roadster parked alongside a freighter. The other ship's in-line warp nacelles were already glowing, and through the cockpit canopy she could see Olivia Bolaji in the pilot's chair, making last-second checks. The ensign caught sight of her and gave a thumbs-up. Pazlar nodded back, and she bent to scoop up the small mission pack she was taking with her; inside was a medical kit and mix of other gear that might come in useful.

Horne's engines hummed and the ship floated up off the deck on its antigravs, waiting for *Monk* to lead the way. Pazlar turned and put a foot on the cargo shuttle's drop ramp just as a voice called out her name. She couldn't stop herself from frowning.

"I'm glad I caught you." Xin Ra-Havreii jogged up to the shuttle and paused, breathing hard. He must have run all the way from main engineering.

"What's wrong?" she asked. For a second, she expected him to insist on coming with them. That was just the kind of hasty decision he would make in order to impress her. Once upon a time, it might have worked.

But instead he shook his head. "Nothing. I . . . I just wanted to tell you something before you go." He nodded toward the open hatch, the vacuum beyond held out by a glowing wall of force. "Be safe." Xin scowled the moment the words left his mouth. "*Ach.* Listen to me. I sound like some addled youth. I'm making a fool of myself!"

She folded her arms. "Xin, this isn't really the right place—"

"Isn't it? You're going into harm's way, we're all in grave bloody danger, stuck in a place that will kill us just for being here. Suddenly, I am understanding that things I've taken for granted . . ."

Just for a moment, the tone in his words made her heart soften. But then she remembered why she had chosen to end their association, and it passed. "Better late than never."

"I have heard it said." He shot a look at the other ship, then back to her. "In case anything happens, if the last words between us were cross ones, Lora, I could not live with that." Xin sighed. "You were right about us. I just didn't want to admit it. We both have to move on." He looked away again. "I'm sorry I couldn't have been better at this. I can fix a lot of things, it seems, but *I* am still a work in progress."

"I didn't mean to hurt you," she offered.

"But you did, and I deserved it, and now I'm growing because of it. That's progress." He reached up and touched her on the arm. "Don't take any wild chances out there. Just come back alive, all right?" He stepped back from the idling shuttle and waved her away. "Go, go. I've wasted enough of your time as it is!"

She nodded her farewell and continued up the ramp, hearing it hiss closed behind her. The *Monk* lifted off the deck and Pazlar ran through the wide, empty cargo compartment and into the cockpit. Slipping easily into the copilot's seat, she watched as Keru guided them out and into open space.

"Okay back there?" he asked, without taking his eyes off the controls.

"I think we will be," she replied.

Titan led the approach to the Solanae asteroid base with a fast pass at high impulse, deliberately offering the plasma nodes on the surface a tempting target at which to fire. The autonomic weapons systems operated just like the ones they had encountered on the Ciari Refuge, bombarding the vessel with fat globules of accelerated star-stuff. But this time, *Titan*'s crew knew what to expect and they could anticipate the patterns of attack. Still, the starship took a few direct hits, and it powered away trailing a pennant of spilled gasses behind it.

But the run served its purpose. Concealed in the ion wake of the *Titan*, *Horne* and *Monk* threaded a swift path through bursts of plasmatic fire, and at the last second, they peeled off from under the bigger ship's sensor shadow, veering away from one another. Too close for the emplaced weapon nodes to target them, the slow cargo shuttle dropped down low to follow the line of the asteroid's surface, while the faster *Horne* wove a complex, jinking pattern in the opposite direction.

Lieutenant Kyzak's last glimpse of the *Monk* was as the other craft passed behind a pinnacle of obsidian-black stone and vanished around the curve of the planetesimal. He swung back just as Sortollo handed him a primed and fully charged TR-120 mag-pulse carbine. The ballistic weapon, a legacy from the Dominion War, would serve them better here than any phaser.

"I hear everyone from North Star is good with firearms," said the security officer. "We could certainly use that today."

"I ride better than I shoot," Kyzak admitted.

"This is not a combat mission," Lieutenant Dakal said firmly. Although everyone on the shuttle but Ensign Bolaji was of the same rank, Pazlar had given command of the *Horne* contingent to the Cardassian science officer, and he was already setting the tone. "Our primary goal is to make the *Whitetree*'s warp core safe. Secondary objective is to liberate the ship if we can."

"And destroy it if we can't," added Sortollo. "We may not have a lot of choice if it's swarming with those drone things."

Kyzak gave a nod. Each of them had been given briefings on *Whitetree*'s prefix codes and emergency command protocols, and the Skagaran was familiar with the helm configuration on a *Saber*-class ship after serving his first tour of duty on board one. If push came to shove, he could fly the vessel out on his own—but he wondered if the Solanae would ever let them get that far.

"Stand by," said Bolaji. "We're coming up on the docking bay. It looks like it's a hollowed-out crater."

Sortollo went to the *Horne*'s transporter alcove and powered it up as Dakal leaned forward over the pilot's shoulder. "Olivia, I want you to make a high-speed pass across the mouth of the crater, then invert and come back around so we can beam in line-of-sight."

"Got it." She worked the ship's archaic electromechanical controls with small, economical movements. "After you've been deployed, I'll go dark and put her down behind one of those rock formations. Send me the go signal when you're ready, and I'll come back and pull you out."

"*Team Two, this is Team One*," Ranul Keru's voice crackled out of the comm panel. "*We're down, solid contact with target hull, burning through now. If they don't know we're here, they will in the next ten seconds. Copy?*"

"Team Two confirms," said Dakal. "Don't wait around for us, sir. We'll see you back on *Titan*."

"*I'll have a glass of* kanar *waiting for you. Lieutenant. Keru out.*"

Dakal gave a low chuckle as the signal cut. "I don't have the heart to tell him I hate the taste of that stuff."

"Well, don't rack up the celebratory drinks too soon—we have a problem," called Sortollo. "There's a lot of bleed-off coming from the *Whitetree*'s warp core, worse than we thought. We try to beam through that, we'll end up as meat slurry."

"Nice." Kyzak's lip curled at the unpleasant image. "What's our alternative?"

"The bridge," said the security officer. "I can beam us onto the command deck, and we come through that way. It just means we'll have a slightly longer walk to main engineering."

"Do it," snapped Dakal. "Ensign, start your run."

Kyzak took a shuddering breath. "All right," he told himself. "Here we go."

"Nervous in the service?" Sortollo shot him a wry smirk.

"I'm just trying to make *you* feel better."

Dakal followed them onto the narrow, cramped transporter pad and nodded to Sortollo. "On her mark."

Kyzak felt the lurch as the *Horne* made a fast, looping turn over the black rock of the Solanae base, and out of the canopy he saw a brief flash of a familiar tritanium hull garlanded by odd sheets of metallic fabric. The *Whitetree* looked like it was trapped in the middle of some strange, complex origami sculpture, and Kyzak wondered what purpose it could serve.

"*Energize*," said Bolaji, and they were swept away.

Seventeen

"Move! *Now!*" shouted Keru, and he sprinted from the cover of the support stanchion, firing from the hip. His mag-pulse rifle bucked in his grip, the recoil effect unfamiliar to a security officer who had trained all his life with energy beam weapons. He kept it on target and watched as electro-stunner rounds slammed home into the chests of two armor-plated Solanae soldiers. Bright, actinic flashes of lightning briefly wreathed the torsos of the aliens and they collapsed to the deck.

The shots had been calibrated with biodata from tricorder readings of the Ciari dissidents, configured to deliver enough shock-force to render a Solanae unconscious for several hours. Across the curved corridor, Dennisar was pinned down by plasma bolts arcing in over his head, the shots streaming from an alien warrior on an overhead walkway. Keru brought up his weapon to draw a bead, but at his back Pazlar had beaten him to the shot. The science officer fired and hit the shooter square in the thorax. The Solanae let out a strangled stream of click-speech and collapsed in a twitching heap.

Dennisar nodded his thanks to Pazlar and the big Orion broke cover. He gestured with a tricorder clipped to his forearm. "We have more of them converging on our position, boss. We don't have a lot of time."

Keru nodded and looked along the line of several large hatches built into the walls of the complex. "Question is, behind which of these are our crew?"

As the question left his lips, he heard a low thudding sound and froze. A moment later it came again. Three knocks against the inside of the nearest hatch.

Dennisar pressed his ear to the door. "I hear movement. Voices. Can't make out the words, though."

"Melora?" Keru pointed at a control panel nearby. "Can you get that open?"

She nodded, and in a few seconds her tricorder was beaming a high-frequency overload pulse into the locking mechanism. With a clatter of bolts, the hatch shifted and then began to draw open.

On reflex, Keru raised his TR-120 once again, just in case the door they were opening was actually to a barracks room full of Solanae reinforcements—but in the next second his bearded face split in a grin as he recognized Counselor Troi and Commander Sarai, standing alongside a rangy Dinac officer.

"Ranul!" Troi came to him, taking his hand. "I knew it was you! I sensed someone familiar coming closer, I hoped I wasn't mistaken. It's good to see you!"

"Likewise," he responded, and he jerked a thumb over his shoulder. "But we don't have time for a reunion. The *Monk* is docked a thousand or so meters from here, so if you'll come with us . . ."

Troi's expression shifted. She said nothing, but she stepped aside so that Keru and the rest of the rescue team could get a clear look at the size of the holding chamber and the number of abductees it held. He saw hundreds of people, not just the crew and the civilians from the *Titan*, but cadets from the *Whitetree* and the Dinac explorer's complement as well.

Dennisar said what they were all thinking: "We can't carry this lot in a single cargo shuttle!"

"Is there something wrong with the transporters?" said Troi.

Pazlar nodded. "It's . . . complicated."

Sarai stepped up, reaching out a hand. "Clearly," she snapped, and with a deft motion the first officer plucked Keru's combadge from his tunic, tapping it with a long finger. "*Titan*, do you read?"

From the *Whitetree*'s ruined bridge, it was a matter of finding their way back along the length of deck two, through the debris-strewn compartments until Lieutenant Kyzak found an unobstructed access panel. The whole ship stank of burned tripolymer and acidic discharges, and Zurin Dakal's nostrils stung with the odor as he moved forward on his hands and knees in the confined space. On the bridge, it had been worse. The empty command deck had a ghostly air to it, and as Dakal had moved from inert console to inert console, he saw that it was because the Solanae had carefully and deliberately severed the links from the ship's "brain" to the rest of its "body." Every panel was a melted mess of slagged components, corroded metal and partly dissolved isolinear chips. He recognized the work of the orb-drones and their caustic bile—which meant the alien automata were probably still lurking somewhere on board.

They emerged inside a Jefferies tube, a long and low gallery following the *Whitetree*'s midline. Color-coded pipes and large cylindrical storage modules crowded in around them. The deck of the ship creaked ominously beneath their boots, as if a great vice were slowly tightening on it, and Dakal hesitated, listening to the vessel moan.

"We need to keep moving," insisted Sortollo. The human was hunched over so he could fit inside the low-ceilinged compartment. He hefted his mag-pulse rifle, using an underslung light to illuminate their path. "If they figure out what we're here for . . ." He let the sentence trail off.

"You're right." Zurin nodded and continued on. He had been given command of away teams and work parties before during his service on *Titan*, but this was the first time he had ever been in charge of something like this: a mission into enemy territory. The very real risk to the lives of him and his fellow officers was palpable; Zurin's chest tightened at the thought of being responsible for them all. It was his duty to get Ethan, Gian and Olivia back safely, he told himself. This was not some away team excursion where the worst he could expect was some unruly local wildlife or unseen environmental hazards; it was battle, and—

His inward focus almost became a deadly distraction then and there. From the corner of his eye, Zurin caught sight of something moving behind one of the larger coolant tanks, and suddenly a pack of the octopoidal drone forms flooded out of the shadows in a hissing wave.

"Look out!" he cried, stumbling, and felt a hand on his back—Kyzak—grabbing him by the scruff of the neck before he could lose his balance.

Bright discharges flashed as Sortollo blind-fired two shock rounds from his weapon into the throng of drones. The blast effect was loud and dazzling in the tight confines, and Zurin grunted as his vision became a haze of purple-black retina burn. He heard Sortollo call out in anguish and pain, and he smelled burned flesh.

Kyzak pulled the trigger on his rifle and put another crackling bolt into the middle of the crawling mass. Zurin blinked furiously to get back his vision and struck out with the butt of his weapon, more by instinct than aim, smacking a fanged monstrosity away from his face before it could sink its teeth into him. Acid venom spattered off the walls, sizzling where it landed.

His stomach tightened as he realized how close they had come to being killed. A sickly sensation passed through him as he stared at the dead drones. Back on *Titan*, Doctor Ree had told him that the sleep disturbances he experienced during the search for the missing ships were the likely result of being taken and returned by the Solanae; Zurin was content that memory was lost to him. It chilled his blood to think of what horrors he might have experienced. *Better never to know*, he thought.

Sortollo spat out something in a human dialect that Zurin didn't recognize, but the tonality made it clear he was uttering a vehement curse. The security officer lurched forward as the attacking drones perished, kicking them aside. "Filthy damned things. Ah!" He clutched at his arm, where his uniform sleeve had disintegrated. A livid wet burn seared his flesh there.

Zurin tore a medpack from a pouch on his waist and found a pan-spectrum anti-infective, spraying it over the injury. Sortollo went pale.

"Stings, don't it?" offered Kyzak.

Sortollo could only choke back a gasp of pain and ride out the wave of agony. After a long moment, the security officer's color returned and he gave Zurin a weary nod. "I'm all right. I can keep going."

Kyzak panned his own light around, beyond the tentacled heap of dead drones. "Don't see any more. These were probably the guard dogs." He nodded at a bulkhead on the far wall. "The upper array of the warp core will be on the other side of that. We're real close now."

Zurin patted Sortollo on the shoulder, stepped in front of him, and left him to get his breath back. Acting quickly, he found the small keypad near the bulkhead and activated the manual retraction system. It was a calculated gamble. If the Solanae had penetrated the *Whitetree*'s computer network as they had attempted aboard the *Titan*, then using the manual switch could alert them to the exact location of the away team—but it was a chance Zurin had to take.

With a thud of magnetic bolts, the bulkhead panel unlocked and dropped away into the deck. A throbbing, blue-white glow flooded the service gallery, spilling in from the reflected pulses falling away down the length of the ship's matter-antimatter stack.

Riker stiffened as he heard Sarai's voice over the communications channel, suddenly daring to hope that Deanna and Tasha were all right.

"Commander," said Vale, leaning forward in the captain's chair. "It's good to hear your voice. Report."

"Abductees are largely intact and well, Captain. The survivors from the Whitetree *and the Dinac explorer are also here. I regret to inform you that most of the* Whitetree*'s command crew have been killed."* Before Vale could speak, Sarai continued: *"Captain, there are far too many people here to be transported aboard a cargo shuttle in a single trip. Commander Pazlar says we cannot be beamed out. Is there another alternative? We are on borrowed time."*

"I think we're all well aware of that," Vale replied, shooting Riker a sideways look. "Is it possible to coopt a Solanae craft of some kind?"

"Pazlar here, Captain," said the science officer. *"We don't have a location for the asteroid base's hangars, other than the one where* Whitetree *is being held. Can we use that?"*

"Negative," said Riker. Before Sarai had contacted them, Lieutenant Dakal had reported in after successfully boarding the *Saber*-class ship. The admiral relayed what Zurin had told them. "*Whitetree* is dead in the water. Whatever the Solanae are doing to her, they've severed connections to all drive systems and channeled ship's power into the main deflector grid."

Sarai's response was grim. *"I'm afraid I have the answer to that question, sir. We saw what the aliens are doing. It is my estimation that the Solanae are attempting to convert the ship's warp core into a subspace rift generator. You understand what will happen if they activate something capable of generating that much energy."*

Vale turned to Tuvok. "Commander, get that information to Dakal's team right now. They need to know what they're walking into."

The Vulcan nodded. "Complying. Captain, you should also be aware that long-range scanners have detected the approach of two objects traveling at near-lightspeed, on an intercept course."

"Ships?"

Tuvok nodded. "Likely so. Because of the unusual properties of this stellar region, sensor readings are confused, but these craft exhibit similar power signatures to the smaller vessels we captured with the transporters. Their size, however, is more equivalent to that of a *Galaxy*-class starship."

"The outpost called for help," said Riker. "How long until they get here?"

"Less than forty minutes," replied the tactical officer.

Vale was shaking her head. "Even if we commit every single auxiliary craft we have to the recovery of those prisoners right now, there's no way we can evacuate them all in under forty minutes."

"And from a location held by an armed enemy force as well." Riker's throat went dry.

"There is a clear equation here," said Tuvok, his tone neutral. "We are currently holding eighteen Solanae in transporter stasis, along with their vessels. If we release them in order to recover the abductees, they will recommence their attack on us. Therefore, we must consider the lives of those attackers against the numbers of those stranded on the asteroid. We can dispose of the Solanae prisoners in a matter of seconds and have *Titan*'s transporters ready for use soon after."

"Ten of ours for each one of theirs." The admiral said

it before he realized the thought had formed in his mind. He met Vale's look. "If it's a matter of us or them . . ."

Christine looked steadily back at him. "If there's more loss of life on both sides of this conflict, we may lose any chance of ever finding a diplomatic solution. We sent the rescue teams out with nonlethal weapons precisely *because* we wanted to keep the casualties low."

Part of him knew she was right to urge restraint, but another part of Will Riker was also shouting inside: *My wife and daughter are over there!* Finally he asked the only question that he could: "Do we have any alternative?"

"Actually . . ." From the front of the bridge, Commander Rager pivoted in her chair to address them. "Captain, I have an idea. But it will be dangerous."

Riker nodded to his former *Enterprise* crewmate to carry on. "Let's hear it, Sariel."

Zurin Dakal gingerly peered in through the open hatch. He looked down on the warp core, the column five decks tall ranging away from him into the heart of the *Whitetree*. He could see the debris-strewn engineering deck below, less than twenty meters from his position. Entire sections of decking, wall panels and consoles had been forcibly ripped out of the ship's structure. In their place, thick energy-conductive conduits were being run from the raw flux of the warp core. The conduits snaked away, some down and out of sight, others away past Zurin's vantage point toward the upper hull. He looked up and flinched in shock.

Where there should have been the inner surface of

the *Whitetree*'s dorsal hull, there was open space, the vacuum of the void held out by a force field. The conduits grew like roots into thicker branches, and these in turn had unfolded into the strange metal sails they had glimpsed as *Horne* made its approach. The data Commander Tuvok had sent to Zurin's tricorder was now confirmed by his own eyes: The starship was being rigged to act as a giant subspace inverter.

He frowned and returned his attention to the activity on the engineering deck, as Kyzak crowded in next to him, a questioning look on his face. Silently, Zurin pointed downward, and the Skagaran followed his lead. Kyzak's eyes widened in alarm.

Figures in silver-gray robes moved back and forth in a strange, shuffling gait, and the Cardassian heard snatches of Solanae click-speech. As they watched, a larger example of the alien race appeared, clad in what had to be battle armor. It was escorting one of the robed Solanae, who in turn was guiding an antigrav sled across the engineering room.

Kyzak pointed. *What's that?*

There were a number of ovoid containers lying on the sled, and each one appeared to be made from a soft, translucent material. Zurin shook his head and shrugged his shoulders. *I do not know.* A jaundice-yellow fluid sloshed around inside the pods, and he was reminded of insect eggs. He found his tricorder and aimed the scanner head, hoping that the interference from the cannibalized warp core would not interfere with the readings.

The alien leading the sled halted at an alcove on the far side of the *Whitetree*'s engineering deck and began transferring the pods one at a time to the wide beaming pad of a cargo transporter.

A fourth figure came into view, hunched and trembling, shoved roughly by another of the armor-clad aliens. A Barzan male wearing a torn, blackened Starfleet undershirt in the sand-yellow of the operations division. The engineer's movements made it clear that he had been badly abused by his captors. The armored Solanae pushed him toward the control console of the cargo transport and barked out a string of harsh, guttural clicks.

Zurin's tricorder completed its analysis, and he felt cold dread as he read the display. The signature of the fluid inside the pods was unmistakable. "Those are biogenic materials," he whispered, remembering the words of the Ciari scientist Kikkir and his warning about the deadly intentions of the Solanae.

"What are they going to do with them?" Kyzak asked the question, even as all the horrible possibilities formed in their minds.

"We can't wait around to find out," said Sortollo, finishing up a field dressing over his injured arm. "Lieutenant, we have to get down there."

Zurin gave a nod. "Agreed."

Gian Sortollo was the security officer; Dakal ordered him to take the lead. Kyzak stood back and watched as Sortollo handed out the monowire descenders. They clipped the devices to their waists and secured a magnotomic plate on the deck behind them. Although the wires were little thicker than an ODN cable, they were strong enough to bear the weight of a shuttlepod, and they would allow the three men to literally *drop in* on the Solanae instead of risking time and exposure by descending via the emergency ladders bolted to the walls.

Sortollo pulled a photon grenade from his backpack and dialed in the detonator setting. "Commander Keru said this worked on the drones before. Let's hope it has the same effect on their creators."

Dakal gave Kyzak a look, and he nodded his assent. "I'm ready."

"Go," said the Cardassian.

Sortollo thumbed the switch and dropped the grenade through the open hatch. Kyzak heard the device clank and clatter against the sides of the tube as it fell the distance to the deck below. He held his breath, and for a moment he thought he could hear some confused bursts of click-snapping as the attention of the Solanae was drawn away.

Then there was a shriek of electromagnetic energy as the grenade went off, and they were moving. Sortollo went through the hatch headfirst, like a diver going off a cliff. Dakal's descent was more careful, and Kyzak went last, his gut lurching as he threw himself out into the empty vertical shaft and let the monowire sing as it played out from the reel.

Aiming down, he saw that Sortollo was already firing mag-pulse shots, knocking over robed Solanae with direct hits. Dakal clipped one of the armored aliens, but the glancing hit did not put him down. As Kyzak's boots hit the deck and the monowire automatically detached, another of the armored Solanae was right on top of him, snatching at the barrel of his TR-120 before he could bring it to bear. He lost his footing and was slammed up against the impulse manifold monitor. A constant string of angry *snap-snap-snap* sounds spilled from the Solanae as it tried to choke the life out of him; but then a stool crashed into the back of the alien and it lost all interest in him, spinning around to confront the Barzan engineer who had dared to attack it. With a savage, power-assisted backhand, the Solanae swatted the engineering officer away, and he crumpled against a guide rail.

Turning back, the alien met the muzzle of Kyzak's rifle and took a mag-pulse round to the chest at point-blank range. The armored figure tottered and fell with a crash. Breathing hard, the lieutenant looked around to see the last of the Solanae go down under another stun discharge. He sprinted across the compartment to the still form of the engineer.

"Hey . . ." Kyzak spotted the rank pips on the Barzan's collar. "Lieutenant Commander? Can you hear me?" He cradled the officer's head, but there was major damage to the breather disks at the engineer's mouth as well as blood misting his right eye. Kyzak fought down a surge of anger. They had tortured this poor man, probably to coerce him into assisting with their plans for the *Whitetree*.

"I'm sorry, I'm sorry," choked the Barzan. "Couldn't fight them anymore, they were in my head, cutting me, burning and burning . . ."

From behind him, Kyzak heard the keening of a tricorder as Sortollo scanned the injured man's life signs. The faltering tone was enough for them to know that he would never leave his ship alive. "It's okay," said Kyzak, holding the dying man's hand. "It's not your fault, sir." He took a breath. "We need to know, what did they want?"

"Portal." The engineer coughed up a line of dark, arterial blood. "Dragging something here. Something . . . big."

"The Refuge," said Dakal quietly.

"And the . . . the transporter." He watched the Barzan's eyes slowly lose focus. "Same time . . . pull something in, they send something back." He coughed again. "The pods. To Casroc. *Casroc*." The last word was a long, breathy gasp, and then nothing.

With infinite care, Kyzak reached out and closed the engineer's eyelids. "Damn it," he muttered.

"They want to transport the biogenic weapons to the Dinac homeworld . . ." Sortollo scowled. "Why?"

"A first strike," said Dakal. "Remember what the Ciari told us? Their government intend to invade and take over worlds in our space. If they have the Refuge and the dissidents, they'll be able to torture the data they need out of them to reconstruct the ability to transit to our space, and the biochemical solution required to survive there."

Kyzak stood up and gave a grim nod. "Meantime, the Dinac are looking for their lost, and they find a germ weapon for their trouble. The Solanae test their nasty new toys, get rid of the only sentient race for light-years around. Not to mention the crews of any Federation ships that might be involved. Then when they punch through, they got themselves an unoccupied planet to use as a base. It makes a sick kinda sense."

Dakal nodded. "Lieutenant Kyzak, contact the *Titan* and tell Captain Vale what we've found here." He pointed toward the cargo transporter. "And everyone stay away from those pods."

Vale watched as the image on the main viewscreen shifted. *Titan* pulled back and away from the chain of linked asteroids and then came back around in a half-turn, until the bow was aimed directly at the section of the complex where the abductees were being held. The captain tapped her combadge and gave Commander Sarai a quick précis of the plan outlined by Commander Rager.

"That's the best option we have?" The Efrosian didn't make any attempt to hide her skepticism.

"It's what we're going with, Number One," Vale told her. "Get everyone out of there. Let Ranul know we're bringing *Monk* back on autopilot. We're going to need you to be ready. We only get a single shot at this."

"Confirmed," said Sarai. *"Do I need to remind you what will happen if you are off by so much as a few meters? We could* all *end up stranded here."*

Despite the seriousness of the moment, Vale felt a smile cross her lips. "I have faith in my people." She looked across the bridge to Commander Rager's station. "Ops, time check."

Rager answered without turning around. "Two minutes thirty seconds."

"You heard her," Vale went on. "Three minutes from now, this will all be over."

"One way," came Sarai's dour reply, *"or another."*

"Another communication coming in," reported Tuvok. "It is Lieutenant Kyzak."

Vale gestured for the Vulcan to switch them over. "This is Captain Vale, go ahead, mister, but make it snappy. We're right in the middle of something here."

"You're gonna want to hear this, Captain," replied the Skagaran, and he quickly relayed what Dakal's team had found in the *Whitetree*'s engineering room. Vale heard the sound of a blast discharge in the background as Kyzak went on. *"Lieutenant Sortollo just, ah,*

neutralized *the delivery system, but we still got enough of this rot here to kill a whole planet."*

Vale and Riker exchanged a troubled look. "Lieutenant Kyzak," began the admiral, "what about the alterations of the warp core? Can you shut them down safely?"

"Zurin's on that right now, sir, but it doesn't look good. The Solanae have already started the process down here. The array for generating the rift is drawing power."

"Confirmed." The voice of Se'al Cethente Qas tinkled like wind-chimes; the Syrath astrophysicist had volunteered to take the science station on the bridge. "I read a low-level energy pulse in progress. Negligible for the moment, but at the current rate of increase it will reach active potentiality in less than ten minutes."

Vale studied the irregular form of the Solanae facility as it grew to fill the viewscreen. Strips of oval windows glittered with oily reflected light from the subspace domain's strange nebulae.

"Cutting impulse engines," reported Rager, and she leaned forward, spreading her hands over her console.

At her side, Aili Lavena worked flight control in tandem, mirroring the other woman's actions. "We're coasting on inertia," said the Pacifican. "Maneuvering on thrusters only now."

"One minute thirty seconds," added Rager.

Vale sat back in her chair. "Do what you can in there, Lieutenant," she said to the comm pickup, then made a throat-cutting gesture for Tuvok to cut the signal.

At her side, Riker tapped out a series of commands on his panel. "Engineering, divert power to structural integrity fields and force fields. Forward docking bay, stand by for contact." He took a breath. "Yellow alert! Sound collision alarm!"

The automatic restraints snaked out over the shoulders of Vale and her crew, securing them in place, and the captain scowled at the still-raw memory of the last time that had happened. *We're not losing any more people today,* she vowed.

On the screen, the largest array of windows in the stone structure were directly ahead of the *Titan*'s bow, and they were approaching with great speed—far faster than seemed optimal. "Sariel?"

"Forty seconds," replied the ops officer.

From the corner of her eye, Vale saw Riker's knuckles whiten as he gripped his chair. "Hey," she said, pitching her voice low. "No sweat. I mean, we've been through this sort of thing before, right? Remember the *Scimitar*?"

"Of course I do," he said, out of the side of his mouth. "That's why I'm worried."

"Ten seconds," called Rager. "All hands, brace for impact!"

"Oh," said Keru, his voice even despite the shock of the sight. "It looks like our ride is here."

"Hang on to something!" Troi bellowed as loudly as she could, her shout carrying across the corridor and the heads of the assembled abductees. Following Christine's orders, Commander Sarai had led them out from the holding chamber and away toward the outer sections of the asteroid base, heading the opposite way from the direction they had traveled to find the *Whitetree*. Encountering a Solanae patrol along the route, the mass of escaped prisoners had overwhelmed the aliens and made it to an area lined with exterior observation galleries. And it was then that the commander had decided to explain exactly *how Titan* intended to rescue the prisoners—when it was too late for anyone to panic.

A ripple of fear went through the assembled group as the starship reared up ahead of the wide windows and came powering in toward them. It showed no signs of slowing.

"Mommy, I'm scared!" cried Tasha, clinging tightly to her chest. The little girl buried her face in Troi's shoulder.

"It's fine," she lied. "Auntie Christine knows what she's doing." Troi watched the leading edge of *Titan*'s saucer-shaped bow loom larger and larger, close enough now that she could read the ship's pennant and see into the officers' lounge.

"That's a fib," Tasha admonished her.

"Yes, it is, little one," she admitted. "But for now let's both pretend it isn't."

Commander Sarai called out one last order. "Everybody brace!"

Troi sank to her knees and pulled Tasha even closer. To her surprise, Sarai came in and held mother and daughter in the safety of an embrace, the three of them pushing into the lee of a support pillar.

She wanted to close her eyes, but she could not look away. Troi saw the mouth of the secondary docking bay along the ventral surface of the primary hull yawning open, lit brightly from within. It looked almost comical, like a ridiculous smile was forming on the face of the vessel; then in the next second that fanciful image was blasted away by sound and fury as the *Titan*'s bow crashed through the windows into the wide observation chamber.

The noise was like the world ending, and Tasha screamed in terror for one brief moment, before decompression got its claws in the platform and the shattered remnants of reinforced quartz-glass were blown out into the vacuum. A hurricane battered at the escapees, ripping the air from their lungs, and Troi experienced a terrible emptiness as all her breath was suddenly stolen. A terrible grinding, crashing cacophony assaulted her ears as *Titan*'s slow collision chewed up the decking of the Solanae station. Light flashed all around and her ears popped. Suddenly there was air again, and everyone was coughing and gasping.

"Force field," managed Sarai, pulling back so they could get to their feet.

Tasha was crying. "That was not fun at all," she wailed.

"No," admitted the first officer. "You are quite correct."

Troi took a shaky step, refusing a helping hand from Keru. "I thought your husband's job was to order people not to do this kind of thing," said the Trill.

Other voices were shouting, and for a moment Troi stood and marveled at what stood before them. A forward slice of *Titan*'s saucer section—just enough of it to bring the open docking bay within reach—had been punched through the complex's exterior gallery. Held there by glittering tractor beams, with a temporary envelope of atmosphere captured under a dome of projected deflector fields, the starship had docked with the alien station—without any of the usual complications of using an airlock.

She could see figures moving inside the docking bay and recognized Lieutenant Ssura as the Caitian nimbly bounded down from the open hatch to the torn deck of the outpost. "If everybody will please board the ship in an orderly fashion," he called, as politely as if he were the conductor on a moon shuttle "then we will be on our way."

"We have good capture," said Rager, blowing out a breath.

Vale let out a dry chuckle. "*Good* is a relative term in this case, I think." She shot a look toward Riker as their restraints retracted. "Admiral, if you could get below and help supervise the recovery?"

"Aye, Captain." He nodded his thanks and rushed to the turbolift. They both knew that Will didn't need to be down there as the abductees boarded, but she couldn't deny him the opportunity to be there when his wife and child came home.

She glanced over her shoulder at Tuvok to make the same offer. "Commander?" Vale nodded toward the turbolift door.

"I will remain," he replied, and he tapped at his console. "Damage to exterior hull was minor, within expected ranges."

"Aili, Sariel," said the captain, "you threaded the needle there. Try not to scratch the paintwork any more backing us out. I only just got this ship."

"Sensors reading movement inside the complex," reported Se'al. "Multiple Solanae life signs converging on this location."

Vale's brief moment of levity vanished. "Warn Commander Keru. We've already outstayed our welcome."

She turned to McCreedy at her station. "Start the preparations for the warp destabilization process."

"Aye, Captain," said the engineer.

"Torpedoes," she added, "did you manage to get them operable in this environment?"

McCreedy frowned, pushing back the spectacles on her nose. "I'm not confident of the refit, Captain. They could detonate in the launch tubes. This damned subspace effect: It's playing havoc with all our systems."

Vale was going to say more, but a chime from the communications system interrupted her. "*Team Two to* Titan, *respond please.*" Lieutenant Dakal's crisp diction cut through the static interference, and she heard the warning tone in the words.

"Go ahead, Zurin. What's the situation?"

"It is not good." Dakal met Kyzak's gaze and then looked away. *If anything*, thought the lieutenant, *he seems more pale than usual*. "The Solanae modifications to *Whitetree*'s warp core are extensive and complex. They have removed all safety interlocks and destroyed the emergency shutdown modules. Simply put, Captain, it cannot be turned off. We have already passed the point of no return."

Kyzak felt a tingle in the scales on his neck, and suddenly he was sharing the Cardassian's lack of color. "Oh. *Crowbait*."

There was a long pause before Captain Vale responded. "*So. It has to be destroyed, then. You're on-site, Lieutenant. What is your best recommendation?*"

"A forced removal of the dilithium crystal matrix.

Without the controlled interface between the matter and antimatter streams, the warp core would immediately annihilate itself, destroying the *Whitetree* in the process, along with a substantial volume of this section of the asteroid complex. If we do this now, before the subspace rift has had time to reach criticality, the entire Solanae scheme to recapture the Ciari refugees will be terminated." Dakal took a breath. "Captain, we can't beam any explosive devices into this area, and it would take too long to fetch something from another part of the ship. Corruption of the engineering console systems caused by sabotage means that a remotely triggered operation is not possible."

Kyzak's blood ran cold. "Zurin, what are you saying?"

"I am saying that someone will need to remain here and manually remove the dilithium matrix."

"And be killed in the process?" said Sortollo.

The Cardassian nodded.

Eighteen

The Dinac crew were the last to leave the Solanae asteroid facility.

Engineer-Commander Guoapa would not explain, but the reason was something ingrained in the character of the fox-like beings, a determination instilled in them on a cultural level that they were always to be the final ones to flee from a sinking ship. Guoapa made sure that the Federation cadets who had come to help her people and learn from them, the ones kidnapped by the scheming invaders from subspace, were safely aboard the *Titan* before her own people scrambled up the ramps and into the open mouth of the docking bay. She had not been able to shake the sense that her race were somehow responsible for all that had happened; and although the reptilian, Ythiss, had refused to be drawn on the matter, Guoapa knew in her bones that she bore the blame. It was Dinac technology, Dinac ships that had brought the Solanae to their space. That there had been deaths among the Federation crew and her own because of it. She prayed to her ancestors that there would be a chance to make this right. Sobasor, her second, sprinted down the ramp and pulled at her arm.

"We must go!" he barked, loudly enough to be heard over the cracking and grinding of torn metal all about them. "They will not wait for you!"

She nodded. "I know. But it sickens me to leave the bodies of our lost in this under-realm." Guoapa closed her eyes and sniffed as she thought of Pohodo, the healer whom she had taken as a flight-mate during the voyage. They had talked amiably of possibilities after the mission was over. Of taking a leave of absence, of a den in the outlands and raising a pack of pups. Foolish, unlikely things, given their natures. But shrouded in sorrow now that she would never know how it might have played out.

"Alarm!" Sobasor shouted and aimed a paw across the wrecked observation bay. A cluster of Solanae warriors in their shiny ceramic armor burst into the chamber and opened fire with their wrist-blasters. Streaks of firelight fell like tiny meteors, cracking off the *Titan*'s exterior hull.

Guoapa could not help but bare her teeth in a snarl of defiant fury, but as much as she wanted to stay and fight, she knew that would not be possible. Following Sobasor and the others, she sprinted up the incline, leaping over broken fragments of decking, and scrambled inside the Federation ship. She felt a peculiar tingle over her fur as she passed within, and immediately her sensitive nostrils were assailed with hundreds of strong scent-traces. She wondered if the beings who formed the great mix of this coalition understood how much odor they put out;

certainly, the humans among them seemed to largely be unaware of it.

The mundanity of the thought snapped her back to the moment. The big hatch came down and she felt the *Titan* starting to move. They were backing out of the great rent in the hull of the alien complex, meter by meter.

"We are all here!" Sobasor gave a breathless yelp. "All but the dead. Those creatures will take no more of us!"

Guoapa moved to a thick portal in the outer hull and watched the departure. *Titan* shivered in retreat as broken stanchions dragged on it, and deck plates tore free. She glimpsed some of the Solanae—the quicker and more intelligent of them, she guessed—turning tail and running for the corridor beyond the wrecked observation bay. Others among them, perhaps blinded by rage at this mass escape, were still firing salvoes of plasmatic energy from their weapons. Even as the compartment came apart around them, they hurled shots against the Federation vessel as if they thought spite alone could halt it.

Then the local force wall that had been projected to keep a thin atmospheric envelope in place snapped off, and the savage force of the vacuum bore down. The Solanae were captured by it and blasted out into space along with a storm of debris, pieces of metal and armored beings alike bouncing off the hull.

Titan pivoted as it withdrew, and the bow of the vessel turned away from the asteroid base. Guoapa's last glimpse of it was the image of a chain of glistening black stones along a thick steel necklace. The potent mix of elation and remorse at surviving went away. The engineer-commander wanted nothing more than to obliterate this nest of the Solanae and the threat they still posed to her people.

At last, she pulled her gaze away from the port and

found Sobasor watching her intently. "We live," she told her old friend, "but I fear we may have traded our lives for the commencement of a war."

Will Riker came through the doors into the secondary docking bay at a full-tilt run, all thought of decorum and poise utterly dismissed. He didn't give a damn if any member of the crew looked askance at an admiral charging through the ship like the devil was on his heels. He knew Deanna and Tasha were safe, on some level sensing it as strongly as the pulse of his own heartbeat—but that wasn't enough. He had to see them, to *feel* it.

His gaze swept the crowded compartment, catching glimpses of Commander Sarai helping Lieutenant Ythiss into the arms of a medical team, of the Dinac crew tending to their own, of Ssura and Keru guiding groups of pale and weary-looking cadets to safety. And then his wife and daughter rose into sight, and Will felt a weight he didn't know he had been carrying roll off his shoulders. The family came together in an embrace, and for long seconds there were no words, only the pure sense of being together once again.

"Hello," offered Tasha, and the word almost broke Will's heart, with all the plaintive simplicity of emotion behind it. "I missed the rest of my classes," she went on. "Will I get into trouble?"

Riker burst out laughing and gave his little girl a kiss, then found another for his wife. "No, no." He saw T'Pel patiently leading the other children that had been taken across the bay, each holding the hand of another as if they had just come back from some innocuous field trip.

"Look! Your teacher missed them too, so that means everyone gets a free pass."

"I knew you'd come for us," said Deanna, her voice thick with emotion.

"I can't lose you," he told her, and he meant every word. "I need you both, now and forever." Will nodded to himself as a moment of understanding came to him. "You're my compass, you two. You keep me grounded."

"It was scary in that place," said his daughter. "But Auntie Christine brought the ship to come get us. Can I say 'thank you' to her?"

Will took a breath and began the process of putting away thc parts of him that were *doting father* and *dutiful husband*, bringing *Admiral Riker* back to the fore. "In a while. We're not out of the woods just yet."

"We're clear of the Solanae complex," said Lavena. "Moving to safe distance."

Vale nodded absently at the report as she got to her feet. The channel with the second away team was still open, and her attention remained on them. "Are we absolutely certain there is no other way to do this?"

Everyone on the command deck had heard Lieutenant Dakal's bleak evaluation of the situation on board the captured *Whitetree*. The other starship was beyond recovery; the only way to neutralize the threat it represented was to destroy it utterly. Under other circumstances, the *Whitetree*'s autodestruct mechanism would be called upon to do the deed, but as Dakal explained, the brutish Solanae cannibalization of the ship's systems had rendered that nonfunctional.

Her mind raced. There had to be something on board the ship that could be used to trigger a collapse of the matter-antimatter stream, something that might enable Dakal's team to get clear before it went up. She put this to him, but the Cardassian's reply was no different.

"Captain, there are plenty of other options. None of which are open to us because of the time factor. This must be done now. *If we delay, the rift formation will become self-perpetuating. As we speak, it's already forming on a microscopic level inside the heart of the warp matrix. At worst, it will succeed as the Solanae wish it to and open a passageway to our spatial realm. At best, a singularity will form that will consume this ship, the asteroid base and everything within a hundred-thousand-kilometer radius."* He didn't need to add that would likely include *Titan* as well. *"If we disrupt the core now, that detonation will only be a fraction of the size. Captain, what are your orders?"*

Vale's stomach flooded with ice and her legs became leaden. She showed nothing of this to the crew standing around her, but she felt sick inside. As captain, she knew the capabilities of every person on Dakal's away team, their skill sets and their talents. She also knew something about all of them, bits of the story of Zurin's youth as a refugee from the Dominion War, Ethan Kyzak's aspirations to become an explorer, Gian Sortollo's dedication to the huge extended family he had back on Earth. But beyond all of that, she knew that for everyone here to have a chance at survival—not just on the *Titan*, but back on the Refuge—she would have to order one of them to die.

Before, Tuvok had spoken about the equation of life against life, and now Vale was balancing that same question in her hands. One officer sworn to serve, who knew the risks when they took the Starfleet oath, weighed against hundreds of others. Far more than that, even, if she considered the possibility of all those the Solanae could kill with their biogenic weapons. In the cold light of harsh reality, it was hardly a question at all.

But these were her people, not numbers in an equation. Men with lives, pasts and futures. Vale did not doubt that they would do whatever she asked of them. No, the doubt was in *her*. As a command officer, she had always known that one day this choice might be laid down before her. That she would come to it during her first mission as a starship captain wasn't something Christine Vale had ever expected.

It has to be done, she told herself. *And you have to say the words.* Vale stopped herself from absently reaching for the four gold pips at her collar. At this moment, they weighed more than worlds.

"Team Two," she said, working to maintain an even tone. "In the absence of any other solution, I'm ordering you to go ahead with the forced removal of the *Whitetree*'s dilithium matrix." Vale hesitated, then said the words that would end a man's life. "Lieutenant Dakal is the only member of the landing party with the training to correctly decouple the matrix. He will remain behind while Lieutenants Sortollo and Kyzak evacuate back to *Horne* and clear the area." The words sounded hollow, as if someone else were speaking them.

"Team Two copies," Dakal replied. *"For the record, Captain, I fully concur."*

"I'm so sorry, Zurin." The words slipped out before she could stop them.

"Don't be," he said. *"Just get everyone home, Captain."* The comm channel closed with a soft click.

Crossing back to the center seat seemed to take forever. "Helm," said Vale. "One quarter impulse. Get us clear. If we're going to pay this price, let's not waste it."

"Wait, *no*," began Kyzak, reaching out to Dakal. "Zurin, you can't just—"

"It is done," insisted the Cardassian, his tone hard and uncompromising. "It's an order. Now I'm giving you another." He pointed across the main engineering area to one of the access ladders leading to the outer hull. "There's a cluster of escape pods on the deck below this one, get down there and launch them all. Take one each, and the moment you're clear of the *Whitetree*, send the recovery signal to the *Horne*. Olivia is still out there waiting. She'll sweep in and beam you both out."

Sortollo was nodding, his face pale. He didn't seem to be able to find any words to offer.

Kyzak had no such issues. "I'm not going to let you die here," he insisted. "Come on, man, *there has to be another way!*" He was almost shouting it. "Program a tricorder as a timer, put a phaser on overload, poke the damn button with a long stick! *Something else!*"

Dakal was infuriatingly calm about the whole thing. "There isn't anything else, Ethan." He gestured at the hatch to the dilithium matrix array. "It's a complicated job, with multiple steps. I can't just try to blow it up and hope for the best! You understand that." And then the mask of stoicism fell away and he was suddenly furious. "Do you think I woke up this morning planning to sacrifice my life? I have a family. I have hopes and dreams, for hunger's sake! I don't want to die here! But we don't have any other choice! I am the only one who can do this. Not you." He stabbed a finger at Sortollo. "Not him. Just *me*. This isn't like before, on the wreck. We can't draw straws."

"It isn't . . ." Kyzak's throat went dry. "It isn't fair. I mean, I only just met you. And I kinda like you, Zurin. I was hoping we could be friends." He managed a smile. "Talk about the prairies, you know?"

"I was never that good a conversationalist," he replied, finding a shaky smile of his own. "Go on, get out of here. *Please*."

"Is . . ." Sortollo frowned. "Is there anything we can do, Lieutenant?"

"There's a letter for my family, on the padd in my quarters." Dakal walked away from them toward the warp core, flexing his hands. "See that they get it, will you?"

"Done." The security guard put his hand on the Skagaran's shoulder. "Kyzak. Come on. Let him do his job."

"It's not right," he said, under his breath.

"No," agreed Sortollo, "but we don't get to decide."

Taking one heavy step after another, Kyzak followed the other lieutenant along the accessway, through the cramped Jefferies tubes to the escape pod bay. Beyond the warp core, they could hear the rattles and bangs of movement in other parts of the ship. It had to be the Solanae, coming to find out why their people had fallen silent.

Part of Kyzak wanted to stay and fight them, but he knew it would be pointless. What Zurin was doing had meaning—but if he and Gian died here just for the sake of stoking his anger, it would be an act of disrespect to the choice Dakal had made.

The two lieutenants clambered inside the box-shaped escape capsules and pulled the hatches shut behind them, automatically triggering the launch process.

Kyzak's gut lurched as the pod was shot out of the *Whitetree*'s hull on jets of ion thrust, spinning and flocking together as the autopilot found a path away from the stricken ship, out of the crater and into open space.

His fingers found the emergency transponder tab on his tricorder and Kyzak pressed down hard, still trying and failing to process what had taken place. Moments later, he saw the fast blur of a small ship race past the escape pod's single viewport; and then the buzz of a transporter effect filled his ears.

"Admiral?"

Riker turned to find Commander Sarai standing before him, at stiff parade-ground attention. "XO," he replied. "Good to have you all back."

"Not all of us, sir," she corrected. "To my regret, I have to inform you that Captain Minecci and—"

He held up his hand. "I was on the bridge when you gave your report to Captain Vale."

"Oh. Yes, of course . . ." For the first time since Riker had met her, Dalit Sarai seemed fatigued. She was actually showing something that was borderline vulnerability, and he found it strangely heartening. The woman whom some of the lower ranks had already christened "the Ice Queen" was proving herself to be more than that, and Riker wondered if he had been too quick to judge her.

"The commander helped keep us together," said Troi. "I don't think we'd be here without her."

Sarai shook her head. "The counselor is being overly generous. I did my duty." She drew herself up. "I wanted to bring them all back, sir. Even the ones who were dead. It's not proper that they stay there . . . with *them*." She jutted her chin toward the hull and the space beyond.

"You're right," said Riker. "And that's why we're going to do our utmost to end this conflict before it escalates any further, before any more are lost."

An alert tone from the ship's intercom drowned him out. *"Attention, all decks, all divisions,"* said Tuvok's voice. *"Stand by for close-order antimatter detonation. Shields at maximum."*

"What?" Troi turned back toward the ports looking out into space, then thought better of it, turning away and covering Tasha's eyes.

But Riker and Sarai did not turn. Barely visible, out past the starboard hull of the *Titan*, they could see a fraction of the Solanae facility. The admiral tapped his combadge. "Tuvok, what's going on?"

"Circumstances have changed, sir," said the Vulcan. *"A difficult response was required."*

"Interlocks open," said Zurin Dakal, speaking aloud to the empty room. His gray fingers danced over the control panel and the heavy duranium clamps set around the edges of the dilithium matrix's outer hatch thudded open one after another. Alarms sounded, warning him of the danger of what he was doing, and the Cardassian grinned. "Yes, I know," he said to the air. "Thanks for the reminder."

Pulsing light bathed him in a steady glow. He stood directly in front of the *Whitetree*'s warp core, before the oval reaction chamber. Inside that module, energy as powerful as the heart of a sun was constantly being created.

Placing his hands on the manual safeties, he turned the first latch ninety degrees from lateral to vertical, then did the same to the second. More alarms sounded now, along with flashing lights. He paused to type in the prefix code Commander Tuvok had provided before they left *Titan*, and the tocsins all fell silent. "Better," he said. "I'd prefer some peace and quiet."

He took a breath and searched his memories for the moments in his past that had made him the most happy. He found instances of times with his family, of the days when they had *not* been on the run from the Jem'Hadar. He found recall of life at Starfleet Academy, of the great challenges he faced there and the people he had come to think of as his friends.

Suddenly, he was recalling someone he had not thought of in some time. Jaza Najem, *Titan*'s former science officer and, for a while, something of a mentor to the younger Zurin Dakal. Jaza had been dead for several years, lost in the incident at Orisha, but the Bajoran's influence lived with Dakal in ways that he could not truly articulate. Jaza had done something that the Cardassian had never thought possible: drawn Dakal out of himself to become a confident, able officer. Cadet Dakal, straight off the Presidio campus with little or no desire to do anything other than blend in, could not have done what Lieutenant Dakal was about to do now. As he placed his hands on the grips of the matrix array, he heard the ghost of Jaza Najem's voice filtering up from the depths of his memories. Telling him this was right. Telling him how proud he was.

"Mother. Father." He heard the crunch and thud of the sealed doors behind him being broken open. "I love you dearly." Dakal tensed, feeling the weight of the dilithium articulation frame. Heavier than he expected. Leaning forward, he took his last breaths. "Thank you, Jaza," he said. He ignored the strident clicking and snapping sounds closing in at his back. "Thank you for teaching me that I am strong enough to do something like this."

Dakal pulled hard on the grips, and the unseated matrix module detached with a crash, suddenly removing the dilithium crystal it contained from the middle of the *Whitetree*'s matter-antimatter reaction stream. Light, bright as a supernova, burst from the opened warp core and bathed him in star-fire. Pillars of raw energy, no longer focused and controlled, collided with incredible force and destroyed one another in a catastrophic release of power.

Ensign Bolaji executed a tight turn that stressed *Horne*'s structural integrity fields to the red line and then powered the *Flyer*-class shuttle away at maximum impulse. As the Solanae station shrank on the aft scanner screen at her elbow, she risked a look over her shoulder to the transporter alcove on the upper tier of the cockpit. The beaming sequence ended and Olivia saw two figures stumble off the pads.

Sortollo caught her eye. "Where's Lieutenant Dakal?" she asked. "The transporter didn't catch him, we have to go back!"

But it was Kyzak who answered. "He's not coming, Ensign."

"What?" The full meaning of the Skagaran's words were barely registering with her when the *Horne*'s scanners bleated a warning. A brilliant flash of light washed out the view on the aft monitor, and a split second later, the shuttlecraft was hit by a bow-wave of violent energy.

Olivia was thrown forward in her seat and her head bounced off the flight systems panel, lighting bursts of stars behind her eyes. The *Horne* rocked and spun out of control, buffeted by the passing of the shock front. The pilot gritted her teeth and shook off the moment of disorientation, taking the throttle and helm in her hands and dragging them back to true. She smelled smoke. "Someone get to that!"

Behind her, Kyzak and Sortollo rose from where they had fallen and the security officer pulled the emergency breaker on an overhead panel. "Done." He coughed out a shaky breath. "Damage report."

"Minor hull stress," said Kyzak, peering at an engineering readout. "We lost the aft phaser strip. Nothing mission-critical."

Olivia eased the little ship into a wider, slower turn, enough to put the Solanae facility off the port bow. Through the canopy, she could see that the explosion had sliced the chain of tethered asteroids in two, one entire link blown apart into a cloud of fragments and dust. Belatedly, she saw that the missing segment had been the one they had traveled to, the one where the *Whitetree* had been confined.

"The ship . . ." She started to speak, then fell silent. It was abundantly clear what had happened. Olivia had seen a recording of a warp core detonation in flight school, and she knew it could be nothing else.

Kyzak pulled himself into one of the crew seats and worked the panel in front of him. "I'm running a scan for spatial anomalies . . ."

"Zurin did that?" Olivia met Sortollo's gaze.

He nodded. "Yeah. If he hadn't, the Solanae would have opened a subspace portal to the Refuge and gone after the Ciari. He just stopped an alien invasion."

"And all it cost was his life," Kyzak said bitterly, scowling at the display. "No subspace fissures detected, no anomalous readings. Whatever the Solanae were going to do with the *Whitetree*, it's all ashes now."

A warbling tone sounded from Olivia's console. "Incoming hail from the *Titan*. They're calling us back." Sortollo and Kyzak exchanged looks. With Dakal gone, neither of them seemed to be sure who was in command of team two anymore. The ensign decided to make the decision herself. "On our way."

Ahead of them, framed against the freakish colors of the aberrant sky, the silver-gray shape of the *Titan* rose up, a beacon of the familiar among the alien.

"Time?" said Riker.

"Solanae starships will be in effective range in twelve-point-three minutes," said Tuvok, without looking down at the tactical panel.

Behind him, at the engineering station, Lieutenant McCreedy double-checked her chrono before replying. "Imbalance effect program will be ready to activate in ninety seconds, sir. White-Blue's probe has been launched and he reports he is ready to lead us in."

The admiral accepted the reports with a nod and turned back to face his captain and his wife. With the recovery of the survivors of the second away team aboard the *Horne* and the cargo shuttle *Monk*, the *Titan* was done here. They had completed the mission, rescuing the abductees, neutralizing the Solanae's ability to strike at the Ciari Refuge—and, hopefully, put a major dent in their ability to continue their campaign of terror and kidnapping. He did not want to think about the price they had paid to get here, but he couldn't stop himself from looking over to the science station where Zurin Dakal had often worked. Riker always considered the young Cardassian to be a fine officer with a bright future, and he had quietly admired Zurin for being the first of his species to serve in Starfleet. He regretted that he had not made a greater effort to learn more about him.

"We are ready to do this, then?" said Commander Sarai, who stood with Commander Keru at her side. Both the XO and the chief of security were armed with holstered phasers.

"We are." Captain Vale got to her feet and Riker followed suit, Troi rising a beat later.

Despite the stress of the situation, both Will's wife and the first officer had refused to stand down after their rescue from the Solanae facility, insisting that they return immediately to their duties—at least until the *Titan* was back in its own universe.

Vale had said nothing, but Riker knew that she appreciated the help. It was not an easy thing to make the call that this situation had forced on her. When Riker had been in the same circumstances, he was not ashamed to admit he had needed all the support his crew could provide.

"Melora, Bowan, do you have the patterns?"

Transporter Chief Radowski stood next to the science officer, the pair of them working through the last few keystrokes on the console. "Aye, Captain," said Commander Pazlar. "We've filtered out two of the Solanae biosignatures from the patterns we're holding in the transporter buffers. Ready to rematerialize."

"Do it." Vale drew herself up and faced the empty space in the middle of the bridge. Radowski tapped a control, and Riker saw Keru and Sarai put their hands on the grips of their weapons as two columns of blue-white light formed out of the air.

Phased particles glittered and vanished, revealing two Solanae in their now-familiar ceramic battle armor. Shock washed over the aliens as they came to terms with where they were and what had happened to them. From their perspective, a moment before they had been aboard one of their interceptor craft, heading in on an attack run against the *Titan*. Now they had been pulled from their ship to find themselves surrounded by alien beings. The irony of the abductors becoming the abducted was not lost on the admiral, and he took a brief moment of cold pleasure from the obvious distress the Solanae were experiencing. He wanted to ask them, *How do* you *like it?*

Troi gave Vale a subtle nod, indicating that she had a line on the emotive state of the aliens, and the captain cleared her throat. "You are our prisoners," said Vale, the universal translator turning her words into their click-speech. "We have recovered the beings you kidnapped from our dimension. We have destroyed the starship you stole from us in order to deny you the ability to coopt its systems. We have retarded your ability to strike back at us. Do you understand?"

The two aliens shifted uneasily. Finally, the shorter of the pair—the one with more ornate armor, Riker noted—leaned forward to speak. "Why have you not terminated us?" The translator rendered the Solanae commander's language into a blank, monotone voice. "This is weakness."

"We know about the threat to the survival of your species," said Troi. "The eventual collapse of this spatial realm will destroy your civilization. We understand why you have struck out against us."

Not for the first time, Riker marveled at Deanna's seemingly bottomless well of compassion. Someone else who had been stolen from their home against their will, someone whose child had been torn away, might not have been able to stand and look those responsible for that act in the eye. Deanna Troi could do so, and offer the olive branch in the same breath. Although it was Riker who had set this in motion, all of them together would need to put aside the events of the past few days if they were to find a way toward a peaceful resolution.

His wife went on. "The need to survive forces difficult choices to be made. But we can help you."

Vale gave him a sideways look. "Your show, Will," she said, out of the corner of her mouth.

Riker stepped forward. "There does not have to be conflict between our civilizations. You do not need to invade by stealth or force of arms. We can coexist."

The Solanae commander cocked his head, listening intently. "How?"

"By my authority, the United Federation of Planets can offer your people a truce," he said. "This is a chance to step back from the brink of a potential war with the races of my galaxy. We can stop the conflict here and now. We can help your species find a new place to inhabit, without having to harm others."

"Do the traitors still live?" snapped the other Solanae. "They who call themselves the Ciari?"

"Yes," said Vale. "We haven't harmed them."

"You should have," spat the alien commander. "We will, when we find them. Open them and take all the knowledge that we need."

"Approaching ships entering weapons range," said Tuvok quietly.

"Don't throw this chance away," Riker insisted. "We don't want to fight you, but if you force us, we will retaliate with all the power at our command."

The Solanae's clawed talons clacked together in a clattering, bony chorus. Sarai shot Troi a questioning look. "What are they doing?"

Troi's expression became a frown. "I believe it is a gesture of . . . mockery."

"They're laughing at us," said Keru.

The commander pointed one curved talon at Riker's face. "We do not fear you, animal. Cunning as you are to have come to our domain, it matters little to us. Try again, and we will be ready for you." It took a step toward him; Sarai's and Keru's weapons were out and aimed in a flash, but the alien paid them no mind. "We want no part of a peace that makes congress with lower life-forms. You are beneath us. You are not our equals. We reject your pathetic attempt to oppose us."

"We have done nothing to you!" said Troi, and for a moment a flash of the angry, threatened mother inside shone through. "But you prey upon us, harm us. *Why*?"

"Because we can," said the Solanae, its bulbous eyes flicking as it looked around the bridge, taking them all in. "We will take what we want from you, when we want to. You cannot stop us. You will never see us coming."

Riker sighed and gestured for Sarai and Keru to back off. "Very well. If that's how this will go, then you've made your choice." He eyed the alien frostily. "But I warn you now. When we get back, we will make sure that everyone knows about you. Every starship crew, every planet and colony, every single starfaring race we have encountered and every one we have yet to meet. We will tell them about you and we will tell them how to stop you." He nodded at the strange nebulae on the main viewscreen. "Remember that, when the stars in your sky go dark. We offered you a chance, and you turned away."

The alien commander made the talon-clacking motion again. "Why do you believe we will ever allow you to leave?"

Vale gave the Solanae a cold smile. "That's not something you get to decide." She turned to Tuvok. "Ready, Commander?"

The Vulcan nodded. "Aye, Captain."

Vale glanced at Radowski. "Bowan, send our guests home. Along with Mister Tuvok's parting gift."

"My pleasure," said the other officer, and he ran his hands up the sliders of the transporter control slaved to a bridge console.

Realizing what was happening to them, the two Solanae warriors surged forward to attack Riker and Vale, but the beaming effect swept them up before they could reach out, and then they were gone.

"Solanae ships on-screen," said Tuvok, bringing up the alien craft on the main viewscreen. Two great stone daggers cut from the same kind of black volcanic rock as the alien space platform grew in size as they approached, each propelled by a plume of fusion fire. Then, without warning, both vessels suddenly slowed, their motions becoming erratic. Their engines flared and went dark. "Transport complete," continued Tuvok. "The interceptors and their crews were beamed directly into the landing bays of both Solanae vessels. In addition, Lieutenant McCreedy's modified torpedoes successfully materialized inside the engine nozzles of the target ships, destroying their drive systems."

Riker felt Deanna's hand on his arm and looked into her dark eyes. "You tried," she said. "And they threw it back at us."

He frowned. "I wanted us to go home with our lost," he said, "not with a new enemy to fight."

"That we are coming back *at all* is enough of a victory for now," said Vale, answering the admiral but speaking to her crew. "Start the clock on the warp imbalance program. Secure all decks and sections. Shields to maximum." She returned to her seat and settled into it.

"Let's get the hell out of here."

Nineteen

Now that circumstances had changed, Christine Vale found her perception of the alien comet-habitat shifting. On her first visit here, the *Titan* crew were entering *terra incognita*, confronting a species they suspected were out to do them harm. That had colored her perceptions, but now that she understood the Solanae—*No, these are the Ciari*, she reminded herself—it was as if she were seeing it anew.

It was remarkable. The hollowed-out interior spaces of the stone-hard permafrost surrounding them was an extraordinary work of ingenuity, fueled by desperation. The dissidents had created an enclosed world, a true refuge in all senses of the word.

But now their isolation was about to end, and the *Titan* would play a key role in that. After the events of the past week, there was little that could remain the same. Life would change forever for not only the Ciari but for the Dinac too—and for the Federation, once the full ramifications of the Solanae threat had been considered.

Vale had been in the hub with Riker as the admiral talked via a real-time communications relay to the commander of the fleet back on Earth. Admiral Akaar's hologram, projected into the seat across the table from them, had seemed like a digital sculpture. Unmoving and silent, he listened to their report and then gave a solemn nod. "I'll get back to you," he said.

That had been three days ago, and so far no word had been forthcoming. In the meantime, while Xin's engineering team and volunteers from the *Whitetree*'s cadet crew repaired the *Titan*'s damage, Sariel had seen to it that the rescued were given quarters and all the medical attention they needed. The corridors of the *Titan* were busy now, with her full crew complement restored and all the extra passengers aboard. More than that, the upbeat mood that had filled the ship earlier in the mission was back.

A day after the *Titan*'s return through the artificially generated subspace rift, a trio of Dinac cutters had appeared, sent out to follow them from Casroc. Led by an engineer-commander Riker had met on their orbital station, the new arrivals were overjoyed to see Guoapa and the crew of the lost explorer alive and well. Those three ships orbited the Refuge in formation with the *Titan*, and Guoapa and the other captain were now with the Starfleet party.

This would be a historic moment, a meeting to be cherished. Unlike the initial encounter, which had taken place with daggers drawn. It wasn't often that a first contact got a second chance.

All around the Federation and Dinac parties, the

stepped terraces of the Ciari amphitheater were filled with hundreds of hooded beings, the quiet broken only by the occasional soft click-snap as one of them whispered something to another.

"Standing room only," noted Riker to the captain.

"Yes," added Counselor Troi, on Vale's right. "I understand that this gathering is being monitored in every habitat chamber throughout the Refuge."

"No pressure, then," muttered Vale, and her words drew the attention of one of the Dinac.

Guoapa eyed her, her tall ears flicking. "It is not easy, to meet a possible ally and see them wearing the face of an enemy."

"No," she agreed. "But arguably, that's the mistake we both made at the start. We looked and saw what we wanted to see. I think the Ciari did the same. We were equally afraid of each other. It could have ended very badly for all of us."

"Your restraint does you credit, Vale," said Guoapa. "I am learning much from you. I confess that I might not have shown such moderation."

Christine smiled slightly. "We're *all* learning, every single day we're out here. Don't worry about it; from what I've seen of the Dinac, your race are very quick studies." She halted as the crowds of refugees parted to allow the two Ciari scientists Kikkir and Tokiz to approach. They still wore the markings on their faces taken on after the elder of their number had ended his life in front of Admiral Riker.

Christine glanced at Will, saw the thinning of his lips. Like her, he found it hard to understand why the older Xikkix had done what he did. Had the alien been seeking some kind of atonement for being party to Riker's abduction years earlier? She wondered if they would ever be able to fully know the mind of these beings. *But we have to try. For our sake . . . and for theirs.*

"We greet you, outworlders," said Kikkir. "It is well that we may begin our association again on better terms."

"On that, we firmly agree," said Riker. "We regret the circumstances that forced our paths to cross, but those events cannot be called back. We can only move forward, and make the best of what lies before us."

"That is so." Tokiz inclined her head, letting her hood fall back. "The actions of your people have preserved the Ciari. Some among our number would have us retreat away and hide once more in the darkness. But a greater voice stirs. We grow tired of being the hunted. We want peace, but not the peace of death."

"Then you require friends," offered Guoapa. "Just as the Dinac did when we took our first steps beyond our star system." She nodded to the *Titan* party. "These Federation beings came to us and offered friendship. It has been a most beneficial association." The engineer-commander glanced at Vale, then away. "The Ciari are within the bounds of our space, and thus we see you as our welcome neighbors. We extend you the same offer of aid as the Federation gave to us. Will you accept alliance with the people of Casroc?"

"We will accept," said Kikkir. "It would be self-destructive not to. What has transpired recently shows the Ciari that we cannot stand alone. Coexistence, yes; not isolation."

Vale smiled, heartened by the honesty of the moment. Even if the militant Solanae, trapped for the moment in their origin domain, were adamant they would reject any overtures for peace, this dissident splinter from their society *would* take the hand of friendship. That gesture might hold the seed of some future amity.

"On behalf of the United Federation of Planets," said Riker, "we would like to welcome both your peoples to the greater galactic community. It is a core principle of the Federation's charter that in unity, different cultures and peoples can be stronger. No matter what their origins, even if we have been opposed in the past. Together, we can achieve great things. We are proud to be able to extend the hand of friendship to the Dinac and the Ciari."

"It is accepted," Kikkir repeated.

The near-silent crowd rose and began to speak as one, their voices growing loud, filling the chamber until it echoed. At Vale's side, Guoapa and her party bared their teeth in wide grins and let out celebratory barks, their tails swishing back and forth.

"Well, what do you know?" Vale said to Riker and Troi, shouting to be heard over the sound. "It looks like we have done some good out here after all."

"To lead and teach, to defend and uphold," said Riker, recalling his own words. "By example." The admiral nodded. "Yes. Today, I think I'll take this as a win."

Partially to keep them occupied, but also because he saw it as an opportunity, Chief Engineer Ra-Havreii had taken it upon himself to appoint Lieutenant Ythiss as a temporary liaison between the *Titan* and the rescued crew from the *Whitetree*. With the Selayan's status as a former *Titan* engineer and the fact the cadets were largely operations trainees, it hadn't taken Ra-Havreii long to put them all to work on every tiny little task that needed doing throughout the vessel.

Torvig observed this from his station in main engineering, seeing quite clearly how much the Efrosian was enjoying having a cohort of young midshipmen snapping to at his every command. Ra-Havreii's darker moods of late melted away, proving a truth that the ensign had come to very early on in his service aboard the ship: The chief engineer was only really happy when he was issuing orders.

For Torvig it meant he had a moment of peace to work on his own tasks, finishing up the laborious job of refitting each and every one of *Titan*'s replicator units. It was not easy, because to produce certain parts for some of the units required a working replicator—but to make *that* replicator operable required certain parts that needed to be replicated, and so on and so on. The Chobilk was afraid he would get sucked into an endless recursive loop of never-ending maintenance.

He was so fixed on his work that when the hologram appeared next to him, he almost dropped the stylus he was carrying in his tail's cyber-manipulator. "White-Blue?"

"Greetings, Friend-Torvig." The abstract avatar-self of the Sentry AI was being projected from one of the engine room's embedded holo-emitters. "Interrogative: May I/We speak with you?"

"Of course. Is there something you require?"

"Negative," said the Sentry. "I/We am transmitting this representation to your coordinates from my probe-shell. I/We desired to speak to you before the operative range was too great for synchronous conversation."

Torvig blinked. The last he had heard, after White-Blue

had expertly performed his "pilot ship" duties guiding the *Titan* back through the perilous wormhole from subspace, the AI had recovered the rest of his modified probes and gone into standby mode. "You're . . . gone?" He felt a sudden jolt of disappointment. "Oh. Where are you now? In an astrogeographic sense, I mean."

"This unit's distributed consciousness is in several different areas simultaneously. The probe fleet I/We configured is currently moving into a number of sectors at the edge of the area colloquially designated 'Alpha Quadrant frontier zone.' "

"Oh," repeated Torvig. "I didn't know that you had left. I mean, I knew you intended to range out and explore, but I didn't think . . ." He trailed off, trying to reframe his thoughts. "I didn't think you would leave without saying goodbye."

"You were in the process of a biological rest cycle when I reached the optimal time for departure," White-Blue responded. "I/We am aware such functions are important to bioforms such as the Choblik. I/We did not wish to interrupt that process."

"You couldn't wait?"

"Interrogative: For what reason?"

"Nothing." Torvig felt deflated. "No reason, really. I mean, it's not like you had a physical presence for me to, you know, wave farewell to." His tail drooped to the deck.

White-Blue was silent for a moment. "Friend-Torvig. This unit detects emotional signifiers in your tone. Regret-sadness. I/We process that there has been an error here. You required a moment of final, locative connection to find closure with this unit's determined course of action. I/We did not provide that. Apologies."

The ensign tried to lighten the moment. "I am sorry to see you go, but we will still be able to communicate, yes?"

"Affirmative, but only asynchronously."

"And . . . you are going to come back, aren't you?"

Again, the AI was silent for some time, as if processing the import of the question. "There are wonders," said the Sentry. "New phenomena. Uncharted worlds. I/We will continue to transmit data on them to *Titan*. It is this unit's hope that you will follow. You have taught SecondGen White-Blue two-point-zero so very much, Friend-Torvig. I/We exist because of you and the crew of your vessel. But there is so much out here. The impetus to explore cannot be denied."

"I understand," said Torvig, and he was at once sad and happy as he said it. "I wish you well. And please. stay in touch?"

"Confirmed," replied the AI, and the hologram faded into nothing.

"Hey, Torvig." He turned to find Ensign Peya Fell approaching. "Are you all right?"

"I suppose so," he replied, a little glumly. "White-Blue left the ship."

"I heard." She nodded. "He helped us parse the data that the Ciari sent up from the Refuge before he warped out."

"What data?"

Fell gestured at the air. "As a goodwill gesture, the dissidents turned over their full database of scientific and technical data on subspace dynamics and field manipulation. There's gigaquads of it! It'll take months just to index it all . . ." She paused. "Will you miss him?"

Torvig nodded. "I think so."

The Deltan gave him a considerate smile. "I came by to see if you wanted to come along to the gathering. It's not really a wake but a farewell for Zurin Dakal. You could say goodbye to your friend there too. I imagine Zurin would be okay with that."

"I am uncertain." The Choblik hesitated. "Is it going to be . . . distressing?"

Peya's smile widened. "Are you joking? Not on this ship!"

Deanna finished her pass over the operations logs and gave a heavy sigh. Her colleagues, Pral glasch Haaj and Huilan Sen'kara, had done a good job keeping things on an even keel during her brief involuntary absence, and both of them had offered separately to cover her scheduled meetings for as long as she needed. But the truth was, Troi didn't want to take a day—*or maybe two*, Huilan insisted—to find her feet. She had been through much worse, and the best solution she knew was to take the advice she so often gave to others. *Go back to your normal routine. Prove to yourself that life as you know it hasn't gone away.*

The fact was, she had already been approached by some *Whitetree* survivors who wanted to unburden themselves about the traumatic events they had gone through. It was Troi's duty, as a counselor, to make herself available to them.

But maybe not right this second. *Tomorrow*, she decided—tomorrow she would get back to work and do what she was best at.

The office door chimed and she frowned. Nobody

knew that she was here. Troi had not officially posted her return to duty. "Come in," she said.

Dalit Sarai stood in the doorway. "Do you have a moment, Counselor?"

"Of course." The taciturn executive officer was, in all honesty, the last person Troi had expected to see. She put down the padd she had been working on and went to the chairs in the office's interview area.

Sarai trailed after her, hesitating before taking the seat opposite. "I saw Lieutenant Ythiss on my way here. He seems to be healing well."

"Doctor Ree was able to reverse the molecular degradation that affected him, and the others," she replied. "We were lucky."

"That is one way of seeing it." She paused, and Troi didn't make any attempt to prompt her. Eventually, Sarai found her way to the point. "I thought about what you said to me, when we were in the Solanae holding area. About my . . . *detachment*."

"I wasn't serious when I said I would order you to come to counseling sessions, Commander," Troi said lightly. "But if you do want to talk, we can."

"You misunderstand," said Sarai. "I'm not here because I want to hear soothing words that will make me feel better about myself. I am here because I want to make sure you do not have the wrong impression of me."

Troi raised an eyebrow. "And what impression is that?"

Sarai smiled, very briefly. "I know what the noncoms call me. 'The Ice Queen.' I've heard worse. Because of the way I comport myself, and the choices I have made in the past, I am thought of as aloof. Some have said cold-blooded."

"I don't think that," Troi said truthfully. "Someone who worked as hard as you did to bring our people home is not someone without empathy. Even if you do insist your telepathic skills are poor."

"We are all being judged," said Sarai, the comment coming from nowhere. "Do you see that, Deanna? All of us, in our own way."

It surprised Troi that the first officer used her first name, and she faltered before replying. "Dalit, you don't have to justify yourself to me."

Sarai showed that smile once more, there and then gone again. "That's a start." Before the counselor could say anything else, the Efrosian woman got up and walked out without another word.

"My door is always open," Troi called after her.

Sarai didn't answer.

"And then . . ." Keru said, barely able to keep a straight face. "And then he said to me, 'But sir . . . didn't you know that all Cardassians have that many?' "

The punch line landed as the doors to the officers' club hissed open to admit Torvig and Peya Fell, as the uproar of the assembled group's laughter sounded off the walls at the memory of Zurin's ribald joke.

Lieutenant Ssura seemed slightly nonplussed, however. "But how does the number of—"

Aili Lavena let out a bubbling giggle. "You're a little sheltered, aren't you? She leaned closer and whispered an explanation of the gag into the Caitian's peaked ears. Ssura's mouth dropped open.

"I am shocked," Doctor Ree said, peering at Keru

with mock seriousness. "Shocked that such an upstanding young fellow would engage in so bawdy a discussion with a Trill known to be a reprobate."

"It's this crew," offered Pazlar, grinning. "We bring out the best in everybody!" She raised her glass. "How about we toast that? To Zurin and the *Titan*. Sailing on forever."

Keru nodded and tapped his chest, where his heart lay. "In here," he said, then pointed at the stars through the windows along the far wall. "And out there."

Peya and Torvig each took a tumbler with a measure of *kanar* in it and joined their comrades. This was an informal gathering, but there were faces from each department scattered around the tables. It was clear from numbers alone that Zurin Dakal had been well liked.

Ensign Modan raised her glass. "To Zurin . . . And to Kekil."

"Nidani Ledrah and Jaza Najem," offered Ree.

"Tane," said Lieutenant Sortollo. "Antillea. Shelley. And Rriarr."

Olivia Bolaji stepped forward. "Tylith and T'Lirin."

Pazlar nodded, and her eyes shone as she did. "All of them. In here, and out there." The assembled group repeated the science officer's toast, and then as one they all knocked back the shots of *kanar*.

A strained, unpleasant silence descended in the aftermath, and eventually it was Torvig who broke it, voicing the same thought that was on all of their minds. "That tasted *awful*."

And suddenly everyone was laughing again. Keru eyed his glass as if it might contain poison. "Ugh. Cardassians actually *like* this stuff?"

Sortollo shook his head, chuckling. "Oh, heck no. Zurin couldn't stand it!"

Pazlar deposited her empty tumbler on the tray of a passing server. "The last joke is on us, it would seem." She caught sight of Lieutenant Kyzak, who sat off to one side, his glass of the alien liquor still untouched.

As the gathering went on, with yet another yarn unfolding from the chief of security's seemingly endless supply of tales, Pazlar took the seat across from Kyzak's. "Not a drinker?" she asked.

"Not today," he replied. "Don't seem right." After a moment, the Skagaran shook his head. "I just met the guy. Now he's free atoms. Don't seem right," he repeated.

"A wake is not about what's *right*," Pazlar told him. "It's about who is *left*. Zurin died for us, so we could be here to see him off. Honor that, but don't dwell on it. Because that only gets you sorrow." The Elaysian's gaze turned inward for a moment. "If we don't move on, we get stuck in the same place, the same patterns."

Kyzak studied her. "You talk like you know from experience."

"Things change," Pazlar admitted. "If you can't accept that, you'll suffer. And so will those around you."

"Then here's to change." The lieutenant downed the shot of *kanar* in one pull, then licked his lips. "Eh . . . not bad."

Pazlar's eyes widened. "You actually enjoyed that?"

Kyzak shrugged. "You should try Skagaran whiskey. Now there's a *real* drink." He paused. "Speaking of moving on: I don't mean to pry, but if you and Commander Ra-Havreii are not—"

She stopped him with a look. "I'm going to take a wild guess and say that, yes, whatever you're about to ask me *is* prying."

"Okay. How about a suggestion instead?"

"I'm listening."

"Word is we're heading back to the nearest starbase to drop off the *Whitetree* crew, and I heard about a great Andorian place there." He smiled, pouring on the charm.

"No." Pazlar shook her head. "I like you, Ethan. But I'm not going down that road. Not for a while." She stood up to walk away. "I think I need some time on my own."

"All right then," he agreed. "Be here if you change your mind."

She smiled back at him. "Just don't hold your breath."

Vale entered the hub, and for a second she thought that the room was empty. In a rare change from the norm, Admiral Riker's aide was nowhere to be seen, and the captain wondered idly if the Caitian was ever really off-duty. Lieutenant Ssura seemed like a good officer, but he was earnest and always fully focused on every tiny detail. It could be wearing.

She was a couple of steps into the hub when she realized that Riker had company. The admiral didn't see her, but Vale caught sight of him standing next to Sariel Rager. He had his hand on the ops officer's shoulder and an unguarded expression on his face.

"I know it wasn't easy," Riker was saying. "For either of us. But I hope that we can put away some of that trauma."

Rager nodded. "We faced our fears, didn't we? And we're still here."

Vale felt awkward. She was intruding on something

private, a moment between these two people as they put to rest a horror from their past.

"Yes. But I won't lie to you, Sariel." Riker sighed. "It's not over. We may have to look our fears in the eye again."

Rager nodded. "I know, sir. But before I felt like it was just me. Now we're all in this, that makes me feel stronger." She gave a shaky smile and turned to leave, catching sight of Vale. "Oh! Captain . . ."

"At ease," said Vale, covering her moment of indecision. "If this is a bad time, I can come back . . ."

Rager shook her head. "No, sir. It's okay."

Riker dismissed Rager with a smile. "We'll talk again, Commander."

The other woman nodded again and left the hub, giving Vale a look as she went on her way. The captain waited until they were alone. "How is she doing?"

"Good," Riker replied. "There were some things she didn't want to say to someone who hadn't been there." His expression darkened. "I can still remember her face, Chris, when I found her in the Solanae lab that first time. Eyes wide open, staring into nothing. But she was awake and conscious all the while, forced to watch them as they . . ." He stopped, then shook off the memory with a shudder. "Sariel was very brave. But she's paid for it. The nightmares never really leave you."

"There's a cost for every step we take out here," Vale noted. "We all know that. Zurin Dakal knew it, and he paid it."

Riker looked out of the ports. "Strange. There was something Kikkir told me, back on the Refuge. He said that before we left to venture into subspace, there were still strong voices among the dissidents calling for the Ciari to cut off all contact with outsiders. But they changed their minds when they heard about Zurin's sacrifice. One noble, selfless act was enough to convince them to break their isolation from the rest of the galaxy."

Vale felt a shadow pass over her spirit. "Was it noble, Will? I *made* him do it. I gave the command, and Zurin walked right into the fire."

"You didn't kill him, Chris." Riker turned back to face her. "Don't think that. Don't go down that road. It will eat you alive."

"He would have done it, even if I hadn't asked him to." Her voice caught on the words. "And I still made it an order."

"Both of you made a choice," said Riker. "The right choice. The *only* choice. But you're the one that has to live with it."

Vale took a long, drawn-out breath, feeling hollow inside. "Sure you don't want to take that chair back?" she asked. "Still time to change your mind."

"You don't mean that."

"No," she said at length. "I don't. I just hate how I feel right now."

"You and every captain since the age of sail. But we honor the deed and we go on." He sat on the edge of his desk. "We pay the cost, and we go on. We've secured the Federation new allies in this sector of space and learned a lot about a potential menace in the process. Think about it: If we had failed here, then it wouldn't be just us that were lost. The Dinac would be under threat, the Ciari dead or captured, and the Federation would be looking the wrong way if and when the Solanae decided to come at us. Now we're ready."

"I guess we can't always hope to make allies

everywhere we go," she allowed. "But if I've learned one thing serving aboard the *Titan* above all else, it's that we can never stop looking for them. We can't stop moving forward, offering the hand of friendship, even when it costs us. The moment we do that . . . If we can't look past our fears, if we let ourselves prejudge"—Vale took in the ship around them—"then all this has been for nothing. And I will never accept that outcome. This crew wants to make history, they want to make a difference. *We're going to do that.*"

Riker smiled. "Spoken like a true captain."

Epilogue

Sarai entered her cabin and did not bother to change the room's illumination levels from their dim, twilight setting. There was something oddly comforting about it, she reflected. After spending a full ship's day under the strong, daylight glare of *Titan*'s bridge, she found the shadows almost restful.

What would Troi think that said about me? she wondered. The first officer dismissed the thought and took some water from the storage pod resting in the alcove where her replicator would normally have been. It was still awaiting repair, and the faint odor of burned polymers hung in the air around it. The thought that the device had been coopted to produce a horde of invasive alien drones made her seriously consider leaving the mechanism in its disassembled state, and Sarai's SI training had made her permanently suspicious of every item of technology that surrounded her. She knew how simple it was to insert some lines of code into the operating systems of a viewscreen or a simple padd and turn it into a covert listening device. In the past, she had done exactly that in the offices of a particularly talkative Romulan senator.

Her kit bag lay in the bottom of the closet where she had put it on her arrival on the *Titan*, the small number of personal items in there still unpacked. Sarai manipulated a section of the hard-sided carrier's exterior in a certain way, and a hidden panel popped open. First she took a small scanner wand from inside and ran her usual sweep of the room. She expected—and found—nothing out of the ordinary, but it was good tradecraft for her to stay in practice. Returning to the bag, she exchanged the wand for a different item.

It resembled an older design of Starfleet combadge but without the familiar delta shield insignia. A casual observer might have thought the bronze oval to be no more than a brooch of uninspired motif, but inside it was a complex amalgam of communicator, encryption processor and signal jammer. Sarai tapped out an acoustic code on the device, and it answered by giving off a quick pulse of vibration. She knew that the unit was now quietly interfacing with the *Titan*'s computer network, masquerading as an innocuous peripheral such as a padd or personal computer. In a few moments, the device pulsed twice, indicating it was ready.

Sarai was now stealthily connected to the starship's long-range subspace transceiver, and an array of cloaking subroutines were at work carefully erasing all record of this action having ever taken place. She raised the communicator to her lips. "Active," she said quietly. "Ready."

"Proceed with your report," said a resonant voice,

masked by the action of encoding software. *"I've already heard what Riker and Vale had to say."*

"I need more time to make a thorough evaluation. But my preliminary observations follow the previous patterns. Both Admiral Riker and Captain Vale have made command decisions that could be considered questionable."

"That ship and its crew have been granted a lot of latitude over the years," said the voice. *"Circumstances have changed now."*

"I . . ." She paused, trying to find the right words. "I am not comfortable with what I am being asked to do."

"Your level of comfort has no bearing on your orders, Commander."

"You're asking me to constantly second-guess *Titan*'s senior officers."

She heard something that might have been a gruff chug of amusement. *"You're the ship's first officer, that's your* job. *Carry on, and keep me informed."*

"Yes, sir," said Sarai, but the channel had already been cut.

She sat in the dimness looking down at the device in her hand, considering the weight of it, and of the mission that had been put upon her.

Acknowledgments

Thanks to Brannon Braga, Michael Jan Friedman, Larry Nemecek, Michael Okuda, Denise Okuda, Debbie Mirek, Geoffrey Mandel, Adam "Mojo" Lebowitz, Robert Bonchune, John Jackson Miller, David Mack, Dayton Ward and Kirsten Beyer for their fiction, reference materials and sterling advice; to the folks at Trek FM, Literary Treks, The G & T Show, Visionary Treks and TrekMate for their ongoing support; and forever with much love to Mandy Mills.

About the Author

James Swallow is a *New York Times* best-selling author and BAFTA nominee. He is proud to be the only British writer to have worked on a *Star Trek* television series, creating the original story concepts for the *Star Trek: Voyager* episodes "One" and "Memorial"; his other *Star Trek* writing includes *The Poisoned Chalice*, *Cast No Shadow*, *Synthesis*, the Scribe award winner *Day of the Vipers*, the novellas *The Stuff of Dreams* and *Myriad Universes: Seeds of Dissent*, the short stories "The Slow Knife," "The Black Flag," "Ordinary Days" and "Closure" for the anthologies *Seven Deadly Sins*, *Shards and Shadows, The Sky's the Limit* and *Distant Shores*, scripting the videogame *Star Trek Invasion*, and over 400 articles in thirteen different *Star Trek* magazines around the world.

As well as a nonfiction book (*Dark Eye: The Films of David Fincher*), James also wrote the *Sundowners* series of original steampunk westerns, *Enigma, Jade Dragon*,

The Butterfly Effect and novels from the worlds of *Doctor Who* (*Peacemaker*), *Warhammer 40,000* (*Fear to Tread, Hammer & Anvil, Nemesis, Black Tide, Red Fury, The Flight of the Eisenstein, Faith & Fire, Deus Encarmine* and *Deus Sanguinius*), *Stargate* (*Halcyon, Relativity, Nightfall* and *Air*), *24* (*Deadline*) and *2000AD* (*Eclipse, Whiteout* and *Blood Relative*). His other credits feature scripts for videogames and audio dramas, including *Deus Ex: Human Revolution, Fable: The Journey, Disney Infinity, Battlestar Galactica, Blake's 7* and *Space 1889.*

James Swallow lives in London and is currently at work on his next book.